SOMETHING IS COMING

THE COSMIC SERIES: BOOK TWO

CJ DEARLOVE

LADY EDITH PUBLISHING

CJ DEARLOVE

Ontario, Canada

Printed Worldwide
First Printing 2024
First Edition 2024

ISBN 978-1-7389734-6-0 (Hardcover)
ISBN 978-1-7389734-4-6 (Paperback)
ISBN 978-1-7389734-5-3 (eBook)

10 9 8 7 6 5 4 3 2 1

Cover Art by Daniel Eyenegho

Interior Book Design by Walt's Book Design
www.waltsbookdesign.com

Content Warning: this book portrays the use of substances and should be read by a mature audience.

Statement on use of Artificial Intelligence:
Not a word of this book was created by AI. An actual human being, with access to the universal consciousness, wrote this book.

SOMETHING
IS COMING

DEDICATION

This book is for the weird.
The strange. The odd, shy, and uncertain.
The too quiet, too loud, and too much.
The nerds, geeks, dorks, and generally awkward.
The kooky, crunchy, out of place, the anxious,
the depressed, the lonely.
May you meet your people and find your home, wherever and
whoever in the universe that is.
And the being said: "You still have much love to share."

"It seems to us that rather than being 'extraterrestrial' in any simple sense, UFOs could well be part of the same larger intelligence which has shaped the tapestry of religion and mythology since the dawn of human consciousness."

Dr. J. Allen Hynek

"There is no story that is not true."

Chinua Achebe

Prologue

"Virtually every abductee receives information about the destruction of the Earth's ecosystem and feels compelled to do something about it."

John E. Mack

Tomi felt disoriented in the bright light, and closed her eyes. When she opened them, the overwhelming light was gone, and was replaced with a light glow emanating from the walls around her.

She looked down at her hands, still putting pressure on Kirsten's stomach. Kirsten's shirt was covered in her dark red blood. *Too much blood*, thought Tomi.

Tomi looked at her face. Kirsten's eyes were open, and instead of fear, she saw life. Love. Kirsten was smiling. Tomi looked down again at her hands and lifted them off Kirsten's stomach. Blood didn't flow from her abdomen. Tomi pulled Kirsten's shirt up to find not an open wound, but instead two round scars, the skin already healing over.

She looked Kirsten in the eyes again, and wrapped her arms around her. "You're okay!" she said.

Tomi started to become aware of her surroundings. Ib and Barry stood beside them, their arms still raised, but they were no longer in the clearing, no longer outside. She had seen this place before. The inside of a UFO.

She turned slightly to see Ete, her big, dark eyes emanating kindness. Tomi stepped forward and took Ete's hand, so much larger than her own. Ete towered over her. She hadn't felt so small with Ete when remote viewing, but now could see clearly how tall and lanky Ete and her kind were.

"You saved her," said Tomi.

She felt Ete smile. "*There's someone I think you'd like to see,*" Tomi heard.

Tomi turned to see her, as radiant and full of life as the last time she saw her, long ago, when Tomi was a child. It was like she glowed, emanating light.

"Grandma," Tomi said, stepping towards her grandmother, hugging her tightly. Tomi breathed in, finding her grandmother's hair smelling just as it had when Tomi was a child. *She's really here, in the flesh*, thought Tomi, incredulous.

After an extended embrace, Esther let go and took a step back.

"Look at you, you are so beautiful and so special, as I always knew you were," Esther said.

"I don't," Tomi stammered, "I don't understand. How? I mean you look younger than I remember you. Where have you been?"

"Well, let's just say it all started with an investigation of Mars. Oh Tomi, there are so many stories to share. All in good time," she said. Esther brushed Tomi's hair with her hand and smiled at her. "I'm so sorry I haven't been around. Please know I've been with you. I've been in, well, in the Other Place. I've been preparing, Tomi," she said, taking her granddaughter's hand, "for our mission."

Tomi looked at Ete, and thought about the dark pyramid that she was to destroy, to pull the lid off the boiling pot, then thought about the napkin her grandmother had used to draw the vibrating pyramid. *Our mission.*

"Now, you and your friends have been through a lot," Esther said sweetly, stroking Tomi's hand. "What kind of grandmother would I be if I didn't have a treat for you?" she said with a smile, as she reached for a helmet that was secured on a panel in the centre of the craft. Tomi remembered Ete wearing this helmet when she had remote viewed being on the craft, the flying saucer.

She held the helmet, black and metallic, out to Tomi. "I believe someone promised you would learn to fly one of these," Esther said, nodding towards Ete. "It's pretty simple, really. Put this helmet on, and think about where you want to go. Let your consciousness travel there. And the craft will take us."

Tomi looked to the wall of the craft, and saw the walls disappear wherever she focused, giving her a view outside. She could see the dark landscape, the mountain still below them, the General and John somewhere down there.

"Anywhere…anywhere on Earth?" Tomi asked.

"Anywhere," said Esther.

Tomi closed her eyes and focused. *I want to go home*, she thought.

She slowly opened her eyes, and saw it approaching: her beautiful, hilly island, her refuge, somewhere in this vast universe. She could see the craft lowering gently, preparing to land towards the top of the hill. Tomi turned to look at her grandmother, and they joined hands. Kirsten stepped to the other side of Tomi, and took her other hand.

"It's…it's the place from my dreams," said Kirsten in wonder. Tomi gave her a knowing smile and squeezed her hand.

As the craft approached the island, Tomi suddenly felt scared, seeing the steep incline of the hill. *The craft will topple over if we try to land*, she thought.

As though the island heard her thoughts, the hill began to fold in on itself, bending inward, creating a giant flat shelf just where the craft would land. Tomi felt a gentle shake as the craft touched down. An area of the floor suddenly carved itself into a rectangle and opened, creating a ramp down to the surface.

Tomi led the way out, and everyone followed. She jumped from the ramp, feeling light as a feather, drifting down to the ground.

She turned to look at Ete. "The air is safe for us? We can breathe here?" she asked.

"*You can, but you don't need to, here*," Ete said telepathically.

Tomi closed her eyes, breathed deeply, and raised her hands to the sky. She let herself fall backwards, like a trust exercise with the ground, with the island, with reality itself. She flopped gently back onto the grass, almost fur-like in its softness, and looked up to the sky. It was a bright blue-sky day, and yet she could see the stars. So many stars it seemed impossible.

She felt a warmth, and sat up to see her grandmother seated beside her, also nestling into the grass. Tomi looked around and saw

Ib sniffing a multicoloured flower, and Barry pointing out a star to Kirsten. And there was Ete, sitting down and yet as tall as a human, settling into a meditation.

Home.

Over her shoulder, Tomi heard a familiar voice call her name. She stood and turned, only to see a cliff and the seas below, stretching off into the horizon, towards the stars. Then she felt it, like the vibrational wave that hits you when a gong is struck. It was a pull, *a subatomic pull*, she thought. *I know this one. I've felt it before.*

She looked around and saw everyone else standing, looking towards the same horizon.

"Do you feel it too?" she asked.

"Yes," said Kirsten. "It called my name."

"Mine too," said Ib.

"*Earth*," said Ete.

"The fourth call," said Tomi, solemnly. "The fourth wave."

Tomi looked around at the landscape, so lush, soft, and perfect, a world like a hammock, cradling you in suspension. She didn't ever want to leave this place of pure beauty, peace, and harmony.

My home, she thought.

Tomi looked at her friends. Her people.

"Our mission. We need to go back," she said, turning to look again towards the horizon, towards the source of the call. "We have to go back to Earth."

Chapter 1

"The extraterrestrial is the human oversoul in its general and particular expression on the planet...It is actually the most intelligent organism on the planet, regulating human culture through the release of ideas out of eternity and into the continuum of history. The UFO is an idea whose purpose is to confound science, because science has begun to threaten the existence of the human species and the entire ecosystem of the planet. And at this point a shock is necessary for the culture – a shock equivalent to the shock of the Resurrection on Roman imperialism."

Terence McKenna

Tomi laid back, feeling her body relax as she nestled into the soft, fur-like grass of the Hilly Island. *Her* hilly island. She grazed her right hand through the grass until it found her grandmother's, and she held it.

Just a few moments ago, this visit to the Hilly Island – her soul's return to the Hilly Island, the one she saw in her past-life regression, the place she'd lived before, the place that felt like home – was interrupted by a call. A message from the Earth: *you're needed here.* The deep-down feeling of joy at returning home was quickly replaced with feelings of duty and responsibility to her Mother Earth.

"Our mission. We need to go back," she had told the group. "We have to go back to Earth."

"We will darling," Esther had replied, stepping forward and putting a hand on her granddaughter's shoulder. "We will go back.

But let's not rush off just this moment. Let's enjoy this place a little longer. And let's have a little heart-to-heart first, you and me. We have so much to catch up on."

Now that's an understatement, thought Tomi. In just the past few months she went from thinking that her grandmother had died when she was a child, to learning that she had in fact disappeared and was never found. She had learned that her grandmother wasn't a bit psychic, as Tomi had thought as a child, but was remarkably gifted, having worked as a psychic spy in Project Stargate. That she, Tomi, had inherited her grandmother's gift, and like her grandmother, had also used it in service of the Intelligence Community. And now, today, she learned that her grandmother was alive, yet somehow had barely aged a day since Tomi had last seen her, decades ago.

Tomi looked into her grandmother's eyes and nodded. She was struck by the depth of kinship she felt with her. It wasn't just the excitement of seeing a beloved relative, but something deeper. *On a soul level,* Tomi thought. *We're connected on a soul level.*

Tomi smiled and tilted her head, inviting her grandmother to have a seat over in some luscious grass. *It's not just a kinship. I feel our connection on a soul level, yet it turns out I know next to nothing about her,* she thought. *About her life. About all those missing years.*

Tomi longed to sit with her grandmother for hours, for days, sharing stories and ideas, and to be able to start processing the hurt, abandonment, and betrayal she'd experienced. Not to mention processing what she had just experienced, seeing Kirsten, her best friend, her soulmate, hot and bleeding out. She longed to be able to speak of these things out loud, knowing her grandmother will listen patiently and empathetically, wrapping her traumas up in a warm and loving hug.

As Tomi eased herself into the soft grass, she looked over at her friends and saw that they didn't mind the delay. Ib and Barry were examining the outside of Ete's spacecraft, pointing and chatting, their faces full of youthful wonder. Tomi watched Barry, a man in his late forties, his tight curly hair an even distribution of black and grey, feel for a seam on the outside of the craft, shaking his head when none was found. She thought back to how stoic and formal he had seemed when she first met him, and how important of a friend he had become to her. She knew she wouldn't have made it here without him.

She watched Ib push his grey, professorly hair out of his face with his hand, his soft green eyes glowing with excitement as he smiled boyishly back at Barry. Ib had never been stoic or formal. Tomi was endeared with his mad-scientist type of awkward the first time she had met him, and he had a warmth and childish curiosity that had always put her at ease.

Tomi looked up the hill and smiled at Kirsten who was skipping and jumping in the soft grass, giggling as she almost floated along the ground in low gravity, her long blond hair bobbing slowly with each step. *What have I done to deserve these people?*, Tomi thought to herself, experiencing a wave of gratitude.

Then there was Ete, who had found her seat again and closed her eyes in meditation. Tomi gazed at her friend who, until her rescue, had existed only in her mind, in her visions. Ete was physically taller and lankier than Tomi had imagined in her remote viewings. Even while seated Ete was taller than Tomi was standing straight up.

As she meditated, Ete's green-blue skin emitted a shimmer. Her huge eyes were closed, with her one long hand buried in the grass, and the other facing up to the sky.

This impossible sky, Tomi thought. She looked up and was shocked to see that the bright blue sky of midday had turned night black. Although the day had turned to night, it wasn't dark. The sky was abounding with stars, swirling galaxies, and colourful gaseous formations, lighting up the night. Tomi looked around and saw that the plants on her Hilly Island, the grass and flowers and trees – almost the island itself – had just the slightest glow to it, the colours taking on a deeper richness at night.

"It's night," Tomi said with a tone of confusion.

"And what a beautiful night it is," said Esther, squeezing Tomi's hand, the two of them laying back in the soft grass. "And that sunset, it was like watching a miracle unfold. There were colours I've never seen before. That I don't have names for."

"But…I don't understand," said Tomi, turning her head on the grass to look at her grandmother. "I didn't see the sunset. It just suddenly switched from day to night."

"Take a breath, take a pause, sweetheart," said Esther, turning her head in the grass to look at her granddaughter. "Be in the moment. Clear your mind. You remember."

Tomi looked back up to the sky, closed her eyes, and drew in a deep breath. The dark of her closed eyes lit up as she remembered the bright midday sun descend behind the sea at the bottom of the Hilly Island, casting lengthening shadows, and revealing the most wonderous, fiery tapestry of colours across the sky, the sea, and the grassy slope. She and her grandmother had traded gasps as they watched the sky both darken and light up in tandem, the light of a billion stars filling the dark expanse.

"The darker it becomes, the brighter the light burns," she remembered her grandmother saying.

Tomi opened her eyes. In an instant she had experienced what should have been hours. She felt disoriented, unsure what was happening with her perception of time. She thought again of the call from Earth. Their mission. She tried to estimate how long they had been here, and started to worry that they should return.

"I know you're feeling the pull to return to Earth," Esther said. "I can feel your anxiety about time."

"It just…feels like time is moving much faster here," said Tomi.

"Maybe," said Esther. "Don't worry, the craft will get us back for the right time."

"How? Does it bend time or something?"

Esther smiled. "I don't really know how it works. But the craft, well, try to think of time as a place, and not a process."

"I've always imagined time like a river."

"Exactly," said Esther. "You can put your foot in the river, and time – well for us humans anyways – flows by like the water. You can put your foot in the same spot again, but time has flowed on. That's the way we experience it. Think about the craft like a boat, or a fish in the river, that can move through the water."

"So it doesn't matter when we go back?"

"All the world's a stage, Tomi, and we all have parts to play. To play in our time, wherever that time is. We will go back soon. But first, we need to talk about the elephant."

"Elephant?" asked Tomi

"I can feel your anger, Tomi. You may not have even realized it yet, but I can feel it, a hot little nugget of anger building in you. Right there," Esther said, pointing at Tomi's navel. "You're angry at me for leaving you. For going missing and not coming back. For missing so much."

Tomi hadn't felt it. At least, she hadn't acknowledged it, but once her grandmother spoke of her anger, she could feel it burning in her stomach, a little nugget of hot plasma. *Where the hell has she been?*, Tomi thought. As she made eye contact with her grandmother, tears began falling from her eyes.

"Oh sweetheart," Esther said, wiping a tear from Tomi's cheek. "You have every right, every reason to be angry. To be hurt. I'm angry at myself, Tomi."

"Where have you been?" asked Tomi, her voice coarse as she spoke through a dry lump in her throat. "Why haven't you aged? I mean, are you really here, or am I dreaming this?"

"You're not dreaming Tomi. I'm here. I'm real, and I'm alive. You see Tomi, I've been in the Other Place. I know Ete has told you about it."

"Ete said it's, well, another place," Tomi said, her voice a little smoother. "'Off to the side', Ete said. I don't really understand it. I sort of assumed it's another dimension, or another plane of existence, whatever that means."

"I'm not really sure myself how to explain it. I kind of think of it like a sharp on a piano, how it raises the note by half. There are some things that words just can't really explain," said Esther. "The Other Place, well, you really need to see it. Experience it. I hope one day I can show it to you. I *need* to show you. For our mission."

"Our mission," said Tomi flatly, remembering the vision Ete had shared with her. "To destroy the underground pyramid?"

Esther nodded. "To help humanity. Preserve humanity. For our growth."

"Why were you gone so long?" asked Tomi, feeling that little anger nugget heating up. "Why didn't you come back sooner?"

Esther tilted her head towards the sky. Tomi followed her gaze, dropping her mouth open in wonder. "Do you remember the sunrise, Tomi?"

"I…I can't believe it," said Tomi, both amazed and exasperated. "How did it go from night to day just like that?"

"Time, Tomi. Time. How long have we been here? It feels like maybe an hour. But maybe we've been here for days. Or longer."

"So the Other Place is like that?" asked Tomi, feeling her muscles loosen, thinking of her grandmother stuck in some kind of a time warp.

"Well, it's different – you'll see – but yes. There's this time distortion. Almost like someone pressed pause. When I went there, I knew I would come back when it was the right time. The right time for our mission. I just had no idea it was going to be so long. I'm so sorry, Tomi. I was so excited to get there, to experience it, I didn't think about the impact on the people I loved. And now, well I just hope it's not too late. Too late for us. To be your Nana again," said Esther, squeezing Tomi's hand.

The nugget of plasma, the deep-down anger Tomi felt, began to cool, her nana's words and presence pouring cool water on it. She smiled at her grandmother through fresh tears. "It's not too late. Nana."

"So you knew you would come back when it was the right time," Tomi said. "Right time for what? Why did you go?"

"You remember, I told you it all started with my investigation of Mars. I will explain it all, in time. There's just so much to tell you, Tomi. But for now, I'll explain that I went because Ete asked me to. Ete said that humanity, our civilization, was decaying faster than they'd anticipated. The pollution, the deforestation, all these stupid nuclear bombs ready to fire at the push of a button. Ete said I was a wise soul, and that the Earth needed more wise souls before it was time."

"Time for what?"

"For humanity to ascend. For the disruptions that are to come." Esther smiled at Tomi. "I would be too old, this human body of mine, so I went to the Other Place to wait until the time came. I just didn't know that the wise soul I was waiting for was yours."

Tomi blushed. She always had trouble taking compliments, being told that she was special. But she knew that if her grandmother said it, she really meant it.

"You were waiting for me." Tomi looked back up to the sky, trying to process this information and decide how she felt. She thought about how her life had changed since she met Ete. Her life now had two distinct phases: Before Ete and After Ete.

If she were in her grandmother's shoes, she would have gone, too, she decided. She looked around at her Hilly Island, at the waves lapping onto the rocks at the bottom of the hill, the foliage swaying slowly and in unison, like a choreographed dance. *Look how far I've gone since meeting Ete*, thought Tomi.

"How did you meet Ete? Was it your investigation of Mars, through remote viewing, the way I did? Did you always know you were psychic, or did you realize it later, like me?"

"Oh, so many questions," Esther said with a laugh. "The way you spoke there, fast and excited, you reminded me of these two beings I saw when I was a child."

"Beings? What do you mean *beings*?" asked Tomi.

"Well, at the time I thought they were ghosts. Now, I just don't know what they were. Ghosts? Some interdimensional being? Just my imagination? I'm not sure."

"Where did you see them?" asked Tomi.

"On my bed! I think I was about eight years old. One night I woke up, and there were these two beings sitting on the end of my bed, talking to each other. All fast and excited, just like you were," Esther said with a laugh.

"That must have been terrifying," Tomi said seriously.

"That's what was so strange," Esther said. "I wasn't afraid. I woke up, and I wasn't surprised at all that they were there."

"You weren't scared?" asked Tomi, incredulous.

"No," said Esther, shaking her head. "It was the strangest thing. I felt as though they should be there. As though it was normal. Like they're always there, but there's usually a curtain between, hiding us from each other. But for some reason, that night the curtain was pulled back. And instead of being afraid, I was annoyed. 'Hey, I can't sleep with you two talking,' I said to them."

"Oh my god," said Tomi, imagining herself throwing her head under the covers and hoping she had been dreaming. "Did they hear you? Did they respond?"

"Oh yes they did. They told me they were talking, and if I didn't like it, I should go sleep on the other side of the room!" Esther said, smiling and shaking her head. "So that's what I did. I grabbed my quilt and my pillow and curled up on the floor."

"And what happened, did they follow?"

"My mother came into my room in the morning to wake me, and asked why I was sleeping on the floor. Then I was spooked. I remembered what had happened, realized I had seen ghosts, and had actually moved onto the floor, like they told me to. I tried to explain to my mother that I had ghosts in my room and that's why I was on the floor."

"What did she say?" asked Tomi.

"She told me there's no such thing as ghosts, and that I must have been dreaming and sleepwalked onto the floor."

"But you felt like it was real," said Tomi. "Something that really happened. That the beings were real?"

"Well after Mama dismissed it, I wasn't so sure. But later, when I was alone with my nana, I told her about it. She didn't make me feel like I was being silly, or making it up. No, she already knew that I was a bit different. That I had 'the sight', as she called it. She recognized it because she had it, too. And now here I am with my amazing granddaughter. And she has the sight, as well."

Tomi looked to the ground. Her nana's nana, too. She wondered how far back it went. If it always skipped generations. If it was only the women.

"Can you tell me more about your grandmother? About your childhood?" asked Tomi. She had a deep desire to hear it all. To visualize her grandmother's life, to see if it helped make sense of her own.

"I'll tell you a few stories from my childhood, and then we should go and get these Earth exiles back to their planet," Esther said, smiling and motioning towards Tomi's friends. "And on another day I will tell you about the witches. About remote viewing, and meeting Ete. About the Other Place. There's so much to share, but for now, maybe just a few stories."

Chapter 2

"As to the Fairy belief, we conceive it to be a complex matter, from which tradition, with its memory of earth-dwellers, is not wholly absent, while more is due to a survival of the pre-Christian Hades, and to the belief in local spirits – the Vuis of Melanesia, the Nereids of ancient and modern Greece, the Lares of Rome, the fateful Mœræ and Hathors – old imaginings of a world not yet dispeopled of its dreams."

Andrew Lang, *Editor of The Secret Commonwealth of Elves, Fauns and Fairies*

Esther's dirty yellow rubber boot caught on the lip of a pothole, making her stumble and drop her string of catfish onto the dusty gravel.

"C'mon," Clarence said with a sigh, turning around to grab his little sister's hand and pull her upright, Clarence towering over his little sister after a recent growth spurt.

Esther choked back tears, wanting to be strong and brave in front of her brother. It was only recently that he had let her come with him on his Friday catfish runs, and she knew that if she annoyed him, he wouldn't let her come next time.

Clarence, seven years older, was impatient with his clumsy little sister. Every Friday Clarence would rush home to change out of his school clothes, grab his pole, and hurry off to his favourite catfish hole near Celanese. He would then take his haul downtown to sell them so that he could go to the cinema with his friends.

While Clarence brushed gravel from Esther's knees, she held up her string of catfish – smaller than Clarence's but enough for a family dinner – and examined it, brushing pebbles from the fish. While Clarence had an entrepreneurial purpose for his string, Esther wanted to get her fish back home to her mother and help her turn them into dinner.

It was one of the ways Esther was trying to make amends with her. Though her mother hadn't brought it up again, Esther still felt uneasy about the night the two ghosts sat chatting on the foot of her bed. Esther brought it up with her mother only once, before bed the next day.

"Mama, what if the ghosts come back again tonight?" she had asked, climbing under her quilt after praying beside her bed.

"I told you, there's no such thing," her mother had said sternly, pulling the quilt up to her neck.

"But I saw them, I heard—"

"If you heard something, it's the devil trying to trick you," her mother had shot back. "I don't want to hear this nonsense again."

The ghosts hadn't come back. Instead, Esther had pulled her head under her covers and cried. She was ashamed. *It wasn't real,* she'd whispered to herself. She had resolved to forget the whole thing, and not speak of it again.

While her mother hadn't brought it up again, Esther felt like her mother was looking at her a little differently. Like she was suspicious. The next Friday when Clarence went to grab his fishing rod, the idea came to her. After begging and pleading, he agreed to let her tag along, so long as she didn't slow him down.

While she hoped bringing home fish would smooth things over with her mother, she found that she looked forward to it all week. Running off with her brother, catching fish and contributing to her family, she felt mature and independent.

Having brushed the loose gravel off her fish, she smiled with pride at her catch.

"C'mon, don't make me miss the show. This way," Clarence said, pulling her back into motion, and towards a small dirt road.

Esther tugged at his sleeve. "Can we go this way, please?" The dirt road, Clarence's preferred route, pointed directly towards Hell's Hollow, a poor neighbourhood hugging the Oostanaula River in Rome, Georgia, where they lived in a small wooden house. The dirt road took them along an old cemetery that gave Esther the creeps. While she always felt nervous passing it, she was extra anxious since her ghostly visit.

"No. You ask every time. This way's faster," Clarence said, unbothered by a few headstones in a field.

"What you got there?" a voice called from behind them.

Esther and Clarence turned to meet the voice, and saw a young man in a red pickup hanging his face out the window and pointing towards Clarence's string of fish.

"Catfish," Clarence said shyly.

"What've you got planned for 'em?" the man said, raising his dark eyebrows.

"Sell them, I guess," said Clarence.

The man eyed up the string of fish while doing some mental math. "I'll give you one-seventy-five," he offered. Clarence hesitated, looking at his catch. "Okay, two even."

Clarence looked back at the man, smiled, stepped towards the truck and handed the man the string. The man reached into his pocket and pulled out two ratty dollar bills.

"Mine aren't for sale," Esther said flatly.

"That's okay little lady, these should do fine," the man said kindly. He tipped his head in the direction of the dirt road. "You two live down there?"

"Yes, sir," said Clarence.

"I always heard there's an old lady lives down there. A witch. Dark magic," the man said. "Heard her house has a yellow door and to steer clear. Any of that true?"

Esther was chilled. A witch, living in her neighbourhood?

"No, sir," Clarence said coldly. "Never heard that. We best go." He turned, grabbed Esther by the hand, and headed down the dirt road.

Esther heard the man yell out, "Thanks for the fish!" over the sound of his truck starting.

"A witch?" Esther said, trying to look her brother in the face while keeping up with his longer strides. "We have a yellow door."

"He was talking about Nana," Clarence said flatly.

Esther stopped in her tracks. "Nana? Is Nana a witch?"

"Don't be stupid," he said, grabbing her hand again to get her moving, the two dollars burning a hole in his pocket. "Nana's not a witch."

"Why would he say that?" she asked.

"Nana's not a witch," he repeated, impatiently. "She's just a bit…weird. Now c'mon, let's get home."

As soon as they finished dinner, Clarence asked to be excused, and rushed out the door to catch his show. Esther's mother, pleased with her daughter's dinner contribution, told her not to worry about dishes, that she would tidy up.

"Esther sweetheart, it's such a beautiful night, will you walk with me down to the river?" her nana asked.

Esther liked walking with her grandmother. She wasn't always racing to catch up like with other adults, since Nana walked slowly and with a cane.

They walked quietly towards the river, her Nana stopping short of the bank, smiling at the slow-moving brown water. While her grandmother had become more frail and moved more slowly than she used to, Esther hardly noticed, her Nana always seeming larger than life to Esther.

She then looked kindly at Esther, and asked gently, "What is it that's troubling you? I can tell when there's something."

She then looked kindly at Esther, and asked gently, "What is it that's troubling you? I can tell when there's something."

Esther froze. She wanted to ask her nana about what the man had said, but didn't want to hurt her feelings. Esther knew she couldn't hide it forever. Her grandmother always seemed to know what was going on in her mind, often before she did.

"Well…we met some man today. He said you are a witch. That he heard you are a witch," she finally said.

The corners of Nana's mouth slowly started to curl, then broke out into a smile as she let out a huge laugh, putting her hand to her mouth to stifle her laughter. Esther was confused by her grandmother's reaction.

"Aren't you hurt? Or angry?" Esther asked.

"Oh, child," Nana said, her voice lighthearted and mischievous, "men have been claiming women are witches for a thousand years. You see, a lot of men seem tough, but they get scared when there's something they can't control. Don't pay them no mind."

Esther thought about what her brother had said. "Clarence said you're not a witch, just weird."

"Did he now?" Nana said, laughing again. "Well that's alright with me, I don't mind being called weird."

"You don't?" Esther said, trying to think of a time someone used the word 'weird' positively.

"Let me tell you a story," Nana said, taking Esther's hand and slowly walking back towards the street. "There were two trees growing on a hill. One grew up straight and tall, and the other grew up crooked. The straight tree would laugh at the crooked one. Even called it ugly and weird. Until one day, a man came with his saw. He looked at both trees, and cut down the straight tree, because he could turn it into lumber. He didn't know what to do with the crooked tree, so he just left it."

Esther walked quietly for a moment. She started to wonder if she was weird, too.

"Have you ever seen ghosts, Nana?"

"Child, I've seen all kinds of things." Nana looked at her and smiled. "Your mom told me you saw something in your room."

"She told me not to talk about it," Esther said, looking at the ground. "She said it was the devil trying to confuse me."

Nana squeezed her hand. "Here's the thing about being weird. It's easier to share these things with other weird people. Like a club. A secret club."

Esther liked the idea of being part of a secret club. "Well, I have a secret," she said, speaking tentatively. "I saw two ghosts in my room. Two little people, they were sitting on my bed. Talking to each other."

"Were you scared?" Nana asked.

"No! It was so strange," Esther said, still surprised.

"I've seen ghosts in my bedroom before, too. And you know what, they never did anything to hurt me. I've even gone with them, and they always bring me back," Nana said. She looked directly at Esther, and Esther saw her eyes twinkle. "Secret, right?"

Esther smiled at her nana, feeling both reassured in what she saw, and intrigued by this club.

"What else did you see?" Esther asked, wanting to be let in on more secrets.

"Oh, different things," Nana said. "Once when I was young, I was out with *my* nana, out walking just like we are. And I still almost can't believe it, except I was there, and I know what I saw. It was a bright, quiet day, and all of a sudden we started to hear voices. We turned, and saw a big wooden ship, a ship that should be in an ocean, except it was flying! Instead of a sail, it had a huge balloon, which I guess is what made it float. And it just sailed along quietly. Except there were some small men on board, and we could hear them talking. Well, my nana was frozen, but I yelled out, 'How did you do that?' You know what they said?"

After a pause, Esther replied, "No, what?"

"*We're from Mars!*" Nana said, raising her hand and waving. "And they just waved and floated by. I mean this was before airplanes. We'd never seen anything fly but birds and bugs. Well, after a minute, my nana started walking. I was excited to get home and tell everyone, but my nana said no. We won't tell anyone about this."

"Why not?" asked Esther.

"Well, I guess she thought people would think we were crazy. So we kept it a secret. Just like you and me," she said, smiling conspiratorially at Esther.

Esther was so engaged listening to her grandmother that she wasn't paying attention to where they were walking. Suddenly, she felt distracted. She looked to her left, and there was the small cemetery.

"Most of the time," Nana said, "it's not about what I see, but what I feel. Like now."

"Now?" asked Esther.

"The graveyard," Nana said, stopping and turning to look at it. "I know it spooks you. Why?"

Esther looked down and responded. "They're…dead. They're buried there."

"Look up," Nana said, pointing towards the cemetery. Esther looked up at the rows of headstones and markers, shaded in dusk. "Each stone there is for a person. People just like you and me. These are our ancestors. They only want the best for us."

Esther nodded. She knew this was true.

"Listen," Nana said. "If you get real quiet, close your eyes and listen closely, you can hear it. Hear them. Feel them. They're sending love to us."

Esther looked up at her nana, whose eyes were closed, a slight smile on her face. She looked back at the cemetery and closed her eyes. She waited, not hearing anything but the crickets and birds.

Then she thought she felt something. A warmth, a stirring, in her belly. She opened her eyes, scanned the headstones, and found she was no longer afraid.

"Come on, it's getting dark, time to get home," her nana said, slowly shuffling over the dirt road.

One summer day Esther and her nana were sitting on the front steps of the house when a man Esther had not seen before pulled up in a red old truck. He turned off the engine, got out of the truck, and tipped his hat to Esther's nana.

"Good mornin', Elizabeth," he said, removing his hat and looking up at the sun, perhaps trying to gauge if it still was in fact morning. He didn't look at Esther, speaking only to her grandmother. "Would you take a ride with me? Some folks need to dig a well and aren't having luck. I'm afraid they're going to be broke before they find some water. They've only got enough for one more hole. Think you'd come and help?"

Esther looked to her grandmother, sitting silently, considering the request.

"Who needs it? And who's there?"

"The Carters," the man said, "you know them. They're good folks. It's just the family, the well diggers, and maybe a couple onlookers. They've dug three dry holes. They have just enough money for one more drill. I told them to wait until I can bring you out there."

Nana sat quietly in thought, finally nodding and standing up as the man opened the door of the truck and waved for her to climb in.

Years later, Esther would realize that her nana was exercising caution when she asked who would be there. She wanted to know who would be witness to her performing an act some people might call witchcraft.

"Well come on," Nana said, turning to Esther who hadn't budged, so curious watching this exchange, wondering what her nana had to do with digging holes. "I can't exactly leave you here alone, can I?"

Esther sat in the middle of the bench seat, watching with interest as the man worked the gear shifter and picked up speed as they left town. She kept looking up to her grandmother, wondering what this was all about, what her grandmother was being asked to do. Her nana's face told her to not bother asking.

"Pull over here a minute," Nana said, pointing. The man pulled to the side of the road, and Esther watched her grandmother get out, tromp into an orchard, and start jiggling and tugging at branches on the trees. She then picked up and tested the resistance of branches she found on the ground. Eventually she found one that was deemed acceptable, and climbed back into the truck. Without words, the man started driving again.

After a little more driving, the man turned into a field, over barely visible tire tracks, through some trees, and into a small clearing, towards a gathering of twenty or so people.

"A couple onlookers?" her nana said.

"There were. I guess word got around that you were coming," said the man, opening the door and exiting the truck. He led Esther and Nana past a group of onlookers, watching and whispering, and past three men leaning on a huge contraption, a machine bigger than any Esther had seen. The man led them to a stern, concerned looking man standing alongside a woman holding a baby. She smiled but her eyes were weary and red.

"Elizabeth, these are the Carters," the man said.

"It's so good of you to come here," Mrs. Carter said with a kind smile, shaking Nana's hand. The man said nothing, other than tipping his cap. Esther felt like he looked at her nana suspiciously, even with contempt, which she didn't like or understand, since Nana was doing them a favour.

"Well, I hear you folks want some water. I'll get to work," Nana said, turning to Esther. "You stand here with Mrs. Carter and don't make a fuss."

Esther watched curiously as her nana walked back to the truck, retrieved the branch she had found at the orchard, then walked into the centre of the field, and closed her eyes. The branch was forked, shaped like a Y, and her nana held the tops of the Y with each hand, letting the long part of the stick hang towards the ground.

She started to take slow, deliberate steps. At first she just walked slowly, until on one step, she let out a "*humph*" sound, and the stick seemed to jump. Esther could hear a few giggles from the onlookers and the men leaning on the drilling machine. Esther heard Mr. Carter make a "*pshhh*" sound, and heard Mrs. Carter whisper, "No," back to him. Esther wanted to yell, scream at all of them for laughing at her nana, but managed to keep it in, knowing how angry Nana would be with her.

Nana dragged her foot on the ground to make a marking. She walked around that first spot, holding the branch, until she again made a sound and the stick jumped. She made another marking. She did this several times, sketching out a path. Esther smiled, thinking her grandmother was done, but her nana then moved up and down in the opposite direction, intersecting the path she had already made. She paced back and forth for some time – *surely hearing the giggles*, Esther thought – until the stick finally jumped again. She again seemed to find a path, marking off another line until it intersected the first line. On that spot she stopped, stood quietly for a few moments, then opened her eyes. She looked towards the Carters and pointed at the first marked line, then the second.

"There's a channel here, and another running here," she said, then pointed down to where her feet stood. "This is where they meet. Drill here."

The men leaning on the huge drill looked at Mr. Carter. Esther looked at his face and saw both fear and anger. It looked like it pained him to do it, but he nodded to the drillers. Her nana returned to her, and they sat down under a tree and watched the drillers get to work, moving the huge contraption into place, firing up the smoky engine, and filling the field with noise. Esther held her hands over her ears.

She watched them get to work, as the huge drill started to corkscrew down into the soil. Esther looked at the Carters and felt their fear. Eventually, they put the drill in reverse, revealing a hole. One of the men tossed a bucket on a rope into the hole, then started to haul it back up. He reached in, pulled the bucket out by the handle, then so that everyone could see, poured the bucketful of water onto the ground.

The onlookers murmured excitedly, then gave a brief applause. Esther looked at Mrs. Carter and saw that she was crying. Mr. Carter laughed and hugged his wife.

Esther got up and hugged her grandmother. "You did it, Nana!" Her nana gave her a quick smile and gestured downwards, telling her to contain her excitement.

Mr. and Mrs. Carter approached Esther and her nana, along with the man who had brought them to this field.

"Mrs. Baptiste," Mrs. Carter said, beaming, "I don't know how we can properly thank you, that was, well…"

"A lucky guess," Nana said, touching the woman's hand.

"My wife is right," Mr. Carter said, his voice deep and genuine, "I don't know how you did it, but you did. I can't tell you how much we needed this. Now, we probably should have discussed your fee."

"Oh, I don't think we need to discuss that now," Nana said, smiling at and stroking the cheek of the baby in Mrs. Carter's arms. "Why don't you grow something on this field first, then we can talk."

They arrived back home just before Esther's mother would be returning from work. Esther asked if she could see the stick that her nana had used.

"Nana, how did you do that, how does the stick work? How did you know where the water was?"

"You just have to listen, child," her nana said. She pointed at the branch. "There's water in this branch, just like there's water in our bodies. Water always remembers. That same water that's in me, in you, in that branch, that water knows the water underground. It just needs reminding, is all."

"I can't wait to tell Mama about today," said Esther, holding the stick just as her grandmother had.

"Well your Mama might not like it," Nana said, "but enough people saw today that she will hear about it anyways. But maybe we don't tell her that I didn't take any money."

"Secret club. I understand. But why didn't you ask for money?" asked Esther.

"You always get more back from kindness than you give out, child, remember that."

Lying in bed, her head under her pillow, Esther realized she wasn't making tears anymore. She had cried her eyes dry.

She slowly moved the pillow off her head, and sat up in the bed. She had jumped into bed so quickly, she had forgotten to close the curtains over her window. She saw it was a dark, clear night, the sky abundant with stars. Esther stared at the stars, thinking of her nana.

When she was younger, her grandmother had told her that the stars were our loved ones, our ancestors, looking back at us. She wasn't sure she believed that anymore, but felt a jolt of hope that her nana was watching over her.

Esther knew she should lay back and get some sleep. Tomorrow they would be at the church for the funeral, then to the cemetery for the burial, and she wanted to be as helpful to her mother as she could.

She had tried her best to be strong and supportive, seeing her mother agonized by Nana's passing. It was only a few weeks since Nana had let her in on the secret club, and shared some of her secrets with Esther.

And now she's gone, and I'm alone, she thought, *there is no club anymore. Just me.*

She scanned the stars, and wondered where her nana was, wishing so deeply she could see her again.

Through her window, a star caught her eye. She leaned her head forward and squinted, sure that this star had a blue glow to it. It was moving slowly, not like a shooting star. It passed gently across the sky, before it sped off to the west and disappeared.

Esther continued watching and wondered, *was that Nana, that light?* She watched the window for a few more minutes to see if it would return, but it didn't. Still, she found herself feeling full and calm, suddenly not thinking about the funeral and saying goodbye. Instead, she felt love.

She lay back in her bed and closed her eyes. *Nana, what will I do without you? Who will understand me?*

She opened her eyes, and saw a blue glow in the corner of her room, near the ceiling. She closed her eyes again to reset her sight, and saw it again. It was moving, floating gently from one corner of her room to another, a vibrant, shining blue orb the size of a grapefruit.

As the orb floated from one side of the room to another, it hovered above Esther's bed, just out of reach. Mouth open in wonder, Esther reached for it anyways, wishing she could feel it, imagining it felt warm. As she reached out, she thought that it grew brighter for a moment, as though it recognized her and was saying hello.

"Nana, is that you?" she whispered. Again, the glow brightened. She reached her arm out a little longer, and the orb slowly backed up towards the ceiling. Though she could have blinked and missed it, Esther was sure she saw the orb wink as it disappeared out of existence.

Esther cried again. This time she cried not because she lost her grandmother, but because she felt her grandmother's love.

When she stopped crying, she whispered, "Our little secret," and fell asleep.

Esther had been so full of rage, so preoccupied with both her anger and her shame, she had missed a turn, and found herself on a street she didn't recognize.

She stopped and looked around. It was a residential street like any other, but it felt eerie. There were no kids playing on the street, nobody sitting on their front porches. The silence and emptiness gave her the creeps. She was about to turn and retrace her steps, when she was spooked by a voice from behind her.

"You look lost, sweetheart," said a kind, elderly voice. "Where are you heading?"

Esther jumped in surprise, turned to find the owner of the voice, but instead saw tall flowers growing in big bunches, so unlike the well-manicured flower gardens on the rest of the street. The rest of town. She saw the stems of a bunch of white flowers part, and a woman's face poked through, an older woman down on her knees, her hands covered in soil.

"Oh, uh," stammered Esther, disoriented and surprised by this interaction. "Home, but I guess I got lost."

"Lost isn't so bad," said the woman, slowly standing up, revealing a short, squat elderly woman wearing a straw hat, wide-brimmed for gardening. "You have to get lost before you can be found. Where is home?"

"Hell's Hollow," Esther replied.

"Oh well that's not far from here," the woman said looking surprised, wondering how this girl had gotten lost. "How did you get lost? Are you new to Rome?"

"No," said Esther, feeling ashamed for not paying attention and getting lost. "I was born here. I just…wasn't paying attention to where I was walking. I was in my head, I guess."

"What was causing you to be so distracted?" asked the woman kindly. "Nothing too serious, I hope."

"No, well, I was just really mad," Esther said. "Am mad. But it's okay, I should go."

The woman smiled at her. "It's pretty hot out, why don't you come in for some sweet tea first."

Esther hesitated, but there was something about this woman, perhaps the way she smiled, that reminded her of her Nana, gone for six years now.

"Okay, thank you," Esther said, stepping towards the walkway to the woman's front door. She passed the mailbox which had the name Fairchild painted neatly on it.

Esther entered the small home, and saw it was very different than her own. The art on the walls looked different, chaotic and almost random. The living room was untidy. Not dirty, but there were books piled on surfaces here and there, with a large bookcase in the room. Esther hadn't seen that many books in a home before. She drew in a breath, and found the home smelled of flowers and herbs.

"Have a seat," said the woman, pointing at the small kitchen table while she pulled glasses off a shelf and a pitcher from the refrigerator. "Just push those books aside."

Esther sat down, and gently slid a few books to the side. She noticed one of the books was about fairies, but it looked like a serious book, not a children's story.

"Now," said the woman, placing a glass in front of Esther and sitting across from her, "what are you so mad about?"

Esther sipped the cold tea and felt refreshed. "Oh, well, it's probably wrong to even say."

"Well now I'm really intrigued," said the woman, with a slight smile. "It's okay child, I'm not one to judge others. Who are you mad at?"

"The Church," Esther said shyly, waiting for a harsh reaction. Instead the woman smiled a little more and nodded. "And the pastor. And me, I guess."

"That's okay," said the woman, taking a drink of tea and maintaining a reassuring look. "I've been mad at the Church once or twice myself. What happened?"

Esther couldn't believe she was having this conversation. She wasn't sure she could tell her mother about how upset she was, and here she was sharing with this stranger. Still, the words spilled out.

"Well, I've been doing a lot at the church, especially the past few years, I help with chores, with the littles at Sunday school. Well today, the pastor asked a few of us what we want to be when we grow up. It came to me and I said a pastor in the Church," Esther said, her eyes welling with tears.

"Oh, I see," said the woman knowingly.

"He said I can't be a pastor. Because I'm a girl. That it says so in the Bible. But when I grow up I could maybe be a deacon, or run the Sunday school. And I was just so hurt, I thought that was my future. I thought I would serve God."

"I'm sorry to say that you aren't the first woman to face that disappointment," the woman said.

"Now I just, I don't want to help anymore. Help anyone," Esther said, feeling the anger in her stomach heating up again.

"Oh, I'm sure you don't mean that," the woman said. "Helping others is one of the most beautiful things you can do. And you don't need a church to do it, anyways."

As the woman spoke, Esther remembered her grandmother speaking to her. Once, when talking about God, Esther asked her if she ever had any doubt.

'No,' her nana had said. 'If you ever have doubt, child, look for the helpers. No matter how terrible the situation, war, famine, disasters, you'll always find helpers. They are God speaking to you.'

"My nana used to say something similar," Esther said, "before she died."

The woman tilted her head and gave Esther a sympathetic look. "Your nana sounds like a smart woman. My name is Alda, by the way."

"I'm Esther. Thanks for listening, and for the tea," she said, emptying her glass.

Before she stood to go, Alda spoke. "And what about you? You said you were mad at yourself. Why?"

"Oh, I…well I sinned," said Esther, her cheeks feeling warm with shame.

"Tell me, what did you do? Remember, I don't judge."

"Well…when he said I couldn't be a pastor, I said a bad word. A really bad word. Well, I didn't say it, I thought it. I'd never even thought that word before," said Esther, looking gravely at the empty glass.

"What was the word?" Alda asked with a small, mischievous smile.

"Oh, I can't say it," said Esther.

"Sure you can," said Alda. Esther thought her eyes twinkled with mischief. "It's just a word. What did you think?"

"Well, when he said that, that it's because I'm a girl, well I thought…*mmmpf* you," she said, avoiding the actual word.

"*Mmmpf* isn't a bad word," said Alda with a playful smile. "What word was it, really?"

"No. I can't."

"Sure you can. Just say it. It's just me and these four walls to hear you," said Alda.

"It was, well, *eff* you," said Esther, shocked she had even said the letter aloud.

"Come on, say it, it'll feel good!"

"Fuck you, I thought, fuck you, and now I will probably go to Hell, even thinking of saying that to a pastor," Esther said, her eyes again welling with tears.

Alda laughed, reached out and put her hand on Esther's. "Esther, if everyone went to hell for thinking or saying a word like that, there would be nobody in Heaven. Anyways, in my opinion, you had every right to think it. I can see already that you're a woman who is close to God. Or Goddess! And the church isn't the only place you can find that."

From that day, Esther spent less time at the church, and more time visiting her friend Alda. She taught Esther about all kinds of different beliefs, different religions and what people around the world think about God, and how so many religions had gone wrong by taking the feminine out. She also taught her about the constellations and planets, and how they affect us, and shared interesting and old books with her. Esther knew, without Alda ever saying, that this was all part of their secret club.

One day after school Esther found Alda in her back garden, placing a small dish on a flat rock. As Esther got closer, she realized Alda was speaking, looking straight forward, talking to a saucer of milk.

"Do you have a cat?" asked Esther. "I've never seen a cat here."

Alda smiled. "It's not for a cat my dear, it's for the fae. They like cream."

"Fae?" asked Esther.

"The fae. The fairies."

Esther looked at the dish, and noticed there were some small, shiny stones placed around the flat rock, and a small piece of a mirror hanging from a nearby branch. She was confused. *Was this a joke?* she wondered.

"You're leaving this for…the fairies. For real?" asked Esther, trying to ask without judgement, as Alda would do, but feeling like there was a joke that had gone over her head.

"For real. I'm leaving this here for them, and maybe they will leave something for me," Alda said. "But, if they ever leave something for you, it's important you don't thank them. If you thank them, it's like there's still an outstanding debt. They like even deals."

"I don't…have you seen them?" asked Esther, still confounded.

"No," said Alda cheerily, stepping away from the flat rock and saucer. "Well, sometimes out the corner of my eye. They're shy. And I know what you're thinking."

"I…you do?"

"Yes," said Alda, "you think I sound crazy. Because fairies are from *Peter Pan*, not the real world, right?"

Esther nodded.

"Let me show you something," said Alda, leading Esther inside. She stood in front of her bookcase, scanned it, and pulled a couple books out.

"Here," she said, sitting on her couch and waving Esther over to join her. She opened the first book and leafed through it, stopping on a page with a black and white picture. "Look at this. This is the

Fairy Flag. It lives at Dunvegan Castle in Scotland. It's said to be a gift from the fairies, and that it has magical powers."

"What kind of powers?" asked Esther, scanning the black and white picture.

"Oh, it can help a woman in having a baby. It can multiply your army. It can save sick animals. All kinds of things, so they say. And this," Alda said, pulling out an old, green book. "This book is a study on fairies and elves, written four hundred years ago."

"Wow," said Esther, gently holding the small, worn old book.

"The point is," said Alda, "where my people are from, they didn't question if fairies or elves were real. They just knew they were real. Like God. Do you believe God is real, Esther?"

"Yes, of course."

"How do you know? Have you seen Her?"

"No," Esther said, still jarred when Alda used feminine pronouns to refer to God. "I believe, I guess. Faith."

"That's right. Belief, faith. If you believe something is real, it is," said Alda. "Even God. Even fairies."

As Esther got older and school became more consuming, she saw Alda less and less. When she was seventeen, her mom took them to Alabama for a couple of weeks to visit family. When she got back to

Rome, she walked to Alda's house to pay her a visit and was surprised to see a motorcycle parked in front of the house.

Usually she would be outside in the garden, or would be at the door to meet Esther, as though she somehow knew the moment Esther would arrive. This time the door was closed. Esther knocked.

She heard heavy footsteps, the door opened, and behind it was a shorty, heavy, and masculine woman wearing a serious expression.

"Can I help you?" she said.

Esther couldn't speak. Not only had she expected Alda to answer, the woman in front of her was like none she had seen. Her straight hair was parted and cut short, looking to Esther more like a man's hairstyle. She wore no makeup, dark pants, and a black leather jacket. *This could be a man's outfit*, she thought.

"I…I'm looking for Alda," she finally got out. "Is she home?"

"You must be Esther," the woman said, her mouth attempting a smile. "She told me all about you. I'm Joanna, her daughter."

Esther was even more surprised. "Her…her daughter?"

"Let me guess," Joanna said as she let out single a deep laugh, "she didn't tell you all about me. That's okay, I suppose it isn't easy to explain your witchy, lesbian, biker daughter."

Esther really didn't know what to say, finding this conversation, this woman, surreal within her experiences growing up in this town.

"Esther," Joanna said, her face now serious as she pulled in a deep breath. "My mom died this past Sunday. I'm so sorry, Esther. I have an idea of how much she meant to you. You meant a lot to her, too. She cherished your visits."

Esther felt dizzy, like the air was sucked out of her, like she was losing her nana all over again.

Joanna put her hand on Esther's shoulder. "But don't worry, you're not alone. She told me to look out for you."

Chapter 3

"It was among the strongest feelings of grief I have ever encountered. The contrast between the vicious coldness of space and the warm nurturing of Earth below filled me with overwhelming sadness. Every day, we are confronted with the knowledge of further destruction of Earth at our hands: the extinction of animal species, of flora and fauna . . . things that took five billion years to evolve, and suddenly we will never see them again because of the interference of mankind. It filled me with dread. My trip to space was supposed to be a celebration; instead, it felt like a funeral."

William Shatner

Tomi turned to look at her grandmother, waiting for her to continue. She had let Esther tell her stories, and as she did, Tomi saw it all visually in her mind, like she was watching old home movies. When her grandmother finally stopped talking, the movie went to black, and Tomi's awareness was brought back to the present – sitting on this soft grass, overlooking her beautiful Hilly Island.

"Nana? What happened next? Did you become friends with Joanna?" asked Tomi, wanting to sit and listen to her grandmother forever.

"Oh, we did," her grandmother said, smiling at how insufficient words can be in defining human relationships. "But maybe that's enough stories for just now."

"No no, you can't bring up the lesbian biker witch and just leave me hanging!" Tomi said, smiling at her grandmother.

Esther made a weak smile before her face began to droop in sadness. "Well," she said, her voice melancholy, "this part gets a bit sad. It was a difficult time."

Tomi put her hand on Esther's. "Oh, I'm sorry for joking, I didn't–"

"I know, don't you worry," Esther said, her voice softening. "Well Joanna lived on the west coast, and didn't stay in town long. But when she left she gave me her phone number, and said she will always be there for me, just like her mother was. Well, a short time later, just when I was graduating high school, my mother died. It was sudden, her heart gave out, the poor woman. She worked so hard her whole life."

"Oh Nana, I'm so sorry," said Tomi, thinking about her own mother's passing, and the complicated feelings that came along with it.

"Thanks, sweetheart," said Esther, smiling gently. "When it's sudden like that, well, of course I had some regrets. Once I knew about the secret club, well I knew not to share that with my mother. But after she passed, I wished I'd shared more. Been closer to her. Anyways, I had just turned eighteen, so was an adult, and didn't quite know what to do. My brother was off in the Navy, so he had his own life to live. And everyone else was dead – mom, Nana, Alda. My Auntie in Alabama that we used to visit offered for me to come live with them. Or I could just stay in Rome by myself. Get a job and start my life. But something, some deep-down feeling, told me to call Joanna."

"Oh I hope you called her," Tomi said. "Wait, is that how you ended up in Oakland?"

Esther nodded and turned to look at the sky, that faraway look we humans get imagining ourselves in young bodies again. "I called her. A week later, she picked me up on her motorcycle. I hopped on the back of her bike, and off we drove to California. I was eighteen and on the back of a motorcycle for the first time in my life. What an adventure it was."

Tomi smiled at her grandmother, imagining her as a young woman on the cusp of adventure. "The image I have of you in my head, well, it's just beautiful."

"Life is often beautiful if we stop to notice. And I promise I will tell you all about Joanna. But on another day. On another planet! I never thought I would be able to say something like that. Look at this – what an adventure we are on, Tomi," Esther said, gazing at their breathtaking surroundings.

A lump in Tomi's throat prevented her from responding. Instead she smiled, wiped a tear, and nodded. This impossible moment with her grandmother filled her with gratitude and made her feel deeply happy. Even if she couldn't stop herself from questioning if this was all real, if this impossible moment was really happening.

Esther stood, stretched, and pulled Tomi up, Tomi's body almost floating as she stood. They turned to see Ete still sitting in meditation, and Tomi's three friends napping in the soft grass beside the shiny white craft.

"I don't know about all of you," said Esther gently, waking the others, "I could stay in this place forever. But we have work to do. We've been called. What say you we get ourselves back to Earth?"

With a wave of her long, lanky arm, a rectangle began to form on the ultra-smooth white exterior of the craft, and a ramp gently descended onto the ground. Ete stepped onto the ramp and into the craft, followed by Ib, Barry, and Esther. Tomi stepped forward, but paused and turned around, taking a last look at her Hilly Island, wondering if she would ever return, in this life or another.

"I'm still waiting to wake up and find that this was all a dream," said Kirsten.

Tomi smiled at her friend, somehow alive and in one piece, healed upon their rescue by Ete and Esther, Kirsten's white shirt stained with dried blood.

"I'm still not sure it isn't," said Tomi, taking Kirsten's hand and leading her onto the craft.

As they stepped aboard, Tomi looked around again at the seamless metallic interior, the sterile-looking cabin void of seats, controls, or windows. Ete waved her arm again, and shiny metallic stools emerged from the floor. The humans all took a seat while Ete moved towards a pillar in the centre of the room, where she picked up the helmet that was affixed to it, the same helmet Tomi had worn to direct the craft to this Hilly Island.

Before putting the helmet on, Ete turned to look at Tomi. "*I hope you don't mind,*" Ete said, her small mouth not moving, the words instead appearing telepathically in Tomi's mind, "*but I will steer us back to Earth. Back to my home.*"

Tomi smiled and nodded at Ete and had a moment of realization, of shock, that she really was sharing this space, this moment, with a flesh-and-blood non-human intelligence. An alien. There she was, right in front of Tomi, so tall and lanky, with skin that seemed to shimmer. While at this point she loved and trusted Ete, this large alien body in front of her made her feel uneasy.

It's the eyes, thought Tomi. *She has two arms, two legs, a neck, a head. We share the same general shape, but those big, catlike eyes are always a shock.*

At that moment, Ete slowly winked a catlike eye at Tomi, and gently pulled the helmet onto her inverted teardrop-shaped head. She stepped away from the pillar, stood at the centre of the room, and closed her eyes. Just as when she had remote viewed the inside of a craft, Tomi focused her gaze on the metallic cabin wall. As though the craft was aware of where Tomi looked, wherever she focused, the wall became transparent. She could see the craft lifting easily from her Hilly Island, and into the black of space, without feeling so much as a bump of turbulence from the craft.

Tomi looked at each of her friends, all of them staring straight ahead, equally transfixed by the view from the craft. Two moons passed through her view, one larger and spherical, the other kidney-shaped, as though a meteor had come by and chipped a portion of it off.

Her view brightened as they passed by a star – *or is it called a sun when it's this close?*, wondered Tomi – churning, burning, and spitting out life-giving energy to her Hilly Island planet.

In what felt like a blink, the solar system in front of them was just a memory. This journey was different from the one here, when Tomi was directing the craft. When Tomi put the helmet on, it seemed as though she thought of the Hilly Island, and in seemingly no time at all, they arrived. Instead of being transported instantaneously, this time it felt like they were travelling, physically moving through space. Tomi looked at Ete, her mind directing the craft through the helmet, and realized that she was doing this for them, taking these humans on a sightseeing journey through a universe their species would never otherwise lay eyes on.

"My…my god," Ib said, as the walls all around them became fully transparent. Tomi looked at Ib, and saw he had his head cocked upwards, his mouth wide open. Tomi followed his gaze to see they were surrounded by stars, flying under a nebula, with stars clustered within what seemed like bright purple smoke.

Tomi wasn't sure how she knew, but she said, "Stars are being born here."

Tomi sensed the craft speeding up as they quickly approached, then zoomed past star after star until it seemed they were alone in a vast ocean of dark and empty. Single stars were soon replaced by full, distant galaxies, some a concentration of light, some spiraling, others incoherent, a jumble of stars. *How many species*, Tomi wondered as galaxies came into and out of view, *how many civilizations are we passing by just now?*

'*The universe is abounding with life,*' she remembered Ete once saying.

Soon the galaxies stopped passing by, and they were again immersed by a vast darkness, punctuated with distant stars. Soon a single spiral galaxy came into view, growing in size and brightness as they sped closer.

It was familiar. Tomi felt her heart speed up as they approached.

"Is that–" Kirsten started.

"The Milky Way," Ib finished. "Home."

My human home, at least, thought Tomi, a pang of sadness and longing flowing through her body, having just left her Hilly Island, the place her soul called home.

"I hope I never forget this moment," Esther said. "Whoever could have imagined this?"

Tomi wiped her eyes to clear her vision, realizing tears has started to well up as they stared down at the most magnificent spiralling of stars, the beckoning Earth somewhere down there.

"I've seen many pictures of what we think the Milky Way looks like, but this…well, none come close to this," Ib said. "I'm not sure anything can come close to this."

Of what we thought it would look like. Of course, Tomi thought. *Humans have never left the galaxy. Could we be the first humans to see it from the outside?*

"Look at the spirals," said Ib, his usual professorial voice sounding more like that of a boy in wonder. "It's the golden ratio. It's Fibonacci. This spiral, it exists throughout nature, from snails and seashells to flowers to hurricanes."

"To galaxies," said Barry.

"To galaxies. And why? Why does the universe do that, repeat the pattern? What does a snail have to do with a galaxy?" wondered Ib.

"Like I said, *who* could have imagined this?" said Esther.

The group fell into silence as the craft entered the Milky Way, passing by star systems, some enclosed in colourful gaseous clouds. They approached and slowly passed by a massive cluster of stars, enmeshed within tall, castle-like pinkish clouds of gas. Tomi thought it looked both beautiful and sinister, familiar and completely new.

"The Pillars of Creation," said Ib, slightly above a whisper. "I can't believe it. I truly can't believe it."

"This…this really puts the Hubble to shame," Barry said, sharing Ib's tone of wonder.

Again the group grew silent, collectively overcome by the sinister beauty, as though their brains didn't know how to record and categorize something of this scale, this magnificence. How does the brain reconcile the incomprehensible?

"Don't forget, Tomi, there is no beauty without danger," said Ete telepathically. At that moment, a massive cluster of rock, metal, and ice hurtled past the front of the craft, chased by smaller pieces of debris. Tomi thought of some of the visions Ete had showed her. She

remembered seeing a comet. And stars. *'Dangerous stars,'* she remembered hearing.

As the debris cleared and darkness again surrounded them, a small orb entered their view. It grew as they approached it, the orb emerging as a swirling of blue, white, and green.

"There she is," said Esther. "Like a tiny, shiny marble glowing in complete darkness."

"It looks so alone," said Kirsten with a hint of sadness. "Just hanging there in the cold dark."

Tomi felt this in her stomach. *Not just alone. Fragile,* she thought. *Vulnerable.*

As they approached, Tomi could start to make out details, with part of the planet covered in shadow, while the blues and whites and greens of the illuminated side seemed richer, deeper than Tomi had expected.

"It's so beautiful," Esther said. "So beautiful and wonderful, but for some reason I just feel so much…sadness."

"It's so alone," said Kirsten again. "So vulnerable."

"Everyone you ever knew or loved, they're all down there," said Barry.

"Look at the atmosphere. I mean, look!" said Esther. "It looks like it's as thick as a piece of paper."

"And you think about how we treat it," said Ib.

They approached quickly, and the Earth filled their whole view. Tomi tried to make out the land, but unlike putting your finger on a globe, the Earth was covered with streams and swirls of clouds, and far bluer ocean than she had ever imagined.

"I think I know what Edgar Mitchell was talking about," said Barry. "After coming back from the moon on Apollo 14, he talked about how seeing the Earth this way, from above, and how it was, well, transcendent. Spiritual. I'm paraphrasing, but he said: 'You develop a global consciousness, a dissatisfaction with the world, and that you want to do something about it.'"

"I want to hug it. Save it," said Tomi, remembering after she said it that that's exactly what she was returning to do.

"My favourite part," said Barry, "Mitchell also said: 'You want to grab all the politicians, drag them up here, and say look at that, you son of a bitch!'"

"Oh isn't he right about that," said Esther. "If only everyone could see this. We would never be the same. What it would do for human consciousness."

Tomi felt her body tense up as they hurtled closer to the Earth. As they started to enter the atmosphere, she gripped the stool under her, waiting for turbulence to start. But instead of the fiery and intense re-entries she had seen in movies, the craft just slipped through the atmosphere, as though the atmosphere was busy and just didn't notice this little craft.

As they descended, they passed through a massive stack of clouds, and again, Tomi didn't feel the craft shake or react to the atmospheric change in the slightest. It felt like they were stationary, and the rest of the universe was on the move around them.

When they emerged below the clouds, they were closer to the surface than Tomi had expected. They had sea below and behind them, and were zooming towards a green, forested landscape, leading towards snowy, rocky peaks. The craft was descending quickly towards one mountain, a huge snowy white peak sticking up out of endless forest.

The mountain got closer. The craft didn't slow down. Tomi realized they were hurtling directly at the rocky peak, that the craft would smash right into the mountain. Her hands were shaking as she gripped the stool below her. She turned to look at her friends, all of them staring ahead, eyes widening in fear. They were going to slam right into it.

Tomi's lungs urgently pulled in air, but before she could scream, the craft met the mountain peak. Then darkness.

After a brief moment of darkness while the craft descended through the mountain – as though the craft was an imagining, a ghost, and not a material, nuts and bolts vehicle – the craft entered a wide, expansive cavern, slowed, and gently landed.

Tomi put her hand to her chest and felt her heart pounding. She looked around to her friends, and let out a gallows-humour laugh, the way people sometimes do after narrowly avoiding a fatal car accident.

"Ete, thank you for that tour of the universe," said Barry, standing up from the stool with his legs shaking, while Ete removed and replaced the helmet, "and for rescuing us, and saving Kirsten, and well, for everything. But maybe next time you could give a heads up about the flying-through-a-mountain part of it?"

Ete looked at Barry and around at the group, towering over them. Tomi could feel Ete's amusement, that Ete had done that intentionally, to play a joke on them. *Interspecies humour can get lost in translation*, thought Tomi.

"*Welcome to my home*," Ete said telepathically to the group, as the rectangular ramp lowered from the bottom of the craft.

As they stepped out and looked around in wonder at this massive cavern, Tomi knew she had been here before. At least her consciousness had been here before, when she had remote viewed Ete's home. Just as when her consciousness had visited, the floor, walls, and ceiling seemed to be all one, as though the interior of the mountain had been scooped out like a spoonful of Jell-O. The huge cavern was lit up as though it were a bright sunny day, yet here they were, in a cavern below a mountain.

"The walls," said Kirsten, "they are glowing."

"The walls, ceiling, and floors," said Barry. "The light comes from everywhere."

"And nowhere," said Esther. "It's beautiful. Nourishing."

"*Please, follow me*," Ete said to the group. Ete began to walk towards one side of the cavern, and as she did Tomi remembered there were other rooms and hallways, rooms with different purposes, like the dark one Ete and her people used for meditation.

The group followed Ete, watching her tall, lanky body looking graceful as she walked, her movements slow and intentional.

"So this is the hangar," said Barry, as they followed Ete. "Look at these craft!"

Past the craft they had arrived in, there were a half dozen other craft parked in this huge cavern. Each was a different shape and size. The craft they had arrived in was a classic disc-shaped UFO. There were other discs, but also a long and cylindrical vehicle, and a small triangular model.

"My god," said Ib. "Anyone else feel like you've entered some science fiction novel?"

They gazed at the exotic crafts, wanting to run over and inspect each one, but Ete didn't slow down to indulge their curiosity, and so they continued to follow.

At the edge of the hangar there were three openings, like open doors. The opening on the left led to a room that didn't glow with the white nourishing light of the hangar, but instead a dark indigo. Tomi remembered this room, where she had joined Ete in meditation. From the second opening came a pinkish glow, while the third shared the same light as the hangar.

Ete led them through the third opening, and they entered a long corridor, the ceiling much shorter than in the hangar, but still expansive, the walls of stone again cut out perfectly smooth, glowing and warm. They passed what Tomi assumed were doors on the left of the corridor, the 'doors' being metal circles, at least ten feet in diameter. Tomi didn't notice any handles or locks.

She was more surprised by the door they approached on the right – a human-sized varnished pine door with a metal knob, the door hinged right into the rock walls. It looked like it belonged on a forest cabin, and not in this deep underground alien bunker.

Ete stopped at the door. "*You all must be exhausted,*" she said telepathically to the group.

Tomi took in a breath, finally assessing her body and her being, and smiled at Ete's understatement.

"Add confused and traumatized to exhausted, and yes, you're right," said Tomi to knowing nods from the group.

"*That's why we wanted you to have a place to rest that would be comfortable and familiar. Please, take a look,*" said Ete.

Tomi smiled at Ete, wondering how they could ever thank her. She reached out, turned the handle, and stepped through the door.

"I can't believe it," said Tomi.

"My god, is this the same? The same cabin?" asked Ib incredulously.

Kirsten grabbed Tomi's hand. "Our mini-vacay cabin!"

Tomi scanned the living room and kitchen, and it seemed like everything, every little detail, was a perfect replica of the cabin in the woods of West Virginia where she, Kirsten, Ib, and Barry had stayed. *My safehouse,* Tomi thought.

As the group looked around in wonder at the cabin, Ete crouched down and entered the doorway, having to tilt her head to avoid hitting the ceiling.

"We believe you will have everything you need here for rest and nourishment. And please do rest, our next steps will need you to be rested, Tomi. We will give you some days," said Ete, *"to rest, eat, just be human. When you are ready, we can discuss what comes next."*

"Thank you Ete," said Tomi in her mind. *"This is perfect."*

"We're under a mountain," said Kirsten. "How will we know when it's day and night?"

Ete stepped carefully through the cabin, looking like a giant entering a Hobbit house, and pulled the curtains back from a window.

"When the sun comes up it's morning," said Ete, teasing her telepathically.

Kirsten stepped towards the window, and found that the view out looked just like the exterior of the cabin in West Virginia, she knew it wasn't real, as though the window was a 3D movie screen. She looked around at the cabin interior, and wondered how Ete's people could have done this, constructed it as a perfect replica.

"Is this, I don't know, some kind of a projection?" asked Kirsten.

"What if everything is a projection?" replied Ete, moving back across the room towards the door, crouching lower to exit the cabin. *"Please communicate with me if you need anything."*

Esther plopped onto the couch and exhaled with relief. Barry came out of the other rooms of the cabin to report that they, too, were exact copies of the rooms at the original cabin, except there was another bed added to Tomi and Kirsten's room, presumably for Esther.

Tomi poured a glass of water from the sink and tasted it. "Water's good," she reported, before chugging the rest of the glass. "It even tastes like the cabin tap water."

"Even better," said Kirsten, pulling two bottles out of the fridge. "There's wine!"

Everyone agreed that the wine would still be there after a good sleep, and headed off to bed. In the bedroom, Kirsten found a set of pyjamas – just where they had been in the real cabin, folded on the closet shelf, when she and Tomi had stayed there – and set off for a shower and to rid herself of her bloodied clothes.

Esther was already snoring on the single bed that had been added to the bedroom when Kirsten returned. Unlike in the rest of the cavern, the lighting in the replica cabin was just as it was in the real cabin. Kirsten followed the light of a candle perched on the nightstand, and crawled into bed beside a groggy but still conscious Tomi.

"You didn't have to wait up for me," whispered Kirsten.

"Please, after today – or, whatever day it is – I don't want to let you out of my sights. I thought you'd died," Tomi whispered, her eyes tearing up. Kirsten wiped away a tear, as Esther snored across the room.

"How do you feel now?" Tomi asked.

"Well tired, of course. Confused. Terrified. The usual," Kirsten said, muffling a laugh. "But it doesn't feel like I was shot, that's for sure."

"Can I see it?" asked Tomi.

Kirsten gave a little nod, and pulled her pyjama shirt up, revealing her abdomen. Tomi put her hand on Kirsten and felt the scar where the bullet had entered. In the candlelight, it looked like a wound that had healed for a year, not a fresh wound.

"What happened?" asked Tomi. "How did this happen?"

Kirsten looked down at the scar, and back to Tomi, Kirsten's face suddenly looking more tired and sullen.

"I'm…I'm not exactly sure," Kirsten said slowly and quietly. She broke eye contact and looked down at the bed. "I mean Ete healed me, I know that, but I don't know how. I wasn't around for most of it."

"You mean you were unconscious," Tomi said. "When exactly did you wake up?"

Kirsten looked back up at Tomi. "No. No, Tomi, I wasn't just unconscious. I think I died. I think I died there in that clearing and went somewhere else. And well, I saw things. Things you see after you die."

Tomi held eye contact, and could feel that Kirsten was troubled. "I can't believe I came that close to losing you," she said, pulling Kirsten in for a hug. "Will you tell me about it?"

"Yeah. I will. But when I'm ready. For now, how about we sleep for a week," Kirsten whispered, falling quickly to sleep, with Tomi soon to follow, facing each other and sharing a pillow.

Chapter 4

"I shall go into a hare,

With sorrow and sighing and mickle care;

And I shall go in the Devil's name,

Ay while I come home again."

Isobel Gowdie, *1662 Scottish Witch Trials*

The group really did sleep for nearly a week. For the first few days they paid little attention to whether it was day or night. They slept for long stretches. When someone would wake, they might go out to the kitchen, make and eat some food, and either head back to bed or end up napping on a couch. After a few days of perpetual rest, they started to wake for longer stretches, make and eat meals together, and chat and joke. Other than the odd mumbled yelling during a nightmare, they avoided talking about their situation or what they had been through, preferring to pretend that they just happened to be vacationing together in a cabin.

Every so often Tomi would receive a telepathic message from Ete checking in on the group, but otherwise they were left to rest and heal.

One evening, the whole group finally awake together, Esther offered to cook up a big dinner. Tomi helped alongside her, relishing the chance to share the kitchen with her grandmother. Ib set the table, folding the napkins and placing wine glasses at each setting, while Kirsten evaluated the wine inventory, made her selections, and started pouring.

Barry was in the living room flipping through records. He pulled one out and put it on the turntable, placing the needle onto the disc.

"Rhiannon rings like a bell through the night, and wouldn't you love to love her?" the stereo played.

Barry stepped towards the kitchen and smiled watching his friends all working together on a meal, laughing and just enjoying life.

While Esther was stirring a pot on the stove, she started to move with the music, and eventually, sing along.

"All your life you've never seen the woman taken by the wind; Would you stay if she promised you heaven?"

Tomi smiled watching her grandmother, someone she knew so intimately and at the same time, not at all.

"I love that song," said Tomi, as the track ended.

"Me too," said Esther, smiling at Tomi. "Did you know that Rhiannon was the Welsh goddess of the moon? She shunned a god and married a mortal. So the god framed her for murdering her son, and made her stand at the entrance to the city and tell everyone she killed her child."

"Really? Wow, I had no idea," said Tomi.

"My friend Joanna taught me that. She used to make me get up and start the record again when it finished. She loved Stevie Nicks."

"Joanna, the witchy biker?" asked Tomi, her eyes widening. Esther nodded. "What do you think about telling us about Joanna over dinner?"

Joanna steered her bike down a small residential street crowded with houses and walk-up apartment buildings. Some kids laughed and chased the bike as she pulled up to a plain two-storey building, the siding white on the bottom half, and a faded orange on the top. She brought the bike to a stop and cut the engine. Esther could hear women down the street calling to their children to get back home.

Joanna engaged the kickstand on the bike, dismounted, let out a roar and lunged at the children, as though she might catch and eat them. The children screamed and ran back towards their mothers, laughing and pushing each other.

Esther dismounted and immediately groaned. She was looking forward to not getting on that bike again anytime soon. Although she felt free and wild on the bike, and for a young woman who had hardly left Georgia before, it was the adventure of a lifetime, after five long days on the road, sleeping on cheap motel mattresses and riding all day, she felt like her body had aged at least a dozen years.

She looked around, taking in her surroundings. Esther had no idea what to expect when they arrived. Unlike her mother, Joanna wasn't much of a talker. Most of their time spent together had either been on the bike, or Joanna snoring the moment she hit the mattress. She felt a cool ocean breeze wrap around her, and she shivered, feeling vulnerable and lost, wondering what she was thinking leaving her home.

"Welcome to Oakland," said Joanna flatly. "This is Ghosttown. Come on, I'll show you where we live."

"We?" asked Esther.

"We. You said you needed a place to live, right? Here, it's up these stairs," Joanna said, motioning to follow her up a set of worn wooden stairs to her second storey apartment. At that moment Esther came to accept that she had in fact crossed the country and was actually starting a new life.

She climbed the wooden stairs, and found a small, messy apartment with clothes strewn around the furniture and floor, a sink full of dishes that Joanna had left at least a week and a half before. The apartment was darkened, with most of the windows covered by tapestry cloths of intricate mandalas and kaleidoscope patterns.

One window was covered by a black cloth with a red five-sided star inside of a circle. Esther didn't know the symbol, but was both intrigued and afraid of it, a duality she often felt in her conversations with Alda, learning about beliefs so different from what she learned at home and at church. She would sometimes worry that by learning about these things she was offending God. She had prayed on it and resolved that she pursued this knowledge to build her understanding so that she could be closer to God. Surely a perfect God wouldn't be insecure, she had decided.

"I'm in here," Joanna said, pointing to the only bedroom. "You can have the couch. There are some blankets in the cupboard over there."

Joanna disappeared into her bedroom, and Esther looked at the couch with a sweater, jeans, and socks strewn on it. Her eyes started to well with tears, wondering what she was doing here, feeling so alone without her family.

"Tomorrow I need to go to the church," Joanna said, popping her head out her bedroom door. "You can come if you want, and I can introduce you to people. Get some sleep."

Joanna paused for a moment, like she was going to say more, and eventually nodded and closed the door behind her. Esther realized that was Joanna's attempt at warmth, and felt more at ease. She was surprised Joanna would be going to church, but looked forward to joining her and finding something familiar.

Joanna slept through the morning, and emerged in the early afternoon. Esther had woken earlier in the morning, finding herself in a foreign place, regretting coming here. She had looked around the apartment and thought she could almost hear her mother *tsk* at the mess. She set about doing the dishes, scrubbing the kitchen, putting all the loose clothes into a laundry bag she found in a closet, and dusted and swept.

When Joanna exited her bedroom, she poured herself some coffee that Esther had made and stepped outside to smoke without saying a word. Esther had the sense that she hadn't noticed that the apartment had been cleaned – it seemed as though Joanna was simply oblivious to her surroundings.

Esther put on her shoes and met Joanna outside.

"Good morning," said Esther, trying to sound cheery. Joanna turned and looked at her as though she had forgotten she had a new roommate.

"Yes," said Joanna, looking like she was uncomfortable in the bright sun. She put on sunglasses and butted out her cigarette in a large coffee can outside her door. "I don't like mornings. Are you coming today? It's not far, we're going to walk."

As they walked Esther commented on the different buildings, the city busier and more full of people than anything she had experienced before.

Joanna nodded or gave one-word answers. When they turned a corner, she said, "It's just two more blocks this way."

"What kind of church is it?" asked Esther. "I grew up Baptist but I'm interested in learning about other denominations."

Joanna just smiled. *I haven't seen that much*, thought Esther, wondering what was funny about her question.

"Anyways, I'm excited," continued Esther. "Y'know, growing up I wanted to be a pastor."

"I know," said Joanna, surprising Esther with a verbal response. "My mother told me. She was very interested in your faith journey."

This time it was Esther who fell silent, thinking about Alda and the day they had met, the day she had learned the crushing truth that she would never be a pastor in her church.

"Here it is," Joanna said, pointing at a two-storey building with blue siding, not unlike Joanna's apartment building, except on the ground floor. Instead of doors to apartments, there was a plain white door with a hand painted sign affixed to the wall beside it.

As they walked towards the door, Esther stopped to read at the sign. Instead of the cross she expected, there was a silhouette of a female figure, starting narrow at the bottom and widening around the hips, curving in, then out again around her two upraised hands. A white line was painted from her feet, curling into a spiral at her widened hips. On each side of the figure was a crescent moon. Above the figure it read: *Church of the Triple Feminine.*

Esther stared at the sign, trying to make sense of where she was.

"Come on," said Joanna, holding the door open, "You won't go to Hell, I promise."

Inside she found a large room with scuffed hardwood floors and cracking plaster walls in serious need of a fresh coat of paint. The room was empty save for two women seated on folding chairs in the middle of the room. Joanna grabbed two more chairs, unfolded them to create a circle, and sat down.

"You're back," said the one woman to Joanna, older with wiry black and grey hair, sitting back in her chair, looking unbothered with anything in the world. The other woman was younger, not much older than Esther, her hair short – *a man's cut,* Esther thought, having never seen a woman from back home in Rome wearing their hair so short until the day she had met Joanna. Both women wore long, colourful tunics and jewelry made from beads and string instead of silver or gold.

"As you can see, we haven't made much progress. Are you going to introduce your friend?"

The three women looked at Esther, still standing, taking in this alien scene.

"This is Esther," Joanna said, pointing Esther towards the empty chair, "my mother's friend, who I told you about."

"Well Esther, welcome to the First Witch's Church of Oakland," said the older woman, her hands raised dramatically as though she were presenting the Sistine Chapel. She had a kind face and a boisterous voice. "Or at least, it will be. I'm Nancy, and this is Mary. How are you with a paintbrush?"

"Oh, um, I'm not much of an artist," said Esther, taking a seat and wishing they weren't all looking at her.

The women smiled and Nancy let out a laugh. "That's fine," she said. "I meant painting the walls. You see we've been working towards this, and we just got possession of this space. And now we have to paint it and turn it into, well, the place we've been called to create."

"I see. I don't…don't know if I understand what this place is?" Esther still didn't know if Joanna and these women were serious. She had trouble understanding people willingly calling themselves a witch, let alone starting a witch church.

"Esther was raised Baptist," said Joanna, ignoring Esther's question. "She wanted to be a pastor."

"Hmm," Nancy hummed, squinting her eyes and looking closer at Esther. "And how did it feel when you found out that was forbidden?"

"I…well I was pretty angry. They said I could teach Sunday school."

Nancy smiled and rolled her eyes. "We all started out as Christians. I was a lot older than you when I realized that I was missing half the story. The feminine. Have you ever heard of Asherah?"

Esther shook her head.

"She was a goddess, worshipped alongside the God of the Bible. Where'd she go?" asked Nancy.

Esther shrugged her shoulders, wondering why she'd never heard of her.

"I know that you've probably only ever thought of witches as a kind of evil, right?" Esther nodded and Nancy continued. "Did you ever wonder why you were taught to fear witches, and not the people who burned them?"

Esther opened her mouth as if to reply, but nothing came out. Why had she never thought of it this way?

"Come on, let's get to work. We can talk while we paint," Nancy said.

"Jesus, Buddha, Hermes, they have so much to teach us," said Nancy, rolling paint onto the wall. "And if you look, they have a lot to teach us about the feminine. So where is that in the Church?"

For the next few weeks, Esther returned to the church each day, helping her new friends transform the rundown space. Most of the time it was just Nancy and Esther working away, since Mary and Joanna had jobs, earning the money needed to get the Church started.

"Once I had a vision. Like a dream, but I was awake, and it felt so real and vivid. I felt like I was covered in this red light. I met Jesus."

Esther looked at Nancy uncertainly, still unsure if this woman was earnest or crazy, or both.

"Can you guess what Jesus looked like?"

Esther stopped painting, having never heard anyone ask the question. Jesus's appearance was common knowledge, she thought. "Brown hair, a beard. Blue eyes."

"In my vision, Jesus was a black woman." Nancy paused painting, looked at Esther, nodded for emphasis, then resumed painting. "I asked her, if you are a woman, why do we always paint you as a man? She said the men took over the Church, coopted it. And lost the message."

On her first days, she would listen to Nancy but say little, wondering if even listening was blasphemous. Over time, Esther started to get more and more comfortable with Nancy's stories and ideas, started to ask questions, and thought more and more about her grandmother.

One day, when Nancy was talking about intuitive women, Esther told her about her Nana. About the man who called her a witch, about the flying ship and the stories she had told her, and about their secret club. Nancy listened quietly, smiling and nodding at points. When Esther finished, Nancy said simply, "I wish I could have met your nana."

After a few minutes of silence, Nancy spoke. "You see Esther, there are so many of us. Women who are descendants of witches, of spiritual and intuitive mothers and grandmothers. We carry on these traditions, generation after generation. Just under the surface so as to not draw too much attention."

Esther thought about her own experiences, the ghosts in her room, the feelings she had experienced, and thought about her grandmother, and her grandmother's grandmother. About Alda and the ideas she had shared. Esther realized she was part of this tradition, and imagined herself an old woman – a *crone*, as Nancy would say – passing this on to her unborn grandchildren.

"A secret club," said Esther.

One day, as the space was almost ready, Mary and Nancy arrived, grunting and cursing, each carrying heavy objects wrapped in blankets. Inside the church they lifted the objects onto a shelf Nancy and Esther had built the day before. They unwrapped them and revealed two clay sculptures, one a bust of a female with a crescent moon on her head, looking almost like horns, the other masculine with prominent antlers protruding from the top of the head.

"Esther, Mary made these herself," said Nancy. "Aren't they gorgeous?"

"Yes," said Esther tentatively, looking over the two figures. She noticed the masculine bust had a sun pendant on his chest. "Who are they?"

Mary, a young woman who seemed to always be smiling, smiled wider. "The god and goddess. Divine masculine and feminine."

"The Triple Goddess and the Horned God," added Nancy.

Esther thought for a moment, wondering how to ask her question. "I…well I thought this was the Church of the Triple Goddess. I guess I'm surprised about the male statue?"

Nancy nodded knowingly. "Yes, we're here to reclaim the divine feminine. But what is feminine if there is no masculine? And vice versa?"

"No father, no mother," added Mary. "You can't have one without the other, can you?"

"Day and night, winter and summer, sun and moon, sea and land," continued Nancy, "and every state in-between. Each of us carries both, because one doesn't exist without the other."

Over time as they prepared the church, Esther started to open herself up to their ideas and beliefs. And having only been able to take a small bag of clothes from back home, started to borrow clothes and take on their appearance. Spending so much time with them inside, she sometimes forgot that they looked odd, countercultural, outside the church doors.

Late one evening, after a long day of work, the four women walked a few blocks to a late-night diner. They were laughing loudly as they entered, the few customers inside looking up at them, and drawing the attention of the man behind the diner counter.

A server came over to grab menus and show them to a table, but was interrupted by the man, who had come from behind the counter to intercept them.

"Good evening, welc–," the server started, interrupted by the owner of the diner.

"We're closing," he said sternly. "You'll have to go."

Esther started to turn to leave, but noticed her friends had not moved.

"It says twenty-four hours on the sign," said Joanna.

The man stared flatly at her. Esther could feel the contempt oozing from him.

"Closed," he said finally.

Nancy hadn't budged, glaring at the man. She put her arm around Esther and pulled her forward.

"You don't want to do that," Nancy said, quiet and firm. She indicated towards Esther. "Do you know who this is?"

The man gave Esther a quick glance, glared back at Nancy, giving his head the slightest shake.

"This is the Head Witch of Rome," she said, staring back flatly.

Esther looked at Nancy, unsure what was happening or what to do.

"I'm sure you don't want her to put a curse on the diner."

The man laughed and rolled his eyes, unimpressed by this threat. The server just stood there holding the paper menus, looking embarrassed and impatient, as though this wasn't the first time the diner owner had refused to serve customers because he didn't like the look of them.

"Okay, I guess it's curse time," Nancy said. She looked at Esther and winked. "Time to do your thing."

Esther was frozen, standing in the middle of a conflict she barely understood. She looked around the diner, and noticed all of the patrons had put down their forks and stopped eating to watch this interaction. She scanned the diner for inspiration.

"Bring me the vinegar," she said finally. Everyone remained frozen. "The vinegar, from the table," she said, pointing at the condiments perched on a nearby table.

Joanna began to move, paused, and looked sternly at the server. "How much longer is your shift?"

"I…I just started," the server stammered.

"You might want to punch out and go home," said Joanna, with a look of concern for her. "Now."

The server stared back for a few moments before looking at the owner, replacing the menus, and exiting through a swinging door into the kitchen.

Joanna picked up the small glass vinegar cruet and placed it upright on her left palm. With her right hand holding her wrist to ensure the vinegar remained upright, she shuffled ceremonially towards Esther. Esther took the vinegar in her hand, looked around at her friends, and closed her eyes.

"Mmmmmmmm," she hummed. She began chanting in a deep, mumbling tone, so that it was harder to tell that she was chanting pure gibberish. She flipped the cruet and began pouring vinegar into her left palm. Her chanting got louder, until she made a fist and let the vinegar drip from her hand.

She opened her eyes, looked at Nancy, who was doing her best to keep a straight face, and said simply, "The curse is on."

"That's enough, out, go!" the owner yelled, and the four women turned and exited, Esther still holding the cruet of vinegar. They waited for the door of the diner to close behind them before they burst out laughing. They found another restaurant that didn't put up a fuss, and spent hours laughing about the Witch of Rome and imitating Esther's vinegar curse.

A month of so later, Esther walked by the diner and noticed the lights were off, with a *Business for Sale* sign on the door.

When the day finally came that the Church of the Triple Goddess opened, there were many more women who came in, some looking like regular working women, but most dressed colourfully like Mary and Nancy. Esther mostly stood back and watched as the others greeted visitors and showed them around.

While she had learned a lot from her new friends about their beliefs, seeing them in action, in practice, was something new, the words and ceremonies still foreign to her.

At one point in the evening Mary came and took Esther by the hand and led her into one of the smaller rooms. On the floor around the room were cedar branches, the green needles arranged to create a circle in the centre of the room. Within the circle, placed on the floor, was a fountain pen, several strips of paper, and a clay bowl. Mary sat down and waved for Esther to sit across from her.

"I want to teach you to make a sigil," Mary said. "It's a symbol that you create, to represent your desires, your intentions. You see, the divine isn't out there, isn't up in the sky somewhere. The divine is inside of us. She's everywhere. And this is a way of communicating with her, sharing your intentions."

"Intentions?"

"Intentions," repeated Mary. "It's all about intentions. What we imagine, what we think and believe, it comes true. We make reality with our intentions."

Esther looked confused and unsure.

"Here, close your eyes."

Esther closed her eyes, and felt Mary take her hand and hold it between both of hers. "Clear your mind. Come to a blank, to darkness. Now imagine; think about what you want out of life. Now or long-term. Do you have it?"

"Yes," said Esther. "I want to know God. Understand God. Understand the universe."

"That's okay," said Mary gently, "you don't have to tell me. Now think about that intention. Hold it in your mind as truth. Not what you want to happen, what *will* happen. See it as truth. And as you do that, in your mind's eye, let a symbol form. A symbol that represents your intention."

Esther tried to imagine a symbol, thinking through all the symbols she knew. She was drawing a blank.

"Don't force it," Mary said. "Clear your mind, and just let it form. Give it all the time it needs."

Esther tried to clear her mind. She began to grow impatient, afraid she would reveal that she wasn't one of them, couldn't understand their ways, until she noticed lines begin to take shape, like wispy clouds moving slowly together. A visual was forming, and she didn't know where it came from.

"When you're ready, you can open your eyes, and draw that symbol on a piece of paper here. That is your sigil."

Esther opened her eyes, the symbol vivid in her mind. She picked up the pen, drew an equilateral triangle, then drew another intersecting triangle higher than the other, both pointing upwards. She looked to Mary and nodded that she was done.

Mary looked at her sigil and smiled. "As above, so below. Now it's time to release that intention. Hold the intention, the sigil in your mind, and burn it."

Mary handed Esther a box of wooden matches. She pulled one out, struck it, and lit the scrap of paper on fire, placing both the paper and match into the clay bowl before she could burn her fingers. Looking at the fire devour the paper, she saw the statue of the Triple Goddess.

Later that night, after closing the church, the four women flopped down into chairs, exhausted but exhilarated by what they had created. Nancy and Joanna were both too tired to celebrate and decided to head home. Esther agreed, but Mary convinced her they were too young to call it a night.

"Come on, I have an idea for how you can get closer to God." Nancy and Joanna said their goodbyes, and Mary smiled at Esther. "Here, have you ever had these?"

Mary pulled a small brown paper bag out of her sack and poured some sort of dried food onto her hand. "Magic mushrooms. Here, eat these."

She held her hand out to Esther to receive the shrivelled bits of dried mushrooms. Esther paused, having no idea what to do. Mary smiled and nodded gently, prompting her to take them. Mary then pulled some out of the bag for herself, popped them into her mouth and started to chew. Esther followed suit, her mouth filling with saliva after biting down.

"Oh, blah!" Esther said, continuing to chew the spongy bits. Mary laughed and nodded, also trying to chew so she could swallow them down. Once the mushrooms were finally ingested, they locked up the church and began to walk around the city.

Esther, still new to living in a big city, walked beside Mary, looking all around and taking in the sights and smells of the city at night. As the psychedelic set in, the city lights started to glow brighter, the sounds of the city becoming more vivid. As they passed by people on the street, Esther would look at them and thought she could feel their energy, their emotional state.

They walked by a man in his mid-thirties wearing a finely-cut suit and sunglasses.

"He thinks he's living to the fullest," Esther said, "but he's actually miserable. He's trying to chase money and things, and feels like a failure when he doesn't have them."

Mary smiled and nodded. A woman pushing a pram with a baby in it walked by next.

"She's so bored, she has nobody to talk to" said Esther.

Next an older couple walked by, walking hand in hand. They smiled at Esther and Mary as they approached.

"Hello! Beautiful evening," said Esther. When they had passed, she said, "Oh Mary, they are happy, they have such beautiful energy, I can feel it."

They walked in silence, taking in the world through their own psychedelic lens. Esther felt deeper in her mind than she'd ever felt before. She would get so deep in thought she would forget that she was a human being out in the world until she was brought back by Mary talking or by the sounds of the city.

Esther heard a noise, and felt like she could see it in the air. It was music, horns, and drums, the sound getting louder as they walked. They came to a park with a bandshell in the middle, a brass band playing an evening concert in the park to a small crowd of people sitting on the grass or on folding lawn chairs.

As the next song started, Mary said, "Let's lay in the grass and listen." They found a big old tree and lay down in the grass underneath. Esther closed her eyes and found an explosion of images. No longer having to focus on walking and navigating the city, her closed eyes allowed her to step into a new world, new universe of images. She lost track of Mary and of her surroundings, and felt like every cell in her body was vibrating.

An image of a starry night sky entered her mind, the sky more purple than black. She saw the Moon, cartoonlike, with a smiling face and stick arms. The Moon waved one of its hands, calling on the music to start, and as it did a musical staff spread out across the sky, each space between the lines filled with vibrant colours, like a rainbow. She noticed that the notes on the staff were vibrating, almost dancing, just as the stars were, with the moon seeming to conduct the music.

"Ohh," she said aloud, her eyes still closed, "I can see the music, it's so beautiful." She heard Mary giggle.

The multicoloured musical staff flowed like a ribbon in the wind, until it finally reached Esther, the music entering through her chest. As it entered, a green glow emerged in her chest; inside was a glowing green lotus flower, the petals tucked closely together. As the glow became brighter and more vivid, the lotus opened in bloom, the light expanding around her like a bubble. She looked up at the dancing Moon and stars, and felt the deepest connection she had ever felt, deeper than with any place, any person, or animal. *They are me,* she thought. *We are so deeply connected!*

Throughout her life, she had felt moments of a deeper connection in prayer, in nature, with her nana and Alda, but in this moment she experienced something beyond faith; a deep and profound knowing. Esther saw that the green lotus flower was spinning. She looked up at the dancing moon, stars, and musical notes.

"What the mushroom is showing me, it's just incredible! Everything is in motion, everything is connected. There are no opposites. There is no I. We're all the same."

Mary giggled a little, then laughed loudly, rolling her body into Esther, waking Esther from her vision.

Esther laughed, and asked, "What? What is it?"

"Oh Esther," Mary said, still laughing. "You're not wrong about the universe. But you're also hilariously high!"

Eventually the psychedelic wore off, and the world looked more and more normal. Mary walked her home to Joanna's apartment, and as they walked they continued to laugh about their experiences. When Esther curled up on the couch to sleep, she had difficulty. While she felt a sense of safety in being sober again, the material world back to normal, she felt a sense of grief for having lost that moment of clarity. It was as though for just a few moments she got to glimpse through a keyhole to find that on the other side of the door there was something bigger, seeing for just a moment that the universe stretches well beyond our comprehension. For the briefest moment Esther knew, saw, felt that we are not separate, we are connected to each other, to it all. We are the universe.

Chapter 5

"Our Earth of factory chimneys and offices, seething with work and business, our earth with a hundred new radiations – this great organism lives, in final analysis, only because of, and for the sake of, a new soul. Beneath a change of age, lies a change of thought. Where are we to look at it, where are we to situate this renovating and subtle alteration which, without appreciably changing our bodies, had made new creatures of us. In one place and only one – in a new intuition involving a total change in the physiognomy of the universe in which we move – in other words, in an awakening. "

Pierre Teilhard de Chardin

"You know, I felt so lucky, so blessed to have had that experience," Esther said. "I mean I was always religious, I had faith, I believed in a hereafter. But that experience, well it felt like I got some confirmation. But it was a struggle for a while after that. I became a bit depressed, more tired by day-to-day life. Chores and hunger and aching muscles, all of that. I didn't see the point, it felt like none of it mattered, like this world was fake and I had just a small glimpse of the real one."

"Wow," said Tomi, reaching across the table and putting her hand on Esther's. "That was a beautiful vision. And I understand that experience. The struggle with life when it starts to feel like you've seen more. How did you get out of it?"

"Time," said Esther. "And talking about it with others and realizing that they'd had similar experiences. It was like a secret club again. Not long after, Tomi, I met your grandfather. I told him about my experience, my feeling of emptiness in life, that I even wondered if this life was some kind of punishment.”

“What did he say?” asked Tomi, knowing so little about her grandfather.

“He was good with words, your grandfather, and so smart. He quoted Albert Camus. He told me, ‘We need to imagine Sisyphus happy.’ That Sisyphus is sentenced to roll that stone up the hill over and over, that was the drudgery, futility of life. But if Sisyphus found joy in his work, if he was happy, it was no longer a punishment.”

“Hmm,” said Ib, “Find your own meaning in meaninglessness.”

“What happened next?” asked Tomi. “Did you stay at the church? Did you get married to Grandpa?”

Esther nodded, reminded that her granddaughter still knew so little about her life. “Your granddad. You know, the first time I met him, he took me to the cinema. I can’t even remember what the film was. Early on he took my hand, and when we touched, my mind was swept away. I had this vision of us driving. We were driving and driving through forests, and eventually, we came over one hill, and there was a small town, surrounded by evergreen trees and rocks, and I knew we had arrived home. And I felt a third person. A baby.”

“Dad?” asked Tomi, relishing finally hearing these family stories.

Esther nodded. “Your granddad was in the military. Well, shortly after that first date, he got notice he was being transferred to Alaska. When he told me, he said he wanted to marry me and have a family with me. And asked me to go. It seemed so quick, such a wild thing to do. But then I remembered the vision. That town surrounded by trees. And I knew that was my next stop. So I said my goodbyes, thanked Joanna for the adventure she had given me, we got into his pickup truck, and drove north."

"Wow," said Tomi, "I had no idea you lived in Alaska. How long were you there?"

"Not long," said Esther, a note of sadness in her voice. "We married and in almost no time I was pregnant with your father. A few months after he was born, your grandfather died in an accident on the base. And suddenly here I was, a single mother with a small military pension, all alone. Alaska was beautiful, but also hard, and lonely. At first I thought about going back to Georgia, but I realized I wasn't the same woman who left Rome on a motorbike years before. So instead I packed us up, and headed back to Oakland."

Tomi had tears in her eyes, imagining her nana losing her husband. "I'm so sorry Nana, that sounds so hard."

"It was," said Esther. "But it was part of my journey. Back in Oakland I found my community. And eventually, that's where I met Ray, who brought me to work at SRI. That's where I became a remote viewer. And how I met Ete. It was all part of my path here. To today."

The group fell silent, reflecting on Esther's story, her unlikely journey to remote viewing. To the mystical.

Kirsten picked up the bottle of wine, saw there was just a little left, and poured it into Esther's glass. "I think you deserve this after sharing all of that."

At that moment there was a knock at the door. Tomi's body jumped at the surprise sound, having for a moment forgotten that they were actually underground in Ete's base, Ete's home, and not actually in a cabin in the woods. The door opened, and Ete stepped in, holding her head crooked to clear the ceiling.

"*You could rest more, we know this,*" said Ete telepathically to the group. "*But tomorrow morning, we should begin. Tomi, it's time. We have a lot of work to do.*"

Tomi looked around at her friends, wishing this dynamic, days spent in rest and conversation, could continue indefinitely. But she knew, felt it was time.

"I know," Tomi said, trying to smile and project confidence. We start work tomorrow. One must imagine Sisyphus happy, I guess."

"*Something is coming,*" Ete said telepathically. "*If you search yourself, you will find that you already know it. You can feel it. And have felt it for some time.*"

The next morning, Ete had gathered the group, led them out through the carved stone hallway, and into a long, dark room – the same room where Tomi had found Ete and her people meditating when she remote viewed this location. While the walls in the hallway and hangar gave off a warm, white glow, this room gave off a deep, inky, indigo light. The light was like nothing Tomi had experienced before.

When Tomi entered the room – this time in the flesh – she found that the floating stools, the ones Ete and her people had sat on to meditate, were arranged in a small circle. She counted six stools, one for each of them. Other than the stools, the room was empty, though Tomi felt like the dark indigo light filled the air, almost like it was taking up space.

When they entered, Ete had motioned for them to take a seat. The stools had no legs. Instead, the seats hovered, floated in the air. Ete sat first, smoothly perching her lanky body onto the seat and crossing her legs. The group turned to watch Tomi follow suit. She eased her way into sitting down, finding placing her weight on a floating platform akin to a trust exercise. With a few nervous chuckles, each of them managed to get seated. They looked to Ete.

Ete sat quietly with her eyes closed for several minutes. While she appeared to be in meditation or deep thought, Tomi felt as though Ete was gathering her strength, working herself up for a difficult conversation. After a period of silence, Ete began speaking telepathically to the group, the words and their meaning seeming to enter their minds out of thin air.

"*Something is coming,*" said Ete again, with a level of gravity that heightened Tomi's anxiety. "*I have shared certain images, certain visions, with Tomi and Esther. These visions explained the cyclical nature of life on Earth. Simply, life on Earth is a circle. It flourishes for a time, until something comes along and almost wipes it out. Then it begins again. This has been the experience of human civilization, one of growth and development, but also one of destruction and rebirth. Yours wasn't the first human civilization. But something is coming that may make it the last."*

The room was silent, each member of the group holding the weight, the heaviness of Ete's words.

Finally Barry broke the silence. "Boy, don't sugar coat it, give it to me straight, doc."

Ete opened her large, catlike eyes to look at Barry. He knew she didn't understand the idiom. "I'm sorry, it's just…that's information that is difficult to hear."

"Ete," said Ib, "when you say something is coming, well…what exactly is coming? Do you know what it is? Or when?"

Ete closed her eyes, and the group felt compelled to close theirs. The darkness of their closed eyes was illuminated with a vision, as though Ete was playing a video in their minds. Beyond the vision, they received more information. A knowing, an awareness of complexity. A depth of emotion accompanying the visual.

First they saw the Earth, surrounded by the darkness of space. They were watching from a distance, just as they had when they had arrived in Ete's craft. Again, they felt the beauty, the vulnerability of this planet. Then a comet entered the picture, looking just like the one they passed by in the craft, but instead of in some far off asteroid belt, it was close, hurtling towards the Earth, leaving behind it a stunning yellow and orange tail.

"This is one way," said Ete. *"It has happened before."*

Just before the comet struck the Earth, the image shifted, replaced by quick scenes of geologic catastrophe: earthquakes rocking cities, the buildings crumbling like they were made of sand. They saw the top of a mountain blowing violently open, rocks flying with ash and lava spewing in all directions. Then tsunamis, islands washed away by the water. Then suddenly it was peaceful, a beautiful sunny day, and they were looking up at a bright, clear blue sky. A bird flew by. Then a swarm, the birds squawking, then crying. The sun got brighter, it grew larger and brighter still, until a wave of flames torched the land and boiled the seas.

Someone gasped.

"*Each time a reset*," said Ete. "*This time, it may not be anything like that. This time, you may do it to yourself. You have already set it in motion.*"

They saw the New York City skyline deep underwater, another huge wave heading towards the tops of the skyscrapers poking out of the turbulent waters. Then they saw drought and blight, a farmer falling to his knees as he watched his crops fail. There were columns of starving, desperate people on the move. Violence and gunshots. Then crowds of people coughing, sweating with fever, dead bodies being burned in piles. The images were awful enough, but with each it was as though they were experiencing it, tapping into the fear and pain the people experienced in each scenario.

Then they saw the Earth again, just as they had viewed it from Ete's craft. It was beautiful and fragile.

Tomi let out a breath, realizing she was holding it through the last images. Suddenly the vibrant, peaceful Earth shook. They could see some kind of disturbance on the land. Then another. Their view changed and they were now on the ground, watching a city disappear in a light brighter than the sun. Full cities were being eradicated in an instant, replaced by mushroom clouds, the sky growing impossibly bright before growing dark with debris.

Another gasp.

"Please, stop. No more," said Kirsten.

Tomi opened her eyes to look at her friend. She was crying. Tomi realized she was crying too.

"We are watchers," said Ete. *We have seen all of these as possible futures, but it is not clear to us yet which it will be. It is not clear yet when. But from what we have received, we know that it will be devastating, and it will be soon."*

Ete went silent, giving them time to process this news. This horror.

After a long silence, Ib began to stammer, trying to get his thoughts out with his brain in overdrive. "I…I've not read it in years, but it's…these lines keep running in my head. 'Surely some revelation is at hand; surely the Second Coming is at hand.' I guess…I just wonder now what Yeats saw."

"We know that this information is difficult to receive," said Ete. *"We do not share this with you to cause you pain. We share it because there is hope. There is something else coming."*

"Something else is coming, thank god," said Barry, "I would really like to hear something hopeful after what you showed us."

Ete looked at Barry. Though her face remained expressionless – at least so far as Barry could discern – he felt care, sympathy coming from Ete.

"*It is hopeful,*" said Ete, telepathically to the group. "*As I told Tomi before, something is coming. A chance for humanity to grow. To avoid cataclysm. To ascend to the next step.*"

"How…what does this mean, Ete?" asked Ib. "What does it mean to ascend? How does it save us?"

Ete closed her eyes. The others closed their eyes as well, getting accustomed to receiving these downloads, these visions shared telepathically from Ete.

When Tomi closed her eyes she found a vibrant image. She saw a human sitting under a tree in meditation. But the picture looked strange, blurred. It was as though everything in the image was moving, vibrating, like they could see individual pixels, and each one of those pixels was vibrating individually. The vision focused in closer, zooming in on the human, their face blurry and unrecognizable with everything vibrating. Tomi could see that the tiny pixels that made up the human body were speeding up, vibrating faster and faster. The human became blurrier, the features impossible to define. As they accelerated their vibration, the pixels began to float apart ever so slightly, the person's body becoming less and less dense. Then it was gone – the tree, the grass, and the sky all remained in place – but the human was gone.

"Where did they go?" asked Tomi.

"*The Other Place*," said Ete.

The image being projected into their minds turned to black, and they were looking at a dark, starry sky. Again, those stars were in motion, the vibrating pixels again. The pixels began to move and swirl, until they came together again in a new form. It was the human. The body looked similar to the person in the previous vision, but somehow brighter, as though the tiny pixels were vibrating so quickly they had transformed into something lighter, more graceful and energetic.

This person, the energetic body, was in a foggy place. Tomi felt that it was the same place – the same tree, grass, and sky that the person had been meditating under – but they had shifted somehow, just far enough to almost be in a different place. The fog acted as a shroud, a porous barrier, hiding this other place behind a cloudy veil. Tomi watched the person, their energetic body, rise – smoothly and gracefully – and begin walking slowly, almost floating through the fog. The vision ended. After a few moments of reflection Tomi opened her eyes.

"So it's…like another plane of existence, kind of in parallel to us? How does going there save us from cataclysm?" asked Tomi, feeling like she had a thousand questions zig-zagging through her mind.

"*Yes*," said Ete, "*going there may save you from cataclysm. But it can accomplish so much more. If humanity can ascend, if you can raise your consciousness and be able to access this higher level, it may save you, physically. But it will also change humanity spiritually. Your civilization has been so focused on making stronger weapons. Now they are so strong that you can kill not just one human, you can kill all humans. Now, imagine a humanity not materially bound. A human consciousness that understands the unity of the universe. A humanity that isn't alone, but part of a community."*

"I'm not sure I understand the visions," said Tomi. "How do we get people there? How does it work? Do we teach them? Everyone?"

"*Not everyone,*" said Ete. "*Just enough. There are many humans who already understand that something is coming. Many humans already feel this shift coming and have been working towards this, even if they didn't know it. There are many who are becoming ready. We need just enough of you to take the first step, and the others will follow.*"

"The hundredth monkey," said Barry.

"*Correct,*" said Ete.

Tomi looked across the room towards Barry, difficult to see in that deep indigo light. "The hundredth monkey? What is that?"

"It's an idea about…well about how ideas spread. There was this idea that if you teach a new behaviour to one, two, three monkeys, you reach a tipping point – the hundredth monkey – where you don't have to teach them anymore. The behaviour then just spreads across the whole population. They all do it."

"*It will be difficult to achieve this tipping point, because it is very difficult for the human to ascend,*" continued Ete, her words appearing in each of their minds. "*But the more of you there are, the easier it becomes. Your consciousness is not solitary. As more of you raise your consciousness, even more will follow.*"

"I have to ask," said Ib, with a curious, professorial voice, "if you want this to spread, why are you talking to us? Why not make contact? Announce yourself to humanity, share this information with the world. Perhaps land on the White House lawn, as they always say."

"*That's not how it will happen,*" said Ete.

"I'm sorry, not how what will happen?" asked Ib, unsure which part Ete was replying to.

"*We will make contact,*" said Ete. "*You humans will need a major ontological shock, and contact is part of that. But contact will not look like landing on the White House lawn. Imagine instead if everyone awakes one day having had the same dream.*"

Ete closed her eyes again to share a vision. As Tomi closed her eyes she saw a vibrant picture form. It was as though Ete was sharing dozens of scenes at once. Tomi saw people sleeping, each scene a different person asleep in their beds. Then each scene zoomed in, and she knew she was now seeing the dream these people were experiencing. Each scene, each dream was the same.

First they dreamed of destruction, with multiple scenes of cataclysm, much like what Tomi and the others had been shown. But there were also flashes of beauty – healthy forests and clean rivers, people living in partnership with the land. They dreamed of families, communities coming together, a deep spirit of unity. They dreamed of unity not only with other humans. They saw the faces of different species, non-human intelligent beings – including Ete – living in communion with humanity. Tomi could feel respect and comradeship from these being. And she felt love. Friendship.

Tomi's view zoomed out again, and now she could see all the people who had been dreaming. Each of them woke with a sense of wonder and curiosity. They rose from their beds and stepped outside. She saw neighbours gathering outside, openly talking to strangers about what they had just experienced, the dream they had all had. It was the day the Others made contact.

The vision ended, and Tomi opened her eyes. "At the end there, when they all came out to talk, and share. I could feel it, it was like I could feel everyone's emotions. Everything had changed. It was such a beautiful feeling."

"It is," said Ete. *"Humans could be living with that feeling permanently. But there is much work to do before the conditions are right. Esther and Tomi, this is where you come in. As Barry might say, how do you feel about being the first monkeys?"*

Tomi looked to her grandmother. In that dark indigo light she could just barely make out Esther's expression. She smiled at Tomi, but her eyes were serious, sombre.

"What does it mean exactly to be the first monkey?" asked Tomi. "What am I signing up for?"

"Starting tomorrow," said Ete, *"and continuing until you ascend, we will gather around you, and we will meditate together. We will help you ignore the human emotions that get in the way, the emotions that weigh you down. Fear, hate, shame, blame. We will help you to meditate deeply, so deeply that you can not only feel the vibration of your body, you*

can control it. And once you can control it, you can change it. At that time, you will ascend to the Other Place."

Tomi remained silent, taking this in. Ete made it sound so simple and so impossible at the same time.

Barry shook his head and muttered to himself, "Huh, so once again Tesla was right."

Tomi turned, looking to Barry to clarify.

"Tesla. He said that if you want to understand the universe, think about energy, frequency, and vibration. He said something like that."

Tomi looked back to Ete. "So, I learn to control my vibration, or frequency or whatever, and I go there. Can everyone do this? I'm not going there alone, right?"

"*Esther will go with you,*" said Ete. "*She has been there before. She will be your guide.*"

Tomi looked at her grandmother again, her warm smile masking her concern for her granddaughter.

"When…wow this is a lot to take in. How will I get back?" asked Tomi.

"*You will have learned to control your body's vibration. Remember, there are no opposites. Descending is the same as ascending. As for when you will return, you will return when the time is right.*"

Tomi's stomach was churning, and her throat felt swollen, a lump forming as she tried to hold in her emotions. She looked at Barry, then to Ib, then to Kirsten. It wasn't long ago that she thought she had lost Kirsten – did lose her, it turns out – and here she was being asked to depart into the unknown, without knowing when she would see her again. Kirsten had tears on her cheeks. She held Tomi's gaze, her face unchanging, until she finally gave the smallest nod.

Tomi looked back at Ete. Ete's large catlike eyes looked back at her. She heard Ete's words in her mind, and somehow knew Ete was not speaking to the group, not sharing this message with the others. This was only for Tomi.

"You do not have to do this," said Ete. *"It is your choice. I am not asking you to do this. The agreement we and others have is to not intervene on Earth. With humans. Observe, yes. Sometimes nudge. But intervene, no. The time is coming for humans to know. But we cannot intervene. We cannot save you. We can only give you the information. It will then be up to humanity. To enter this larger community, to ascend to a bigger reality. It will be humanity's choice. Just as this is your choice, Tomi."*

Tomi broke eye contact and looked to the stone floor, oozing indigo light. "Okay," she said, her voice straining to break through the lump in her throat. "I will do it. Well, I will try to do it."

"No," said Kirsten, looking to Tomi. "I know you. You won't try. You *will* do it."

Tomi smiled back gratefully. A question struck her, and she turned to look again at Ete.

"What about the pyramid?" Tomi asked. "Remember, you showed me the underground pyramid and said I would destroy it. What happened to that?"

Ete closed her eyes and again shared a vision with the group. Tomi closed her eyes and saw both her and Ete standing in front of the huge, dark pyramid built deep underground. She was surprised by her vantage point, watching herself from the outside, as though there had been a camera crew there filming them.

The vision zoomed to focus on the pyramid, and just as in Tomi's remote viewing of the pyramid, it was moving slightly, vibrating. Those vibrations created a frequency, and Tomi could see the waves of this frequency moving through the air. The vision disappeared, and instead of seeing, Tomi felt it. She could feel the waves hit her body. The waves made her feel sullen, heavier. She could feel the weight of her body, the pull of gravity below her more pronounced. When the waves stopped Tomi again felt curious and connected. She opened her eyes.

"It…suppresses us, somehow," said Tomi. "I could feel it."

"Me too," said Esther. The others agreed.

"You had said we need to destroy it," Tomi said, her eyes locked with Ete's.

"*I said that* you *will destroy it*," said Ete.

Tomi nodded and looked at the ground, wondering what on Earth Ete saw in her to believe that she could do these things. "It needs to be destroyed before the dream. The collective dream. Contact. It will make it easier for people to understand. To ascend. Is that right?"

"*That is right*," said Ete. "*And it will open up your minds. To be able to communicate, to perceive more. What you humans would call psychic. And Tomi, when that happens, when information and experience become collective, you can reach new levels of empathy. A new experience of love. But there is work to do before that is possible. First, you, the mind-body-spirit known as Tomi, must learn to ascend. And while you do that, your friends will have important work to do as well."*

"Oh?" said Kirsten, who had been silently devastated by this conversation, imagining Tomi ascending, leaving not only her side, but leaving her entire reality, her whole plane of existence, while she was sent home, alone, back to everyday reality.

"Kirsten, the work Tomi will do is difficult, frustrating, tiring," said Ete. *"It will take a toll on her in many ways. Perhaps you could stay with her, take care of her, make sure she is nourished and rested."*

Kirsten looked at Tomi and smiled. "I would be honoured," she said.

"I'm sure I speak for Ib when I say that both of us are happy to pitch in as well," said Barry, smiling and nodding to Tomi, wanting her to know she wasn't in this alone.

"Ib and Barry, your help will be crucial," said Ete. *"If you and Ib choose to help Tomi, you will have your own mission. When Tomi returns from her journey, it will be time for her to destroy the pyramid. Perhaps you two could use this time to find the tool, or the weapon, that will allow her to destroy it."*

Ib looked to Barry, then back to Ete. "What sort of weapon? Do you have a little more information than that?"

"We have been watching, looking for the answer to your question. We have not found it. What we do know is this: it is ancient, and it is destructive."

Barry and Ib remained silent, hoping there would be more information to follow.

Finally Barry said, "So…that's it? We go back into the real world – sorry, the surface, human world – and just look for some ancient, destructive, pyramid-destroying weapon?"

"Yes," said Ete simply. *"We will return you to the surface tomorrow and you can begin."*

"Tomorrow," Ib mumbled quietly, looking at Tomi, then around at the group. "So, I guess this chapter is over, then. We all go our ways. Tomi and Esther to the Other Place. Kirsten staying in…in whatever you call this place. And Barry and I go – well go wherever we need to go, I guess."

"That is correct," said Ete. *"You are entering the next phase of your mission. But it is important that you understand that these are suggestions. In the end it's your mission, your choice."*

"And, so…so if we do this, it's going to work? Humanity will be spared destruction? Spared a cataclysm?" asked Ib.

"We have watched it, we have seen that it can work," said Ete.

"Can work?" said Ib. "But not will work."

"Correct," said Ete.

Ib looked at Barry. Barry, who Ib had brought on to work at PSI to be his righthand man, but who had also become his best and most reliable friend. Barry nodded to Ib.

Ib looked up in thought, then smiled. "You know, I've always liked to imagine that if I had been born in another time, that if I saw Shackleton's advertisement, that I would have had the courage to sign up. I feel like I'm getting that chance. So, yes. Of course we will do it, we will sign up for this journey. Of course we will help Tomi."

Tomi smiled at Ib, crying both at his kindness, and at the idea of saying goodbye. "That's so sweet. But Shackleton?" asked Tomi. "What's that?"

"Ernest Shackleton, a famous captain and explorer," said Ib. "In the early twentieth century led a famously disastrous voyage to try to reach the South Pole. He put a small advertisement in a newspaper to find a crew for the journey. It said something like: 'Men wanted for hazardous journey. Poor wages, bitter cold, months of darkness, safe return doubtful, honour and fame in case of success.'"

"Tomi," said Barry, his voice cracking lightly as he spoke through his emotions. "For you, I'll agree to those terms. Sign me up."

Chapter 6

"When a human dies, the soul moves through the universe trying to describe how a body trembles when it's lost, softens when it's safe, how a wound would heal given nothing but time? Do you understand? Nothing in space can imagine it. No comet, no nebula, no ray of light can fathom the landscape of awe, the heat of shame. The fingertips pulling the first gray hair and throwing it away.

I can't imagine it, the stars say.

Tell us again about goosebumps. Tell us again about pain."

Andrea Gibson, *from the poem Tincture*

Barry was the first to enter the replica cabin, which the group had taken to calling Ete's Cabin. He stepped into the living room area, looked at the window and saw that it was already evening, the replica sun setting below the replica treeline.

Barry made a noise, a mix of a sigh and a grunt. "I guess this is it, our last evening together. Tomi, I –"

Tomi caught him off guard with a big hug. She turned to Ib beside her, and gave him a hug, too. As she stepped back, she wiped tears from her cheek.

"I want you to…" her voice cracked under heavy emotions. She breathed deeply and cleared her throat. "I want you to think about if you really want to do this. I mean it hasn't been that long, you could still go back to your jobs as PSI. You could just go home, live your lives. It would be safer."

"Tomi, don't even think of it," said Ib, feeling more confident and composed than he had in their meeting with Ete.

"Besides, we are so far down the rabbit hole," said Barry, "and well, I want to see more of Wonderland. I don't know how I could go home and pretend I hadn't seen what I have."

Esther and Kirsten got to work on dinner while Ib and Barry shared some ideas for their next steps. Tomi sat on the couch with them, half listening to their conversation, half watching dinner prep, and feeling both sad and grateful.

They enjoyed the food and wine, and while there were some laughs and stories told, there was a heaviness weighing on everyone. Tomi's stomach felt elevated, like getting to the top of the roller coaster and feeling that moment of hesitation before your body suddenly plunges downward. Everything was about to change. Still, they enjoyed some wine and stayed up late despite yawns and red eyes. Esther headed to bed first, then Kirsten, and finally Barry and Ib. Tomi sat in the living room for a few moments, reflecting on these friendships, feeling afraid she would lose them. Afraid she was putting these people in danger.

Eventually she went into the bedroom and passed by her grandmother's bed, hearing Esther snore rhythmically. She followed the light of the candle on the nightstand, and found Kirsten looking at her, awake.

"Hey, you didn't have to wait up for me," Tomi said, sliding under the blankets.

"I did," said Kirsten. "For one, I wanted to make sure you were okay. I mean, that was a lot today, Tomi. A lot to take in. How are you feeling?"

Tomi looked up at the ceiling, considering the question. "It's funny. I should be terrified. Totally freaked out. But mostly I'm just feeling sad. In my life, well, everyone always leaves me. I just don't want that again."

Kirsten frowned her face and nodded empathetically. "I get that. I do. I'd like to tell you something, and well, I think maybe it will help. Reassure you."

"I could use that. What is it you want to tell me?" Tomi asked, rolling onto her side to face Kirsten.

"I'm ready to tell you about what I experienced. When I was shot and…and died. What I saw before I came back," said Kirsten.

Tomi pursed her lips. She didn't like thinking about that night, about that moment where Tomi thought she had lost her. "What did you see?" asked Tomi.

"Well, that's just the thing," said Kirsten. "When I died, I saw you."

"I remember hearing the gunshot," Kirsten said.

Tomi flinched, as though she heard it again.

"And I thought I'd just fallen. It didn't hurt at first. Then it hurt so much. I remember your face over me, you were holding my stomach. I was still confused about what had happened. Then I started floating. And the pain was gone. It was like I was hovering in the air, looking down at myself. Looking at you yelling, trying to save me. And then there was a flash."

Tomi nodded. "There was a flash. I was holding you, there was a flash, and then I was inside Ete's craft."

Kirsten nodded. "Maybe it was the same one. I don't know. I just saw a flash, then this really beautiful light. I floated towards it, and the closer I got, the more it was like I was being pulled, faster and faster. You, the soldiers, the craft, the field, it was long gone. Everything was a blur, it was like I was zooming through a tunnel heading towards the light. And you know what's crazy?"

Tomi shook her head gently. She felt so honoured to have Kirsten share this with her. She remembered the relief she felt when she first talked to Kirsten about her experiences and found someone who not only believed her, but had her own strange and mystical experiences. She became the start of Tomi's secret club.

"As I was flying towards the light, it's like my whole life, everything was gone. No heavy body, I wasn't worried about what I was missing. I didn't care that I'd died, I wasn't angry that I'd been shot. I was just excited."

"What were you excited for?" asked Tomi.

"Like, I was going home or something," said Kirsten. "Like my job was done. I'd clocked out and now I got to go home. And finally I got there, to the source of the light, and this place Tomi, how do I say this? It felt like I'd woken up from a dream and was in a place I'd always been. Does that make any sense?"

Tomi smiled and nodded. "It totally does. When I had my past life regression, I saw this in between place, like where we go in between lives, and when I was there, well it felt like I'd just been visiting Earth. That I actually belonged there. Like a part of me was always there."

Kirsten nodded, feeling lucky she had a friend who would not only listen, but understand. Her secret club. "It was like everything there was soft. And iridescent. And I felt so light. It was like I was giving off a light, and at the same time light was entering me. I felt so connected to everything. Not just connected. Reconnected.

"And, this also might not make sense, but it seemed realer than real. Like that was actually the real place. I thought about how to describe it, and thought about my eye surgery. So here goes. I used to wear glasses, and five years ago or so, I had my vision corrected with laser eye surgery. My vision wasn't that bad, or at least I didn't think it was that bad. Things in the distance were just a bit blurry. But I was so used to it that it just felt normal! Anyways, I had the surgery in the morning, slept all day, then in the evening, I went outside for a walk. It was the same place I'd been living, the same street, but everything felt different. Totally surreal. Objects far off were crystal clear. I could see so much detail, tiny things I'd never noticed before, even though I was on that street every day. I had no idea how much I had been missing. It sort of felt like that. Realer than real."

"Truer than true," said Tomi, thinking of some of her remote viewing sessions where it felt like she switched from an old tube television to ultra-high definition.

"And then there was this being," Kirsten said. "This being in a dark robe approached me. I couldn't make out their face, any details. They floated. I mean the figure had legs, well, sort of, they kind of fuzzed out at the feet. I looked down and realized I didn't have feet either, I was just floating there. Anyways, the being pointed their hand out, and right there where they pointed, it was like a screen appeared, and right there it started playing: it was a recap of my life, and I was watching it. It was just like people say. The scenes whizzed by so fast. I could see my mother and father, just before I was born, then I saw my birth, then some of my childhood. It was so amazing to see it, there was much I had forgotten, so many things that made more sense in hindsight. But then the being snapped its fingers, and the screen disappeared. And, boy, was I pissed!"

"Hah!" Tomi laughed then covered her mouth, not wanting to wake her grandmother, snoring across the room. "Did you say something about it?"

"Oh, you know how I can go full Karen, of course I did," said Kirsten. "I said, 'No! I want to see the rest!' 'Well,' the being pulled off its hood, and said in the gentlest voice, 'You will see the rest. But not now. Right now, I need you.'"

"The being said it needed you?" asked Tomi.

Kirsten nodded. "When it took its hood off, and I could see the eyes, well, I wouldn't say it looked like you, but I *knew* it was you. Like a part of your soul was there in that place waiting for me. And so when I realized it was you, it said again, 'I need you, Kirsten. You need to go back. I can't do it without you.'"

"Wow, Kirsten, wow. You know you didn't have to die to hear me say that," said Tomi lightly, escaping for a moment the heaviness of this experience.

Kirsten smiled. "You told me: 'You need to follow me wherever I go. There are people and beings that want to hurt me.'" Kirsten took Tomi's hand in her own. "You told me that you have an innocence, that you can be manipulated to serve an agenda. That you could easily be led down the wrong path. You said you needed love to keep you on the right path."

Tomi felt fear deep in her core, hearing this advice – that she apparently gave – to protect herself. That she was vulnerable to harm. Naïve. She smiled, not wanting Kirsten to feel bad for telling her this.

"I think I was right," Tomi squeaked out, her throat choked up with emotions.

"Then you told me to go back," Kirsten said. "But I knew it was my choice. And, you know I'm embarrassed to say, it was hard. I knew I needed to go back for you, but here I was, this place felt like the real place. It felt so good to be there. But of course I came back. Suddenly I was flying back through the tunnel, away from the light. For a moment it felt like I was falling, and then wham, it was like somebody turned the switch for gravity on, and there I was, lying on the floor of Ete's craft. And I could immediately feel that I was fine, it was like I hadn't been shot. And I looked up and there you were."

Tomi was crying, thinking about that moment.

"And there you were." Tomi turned her head over on the pillow, looking up at the ceiling. "I just…wow, I just don't know what to say. Except, thank you for coming back."

"No biggie," Kirsten said with a teasing poke.

"How…how do you feel about it now?" asked Tomi, turning her head again to look at Kirsten.

"It's…I'm okay," said Kirsten. "It's just, well it's like my eyes are blurry again. I just felt so connected there. It felt just so real. I don't know, it just feels like I saw something I wasn't supposed to. Like it turns out that what I thought was real life is actually a theatre, and I accidentally saw backstage. It's hard to not think about it."

Tomi nodded. She knew the feeling.

"And how do you feel about today. About the meeting with Ete. About the plan?" asked Tomi.

"Well, you – your soul, your higher self, whatever – told me to follow you," said Kirsten. "Which means you need to go. I know you're supposed to be the first monkey. But I'll be damned if I'm not the second."

Tomi was the last one up the next morning. Seeing she was alone in the bedroom, she came out to the kitchen where she found Esther making maple and fruit oatmeal, with Ib and Kirsten already at the table, pouring coffee and chattering with small talk.

Everyone gave their good mornings and continued their banter when Tomi sat down. While everyone acted like it was any other morning, a heavy cloud hovered over them, knowing that after breakfast this period of togetherness, of living like a loving, caring family, would be coming to an end.

"Esther, you really are a magician with food," said Barry.

"I agree with Barry's assessment," said Ib, "you are a magician, Esther. And I must say, Ete stocked this kitchen very well for us. Except one thing: there is a distinct lack of meat, which for a Dane feels a little sacrilegious."

"It's interesting," said Esther. "There are some people who believe that eating meat has a negative effect on meditation, on your capacity for spiritual growth. Perhaps that's why they haven't provided meat? I mean, they provided us with all this other fresh food."

"Yeah, where do you think they got the produce from?" asked Kirsten, analyzing a berry held between her thumb and index finger. "I mean we're how far underground, and we have blueberries. I mean, did Ete just get in her craft and swing by Whole Foods?"

"Nobody pay attention to the ten foot alien pushing a shopping cart!" Barry joked. "Quite an experience though, isn't it? Enjoying blueberries somewhere under a mountain in an alien base. Base?

Maybe home is a better word. Lair? Whatever this place is, my compliments to the greengrocer."

Tomi smiled at Barry. "You know, sitting here I sometimes forget where we are. I just let my mind believe we're on vacation in the real cabin. Just enjoying ourselves. Enjoying our lives."

"Perhaps enjoying a campfire with Sixto in the evening," said Ib, smiling through sadness. "Let's promise that when we get through this, if somehow we get through it and the cabin is still standing, we really do go there. Enjoy our lives, as you say."

Kirsten pulled her napkin from her lap, used it to wipe her eyes, and put it on her plate. She felt more tears coming, and didn't want to bring the rest of the table down, so she reached for empty plates to divert her attention with a task. As Kirsten reached for her plate, Esther placed her hand on Kirsten's.

"Before you do that, I just…I want to say that this, whatever this time was here, well, it's been wonderful. Of course getting to spend this time with Tomi has been like a dream. But I also want to say to you three, Kirsten, Barry, and Ib, how much I've enjoyed your company. And how thankful I am that Tomi has had you in her life, looking out for her. I mean it – thank you."

Ib gave his head a small, humble bow.

Barry tried to speak, but stumbled as he got choked up with emotions. "And I just want to say that this…this time together, well it's felt…felt like–"

"Felt like family," finished Tomi. She placed her right hand on Ib's, and her left on Barry's. "This has felt like family."

"It is family," said Kirsten, no longer trying to hide her tears.

After a moment of uneasy silence as they looked around in appreciation of each other, Kirsten said "well, I'll work on clearing these," and she started collecting dirty plates. Ib and Barry gathered the few belongings they had, and without a word, the group quietly exited Ete's Cabin, stepping into the bright stone hallway, and headed towards the hangar.

They took a few steps into the hangar and stopped, pausing to take in this huge room, this massive cavern hidden deep under a mountain, all surfaces glowing, illuminating the shiny metallic crafts parked neatly and spaced evenly around the hangar. Tomi heard Kirsten gasp just as she noticed Ete standing beside a craft across the room.

"Look, it's Ete. With another Ete!"

Tomi looked around and spotted Ete, who was standing beside another individual, the first time the group had seen another of Ete's kind.

"My god," whispered Ib, "this one is actually taller than Ete. I didn't think that was possible."

As they crossed the hangar and approached, Tomi tried to smile at the other being, while also trying to not look like she was staring. The being was indeed taller than Ete, by nearly a foot she estimated, and while they shared the same shimmering skin and catlike eyes, this one appeared to be older, stooped, a little more frail.

"*Please, meet my friend Cuso,*" said Ete. As is often the case, Ete shared more than words when she spoke telepathically. Along with the words came more information, even feelings and emotions. In this case, Tomi knew that Cuso was considered a wise elder among Ete's community, and that though they had earned rest for their body, they continued to contribute, as they were doing with this task.

"Hello," and "Pleased to meet you," they each said, overlapping their greetings, uncoordinated as they looked on in awe. Cuso was silent, giving a slow nod of their head and a slow blink of their eyes. Instead of words, a feeling of welcome, of best intentions, emanated from Cuso.

"*It is time,*" said Ete. "*Ib and Barry, Cuso will take you in this craft, and deliver you wherever you want to go, wherever you think is best to start your mission. You can go ahead and get into this craft.*"

Ete gestured to the closest craft, smaller than the one they had arrived in – *about the size of a VW Wagoneer*, Tomi thought – but darker, the exterior a deep flat black, and shaped like a bell. It rested on four legs, and at the bottom of the bell was a small entrance with a ladder extended to the floor.

Barry and Ib turned to look at Tomi, Kirsten, and Esther, each of them already crying. They exchanged hugs and whispered good wishes.

"Promise me," said Tomi, "both of you, promise me I will see you again. Soon."

"I promise," said Barry. He grinned at Ete. "We just have to find something ancient and highly destructive, how hard could that be, right?"

Tomi laughed and sniffed. "I believe in you two. I really do."

"And Ete," said Ib. "In my language, we say, 'tak for det,' which in English is, 'thanks for that,' but it really means thanks for everything, for your hospitality. Well, I say, tusind tak for det. A thousand thanks for everything."

Ib held out his hand. Ete hesitated for a moment, then extended her long, lanky arm, and shook Ib's hand, her long fingers extending partway up his forearm. Barry followed Ib and thanked Ete. Cuso had already climbed into the bell-shaped craft, and Ib and Barry walked to the ladder.

They turned to wave a final goodbye, when Tomi suddenly shouted, "Minear! Yes! Don't go yet! Wait just a moment!"

Tomi turned and ran towards the hallway, exiting from view as she sprinted towards Ete's Cabin. After a minute, she came running back out of the hallway, and towards the craft.

She huffed a little as she spoke out of breath after her sprint. "Minear. Ancient and destructive. Go to Arthur Minear and show him this." Tomi held out her hand. On her palm was the triangular chunk of green stone, the piece of the Emerald Tablet, the piece that should connect to the piece Arthur Minear had found, had shown to Tomi when they had their video call. "Tell him I sent you. I trust him. I think he will help you."

Ib took the stone from her hand and held it in his palm, rubbing his thumb over the tiny characters carved in the small surface. "Of course," said Ib. "Tomi, you're brilliant." He hugged her one last time and climbed up the ladder and into the craft.

When they were both inside, the steps of the ladder pulled together and tucked into the craft. The doorway closed, seeming to create a seamless closure. Tomi stepped back as the craft began to climb slowly, silently, as though she were witnessing a magic trick. As it rose in the giant cavern, the legs of the craft pulled in, again creating a seamless exterior, as though the skin of the vehicle formed a single layer with no gaps whatsoever.

Tomi's eyes followed the craft, watching it gain speed as it rose towards the roof of the hangar. The roof, just like the walls and floor, gave off a bright, light glow, illuminating the giant space. Her eyes rose to the ceiling, where she saw the faintest line where the light glowed a slightly different colour, a brighter yellow. The line was circular, forming a swirl pattern, the line continuously spreading out while paradoxically closing in on itself. As the craft sped towards the stone roof of the hangar, Tomi lost her focus on the craft, as though it became blurry, then in an instant it was gone, as though it passed right through the stone, through the swirl pattern, and was absorbed into the mountain.

She stared up at the high, rocky ceiling for a few moments, realizing that her friends had in fact departed. Then Tomi turned around, and held eye contact with Ete.

"*I know*," Tomi said in her mind, directing her thoughts towards Ete. "*It's time to get to work.*"

Chapter 7

"Often I have woken to myself out of the body, become detached from all else and entered into myself, and I have seen beauty of surpassing greatness, and have felt assured that then especially I belonged to the higher reality, engaged in the noblest life and identified with the Divine."

Plotinus

In the deep indigo light, Tomi closed her eyes and was immersed in inner darkness. She opened her eyes again to look at her stool, making sure it hadn't moved. She remembered the way the floating stools had moved and shuffled around the room when she had remote viewed this space, and wondered if her stool would move when she closed her eyes.

The stool had not moved, floating just a foot or so off the floor, the seat wide enough for her to cross her legs. She looked around the room and saw that everyone had their eyes closed. Ete and her three friends looked to already be deep in meditation, as though they could slip into a deep state by simply closing their eyes. Her grandmother sat cross-legged on her stool, her face calm and relaxed. She looked at Kirsten, her eyes closed, her face looking more determined than relaxed.

Ete had to fetch a seventh stool when Kirsten had asked – or almost demanded – to participate. Ete had thought Kirsten's role would be to keep Tomi and Esther cared for and comfortable in the cabin, and hadn't expected her to want to spend hours each day in deep meditation.

"I'd like to stay," Kirsten had said. "And help."

"*Tomi has all the support she needs here*," Ete had said telepathically to both Kirsten and Tomi. "*I assure you it is not necessary.*"

"Esther is participating. And you brought three of your people for this," said Kirsten, looking at the tall beings standing behind Ete. "Why? What role do they play?"

"*Tomi and Esther, but especially Tomi, will have to work hard to deepen their meditation, to get to a state where ascension is possible*," Ete said. "*We will meditate with her, as a group, our consciousness supporting her.*"

"Right," Kirsten had said. "So it couldn't hurt if I meditated to support her also. I want to help."

"*Of course*," said Ete, and off she went to fetch another stool from around a bend in the room. Kirsten looked at Tomi, shrugged, and smiled. Tomi wondered if Ete's telepathic abilities let her know the real reason Kirsten wanted to participate: she wanted to ascend, also, because Kirsten didn't want to be separated from Tomi.

Tomi jiggled her legs, straightened her spine, and closed her eyes. *Basics,* she thought to herself, *back to basics. Just start with your breathing.* She started to imagine what she looked like, perched on a floating stool, immersed in this inky indigo light. Light that just emanates from the stone walls. She thought about the mountain above their heads, and thought she could feel the weight of it on her shoulders.

"*Tomi.*"

Her body jumped as Ete's words popped into her mind, surprising her.

"*Tomi, you are feeling the weight of expectation. This is understandable. But it's a feeling that has no benefit in this work.*"

"*I know,*" said Tomi in reply, still feeling uncomfortable with speaking telepathically, not entirely sure when she was speaking and when she was having a private thought. "*It's the ego stuff. I need to put my ego aside. I will get there.*"

"*I know that you will,*" said Ete.

"*How do you know?*" asked Tomi. "*How are you so sure, so confident in all of this?*"

"*We've seen it, Tomi. You know that we spend a lot of time in meditation, and when we do, we watch. We gather information. And we saw it. We saw you destroy the pyramid. We saw you saving your people,*" said Ete.

"*So in meditation, you see the future? And it's certain? Is that what you're saying?*" asked Tomi.

"*No,*" said Ete. "*The universe is far too mysterious for that. We see what is possible.*"

"*So…it's only a possibility?*" asked Tomi. "*I mean, is it likely? Do you know the odds?*"

"Tomi, a possibility in the universe is a beautiful thing," said Ete. As Ete spoke, she shared a vision with Tomi. In her mind's eye, Tomi saw the universe, the early universe. It was chaotic, violent, hostile, matter slamming into matter, explosions.

"It looks like life should be impossible," Tomi said. The vision then shifted, zooming in on early life: proteins, fragile yet spreading through a hostile universe.

"Statistically impossible," said Ete. *"You asked about odds, Tomi. The odds were that we, that life, shouldn't exist. And yet here we are, in a universe so perfectly fit for life that it's exploding with it. A possibility is a beautiful thing."*

Tomi meditated on the idea of a possibility for a while, then tried to cast the idea aside for now, clearing her mind and drawing a deep breath. But she struggled to keep her mind clear, with more questions and doubts creeping in. As a trained remote viewer, she had become skilled at settling her mind and getting herself in deep meditative states. But today her mind was too active, too curious.

"Ete?" Tomi said in her mind, wondering if they were still telepathically connected.

"Yes, Tomi?" came Ete's reply.

"I'm still not sure I understand how raising my vibration can make me travel," Tomi said.

"It may help to not think of it as travelling, Ete said. *Everything in the universe is in constant motion, including you, at the biggest and at the smallest levels. Imagine if you could just slightly change that movement. You stay the same, stay in the same place in the universe, but*

your movement, your frequency changes. And it will turn out that there is a whole other world, a whole other reality that exists at that new frequency."

Tomi thought about the old TV set her grandmother had, a big wooden cabinet with two big clicking dials. She loved the feeling of turning the dial and feeling it click on the next channel.

"Just like that, Tomi," said Ete, seemingly able to look in on Tomi's memory. *"Like changing the channel."*

Tomi tried to quiet her mind again, but her mind wasn't satisfied. *"Is this Other Place, is it the only one?"* she asked Ete.

Tomi felt amusement coming from her, as though Ete had laughed telepathically. *"Oh Tomi, how special would we be if that were the case. You remember what I told you before: the universe is abounding with life."*

Again Ete shared a vision to Tomi's mind. Tomi saw a picture, a pencil sketch being drawn on a light table. Though she had never seen it, and had only heard about it from her grandmother, Tomi knew the drawing was of Alda's house, her front garden in full bloom. Then another page was placed on top of the first, and a new drawing was made, a field of wildflowers, but no house, then another page and another drawing, and another, each one looking less and less familiar, flipping faster and faster. But with the backlighting from the light table, the pages were not fully opaque; instead, looking closely, she could see impression of the drawings on the pages underneath.

"I understand. If there are so many, layers, or other places, how will I know where I'm going?" Tomi asked.

"It is true, there are so many, but you can't get lost. The Other Place we speak of is the only one we can access from here, from this reality," said Ete. *"From this physical form."*

Tomi reset her breathing, and tried to clear her mind again. She thought about the things Ete had shown her in her remote viewing sessions, seeing the way souls reincarnate, using these incarnations to learn and grow, working towards a next level, a next step in understanding. She wondered how many lives she had lived, how many levels she had climbed, what mysteries awaited at higher levels than this.

"Ete, I'm sorry," said Tomi in her mind, directing it towards Ete. *"I'm sorry but I'm struggling to concentrate. I have so many questions about the Other Place, about how all of this works, what happens when I get there. I feel like I need to know more before I can do this."*

"I know you feel you need that, but you already have everything you need. Tomi, we could spend a lifetime sharing with you everything we know, and you still wouldn't know enough for what is ahead. There is just so much about the universe that is unknowable."

"I know," replied Tomi. *"It's just, finding how much is unknowable is a little frustrating."*

"When you can replace frustration with appreciation, with love for the beauty of the unknowable, you will be one step closer to ascending," said Ete. *"Why don't you stop for today and get some rest?"*

"Thank you," replied Tomi, trying to take Ete's advice and focus on appreciation over frustration. *"Thank you for today."*

Tomi opened her eyes, adjusting again to the dark indigo light. She scanned the six others and saw Ete and her three friends, and Kirsten all still with their eyes closed in meditation. She looked at her grandmother across from her, and had difficulty making out the details on her face. It was as though she were blurry. Tomi rubbed her eyes, opened them, and found her grandmother still looked blurry. She closed her eyes again, rubbing them slowly, thinking she had something in her eye.

"Today's session is now complete. Tomi has completed today's practice and will now rest," said Ete telepathically to the group. The words appeared gently, as though Ete had turned the volume of her telepathy down, since Kirsten and Esther were still deep in meditation.

Tomi opened her eyes again and looked at Kirsten, seeing her face clearly, her body starting to move just slightly as she awakened. She looked again at Esther and felt relieved that she could see her clearly, chalking the blurriness up to sleepy eyes.

Tomi was the first into Ete's Cabin and headed straight into the bathroom, sitting on the toilet lid and taking a moment to herself to regain her composure. She was frustrated, angry with herself, feeling like she wasted the day, unable to get her mind under control. She balled up her hand and punched her thigh, releasing some negative energy.

After a few minutes of breathing to regulate herself, she opened the door and stepped into the living room. Esther was there on the couch with two mugs. She smiled at Tomi and patted the space beside her, calling her to sit down.

"Peppermint tea for you," Esther said, turning the mug so the handle faced Tomi.

Tomi picked up the mug and blew on the hot tea, looking to the kitchen and seeing Kirsten getting to work on making dinner.

"She's a really good friend," Esther said about Kirsten. "You're lucky to have her. When they trained me to ascend, to go to the Other Place, I was there by myself."

"Hmm," Tomi said as she swallowed tea. "There? Weren't you here?"

Esther thought for a moment. "I don't think so. It was underground, like this. But it seemed smaller. I don't think this is their only home."

I know so little about them, thought Tomi. *About all of this.*

"What if I'm not ready," Tomi said. "What if I can't do it? I couldn't focus at all today. I know so little about this, what's happening, where I'm going. I don't know how to get there when I don't even understand what 'there' is."

Esther sipped her tea, listening and nodding with a slight grin, the ones adults have when they hear out a child's ideas before explaining to them how the world really works.

"Thomasina," Esther said grandmotherly, perhaps the only person who could get away with using Tomi's full name, "I don't want you to ever doubt that you can do something. I know you can. I've been watching you. I don't say this just as your grandmother. I know how special you are."

Tomi curled her lips down and looked at her mug. "You said you watched me from the Other Place? How?"

"Okay, let's say we're here," said Esther, placing her mug on the table. She took Tomi's mug and placed it beside hers. "And this mug is the Other Place. Imagine between them there's a curtain, or a veil, so most of the time, you don't notice the other one is even there. Sometimes from the Other Place, if you really focus, you can peek around the curtain and get a little glimpse of the other mug. But it was kind of unpredictable. I didn't always know when I was seeing you, if I was seeing the future or past or what."

Tomi looked at her grandmother, her eyes wet with tears. "Sometimes I thought I could feel you. Nana, what's it like there? The Other Place? Where am I going?"

"It's…oh, it's so hard to describe," said Esther, her eyes bright with wonder. "So hard to describe because it's so unlike here, with our heavy physical bodies. It's more a place of feeling, I suppose. Instead of seeing or touching something, there's just more of a feeling for things. A knowing. As though there's so much more information around you and you can pick it all up in a way you don't here."

"So you don't see or touch, do you not have a body? I'm not sure I understand," said Tomi.

"You have a body," said Esther, "you do, but it's not physical in the same way. It's lighter, more like energy instead of…meat, I suppose. It's as though here we need our senses to kind of navigate things. But, you and I both know there is more out there than the five senses can tell us, right? I mean, think of all the things you've seen through remote viewing, and you never once used your eyes. Think of it a little bit like remote viewing, except maybe a thousand times more intense."

Tomi remembered her past life regression with Marja, where she saw herself in a previous life on her Hilly Island. She had called herself a 'shimmer', an energy being that floated around, without a physical body and yet still bodied. She longed for that weightless feeling.

"And what about time?" asked Tomi. "You said before there is a distortion?"

"It's…again, hard to explain. It's sort of outside of the spacetime collective we have here. It's not linear time, but time still exists. That's what I meant when I said I could see you, get glimpses of you, but I didn't know when it was, because it felt like time here and time there didn't really match up."

"So you could see things, like you had access to points in time, but couldn't control it?"

"Yes. You can access so much information there, but it's hard to navigate, really. You can get glimpses, and with deep concentration, even more. But you can't just pick a time and place and know everything there is to know. I think of it like grade school. You know, maybe here on Earth, on this physical level, we're in the second or third grade and we're learning addition and subtraction, maybe some advanced kids are doing multiplication and division. But when we go to the Other Place, suddenly we're hit with algebra. There's all this new information, but it's not easy to make sense of it."

"And maybe somewhere else, way beyond, it's trigonometry," said Tomi. She eased into the couch and took a long sip of her tea, letting her mind wander a moment, trying to imagine what it will feel like to have a body that is more energetic than material. "So…what do you do there?" she asked.

"You live," said Esther, smiling. "You know, in our lives here, we spend a lot of time taking care of our bodies. Growing food, cooking, grooming, bathing, making clothes. We have to carve out time to focus on our minds, on our souls. Those physical concerns that are core to our lives here are replaced by a more mental, more spiritual existence."

Tomi nodded, feeling comforted by her grandmother's words, and for the first time, a little excited to experience this. Despite all she'd experienced with Ete and her grandmother, part of her still wondered if the Other Place was actually *real*. She started to look forward to trying again tomorrow, and felt some of the tension from the day release in her body. Esther got up to help Kirsten in the kitchen, the two of them dancing as they worked, and Tomi stretched out on the couch.

The next morning, Tomi was woken by sunlight shining on her face. The light came in the window and brushed her cheek with warmth. For a moment she forgot where she was, enjoying the sun's rays, until she remembered that the sun was in fact some sort of projection, a replica sun shining on a replica cabin, and she was somewhere underground. She sat up and was pleased to feel a lightness, an anticipation for the day that she had lacked the previous morning.

After breakfast they exited Ete's Cabin, walked down the large hallway, and turned right into the meditation room. Ete and her three friends were already seated on the floating meditation stools. Without opening her eyes, Ete waved her long, slender hand towards the three empty seats.

Tomi climbed onto her stool, pulled her legs up and crossed them, and watched as Kirsten and Esther did the same, closing their eyes once they got settled. This time Tomi didn't close her eyes right away. Instead she looked up at the ceiling, taking in the deep, inky indigo light emanating from all surfaces. At some point her eyes closed and the dark indigo light created a blank canvas in her mind's eye. The indigo light was replaced by the deep darkness of space, punctuated by the glow of stars many light years away.

Tomi's vision panned across the starry sky, and the Moon came into view, not a dinner plate-sized small moon as we see from Earth, but taking up most of her field of vision, as though she were aboard Apollo 10, looking out the window as it approached the Moon. Seeing it up close for the first time.

Where is this vision coming from? wondered Tomi. Somehow she knew this was not something sent by Etc. It was coming from somewhere else.

As the surface of the moon drifted across her vision, Tomi heard her grandmother's voice. Esther's voice sounded weak, groggy, as though she were talking in her sleep, or from a deep state of meditation. Tomi realized the voice wasn't telepathy, her grandmother wasn't speaking to her. Tomi knew she was listening to Esther have a conversation with somebody else. She was experiencing her grandmother's memory.

I'm approaching the moon, she heard Esther say. *It's so bright. So beautiful. The details of the craters are so clear from here.*

Okay Esther, said a man's voice. *Our focus in this session will be the far side of the moon. Can you direct yourself around the front of the moon to the back?*

Tomi knew the man's voice, she was sure of it, but couldn't place it.

Okay, I'm swinging around it now, said Esther. *I'm so deep, I can see so clearly. I'm flying above the surface. I can see the line, the dividing line, the moon is bright on one side and darker on the other.*

That's great but remember to watch for overlay, the man's voice said. *Just describe the impressions.*

Overlay, thought Tomi, a term referring to the brain's tendency to make conclusions in remote viewing based on the subject's memories or impressions. *Nana is remote viewing the moon, and the man is the moderator of the session,* Tomi concluded.

Tomi remembered when Ray had shown her the drawings Esther had given him, pen sketches drawn on napkins. She remembered one had something to do with the moon. And she thought about her grandmother's old letters, remembering the one Ray had sent to Esther where he asked about her session remote viewing the moon, wondering about the conclusion she had drawn from it.

But Tomi wasn't seeing her grandmother lying on a couch in meditation; she was seeing the dark side of the moon, just as her grandmother had seen it. *I'm watching her memory*, Tomi thought.

What was that? Esther said. *I thought I saw a flash. A blue flash. It's…harder to make out surface details compared to the bright side, but I can see some…there's a flash again. I think it came from a big crater, I can see it, it's kind of shadowed.*

Can you get closer and get a better look? said the man.

Tomi's vision focused in on a large crater where she, too, saw flashes of blue light. Her view zoomed closer, as though she were aboard the lunar lander and she was descending towards the surface. As they got closer the light flashed again, leaving impressions of the surface. There seemed to be something in the crater. Around the crater there were structures, several of them, tall, like multi-storied buildings, but jutting out at the top, as though modeled after the shape of a mushroom.

What do you see? asked the man's voice.

The crater, Esther said. *There's something in the middle, something circular, dark. I can't quite make it out visually, but I have a feeling that it's an entrance of some sort.*

What else do you see?

There are structures, tall structures, shaped like a tree, or mushroom. They are bigger at the top, said Esther. *There's one that's pulling me towards it. Like there's something I need to see here.*

Follow it, said the man.

Tomi's vision pulled in towards one of the towers. It was tall and dark, but as they closed in she could see that the bulge part of the structure was ringed with windows. She zoomed closer and closer, right through the glass, and inside the structure. It was a small room with all-metallic surfaces. Under the window was a panel with various small lights, but the details were fuzzy. Tomi felt a sudden jolt of anxiety, realizing there was a being in the room.

There's…there's a being, she heard Esther say. *In the corner of the room. It's small, short, like an elementary school child. It's, now it's turned to look at me. It…has big eyes. Dark, I can't make out detail in them. An almond shaped face. I feel fear.*

Remember, it can't hurt you, said the man. *Just report your impressions.*

No, not my own fear, said Esther. *I feel the being's fear. It can see me. I surprised it.*

Can you communicate with it? Try to ask it a question? Ask it what it is doing there, said the man.

When Tomi heard Esther and the man speak, it felt like she could hear the words in her mind. When Esther tried to speak to the being, Tomi instead felt them.

Hello, Esther said to the being. *What are you doing here on the Moon?*

The being did not respond.

Tell me, what are humans to you? What is your relationship to us?

Like your relationship with your garden, said the being.

Suddenly the vision faded and turned to black, the voices of her grandmother and the man gone. Tomi spent some time in this darkness, trying to put this vision behind her, focusing on her task. As she moved deeper in her meditation, her awareness of her body faded. She felt as though she were open to receiving information in a way she hadn't experienced before.

Like tiny puzzle pieces coming together, an image formed in her mind. Tomi saw a small wooden house tucked under some trees, facing into a clearing. It was old and beautiful, with a thatch roof. It reminded Tomi of an illustration from a child's fairytale book.

A figure appeared out of the woods, short and dark. It walked as though it didn't have knees, the short legs bending only at the hips. Tomi tried to look at its face, but it too was covered, as though it wore a black full-body suit, the suit made from a hard, molded material. The being waved its arm, indicating Tomi should follow it inside. It then picked up a piece of wood with each hand from a pile of chopped firewood, and entered the small cottage. Tomi entered the cottage, and found a small room with rough wooden floors, a small red rug placed in front of the hearth. The being sat on the rug and placed the two pieces of wood on the dying fire.

Tomi sat down on the rug and faced the being. Despite its odd appearance, Tomi felt no fear with this being. Instead she felt a familiarity, a closeness, a relationship of mutual care.

"*You are one of my guides*," Tomi said, a knowing coming to her as she spoke. The being nodded its head, still covered by a dark mask. "*You watch out for me, protect me. It's coming to me now. What is your name?*"

"*Burden.*" The name appeared in Tomi's mind.

"*Why the name Burden, I wonder*," Tomi thought.

The words, "*You gave it to me*," appeared in her mind.

As Tomi wondered what Burden meant, she heard, "*I have a gift for you.*"

Burden extended a hand holding a white gift box, the lid wrapped with red ribbon and topped with a bow. Tomi lifted the lid off the box and pulled out the gift.

"*A gun?*" she said, surprised to be holding a black handgun. She thought it looked like John's service weapon. "*Why are you giving me a gun?*"

"*Don't forget the danger*," Burden said telepathically. "*Amidst such beauty you have seen, there lurks so much danger.*"

"*But…is the danger real?*" Tomi asked, thinking of Arthur Minear talking of cataclysm, of the visions Ete shared.

"*Would you be doing this if it weren't real?*" Burden replied.

Tomi looked at the gun. "*I don't want this*," she said, opening her hand and letting the gun fall, the gun dissolving into thin air before it hit the ground. The vision faded rapidly and Burden and their cabin were gone, replaced again by darkness.

After a few minutes, the darkness was again pierced by small lights. Stars. She thought about pushing this image out, wanting to pause and make sense of the strange visions she'd had, but was too curious to put a halt to it. She felt movement. She was streaming through space at high speed. The Earth came into focus, and she accelerated towards it. The Earth grew larger, and she felt a warmth as she pushed through the cold of space towards this oasis of life.

Suddenly that warm feeling turned cold. She turned her view around to look behind her, and saw that she was being pursued by a giant hunk of rock covered in ice, a tail of debris and dust chasing behind it. Tomi felt herself move out of the way, and watched the comet zip past her.

It's going to hit, she thought, feeling panicked. The comet barreled towards the Earth like a bullet out of a gun. Tomi audibly gasped as she watched the massive object pound the Earth, like one of the cataclysms Ete had shown them.

Stop, Tomi thought, and the image faded again to black. Tomi opened her eyes and rubbed them. She saw Kirsten and Esther had opened their eyes as well, likely awakened by Tomi's gasp. Ete and her friends remained seated with their eyes closed.

Ete's eyes were still closed as she spoke telepathically to them. *"The deeper you go, the more you will see,"* Ete said. *"Not all of it is pleasant, I'm afraid. There is information all around you all the time. Tomorrow we will work on moving past these distractions."*

When they returned to Ete's Cabin, Kirsten made a sweet potato and chickpea stew. Tomi and Esther helped, but they were all so drained of energy from the day of meditation, they worked away in silence. Once they started eating dinner, Tomi perked up and started to share what she had seen in her meditation. She told Esther about experiencing her remote viewing session of the moon.

"That's so interesting," said Esther. "I haven't thought about that for some time. At least, I don't think it was on my mind today. I wonder why you would see that?"

"A while ago," said Tomi, "I went through some old letters that Ray had sent you, back when you worked together at SRI on remote viewing. In one of them he mentioned this session, remote viewing the back side of the moon. He wrote that he wasn't there for it, and wanted to hear about it from you. He said that you had come to a different conclusion about the beings on the moon than Ingo Swann had come to when he did the same viewing. What was your conclusion? What did he mean?"

"Now let me think," said Esther, taking a few moments to bring details from decades past to mind. "Well Ingo, he was an incredible remote viewer, incredible psychic. Anyways, he had a similar session, again where he encountered a being and asked its intention. And it turned out, in both sessions it said the same thing. Something like they see humans the way we see gardens."

"Yes," said Tomi. "I heard that and that's when the vision ended. What does that mean?"

"Well as I recall," said Esther, "Ingo took that as a negative. He felt that they were saying they had a mastery over us. Like they harvest us, as from a garden."

"But you didn't take it that way?" asked Kirsten.

Esther shook her head and took a sip of red wine. "No. Where he interpreted harvest, I interpreted growth. When I think of a garden, I think of tending to it, nurturing it, helping it grow. For some reason, I felt the being wasn't talking about our bodies. It was talking about our souls. Like they have some interest, or some mission, with human souls. But I saw it as growth, tending to the garden."

"You didn't think they were hostile," said Tomi.

"No," said Esther. "Not these ones."

"And the moderator. I heard a man's voice. It was familiar. Do you remember who was leading you in that session?" asked Tomi.

Esther thought for a moment. "I'm not sure, I don't remember his name. He was a military man. Younger. But the name is escaping me."

They cleaned up the dishes, and despite there being some sunlight still coming in the window, Tomi said she was ready for bed.

"Not just yet. My job is to take care of you, right? Your body has been scrunched up in meditation all day. Let's do some stretches first. Just like a garden, you have to tend to your body, too," Kirsten said, nodding at Esther.

Kirsten led them in some evening yoga in the dying light of day. She then drew Tomi a bath and got her to bed. Tomi fell asleep immediately and Kirsten tucked the end of the blanket under Tomi's feet before climbing in beside her, the replica moon bright and full through the bedroom window.

As the days rolled on, Tomi's meditations went deeper, her experiences increasingly 'mystical,' a word Tomi found herself using more and more in describing them. She would find ideas, information, visions entering her consciousness. Sometimes she would accept and experience them, her curiosity winning out, indulging her desire to find answers, to find a deeper understanding of the universe. At other times, she concentrated on pushing them aside, not letting herself be distracted by noise.

On some days, she would feel herself connected to Ete, as though she could sense Ete organizing everyone participating like a conductor, somehow harmonizing and sharing their energy with Tomi. At other times Tomi would be in a deep state of meditation, completely forgetting the people around her.

One day, she found herself in a state so deep that she had fully lost awareness of her body. She felt nothing, as though she had disconnected from her physical self, her consciousness simply existing in this place, this room. It was both exhilarating and terrifying.

"*You are doing well,*" said Ete, her voice entering Tomi's awareness. "*Stay in this space for some time, and when you are ready, you will reconnect with your body. But when you do, you mustn't focus on the body as a whole. Your body isn't muscles and bones and skin. Your body is a trillion tiny particles. Each of them are energized and in motion. Let yourself feel each and every one of them. Experience them. Be them."*

When Tomi tried to reconnect with her body, to regain her awareness, she felt vibration, but it was still her whole body she felt, not the trillion tiny pieces that Ete described. Several times in the proceeding days she tried this again, to reach this sensation Ete described, without success.

After one unsuccessful attempt, Ete entered Tomi's mind and shared a vision. The vision was dark and it took her a moment to recognize it. Tomi was looking at herself, as though she were seeing through Ete's eyes, looking at her across the indigo room. There she was, her eyes closed, her body seated on the floating stool, the stool slowly and gently rising and falling, but staying in one place.

Suddenly the vision changed, zooming in as though she dove inside her own body, first seeing the muscles and bones and veins carrying her blood. Then zooming closer, like looking through a microscope, seeing herself at the cellular level, the small units of physical life that construct her body. Then zooming in again, she saw the building blocks of matter, their movements unpredictable, always on the move. The scene shifted again. As though coming back to the widest lens, she could see the cosmos. Stars, planets, galaxies.

I understand. I have a universe inside of me, Tomi thought. *I am a universe.*

The vision faded, and Tomi started to regain awareness of her body. She felt the vibration. She had felt her body vibrate, shake before. Once while highly fevered with a flu she felt her body vibrating. In meditation, she had often become aware of her body's natural vibrations. But this was different.

It wasn't her body vibrating as a single unit. This time, she could feel each cell of her body, each electron constant in motion. As though she could feel the movement of a trillion particles, experiencing them individually and in unison at once. Tomi felt the resonance, each one vibrating at the same rate, her body in unison.

She remained in this state for some time. It felt both alien and familiar, a sensation that had always been there but only now was she aware of it. Eventually she let the feeling dissipate, replaced by a more typical awareness of her physical body.

As she came out of her meditation, she opened her eyes and looked around. Everyone else still had their eyes closed in meditation, except for Kirsten. She could see Kirsten's eyes open. Not only open, wide open, as she stared at Tomi, her face carrying a look of shock or confusion.

Tomi stood up from her stool quietly, so as not to disturb the others, and walked with Kirsten out of the room and down the hall towards Ete's Cabin.

"What is it?" asked Tomi, taking Kirsten's hand.

Kirsten stopped walking and pulled Tomi's arm so she could face her. She spoke quietly, in a near whisper.

"Tomi, something told me to stop meditating and open my eyes. I looked around and at first everything seemed normal. I watched for a while, and noticed that you seemed lighter. Like your face, your skin was glowing a bit. It was luminous."

"Wow, that's…wild," Tomi said, touching her cheeks as though she'd just tried a new moisturizer, "I do like the idea of being luminous."

"Yeah," Kirsten said, her demeanour still serious. "And then I saw you float."

Tomi stopped smiling. "Like the floating stool, it was moving?"

"No," said Kirsten. "You floated above the stool. Off the stool. Tomi, I…think I saw you levitate."

Tomi chased that feeling, to get to that stage where she was experiencing every particle in her body buzzing. *I was close,* Tomi thought as she settled onto her floating stool, frustrated with her inability to repeat the experience for – *how many days?* Despite the replica sun and moon, Tomi had lost track of how long they had been doing this. She thought that she should have kept track of the days with chalk five-counts on the wall, like a prisoner from an old movie.

Tomi closed her eyes with the rest of the group, and began breathing exercises.

"*You must rid yourself of frustration*," Ete said to Tomi, the words appearing in her relaxing mind. "*Frustration is not an emotion that will serve you in ascending.*"

"How do you mean?" Tomi asked. *"You mean I should suppress it?"*

"Oh no," said Ete, *"suppressing only moves it, like trying to keep it hidden from yourself. Remember what I said, there are no opposites in the universe, only degrees of the same thing. You need to take that negative emotion and pull on it until you find yourself at a higher degree, pull yourself to the positive."*

"That…kind of sounds like finding the opposite," Tomi said.

"What is hate, Tomi, but degree on a continuum of love? Loneliness but a lower degree of connection? These emotions, hate, shame, fear, these are low vibration emotions. You need to change the degree to a higher vibration emotion."

"I think I understand," said Tomi. *"Do these negative emotions not exist in the Other Place, then?"*

"They exist everywhere," said Ete, *"to one degree or another, but yes, in the Other Place, you have access to higher degrees."*

"Can…can these emotions seep through?" asked Tomi. *"You said we basically share the same space. Can one realm impact the other?"*

"Oh yes," said Ete. *"We are separated by a veil, not a wall. Many things can seep in, back and forth, up and down. It's not only emotion that can cross through. Also actions. From small to large. Your nuclear bombs for example. How could such a thing be contained to this reality?"*

Tomi pictured a mushroom cloud, total destruction, heat and radiation and the pain of thousands of people crying in horror all at once. She wondered what that felt like in the Other Place, and felt shame for what humans have done to this planet, imagining beings in other realms cursing us for such wanton destruction.

Tomi breathed deeply, resetting her meditation, her eyes closed, seeing nothing but darkness. *Shame*, she thought to herself. *I have to take this emotion and find its positive. I'm feeling shame because we harm other beings, but I want to care for and connect to other life.*

Tomi thought of connecting with other living things. She thought about connecting with people, thinking about her grandmother, her friends, feeling love and care for them. She thought about animals, the pets she had loved. She thought about the time she was in the grocery store and found a little girl crying because she couldn't find her mom. Tomi had wiped her tears, took her hand, and had the staff make an announcement. When her mother was found, she had given Tomi a hug, crying in relief.

As these scenes played in her mind, they became less visual and more experiential; Tomi felt these experiences, reliving the positive emotions. She became immersed in the feeling, gently cradling her, making her feel lighter. Tomi gave up control of the experience, and let these emotions continue to flow, continue to hold her until she was again so deep in meditation that she lost awareness of her body.

For a moment she felt a pang of fear, as though she had become disconnected from her physical body, afraid of somehow losing it and not being able to return. Instead of suppressing her fear, she pulled on it and found she could turn fear into curiosity and wonder about what came next.

Then the buzzing returned. One by one she could feel the movement, the vibration of her body at a microscopic level, as though she could experience a trillion sensations all at once. She stayed in this state for some time, willing her body to vibrate faster, higher.

"*You can't do it alone*," Ete said telepathically. "*Tomi can't do this alone. Remember, everything is in motion, Tomi, and everything is connected. Everything is in a constant state of motion. If you can connect with it, you can borrow it, and increase your vibration through unity.*"

Resonance, thought Tomi. She remembered learning in high school how the vibration of one object can change the vibration of another object. Her teacher showed them how hitting one tuning fork could start the other.

Tomi held herself in this vibrational state while she softened her focus on her own body. She allowed her awareness to grow, not of the physical things around her, but of the energetic movement all around her. As she expanded her awareness, she thought she could feel Esther, feel her grandmother's love. She could see it flowing across the room, wrapping around her body, and connecting back with Esther, making a figure eight. Then she felt Kirsten. Tomi felt warmth, as though Kirsten were hugging her.

She became aware of the energy flowing from Ete, and Ete's friends, compassion and empathy emanating towards her. In her mind's eye she saw the flow of energy swirling around the room, wrapping around her body and raising it higher, as though she were the tuning fork, taking on their energy and making it her own. Tomi imagined her body so energized, so lightened, that she floated towards the ceiling.

She revelled in the way her body buzzed. It felt like each particle in her body had been replaced by bees, buzzing and flying in circles faster and faster. She saw her grandmother riding this swirl of energy, raising up towards her. Tomi saw her own hand reach out and take her grandmother's hand. She felt a jolt of energy, as though Esther shared a spark with her, a zap that made her body vibrate even faster. She felt herself ascending upwards, spinning slowly in a spiral.

Then she felt something shift. There was a subtle motion, a gentle movement, that shift to a stop feeling of an elevator levelling on the next floor. Suddenly, everything felt different.

Like elevator doors opening to reveal a new level, Tomi opened her eyes. She gasped. She had arrived in the Other Place.

Kirsten was still deep in meditation, deeper than she had been able to achieve before. Today she felt particularly focused, and at times felt some sort of energetic connection with the others in the room, a deep awareness of the energy being shared in the room. Then something shifted, and she felt that energy crash away. The room felt suddenly empty. A deep feeling of isolation washed over her.

She took a deep breath, wiggled her fingers and toes, and opened her eyes to see four tall, lanky aliens sitting cross-legged on their stools in the indigo light room. To her right and to her left she found two empty stools, floating in place.

Chapter 8

"A fire broke out backstage in a theatre. The clown came out to warn the public; they thought it was a joke and applauded. He repeated it; the acclaim was even greater. I think that's just how the world will come to an end: to general applause from wits who believe it's a joke."

Søren Kierkegaard

b heard footsteps and the sound of cupboards closing above him. He opened his eyes and winced.

"Ah, tømmermænd," Ib grunted, putting his hands over his face.

"Tumor…what?" scratched Barry through a rough throat, rubbing his temples.

"My head," said Ib. "Tømmermænd, it means woodworkers, like they are hammering on your brain. It's what we call a hangover. Why do I feel like I'm hungover?"

"Me too," said Barry, sitting up on a loveseat and rubbing his forehead, while Ib pulled himself up on the couch he had been sleeping on.

"Where are we?" asked Ib, looking around at what seemed to be a basement rec room.

Barry scanned the room. "Oh my god. This is my mother's house. Her basement." He looked up as he heard the sound of a chair scraping on a hard floor. "And it sounds like she's home."

Ib placed his face in his hands, rubbing his eyes like a toddler waking up. He smacked his tongue on the roof of his mouth, dry and like sandpaper. "What…how did we get here?"

Barry's mouth hung open as he tried to pull up his last memory. "The craft. Cuso. They must have brought us here. But why? How did they know?"

Ib shook his head then winced, having irritated his headache. "I don't know. I'm trying to remember the journey here but it's so fuzzy. I remember being on the craft and emerging from the mountain. I think we were discussing coming back to Durham to plan our next steps. Or did I dream that discussion? It's hard to tell. It's so fuzzy."

Barry had a confused look on his face, unable to recall the details. "I remember being in the hangar. Tomi gave you something." Barry huffed out a laugh. "Unless Tomi and Ete and the UFO and all of it were a dream."

Ib felt into the pocket of his corduroy pants. He pulled out the stone and smiled at it as he rubbed his thumb on the text. "The Emerald Tablet. I don't think this came from a dream."

Barry heard a faint beeping – *the microwave, Mom's probably warming up her coffee,* he thought – and looked up at the ceiling.

"I don't even know how long we've been gone," Barry said, lowering his voice to a near whisper. "I visited her before we left for the cabin. I told her we would be there for a few days. When was that?"

Ib widened his eyes, trying to put the madness of the past – however long it had been – into a sequence. "We went to the cabin…why can't I remember the date? It was autumn. Early October I think." Ib smiled. "Twenty twenty-three. At least I can remember the year."

"We were at the cabin, what, a few days? The run-in with John and the General. The craft and the Hilly Island," said Barry, things starting to line up for him.

"Then back to Earth," continued Ib, laughing at how ridiculous that sounded. "Then Ete's underground home and Ete's Cabin. Two, maybe two and a half weeks?"

Barry nodded. "At most three weeks? Mom's probably been worried sick that I haven't checked in."

"What are you going to tell her?" Ib asked.

Barry thought for a moment, then looked at Ib and laughed. "Sorry Ma, I was kidnapped by an alien!"

Ib broke out into laughter and bumped the coffee table in front of him.

"Hello?" came a fragile voice from the top of the stairs. "Is someone down there? If someone's down there I'm calling the police!"

"Ma, it's me, it's okay, don't call the police," said Barry, standing up quickly and almost losing his balance. There was a moment of silence. "Ma?"

"B…Bartholemew?"

"Yes, I'm here with my friend Ib, you remember Ib from PSI," Barry said, waving at Ib to stand up. Barry's mother, a frail woman in her seventies, hurried down the stairs to the basement. She stopped at the bottom and looked at Barry, her eyes wide and filled with tears.

"Bartholomew!" she choked out, stepping forward to wrap her son in a hug, squeezing him as though she wanted to make sure he was real.

"I'm so sorry," Barry said, hugging her back. "I've been gone a bit, you must have been worried."

His mother took a step back and gave him a backhand to his shoulder, surprisingly strong for her physical appearance. "A bit? A bit? Do you call over two years a bit?"

Ib scooped coffee grounds into the drip coffee maker while Barry's mother, Corrinne, whisked eggs beside a hot frying pan. Barry came into the kitchen with a bottle of Tylenol and handed it to Ib. "For the woodworkers, or whatever it was."

"Oh, fantastisk," said Ib, fiddling with the childproof cap, Danish words coming easier to him with his headache.

"Go, sit down, let me serve you breakfast," said Corrinne, shooing them towards the kitchen table. "What time did you get in last night?

Barry looked at Ib who shrugged. "It was late, we didn't want to wake you, so we slept on the couches downstairs."

"I don't mind, but I'm surprised you didn't just go to your apartment," Corrinne said, dropping bread into the steel toaster.

"Yeah, I…didn't have a key on me," Barry said. He swirled his finger around the rim of his empty mug and laughed. "I'd be awfully surprised if my landlord hasn't evicted me after all this time."

"Oh no," said Corrinne. "I have a key hanging on the shelf by the door. Your apartment is fine, I've been watering the plants."

"I don't understand, you haven't been paying my rent, have you?" asked Barry, worried he had left his mother with a financial burden.

Corrinne shook her head. "You really look like you need coffee," she said, putting her hand on Ib's shoulder and filling his mug. She paused to look at Barry, then smiled and poured him coffee. "Two years you've been away and the first thing you do when you return is go out on a bender? Aren't you two a bit old for that?"

"Oh, we didn't–" started Barry.

"Very immature, I agree," said Ib, interrupting Barry, knowing that a hangover from drinking was easier to explain than a hangover from UFO travel.

"Well, I'm just so glad to see you," Corrinne said, stepping back to the kitchen, pulling out two plates and dishing scrambled eggs and toast onto them. "My Bartholomew. I had your letters of course, but that's no replacement for you being here."

Barry shot Ib a puzzled look. "Letters?"

"I know you weren't able to write much, with the nature of your mission, but I cherished each one. I saved them all." Corrinne brought the two plates over to the table and placed them in front of her son and his friend. She opened a hutch beside the kitchen table, pulled out a small stack of neatly opened envelopes, and handed them to Barry.

"My mission," said Barry, trying to not act confused, but wondering what his mother believed he had been doing for the past two years. He pulled a rubber band holding the letters together and looked at the first envelope. Ib picked up the next one. Barry flipped from one side of the envelope to the other, looking for an address, return address, postage, any information about his whereabouts, but found them all blank. "What do you know about my mission?"

"Not much really, which I understand is how it had to be. I just know what the man told me," Corrinne said, bringing a mason jar of peach jam over to the table and finally sitting down, her aged face glowing with her son's return.

"What man? When?" asked Barry, examining the short letter that *he* had apparently penned to his mother. The letter was short; it told her he was safe, happy, and wishes he could share more but his mission was top secret. He hoped he would be home soon. It even looked like his handwriting, but it was signed Bartholomew. Even though his mother called him by his given name, he would never have signed it that way. "What did the man tell you?"

"Not long after you left on that vacation to some cabin, a man came to visit me. He showed me a badge and said he was from some agency, I don't remember which, one of the letter ones. He said you had been working for them as a contractor, through your job, and a mission came up and you were urgently needed overseas. That it was top secret and that I wouldn't hear much from you. That you would be gone for an unknown time, but that you were safe," Corrinne said.

She had tears in her eyes, but smiled. "He said I should be proud of you, that you were serving your country. I've missed you, but that was always nice to think of you serving your country. Out doing some good. Can you tell me about it now? Oh, I'm just so glad you came back safe."

Barry had teared up, thinking of his poor mother worrying about him for two years. *How long were they on the Hilly Island? How long were they underground? How had all this time passed?*

"I wish I could tell you," he said, pursing his lips together, struggling to comprehend what had happened; imagining his mother alone, having to lie to her after abandoning her for so long. "But it's top secret. Maybe one day but for now, well, I'm just glad to be home. What did this man look like?"

Barry's mother squeezed his hand, then raised her eyes to the ceiling, straining to remember. "I don't know, it was some time ago. And he wasn't here long. He had a dark suit and a dark tie. He was very polite. He said your rent, bills, everything would be taken care of while you were gone. He said to not worry about anything."

Barry looked meaningfully at Ib, searching for answers but finding Ib looking as confused as he was. Barry cleared his throat and tucked the last letter back into the envelope. He looked down at the breakfast his mother had prepared for him. "I've uh…I've been travelling for a while, I think I've got my time zones confused. What's the date today?"

"Oh, it's Saturday of course, let's see, what's the number?" Corrine said, reaching for a calendar from the hutch beside the kitchen table. She flipped it open. "That's right, it's the twenty-first."

"June twenty-first," Ib said, looking at the open calendar. "Twenty twenty-six."

Ib paid the fare and got out of the taxi. He stood on the sidewalk, assessing his home, a two-story red brick townhouse. He looked at the small gardens on each side of the front steps, and saw a well-tended garden bed of flowers, not an overrun mess of weeds that he had expected after a two-year absence. He looked around and found the street quiet, no neighbours out to notice his arrival. He walked up the stairs towards his front door.

He pulled his keys out of his pocket, jingled them to find the right one, and put it in the keyhole. It went in, but with some resistance. He tried to turn the key, but it wouldn't budge. He looked again at the unit number; it was definitely his home.

Ib looked around again, saw nobody, and pressed his hands up against the window to peer inside. It was his living room, but with different furniture and a TV twice the size of what he had had. *What happened to my home?* he whispered to himself.

He pulled out his phone and remembered that the battery was dead. He shrugged, put his phone back in his pocket, and started the long walk back to Corrinne's house.

It took nearly an hour to return, and by the time he arrived, his headache was pounding again. Barry found him a pillow and some blankets, and left Ib to sleep and recover in his mother's basement.

Barry had spent the day with his mother, catching up on the time that he had missed. Corrinne had made the bed in her spare bedroom for him, and they all called it an early night.

Both Ib and Barry slept well into the morning, eventually emerging to find coffee made and a note that Corrinne had left for church. They poured some coffee and sat down to assess their situation.

"So," said Ib, "some mystery man came to give your mother a cover story and paid your bills while you were away. Meanwhile, my home was emptied and rented out. With terrible new wallpaper. So I wonder what my cover story is. Am I supposed to be dead?"

Barry shook his head. "I don't know. It's more than two years, Ib. "How is this even possible?" Barry thought quietly for a moment. "Ma was telling me that she got a computer so that she could have video calls with my sister and her kids. Let me see if I can find it."

Barry left the kitchen for a few minutes, and returned with an oversized laptop. He opened it to find it hadn't been secured with a password, and was already connected to Wi-Fi. "Well that was easy," he said. "Remind me to talk to my mother about digital security."

He opened a browser and searched for *Dr Ib Johanson*. He scrolled a little, then looked wide-eyed at Ib. "I found something. It looks like a press release, but it's in Danish, I think."

Ib stood up and pulled his chair beside Barry's. He squinted his eyes, looked around, and found Corrinne's reading glasses placed on the hutch beside the table. He put them on and started translating for Barry.

"This was from December of twenty-twenty-three. It says: 'Aarhus Universitet is pleased to announce the appointment of Dr. Ib Johanson as a faculty member in the Department of Psychology. Dr. Johanson has been working in the United States as a researcher at the Perceptual Studies Institute in Durham, North Carolina, and is pleased to return to his native Denmark.'"

"Well, congratulations on the job," said Barry with a laugh. "I'm glad to hear that you're not dead."

"Me too, I suppose," said Ib. "They even quote me: 'I am so pleased to return to Denmark, and I am looking forward to continuing my research and lecturing the next generation of academics in beautiful Aarhus, said Dr. Johanson.' Funny, I don't remember saying that."

"This is just bizarre," said Barry. "I mean, who had the power, the ability, to get a university in Denmark to put out this press release? I mean, doesn't the University notice you aren't there?"

Ib put his hand over his mouth, staring off in thought. "If they hadn't done something like this, we would have become missing persons. If that man hadn't visited your mother, she would have called the police. Maybe they learned after Esther went missing and became a missing person case. This way it just sounds like we went away somewhere. No questions asked."

"And you going to teach back in Denmark certainly sounds plausible," said Barry.

"It does," said Ib. "To be honest, it sounds kind of nice right now. Just a quiet, ordinary life. Plus, Aarhus is a beautiful city. Terrible football team, though."

"They probably just need a new quarterback," Barry said with a smile. "Hey, I wonder what happened to Tomi and Kirsten? What their cover story is."

Barry searched for Tomi. "Nothing. I can't find anything about her. No social media, nothing. It's like she didn't exist. Nothing about John either, which makes sense with his job and security clearance. Let me try Kirsten."

Barry searched and found that Kirsten *did* have social media accounts. And hers had been active. He found her Instagram page, which was set to public. Each month or so since they had been missing, there was another picture of Kirsten in some exotic location. Vietnam, then Nepal, New Zealand, Tanzania. The pictures didn't have much text beyond a few words about her 'world travels continued'.

"So Kirsten is jet-setting around the world," Barry said. "Sounds nice. Again, no questions."

Barry stood up, bringing his mug over to the kitchen to get more coffee. Ib slid the laptop in front of him, and signed into his email account. Barry watched as Ib's face turned grey, his mouth opened, and he moved his face closer to the screen. "What the–" mumbled Ib.

"What is it now?" asked Barry, returning to the table to look at the laptop screen.

"Nothing but junk in my inbox for months. Until today." Ib turned the laptop to show Barry. Barry read the short email, then read it again. He looked at Ib and shook his head in disbelief.

"Is that from who I think it's from?" asked Barry. Ib nodded in confirmation, then shook his head in confusion. "Well, that's…interesting. It looks like you have a stop to make before we visit Arthur Minear," said Barry.

Barry and Ib sat on the couch in his mother's basement, speaking softly so that she didn't overhear them while she worked on dinner upstairs.

"Let's go over it one more time," said Barry. "We get you a plane ticket to Denmark. You go have your meeting and find out what she has to say. In the meantime, I will stay here and tie up some loose ends. I will free up some money for our mission. And I will reach out to a couple of contacts I have and see if I can find out what's going on. There are cover stories for you, me, and Kirsten, and I want to find out about Tomi's cover story. And who this man in black was that visited my mother."

Ib nodded. "And then we meet in the UK, and we will find Arthur Minear, as Tomi suggested. And from there, well, who knows?"

"We go find something ancient and destructive," said Barry. "Whatever that means. Here, let's see about ordering you a plane ticket. Are you ready to go back home?"

"As long as I don't get off the plane feeling like I did after getting off Cuso's craft," said Ib with a smile.

Barry put the computer on his lap and brought up a travel website. "Look at this," he said, tilting the screen towards Ib. "This popped up."

Ib read the message aloud. "Notice: Many Trans-Pacific flights are currently cancelled due to atmospheric conditions." Ib looked at Barry, puzzled and concerned.

Barry opened another browser window to find out what was going on. "Kīlauea," Barry said. "Hawaii. Has been erupting for a month, filling the atmosphere with ash and dust, limiting air travel. Most people were evacuated in time. And Mount Paektu in North Korea. Because it's North Korea they don't know if anyone was hurt or killed. It hadn't erupted in a thousand years. Wildfires in Siberia are also adding to the air quality over the Pacific."

"My god," said Ib. "What all have we missed?"

"This article is saying they are closely monitoring Mount Shasta and Mount Hood as there have been geologic events recorded that indicate they may soon erupt." Barry became quiet, and continued reading. "Trans-Atlantic flights are fine, but most commercial flights over the Pacific are grounded."

"Well, I guess that's the good news, we can get to where we need to go," said Ib.

"Yes, but you will need to bring a jacket," said Barry, looking up from the screen at Ib. "Some anomalies with the Gulf Stream current, Europe is unseasonably cold. Coldest spring in a century."

Ib's face was pale taking all this in. "Something is coming," he said, quoting Ete.

"So you'll catch the shuttle to Dulles, Dulles to Frankfurt, then a short flight from Frankfurt to Copenhagen," said Barry.

"Yes, I have the itinerary," Ib said, patting the breast pocket of his blazer, freshly purchased. Since his home had been emptied, he had no idea where his belongings had ended up. On the way to the airport he had Barry take him to a department store so that he could buy some new clothes and a piece of luggage for his trip.

"From there I'm sure you can find your way. Keep me updated on Signal. And only Signal because it's secure. I'll catch a flight in a few days to the UK, and we will meet there," Barry said, pulling up to the Departures unloading zone at Charlotte Douglas International Airport.

Ib nodded, turned and looked at the doors to the airport, but didn't move. He looked back to Barry. "I guess this is the start of our big adventure," Ib said, his voice more melancholy than excited. He looked down at his feet and the new brown leather shoes he had bought just a couple of hours ago.

Barry shared the heavy feeling Ib had. "Ib, you ever wonder, why us? What this is all about, and what role we play in all this? I mean look at them," Barry said, pointing at the people crossing in front of the parked car, entering and exiting the terminal building, "they're oblivious. Contented."

"Does it make you jealous?" said Ib with half a laugh.

"Sometimes, yeah," said Barry, bopping his hand on the steering wheel of his Saab, accidentally tapping the horn and surprising a few people outside the car.

"Me too," said Ib. "But just sometimes, really. I don't know what's ahead for me. For us. And I'm nervous. Pit in my stomach nervous. But also Barry, the things we've seen! I've lost my job, my home, and all my possessions are now in this piece of luggage. And I wouldn't trade it for what we've experienced."

Barry nodded, thinking of the sight of the craft overhead that night on the mountain clearing. He had felt like a boy again, confident that magic is real. "Me either. You best catch your plane. Safe flight."

"We'll be in touch," Ib said, stepping out of the car and collecting his new luggage from the back seat. He turned to head towards the entrance, stopped, and turned back to the car, leaning his face into the open passenger window.

"I don't know what I'm walking into," Ib said, reaching into his pocket and handing something to Barry, "so I want you to hold onto this. Safe drive."

Barry watched him enter through the glass doors of the terminal while he rubbed his thumb over the tiny text on the small piece of the Emerald Tablet. He took a deep breath, waited for a gap in pedestrians, and drove on, exiting the airport. As he got onto the interstate, his phone chimed. He glanced at it and saw it was a message on Signal. His contact had replied. He looked at the road again, then back at his phone.

Yes, I will meet. Lucky Strike Tower. 2 hours, the message said.

Barry put down his phone and pressed on the gas. He should make it just in time.

He fought traffic and found a place to park just a few minutes after he should have arrived. *I hope she's still there,* he thought, reaching for a hat in his backseat. He hustled across the American Tobacco Campus, towards the Lucky Strike Tower, a tall brick chimney that dominated the view of the area.

There were a few empty tables at the base of the Tower. He scanned the area, and saw a figure dressed in dark clothes and a dark baseball cap walking away.

Barry jogged a few paces to catch up to them, and said quietly, "Meena?"

The person stopped, turned around, and took her sunglasses off. "Barry. You're late."

Barry and Meena walked back to the Tower and sat down at one of the tables, finding one tucked into a corner, out of view.

"I never thought I would hear from you again," Meena said. "Not long after the last time we met, you were just gone. You were all gone."

"I can't really explain what happened," Barry said, then laughed, "I'm not even sure I could if I tried! But I'm thankful you came to meet with me. The last time we met you told me about a file your husband had, a file on Tomi and how she was being used by them, that she was an asset of the government. Of the General. Well things kind of came to a head, and now I'm trying to understand what happened here."

Meena looked around. "I'm not sure I can help you. What do you want to know?"

"First, someone came to see my mother. A man came and told her that I was on some kind of intelligence mission, top secret. And my sweet but gullible mother believed him. She said it was a man in a suit. Do you have any idea who that could have been?"

Meena shook her head. "No, I'm sorry. Summit told me you were hired for some kind of assignment. That was also when he told me that Ib had resigned from PSI and was returning home."

"So he told you that," said Barry. "I wonder what he knew. What about Tomi and John?"

Meena cleared her throat and scanned the area again. Her voice was quieter. "He told me that John had been offered a new job and was reassigned overseas. The Middle East. And that Tomi had gone with him."

"So that's the story is it? Did…how do I say this. Did it seem like he believed that?" asked Barry.

Meena frowned and looked at the table. "I don't think so. I said to him, 'Just like that? They are just gone?' and he just shrugged and nodded. I know my husband well, and I think by now I can tell when I'm getting the full story, or the story I'm supposed to get. And it just didn't feel right."

"Have you seen John since then? Heard anything about him?" asked Barry.

Meena shook her head. "Nothing. Summit has never mentioned them since. Like we never knew them. Like they never existed. Barry, where is she? Is she okay?"

Barry smiled at her concern for Tomi. "I can't tell you where she is. Not because I won't, I don't exactly know where she is right now. But I believe she is well. I do."

Meena smiled and nodded.

Barry looked up at the Lucky Strike Tower. "Do you remember that day at PSI, Meena? When we had you all try to remote view this place? When Ib put Tomi's sketch up on the screen, and she had drawn this?"

"It was as if she had camped out here with an easel," Meena said, her voice soft with wonder. "And when she drew your watch with the right time on it. I remember. I don't think I'll ever forget."

Ib checked his luggage, got his boarding card, and made his way through airport security without incident. He had some time to kill before his first flight, so he bought an overpriced sandwich and coffee, and wandered into a bookstore near his gate, thinking he should find something to read for his three flights home.

The bookstore was relatively empty, just a couple at the register paying for some magazines. As Ib walked past a newsstand with international newspapers on display, he scanned the headlines. There were articles about economic slowdowns due to supply chain shortages. The main headline on the Guardian read: *Suez Crisis Enters Second Month*.

Something is coming, thought Ib. He took a few more steps into the bookstore and started to scan the contents of a bookshelf. As he ran his knuckle along the spines of the neatly displayed books, a man stepped beside him, looking at the same set of books.

"Don't look over," the man said quietly, pulling a book off a shelf. "Grab a book and act like you're reading it."

Ib felt his blood run cold, but did as the man said. He looked at the book but couldn't make out the words, nervousness washing over him.

"Ib, it's me, John," the man said. Ib's head started to turn towards him. "Just look at the book. I'm not supposed to be talking to you. So I'll make this quick. I just want to know that she's okay."

Ib started to turn his head again and stopped himself. "I, uhh—" he stammered.

"I know you probably don't think much of me, or trust me," John said. "But whatever you think of me, you have to understand that I care deeply about her. I just want to know that she's okay. That she's safe."

Ib stared at the book in his hand. *You're right, I don't trust you*, he thought. But he wasn't unmoved by John's words. Perhaps there was more to it. Perhaps he really had loved her. "She is safe. She is safe, and she is extraordinary."

John nodded subtly. "Thank you. Keep her safe, Ib. And yourself. Just…keep your head down, okay?"

"John, why the hell does it say on the internet that I'm teaching at a university in Denmark?" asked Ib, whispering, but angrily.

"It's part of the agreement we have. You were claimed by them, so we cleaned it up. It's just how it works. It's how you keep a secret this big. And my advice for you? Do that. Go home, be a teacher, live a quiet life."

John put the book he was holding back on the shelf and tapped his fingers on a few others, as though he were scanning the titles.

"By the way, the book? A little on the nose, isn't it?" John said as he turned to leave.

Ib let out a deep breath, realizing he had been mostly holding his breath through this whole interaction with John. He turned to look behind him, as casual as he could muster, but John was already gone, slipping into the crowd of the busy airport. He looked down at the book in his hand, the one he had pulled randomly from the shelf: *The Best-Documented UFO Encounters.*

Chapter 9

"This idea can shake our society to the very roots of its culture. Witnesses are no longer afraid to come forward with personal stories of abductions, of spiritual exchanges with aliens, even of sexual interaction with them. Such reports are folklore in the making. I have discovered that they form a striking parallel to the tales of meetings with elves and jinn of medieval times, with the denizens of 'Magonia,' the land beyond the clouds of ancient chronicles. But they are something else, too: a portent of important things to come."

Jacques F. Vallée

Tomi opened her eyes to the Other Place. It was bright, the sun shining proudly, illuminating everything around her in a yellow, nourishing light. She didn't need to close her eyes or blink for her vision to adjust. *Do I even have eyes here?* she wondered to herself. *I can see, but it feels different.*

She had a body. She could feel it buzzing, vibrating at that high, transcendent level, as it had when she was ascending in the indigo meditation room. *But it feels different,* she thought. She looked down, expecting to see her legs crossed as they had been when she started her meditation, her black yoga pants ending at her calves and her feet bare.

Instead, she saw her bare legs crossed, the yoga pants gone, and her body no longer flesh and blood, but instead some mix of matter and energy. Her body seemed to glow, shimmer when she looked at it. When she didn't look at it directly the substance, the contents of her body seemed to disappear. In her periphery she could see the outline of her hands or feet, but they were almost transparent. It was like her body didn't have a physical form if you weren't looking directly at it.

Tomi stood up and was surprised by how easy it was, as though the Earth's gravity wasn't tugging on her quite so tightly. Her movements were slow, smooth, and graceful. She gently scanned around her, finding her surroundings foggy; not wet or damp, but unclear in the periphery. As though she were immersed in a cloud. When she focused, the fog dissipated, and she could begin to make out her surroundings. She was standing on a flat, rocky surface, somewhere on a mountain – *probably the mountain above Ete's home*, she thought. The sun shone brightly above her, illuminating the fog. She felt like it was wrapping her in warmth.

Even though she was immersed by fog, her surroundings dreamlike, she had that high definition vision she had experienced before. It was as though this new reality was more real than the real she had always known. She remembered Kirsten's story about having laser eye surgery and finding details that she didn't know she had been missing.

"It's so beautiful," Tomi said aloud to herself. "So graceful."

"Isn't it something, my Thomasina?" said Esther, emerging out of the fog from Tomi's right.

Tomi turned slowly – her movements unhurried and smooth – to look at her grandmother. Her grandmother placed her hand on Tomi's cheek; instead of the paper-like skin of her hands, Tomi instead felt as though the side of her face buzzed even more, vibrated even higher.

"My dear, how do you feel?"

Just as with her own body, when Tomi focused on a part of her grandmother's body it looked to be solid – illuminated, energetic, shimmering – but where she didn't focus her grandmother's body seemed almost transparent.

"I…I feel so wonderful," said Tomi. "I just feel so positive, so happy. I mean I know there are sad things. I can remember everything from our…place, our reality, whatever you want to call it. I remember the bad things. But I seem to have this new perspective. And I just feel so…content. Why is that?"

Tomi watched Esther's mouth slowly curl up into a wide smile. "Time, perhaps."

Time, Tomi thought. *What about time?* She thought back on her life. Time was ever present. Time ruled everything, governed her actions, made everything measurable. Marked a beginning and end, birth and death. Time steamed forward like a train barrelling down tracks cut through a dense forest. Tomi felt like she had just had a lobotomy; as though the part of her brain where she stressed and obsessed about time had been completely removed. Or turned off at least. She knew something used to be there, but whatever it was, it was gone. It felt liberating.

"Time," Tomi agreed. "It's still there, I think. I feel like I still know it."

"But it doesn't matter much, does it?" asked Esther.

Tomi shook her head, turning it slowly back and forth. She looked around at the warm, illuminated fog. Gazing through it, she saw traces of material reality; the rocky ground, the plants, and the trees, still present but behind a veil; hiding, but there when you look for it.

She looked back at Esther and was surprised by another change in her thinking and feeling; her grandmother stood before her, her body naked, and Tomi felt no concern, no shame by it. She was naked too, and back there – in *the Material Place*, she decided she would call it – she would have been mortified. But it was different. Her body was different here. She saw the simple beauty, the utility of it. *Another lobotomy,* she thought.

"Our bodies," Tomi said, "it's like they are physical, but also energetic. What are we?"

"Light? Energy? I've heard it called plasma bodies. In a funny way here, I don't really care. I just feel so…what's the word?"

"Grateful," finished Tomi.

"Yes, that's perfect," said Esther. "So grateful for my body. We are so beautiful."

"We always were!" said Tomi. She smiled, thinking about all the hang-ups she'd had over the years about her physical body, the time and energy spent obsessing about it. She started to laugh, the way people will share a silly belief they held as a child, and laugh at how misguided they were.

"I'm not cold," said Tomi. "I don't feel wind or a chill. I'm just comfortable. Why?"

Esther nodded, lips still curled up in a smile. "There isn't really weather here, not in the same way. That's why Ete thinks we, us humans, can be safe here. Or safer at least."

"Safer? Are there dangers here?" asked Tomi.

"Of course. You can't have safety without danger," Esther said.

Of course, thought Tomi, though she struggled to imagine anything truly dangerous in this place. She felt so secure, at peace. The way her body was vibrating, it felt synchronized with her surroundings, as though she had melded with the universe. *It feels musical,* thought Tomi. *Hymnal.*

"So, Nana, what…" Tomi started to say, trailing off before saying the word 'do'. She scanned her brain, looking for the word, the concept of *do*, and like time and bodily shame, it too had been lobotomized. The word, the concept was still there, but was no longer an obsession. That human need to always be *doing* something was just gone, again feeling like a silly childhood belief. Instead, she just wanted to *be*. To connect and share and grow. She smiled at her grandmother.

"What now?" Tomi finished.

Kirsten stared at the large oblong drum hanging from the wall. The deer hide of the drum was stretched tight around the shell, a random pattern of dark red stain spread across the hide.

Kirsten had felt the deep vibration of the drum in the past, when her therapist had given her a sound bath, holding the drum over her horizontal body and beating the drum softly to start, eventually washing Kirsten in sound vibration. Today Kirsten was in the counselling room, sitting across from Casey, a middle-aged woman whose crow's feet around her eyes and salt and pepper hair betrayed her youthful presence.

Kirsten was silent and avoiding eye contact with Casey, having just dumped the most outrageous story on her. She had told her about a woman named Tomi, a psychic spy and secret asset of the US Intelligence Community, who took Kirsten on the run from authorities until they were caught. Kirsten was shot and died before they were rescued by a subterranean non-human entity who took them on a tour of the universe including a stop on the Hilly Island planet of Kirsten's dreams, before returning to Earth. There, in a cavern under a mountain, they taught Tomi how to ascend to another dimension, then, when Tomi and her grandmother vanished, they just dropped Kirsten back into her apartment and her normal life in Durham, North Carolina. More than two years later.

I sound like a complete fucking nutjob, Kirsten thought to herself. Not that Casey had denied Kirsten's experiences in the past. As an experiencer, someone whose family had been subject to UFO abductions, Kirsten had struggled to find a therapist who would take her claims seriously and not point towards deeper mental health issues. Finding Casey, a spiritual psychotherapist open to experiences that were spiritual, mystical, or unexplainable, was like desperately needing help in a foreign city, and finally finding someone who not only spoke your language, but listened with kindness. Finding Casey had been both a relief and a major step for Kirsten, eventually becoming comfortable with identifying herself as an 'experiencer'.

While Kirsten had discussed alien abductions with Casey in the past and had been met with acceptance, it had been at least a year before she had met Tomi that she had last had therapy with Casey. Here she was, several years later, calling Casey out of the blue and asking for a same-day appointment, dishing this wild cosmic adventure. How could she not be afraid of not being believed, or checked in to a hospital to treat delusions? Kisten was not going to break the silence, and waited for Casey to pass her judgement.

Finally, she spoke. "And was your home just the way you'd left it?"

"My home?" asked Kirsten, finally making eye contact again, her face puzzled by the question.

"Well, you said when you returned home, that a long time had passed. That you've been gone what, two years? Was someone paying your mortgage, your utilities?" asked Casey curiously.

Kirsten looked down and shook her head. "Yeah, yeah my place was the same. A bit dusty and my plants were dead. And I think someone cleaned out my fridge. And…well, I don't know who was paying. I hadn't even thought of that yet."

Kirsten had woken up at home in her bed yesterday without explanation. She remembered the indigo meditation room, remembered opening her eyes and seeing that Tomi and Esther had vanished. She remembered Ete telling her that Tomi had gone to the Other Place, and that Kirsten would see her again. Kirsten remembered packing her things in Ete's Cabin in preparation to return, but didn't remember getting on a craft, didn't remember being taken home and put to bed. But there she was when she woke up. Alone and disoriented.

She had woken up with a terrible headache, and couldn't look at screens for the first few hours. As the headache faded, she had checked her phone and found it overwhelmed with notifications, reactions to an Instagram post. She had opened the app and found that 'she' had posted to Instagram the night before with an image of the *Welcome to Durham: City of Medicine* sign. She had written the caption: *So grateful for the amazing adventures, but there's no place like home.*

Kirsten's stomach had twisted into a knot. She had no recollection of posting this photo. She scrolled to her previous post: an elephant bathing in a river. The location tag said Koh Chang, Thailand. The post previous to that showed a small boat with flowers, incense, and a candle burning, floating on water. The location tag was Haridwar, India.

On and on the posts went. Most were of buildings or local people she had 'met', but a few were selfies of her; often unclear or filtered, but definitely *her*. They showed Kirsten in Australia, Korea, Morocco, and other exotic locations she had no recollection of visiting. No, she had been in Ete's underground home, and before that the craft, and before that the cabin. Her breathing had become short as she started to panic, feeling so disoriented and isolated.

When she had noticed the date on her phone's lock screen, she froze for an hour. When she could move, she had called Casey and asked for her earliest appointment.

"And so your Instagram has you travelling the world for all this time," Casey said. "But you're certain of where you've been. Who, then, do you think was posting on your behalf?"

"I don't know," Kirsten said doubtfully. "It's like, someone created a cover story for me. For my whereabouts. I don't know if Ete's people did it somehow, or the government, I just don't know," Kirsten said, feeling her body sink as a tiny grain of doubt started to grow inside of her. What if she truly was delusional? "I know. I sound insane."

Casey smiled kindly and drew a breath. "Kirsten, I've known you for a long time. You've shared a lot with me, and I've never questioned what you were telling me. And I won't now. I can see that you experienced something…profound. And troubling. I know you are being honest about what you believe happened, I can hear that. But it may be wise to explore the more likely scenario: that you were in fact travelling, and something happened to your memory. Perhaps you hit your head or had some kind of accident. Perhaps this whole experience you had, with Tomi and Ete and other dimensions, perhaps you did experience it, but as a dream or vision. Perhaps in connection to the injury."

Kirsten was crying and nodding, agreeing that this was a more likely explanation. But if that were true, had she concocted that whole experience? How far back did it go? Had she ever even known Tomi?

"Kirsten, I want you to call your doctor and make an appointment to have yourself examined for potential injuries," Casey continued gently. "That will give us more information about what we might be dealing with. And we can go from there, okay?"

Kirsten nodded, sniffling as her tears stopped falling. "I just wish I could contact Tomi. And clear it all up."

"Come back on Friday," Casey said, "and we'll get deeper into all of this, including Tomi. It's going to be okay Kirsten, we'll figure this all out."

Casey asked a few more questions about Kirsten's wellbeing to make sure she was safe, booked her next appointment, then Kirsten ordered an Uber to bring her home. Her car had been in her parking spot at home – which was peculiar, because the last she had seen her car it was parked outside the cabin in West Virginia – but she felt uncomfortable driving, feeling so disoriented, questioning her mental competence.

A few minutes into her Uber ride she broke the silence, excitedly blurting out, "Wait, I have a couple stops to make!"

Ib and Barry! she screamed in her mind. If she could just find Ib and Barry, she knew she would feel immediately grounded. Safe. They had returned to the surface, to the everyday world before her. They could confirm that she hadn't dreamt this, that her mind hadn't invented this wild story.

First they stopped at Barry's apartment. She knocked and knocked, but there was no answer, and no signs of life. She then had the driver take her to Ib's home. This time after knocking she heard the click of the door lock unlatching. *Ib,* she thought. *He's here!*

Instead of a tall, consistently dishevelled professor, it was a young woman who answered the door, explaining that she and her partner had lived there for almost two years, and had no information on the previous tenant. *Had he ever really lived here?* Kirsten wondered, questioning her memory.

When she arrived home she tried calling both Ib and Barry, but both numbers had been disconnected. She searched the internet for news of them, and only found a single post from a Danish university about Ib being appointed a professor. She sent him an email to the address on a staff listing of the university, only to have the email bounce right back, saying the user doesn't exist.

Where are you guys? she thought to herself, crying tears of desperation. She thought back to the day they had left, when they went off with Cuso in the craft, after Tomi had told them to find Arthur Minear. *Minear*, she thought. *Maybe they went to Minear.* She searched and searched, and only found discussion about how private and difficult to contact Arthur Minear was.

That's it, she thought to herself, closing her laptop and feeling defeated. *I'll never find them.* These people who had felt like family suddenly felt like apparitions. Ghosts.

That night she couldn't sleep. She got up and lit some sandalwood incense, which usually helped Kirsten relax. She sat in her wooden rocking chair parked beside her bedroom window. She tried to read but struggled to concentrate, so she looked out the window at the few stars visible in the sky, drown out by the light of the city, while she rocked.

One star in the sky shone bright, and as she focused on it, she could see the light had a reddish hue. *Mars*, Kirsten thought. She thought again of Tomi and her investigation of Mars, her first meeting with Ete, the one that had put these things in motion and disrupted so many lives.

"Where are you right now, Tomi?" Kirsten said quietly while looking at Mars, bright red in the dark and cold of space. She wished desperately that she could see Tomi. She felt so confused, disoriented, and knew just being near Tomi would make her feel settled and sure. Kirsten appreciated that Casey hadn't disbelieved her outright, but it wasn't the same as the confidence that comes from being with your best friend. Your person.

In her periphery Kirsten saw something. A light. She looked over at her incense, a small orange heater on the top of each stick, the smoke curling and intertwining vertically. Then she saw it: a small, glowing blue orb, floating and moving slowly around the far side of her room.

It wasn't much bigger than a billiard ball. It glowed in an elegant sapphire blue, and seemed transparent, like an old glass fishing float. Kirsten leaned forward in her chair. It was too small, and seemed hazy, too cloudy inside the sphere to make out anything inside, but she had a knowing, a certainty of what this was.

"Tomi," said Kirsten in a whisper, then louder. "Tomi!" As though reacting to her call, the sphere began to reverse its course, moving away from Kirsten, before winking out of existence. In the blink of an eye, Kirsten was alone again in her room.

"I know it was you," Kirsten said quietly, even though the orb was gone. Kirsten felt energized for a moment, before a wave of sadness and longing came over her. She thought about her near-death experience, the Tomi figure, who came to tell her she needed to follow her wherever she went. To protect her and to keep her on the right path.

Kirsten got back into bed. She smiled to herself and let out a deep, relaxing sigh. She knew what she had to do.

"Okay Tomi, message received. I will follow you," Kirsten said quietly, closing her eyes and pulling her covers up to her chin, ready for a good sleep. "I'll see you in the Other Place."

"Mmm, let's just sit here a while," said Esther.

Tomi looked on as her grandmother tilted her face to the sky while her body – somehow solid and weightless simultaneously – seemed to melt gently to the ground. Her contented face was illuminated by the sun. Tomi thought her nana looked like she was being bathed in peace.

She followed suit, and felt herself gently ease onto the ground, her body flowing like hot wax running down a candle until it stopped and cooled as a solid. Tomi ran her hand along the rock and found her hand eased right into it, like running your hand over a soft mattress. She felt her herself being held gently by the stone, cradling her body.

Tomi closed her eyes and was immediately at peace. It was a calmness she had achieved in some of her deepest meditations, but here she seemed to reach it almost instantly. Previously she had her ego to contend with; quieting her mind, pulling herself out of her here and now, her individual desires and fears, bodily irritations and noises distracting her from a deep inner peace. No, it was as though she could close her eyes and the world around her disappeared, just stopped existing.

Tomi lost herself in this peace, understanding more than ever what it was to just *be*. She didn't know how much time passed because it didn't matter. Time was nothing she needed to concern herself with.

Then she felt something. A disturbance, but not something in her environment or her surroundings; there was a disturbance in her consciousness, like something tugged on it, pulling her out of her peaceful trance.

Kirsten, Tomi thought. She knew it was Kirsten, as though Kirsten had contacted her, consciousness to consciousness. *The information field*, Ray had called it in one of his letters to Esther.

There's a disturbance in the Force, Tomi thought, smiling to herself and wishing she could laugh about it with Kirsten. But she knew Kirsten wasn't laughing. She could feel Kirsten's emotions as though they were her own: sadness, loneliness, desperation.

She opened her eyes and looked at her grandmother. Esther was sitting still, her body seeming to shimmer like sunshine moving across still water. Esther opened her eyes and smiled at Tomi. She was basking in sharing this moment with her granddaughter.

"Nana, you said that when you were here you looked in on me. How did you do that?" asked Tomi.

"I thought you might ask that," Esther said. "It's not perfect or precise. Maybe it's something you can get better at, but I was never able to choose a time or place. I would just be shown a glimpse. Okay, close your eyes."

Esther shuffled forward, her knees touching Tomi's, the two women facing each other in liberation pose. Esther placed her palms onto Tomi's palms, Tomi's hands facing to the sky.

"I would tell you to clear your mind, guide you into a deep meditation, but here we don't need to. It's so easy to get into that state. Just focus on your being, your vibration. Feel it and revel in it, enjoy the way it buzzes. Fall in love with the energy inside of you."

Tomi did revel in it. Her body, whatever it was made of, felt simply perfect, cradled so softly. *Suspended by the universe*, Tomi thought. She sat in silence for a time, feeling the incredible activity of her body, her essence vibrating rapidly, yet she was fully at peace.

"When you are ready, feel the way the vibration of your body mirrors the vibration around you. Appreciate how it resonates. Feel your body start to extend below you, through the ground below us, stretching out farther and farther, until your body is in tune with all that surrounds you," said Esther.

She lost track of where her own body ended and the Earth below her began. She thought if someone were walking, stepping on the ground far off in the distance, she would feel it just as clearly as if they had stepped directly beside her, she was so synchronized with her surroundings. Tomi thought about the time in the forest when Kirsten had told her about the mycelium network, that information network hidden just below our feet, the underground collective wisdom of the forest. She remembered being on the mountain in West Virginia, and feeling herself stretching out through the mycelium network, becoming one with the life all around her, feeling the Earth below her not as a ball of rock but something alive, conscious, miraculous.

"Now Tomi, start to become aware of the transfer of energy, the transfer of information. Become aware of it, but realize it's not new; it's always been there, and you've always had access to it," said Esther, pausing to connect to this herself. "You know that we are all one; you have felt that. Our souls, our consciousness, our human lives, we think they are separate, independent. But that is only our perception. A deception maybe. We are forever and always part of the great consciousness, the universe, whatever you want to call it. Everything is conscious Tomi, everything is connected. You are as conscious as the mountain below us, the Earth below it, the air around us. You will find that consciousness is everywhere, fully interconnected, permeating everything. This means that no information, no experience is had in solitude. No idea can ever truly be held as secret. Do you feel it, Tomi?"

Tomi was quiet, thinking back to some of the experiences she'd had the past year, the depth of her meditations, the deep feeling of connection and unity her nana described. But here, in this place, it was so much richer, so much clearer. *Like the Wizard of Oz,* Tomi thought, *changing from black and white to colour film.*

"I feel it," said Tomi, her voice oozing with gratitude. "Do I ever feel it."

"Feel your consciousness, your here and now, feel it flow, mix and merge into it. Then, go with intention. Think about who and when and where. Try to be as clear as you can, because navigating it is, well, a challenge. Unpredictable. Sometimes I would end up where I hoped, or generally found what I intended – like when I would find you, get a glimpse of your life. Other times I would stumble onto something altogether different."

Tomi felt bound in this state, deeply joined with this network of consciousness, but resistant to let herself go, like she was wading into a river, and if she took another step she would get pulled into the current and carried wherever the river flowed.

"Feel the way it flows. Think about what you are looking for. And let yourself go. Find what you're looking for…" said Esther, her voice trailing off as Tomi felt herself take that step.

Instead of feeling as though she, Tomi, were carried away by the current, she found that she became part of the current, her consciousness like water joining water, a single drop now indistinguishable from whole river. She saw blue, deep shades of blue in her vision, swirling around randomly at first, then settling into a transparent blue. Details emerged. It looked as though she were within a blue bubble, and everything she saw was viewed from within that transparent blue sphere, looking out.

Tomi saw it was a bedroom. She could see a tall wooden dresser, a folded sweater placed on top beside a watch and some jewelry. Tomi's vision felt limited; she felt like she was a fly, buzzing slowly around the room, the room gigantic when viewed from a tiny perspective, her peripheral vision distorted by the curve of the sphere.

Tomi could smell something. It was incense. *Sandalwood. Kirsten's favourite*, Tomi thought. Like a big housefly making a slow arc, Tomi's vision panned around the room, everything seen through that blue sphere. Her view floated past the dresser and curved right, towards a small table. She saw two lines of smoke curling, swirling up from a pair of burning incense sticks. As though she were a fly avoiding the smoke, her vision curved around again, and there she was: Kirsten, sitting in a rocking chair by her bedroom window. Kirsten wasn't sitting back and rocking. She was sitting forward, staring straight ahead, her mouth open. Moving. Talking.

Did she say my name? wondered Tomi.

Tomi was filled with the urge to fly right towards her, and felt frustrated at how slow her vision was moving. *Get closer!* Tomi yelled in her mind. Instead of moving closer, it felt like the bubble she was in suddenly reversed direction and pulled away from Kirsten. The bedroom was gone, and the transparent blue became dark again. She was back on the mountain with her grandmother, meditating in the Other Place.

For the first time in the Other Place, Tomi's negative emotions took hold. She had seen Kirsten, she could feel a deep sadness coming from her, and instead of connecting with her, she had disappeared.

Tomi scooched herself back from her grandmother, tucked her legs up and wrapped her arms around them and buried her head into her thighs. She knew she had ruined it; she had let herself get excited, frustrated, too many emotions tied up in her ego, and she lost the vision.

She felt her grandmother's hands on her calf. Instead of a feeling of physical touch, skin on skin, she felt the vibration of her grandmother's body start to merge with her own. Esther's hands were buzzing, and her touch felt like a gentle zap of energy.

"Tomi, you are fading," Esther said. "In the same way higher vibration brought us here, lower vibration can bring us back. You must stay centred, stay peaceful. Stay tuned in to the frequencies around you. And leave draining thoughts back home."

Tomi lifted her head from her legs and looked at her grandmother sitting in front of her, her naked body almost fuzzy from vibration. Her skin seemed to shimmer, her head eclipsing the sun in the sky. Tomi thought it looked like her grandmother had a halo.

Joy erupted in her belly and quickly filled her up, sending a rush of energy through her body. *She is just so beautiful, so strong and loving,* thought Tomi. Tomi imagined – or felt, she wasn't sure – her grandmother's beauty, her strength. Her love flowed through her grandmother's hands and circulated through her body. The frustration, the sadness she felt had just flown away. Tomi let out a laugh, making her grandmother smile wider.

"What is so funny?" Esther asked.

"Not funny. Joyous. I just…" Tomi said, pausing for the right words, "I just feel this gratitude to be descended from you. Perhaps that sounds strange–"

"Not at all," Esther interrupted. "I'm grateful to my Nana, too. To all our ancestors. How improbable it all is. And yet here we are."

"And yet here we are," Tomi agreed. She looked around at her surroundings, mostly clouded in fog. "Where exactly is here, anyways? And where is…well, everyone?"

The bathroom was dark but for one tealight candle, burning inside a stained glass candle box, sending red light to flicker along the white tiles surrounding the bathtub. Kirsten dropped sandalwood oil into the full tub, and swirled the water around. She turned on the hot water again, liking her baths to be near scalding. Plus, she didn't want to end up cold, hoping this would be a long meditation.

She pulled off her robe, put one leg into the tub, and waited for a moment to adapt to the heat before she introduced her left leg. She settled into the deep clawfoot tub, the water covering her body up to her chin. She closed her eyes and focused on the sound of rain playing from a speaker.

This was the first meditation since the orb in her bedroom, the first since she decided – determined – that she would commit herself to this practice until she also ascended. She was going to find Tomi.

Though she was determined, it had taken her the full day to work herself up to this. She had a complicated relationship with meditation. Years ago, it felt unsafe. While sometimes she could find it relaxing, the openness required for meditation left her vulnerable to difficult memories and emotions. Trauma crept in. Traumas from childhood, from the abductions, traumas from being a woman in this world. She was open, vulnerable, and sometimes meditation would leave her shaken.

Through years of therapy, she had worked through and processed these memories, but meditation still gave her anxiety. Even those days of meditation in Ete's home, in the indigo room, she had approached it cautiously, not letting herself get too deep, the anxiety of what could manifest always holding her back. *But… Tomi,* she had said to herself, and she ran a bath.

Kirsten wasn't sure where to begin. She didn't have Ete here to guide her. She thought she would stick to some basics for this first meditation. She started with breath work, visualizing her body pulling in a breath, the air she breathed in becoming fuel to fire up her chakras. One by one she saw them glowing red, orange, yellow, green, blue, indigo, then violet.

She felt light, energized and powerful, braver because of the warm bathwater embracing her body. She held the visual of the brightened chakras, energized, her root connected to the centre of the Earth, her crown connected to the greater universe.

Her vision faded to black and she maintained her energized state. In time, colours and shapes started to form in her mind's eye. Her initial reaction was to brush them away – her trauma response – but she continued to breathe until she was ready to welcome them in. She offered a deal: I will stay open if you go slow.

Like sparks, little flashes of colours formed in her inner vision, slowly connecting into lines and shapes. Kirsten breathed out her anxiety, and imagined herself breathing in white light. She felt even more energized as the picture, the vision took shape.

It was a forest, an old forest with tall trees, their treetops shading the forest into a look of dusk. Just in front of her was a bushy archway, foliage grown to form an entrance. Kirsten imagined herself moving forward. The image in her mind became clearer and clearer, no longer lines and shapes, but an increasingly vivid visual. As though she were in that forest.

As she moved forward, she could see that just inside the foliage archway was the start of a smooth stone staircase, descending into the ground. Stone walls stood straight up on each side of the staircase, with leafy vines growing down the stone walls. The staircase curved as it descended, so she was unable to see what was at the bottom.

Kirsten saw her feet, bare at the top of the staircase, descending down the stone steps, damp in the cool forest shade. With the curve of the staircase, she couldn't see what lay beyond a few steps in front of her. The first few steps were pristine, the stone cut smooth as though it was sliced butter. As she descended, the steps became chipped, then crumbling, until the steps were no more than heaps of rubble. *This is a message to me,* Kirsten thought, unsure where it came from, but feeling a knowing that it was true. *This is what happens to my path when I neglect it.*

Down she ambled until she came to an old wooden door at least twice her height. She reached for it, felt the mechanical click of the antique iron handle, and pushed the door open.

Her mind's eye lit up with vibrant light. She was standing just past the doorway in an open grassy field, bathed in orange light. Kirsten's vision panned up from the field, across the deepest blue sky, and up to the Sun. Instead of having to turn away, she could stare straight at the sun, its rays not hurting her eyes as they normally would. For the first time she could stare straight at it, hold the Sun's gaze.

The Sun glowed brighter, as vibrant rays of sunshine reached out to the Earth, right down to Kirsten, the orange-gold beams hugging her in light. She felt so supported, so loved, and energized by the light. She saw her hand reach out to touch one of the beams, an arm of the Sun's fiery core. It was more of a knowing than a physical feeling, but the Sun's beams were warm, not burning, soft, but sturdy.

"*You want to wrap me in love,*" Kirsten found herself saying to the Sun.

"*I do,*" came the reply, entering Kirsten's consciousness as warm, gentle words. "*I know life on Earth can be so hard. I want you to know that you are loved perfectly.*"

"*Thank you,*" Kirsten said in her mind, seeing her hands touching the Sun's warm beams, still wrapping her in light.

"*I wish in your life, in your reality, that I could be this nourishing,*" Kirsten heard the Sun say. "*But in your reality I'm as likely to have a fit and melt all human life on Earth as I am to maintain a level long enough for your species to move on. That's the way it is here, it's a cycle, and I'm sorry. I'm always sorry when it happens.*"

"*It's okay,*" Kirsten heard herself say. "*You are so nourishing and perfect. I see the love behind the danger.*"

The Sun's beams receded back into the sky, Kirsten still basking in the warm, loving sunlight. She understood then that the Sun was alive, a conscious being.

A dark figure emerged from the bright sunlight, a figure wearing a hooded cloak draped down to the ground. Although Kirsten's meditative vision was showing itself in fine detail, the face of the figure was blurry; yet, Kirsten felt that she recognized it, somehow recognized its energy rather than its appearance. This being was both ancient and familiar.

The being held out its arm, its hand shrouded by the baggy sleeve of the cloak. Kirsten felt no fear and reached her hand out, into the sleeve of the cloak, and took its hand. The being looked up towards the Sun, and Kirsten followed suit, feeling energized and lightened. She felt the energy flowing between her and the being, she felt the light from the Sun reflecting off her body, off everything around her.

As so many have in states of awakening, Kirsten was overcome by a deep sense of unity, of interconnectedness, individually experiencing the transfer of energy, of consciousness throughout an entangled universe. *Remember this feeling*, she thought to herself. *This will help me in my mission. To ascend and find Tomi.*

The being disengaged its hand from Kirsten's, lifted its hand up, the long cloak sleeve dangling, and touched its index finger to her forehead, where that indigo chakra had glowed earlier.

A new vision took form. She was in a place, a soft place. It was the place she had been when she had her near-death experience. *The in-between place,* Tomi had called it. She saw herself with others, their bodies only energy, but familiar. They were family.

Then she moved to another place, a round room. There was another energy being there, and this one she recognized. It was the cloaked being that had touched her forehead. Kirsten knew that this being was a guide, helping her choose, to select this life she is currently living. Her life on Earth.

As though it were projecting a movie on the walls, the being shared visions, clips of her coming life on Earth. She saw many of her memories, things she had indeed experienced. She saw other visions that hadn't come yet, and often didn't make sense, as though she was watching a clip from minute seventy-four in a movie, missing the context and unaware of the plot.

The being removed its finger from her forehead. The vision ended, and she was returned to the field, caressed by sunlight and facing the cloaked being. She could feel that it was over, that the vision was coming to an end. Before the being receded, it spoke, the words landing clearly in her meditative mind.

"*Do you remember now?*" the being asked.

"*Yes,*" Kirsten responded, hearing her own voice in her mind. "*It turns out I never forgot.*"

As the being receded from the vision, Kirsten saw herself turn and reverse her course, heading back through the old wooden door and up the stairs. She had been in a deep meditation, and as she worked herself back to being aware of her physical surroundings, she could feel that the bath had grown cold.

She pulled the drain, stepped out of the tub, and wrapped a towel around herself. From under the sink, she pulled out her toiletries travel bag. She would pack first thing in the morning. And cancel her appointment with Casey. She knew where she needed to go to get help, to find Tomi. It turned out she had always known where she needed to go; she had seen a clip of it when she was choosing this life.

"Who?" asked Esther, smiling mischievously.

"Well, everyone," said Tomi. "I mean surely there are more humans in the Other Place than the two of us."

Esther nodded. "There are others. We aren't the first humans to make the jump. But in many ways this is a private place. A spiritual place more than a gathering place."

"And what about…non-humans," Tomi asked.

"There are many other beings here, other species, yes," said Esther. "Some that live only here, some that travel back and forth, though much easier than us humans can. We humans can visit and stay for a while, but we need to return."

"To the Material Place," said Tomi. "That's what I'm calling it. If we can't stay, and it's so hard to get here, why come at all? I mean, what's the benefit of being here?"

Esther looked up to the sky to consider her answer. "Knowledge. Understanding. I suppose some of the benefits I only felt when I returned to…to the Material Place. I returned with a new understanding of, well, everything, of life, the universe. As a people, a species, you can learn more, see more because you can connect easier. That's why Ete's people come here. They are watchers, and from here they can watch more, see dangers from a greater distance. It's for survival."

Tomi turned her face up towards the sun, her movements slow and gentle. The sun had hardly moved in the sky since she had opened her eyes in the Other Place, as though the Earth below her had slowed its revolution to a crawl.

"Why don't we take a walk," said Esther, standing gracefully and extending her hand to help Tomi up. Tomi didn't need help. This Other Place body, whatever it was made of, was so light and loose, she shot up like a spring in slow motion. "How about I tell you the story of how I met Ray while we walk?"

Tomi smiled and nodded. She locked her arm with her grandmother's, and they stepped slowly and intentionally into the fog.

Chapter 10

"The materialist interpretation of the world and of science itself is protected not by the facts or by the data of our honest experiences, but by what is essentially social and professional peer pressure, something more akin to the grade-school playground or high school prom. The world is preserved through eyes rolling back, snide remarks, arrogant smirks and subtle, or not so subtle, social cues, and a kind of professional (or conjugal) shaming."

Jeffrey Kripal

Esther set the electric coffee urn on the long table, placing it beside the package of wafer cookies. She plugged it in and flipped it on, the same routine week in, week out for countless years. She noticed a scrape on the wall behind the table, and remembered rolling paint onto just that spot so many years ago.

Just a kid then, she thought, smiling at the memory, a legal adult who had barely been out of her hometown, let alone home state, painting and renovating to create a church for witches here in Oakland. She was the last of them – the ones who rolled up their sleeves and created this place – Joanna, Nancy, and Mary all having passed on or left Oakland for one reason or another. Even the church had changed names a few times, now: The Gathering Place, where pagans, witches, animists, and the general 'spiritual but not religious' could find a community with their interests.

Hosting this support group was a volunteer role, though she did work a few hours a week for The Gathering Place and a half dozen other faith communities, keeping their books, making bulletins, and providing admin support. The hours were enough to support her and her son, and flexible enough for a single parent, though she never lacked requests for her time. While she had not become a pastor as she had hoped as a child, Esther had become a resource for many, a spiritual guide, someone with deep insights and remarkable intuition. Like hosting the support group, it was not a role she sought out, and not one she was ever paid for. Instead, the community chose her.

The support group – a weekly drop-in group for 'experiencers' – became her group almost by accident. One day, years prior, Esther had been in the office updating The Gathering Place's books, when the group facilitator didn't show up. The group members had already come in, set the chairs in a circle, made coffee, and waited. Still the facilitator didn't arrive. They asked Esther to step in as the facilitator that week.

When the group learned that the usual facilitator would be unable to return permanently, they immediately asked Esther if she would continue.

It had come as a surprise to her. The group used the word 'experiencer' loosely in that it was a supportive group for people who had experienced a range of phenomena, from UFOs and abductions to cryptids and ghosts to mediums and channelers. The commonality was the personal experience, both of the phenomenon itself, and of the social derision that comes with talking about these types of experiences. In a society that had settled on and enforced disbelief, this was a safe place, where you could be among others who have also had the universe wink at them.

The seats arranged and refreshments ready, Esther opened the door and welcomed four group members waiting outside. As they entered and got themselves coffee, a few more trickled in, including a new face. There were eight or nine regulars, with another dozen who came periodically, and every so often a new person would attend. After a few minutes of coffee and small talk, Esther took her seat and invited everyone to join her in the circle.

"Welcome everyone to our Experiencer Group. To those who have been here before, welcome back, and to those coming for the first time, welcome home," Esther said, smiling to the newcomer, a thin man in a brown suit, with salt and pepper frizzy hair and thick round glasses.

"Now, a few ground rules. First, we believe each other, period. We aren't here to judge, but to support each other through our experiences. Second, we respect confidentiality. What's said here stays here. And finally, we all have a lot to say, and we welcome you to say it, but we also make space for others, especially those new to the group. Are we all agreed?"

Group members nodded, with one man, Neander, saying, "Yes, mom," grinning to show he was trying to make a joke. Esther gave him a stern look, thinking but not saying, *you're the reason I had to make the rules.*

"Now, just to get the conversation started, I was doing some reading today and I came across this quote, by the writer Philip K. Dick. He wrote: 'It is sometimes an appropriate response to reality to go insane.'"

The group laughed, with some nodding.

Esther continued. "Well, most of the time I agree with him, but I thought I'd share that with you today as a reminder: we're not insane. There are a lot of things that are insane in this world – war, pollution, poverty despite abundance – but seeing something, or experiencing something rare and profound, that's not insane. The supernatural is natural. The paranormal is normal." Esther held the space for a moment, letting the message hover in the air. "Now…who would like to begin?"

Cormac, a stout man with a white beard and a band of white hair around the back and sides of his head, shared a recollection of an encounter he had as a child growing up in Ireland, playing in a field behind their house.

"Nora, my older sister, challenged me on who could climb higher in a tree, this one big tree that stood in that field. Well, I thought I was the best climber, so off we went. We didn't get far up the tree when Nora slipped a little. She held on, but she grabbed onto one smaller branch, and it snapped from the tree. She dropped that branch onto the ground below, and the moment it hit the ground, we heard someone yelling. I couldn't make out what he was saying, but I had the impression he was yelling at Nora, or both me and Nora, and so we both started climbing down the tree. Well, I got down a branch and could see past the leaves on the tree, and that's when I saw him: he was a little man, coming down a small hill, a mound, heading towards the tree. He had golden hair and a golden beard, and he looked like a person, looked human, but he was small, and almost shiny. There was something so strange about him. I panicked, and I jumped out of the tree. Nora saw him and screamed, and she jumped out after me. She landed funny and hurt her knee, and I remember she had her arm around me so I could help her walk. Help her run I should say, we moved as fast as we could and didn't look back.

"We headed straight home and in the door. We were screaming when we came in the house, I remember my grandmother, who lived with us, was angry with the noise. We told her what happened, told her about the tree and the little man yelling at us. Here we were riled up, but strangely she wasn't concerned. She waved her hand, she said that's the aos sí. The Folk, she called them. She didn't explain, she just said that must be their tree, and to not go near it again. She said if you leave what's theirs, then they won't bother us. Nora and I were fine with that as we were not planning to go back. We were terrified.

"Now, the regulars at this meeting know that I've been learning Irish, since it wasn't taught when I was younger. And that this was a very different type of experience than I usually share here. You see," Cormac continued, now addressing the newcomer to the group, the man with the thick glasses, "I was actually a Catholic monk, a Dominican…"

Esther almost jumped in to keep Cormac on track. He spoke slowly and thoughtfully, and with his lyrical Irish accent, people hung on every word, with his kind, jovial old man demeanour making it seem disrespectful to interrupt. If you didn't interrupt, however, the meeting would be over before anyone else got to speak. Instead, Esther gave Cormac a knowing look, and he got back on track.

"Yes, so I was practicing my Irish, and I saw 'aos sí,' and wham, I'd completely forgotten until I saw the words. I did some research this week, and aos sí means 'people of the mound,' as they were thought to live underground under small hills. And I thought, isn't that interesting. We saw him coming from the direction of the little hill. The mound."

Cormac stopped talking, distracted by Neander who wore a smirk and made a groaning sound. Esther shot him a look.

"The first rule is that we believe people, remember?" Esther said to Neander.

"Yes, I'm sorry. Sorry Cormac," he said, exaggeratingly looking to Cormac, whose jolly nature had him smiling back kindly. Neander wore a colourful Hawaiian-style shirt and cargo shorts, and round steampunk style sunglasses, the sides also dark to block out peripheral light. "It's just…I've seen a lot, I believe in a lot of out there things, but leprechauns, I mean, I've heard a lot at this group, but…"

"Neander–" started Esther, before being interrupted.

"I mean if fairies and leprechauns exist, why isn't there any evidence, any picture, a trail cam, security camera, something? I mean I'm not a UFO experiencer, but at least there are pictures, videos, radar. But I hear people talk about fairies like they are real. I think this group is for experiencers, not to talk about folklore," said Neander.

"It's said they don't live in this world, that the aos sí inhabit a kind of parallel reality," Cormac added kindly, as though Neander just needed this additional piece of information.

Esther smiled at Cormac, her nature having her sprinkle extra kindness on anyone who may be wounded. "That's how a friend of mine, a kind of teacher, once explained it to me, while she was leaving out food for the fairies."

Neander leaned forward in his chair. "I just think there's an important difference between a real phenomenon, I mean something well documented, that many people experience, and folklore or fairy tales. Esther, please tell me you don't actually, deep down inside, believe in fairies and elves."

Esther leaned forward in her chair and looked around the circle as she spoke, addressing the whole group. "Let me ask you: why is it that when the enlightenment arrived in an area – usually by force – magic disappeared? Those creatures all disappeared, and they just became folklore. Yet they haven't actually disappeared. They keep on popping up. People keep seeing these things. They experience them. How can we say they aren't real? The fauns, the elves, the fairies, the gods and demigods, flying machines to UFOs, they've always been with us."

"And yet we have no evidence for these beings," said Neander.

"We have experience," said Esther, her voice ringing with wonder. "Why is it that first person testimony is enough in a court of law, someone saying 'I saw this,' can get a person on death row. But thousands – millions – of people across distances and cultures experience something outside of our known reality, and suddenly first-person testimony isn't evidence? Remember, this is an experiencer group Neander, where experience matters."

"Of course, you're right. And you don't need to tell me about experiences. Do you know where the name Neander came from?" he asked, looking around the circle. "Eighteen years ago I had a truly profound experience. I was electrocuted on a downed power line. Dead. Heart stopped, I was completely dead. And I went somewhere. I don't know if it was Heaven, but it felt perfect. And real. I mean really real. This place, this life here, this isn't the real place. This place, this life is just play, and our real life is up there."

"All the world's a stage," said Cormac.

"And all the men and women merely players," Neander replied, nodding. He then paused, looking at each member of the group, his eyes hidden behind his dark glasses. "Of course, I didn't die. They brought me back. And every day for eighteen years, I have had to live with this knowledge. The grief I feel after losing that feeling. I experienced Heaven, or at least got a lot closer to it. I saw what was real, then it's just pulled away. And instead I'm stuck in the place that feel phony. Honestly, it's hard to go on some days."

Several group members shared similar feelings following their experiences, and tried to speak to the importance of finding meaning in life, worried that Neander may opt out of this life to return to that experience. Finally, Cormac spoke.

"My best advice, Neander, is to chop wood, carry water."

Esther nodded and repeated, "Chop wood, carry water."

Neander looked from one to the other. "I don't understand."

Esther waved to Cormac, inviting him to explain. As he spoke, she could almost see him in the monk robes he wore long ago

"There were two monks, one novice and one master. The novice said to the master, 'What does one do before enlightenment?' 'Chop wood. Carry water,' replied the master. Then the novice asks, 'What, then, does one do after enlightenment?" The master replied, 'Chop wood. Carry water.'"

The group sat with this for a moment, a few people nodding and *hmm*ing. Then the new person, the man with the thick round glasses spoke for the first time.

"Where did the name Neander come from?" he asked, everyone looking back to Neander, remembering the question he introduced this story with.

"When they brought me back, I didn't feel myself anymore. Like I was a different person, the knowledge, the experience had changed me so much. I felt like I needed a new name to really mark it. Think Neander Valley, where they first found Neandertals. It means 'new man.' It just felt right."

The man with the frizzy hair and thick round glasses came back to the group three weeks in a row, but hardly said a word. Esther became increasingly intrigued by him, feeling some sort of connection, a familiarity, but he came right on time and left immediately, not giving her a chance to talk with him. On the fourth week she was determined to corner him before he left, so she took the seat closest to the door.

The meeting started with a semi-regular member named Maeve, a short woman with long brown hair. She usually had an upbeat demeanor and a kind perspective to share, but on this day, she appeared stressed and unrested.

"Those who have heard me share before know that I'm an experiencer of ghosts. All my life, I've had experiences of seeing, feeling, hearing ghosts. And I don't mean I'm a medium, I don't usually get messages from them, they're not attached to a certain person. Just…ghosts, you know? Well lately, that's changed. I feel like I'm getting messages."

"Messages from the ghosts?" Esther asked kindly. Sometimes she asked simple clarifying questions to show the speaker she was not only listening, she wanted to hear them.

"No, from…I don't know. Someone or something. It started a few weeks ago during meditations. I would get these messages, like reminders of some of my experiences. And it was like the messages had a task attached to them: remember this experience and write it down. Write your experiences into a book and share them."

"Interesting," said Esther. "And have you been writing them down?"

Maeve nodded. "I started to. Then I started getting messages in my dreams, or when I would be out for a walk, wherever and whenever, just these snippets, like I could see the words as though they were already written. And a few times when I've been meditating, well it's not just messages. It feels like I'm talking to this…I don't know, this consciousness. I mean it's amazing, I'm getting all of these ideas, I'm feeling so creative, but then also I think, maybe I'm just going crazy. I'm literally just having conversations with myself in my head."

"Oh Maeve," said Esther, nurturing in the way she spoke, "if I had a quarter for every time I thought I was going crazy. Or for every time I've had a conversation in my head! It sounds like you're channeling, dear. Some being, some consciousness, has picked you."

Before Maeve responded, another group member jumped in. Though he only attended periodically, Esther knew his full name, Dick Harris, as he always introduced himself with his full name, as though he wanted to make sure it was known and remembered.

"You know, what you describe is quite similar to what a lot of UFO experiencers describe. Oh, sorry, I should introduce myself, I'm Dick Harris," he said, nodding at people around the circle. "The downloads, Maeve, the receiving of information, many people who see a UFO will at the time, or even a few days later, receive messages or information. That's something I've been told from people on the inside."

Esther's face frowned for a moment before she masked herself in a resting smile again. When Dick would share, he would often reference information he was getting from high up in the CIA, the Air Force, NASA. Although Esther's first rule of the group was to believe others, she didn't trust Dick.

"Have you had any UFO experiences lately?" he asked casually.

Maeve shook her head.

"Well, it sounds like it's a good thing. You've been chosen for some purpose. I'd be flattered."

Maeve shook her head again. "No. Well yes, I felt that at first. I tried asking it, 'Why me, why are you sharing these ideas with me?' And all I got back was, 'Why not you?'"

"Exactly. Why not you?" Dick said reassuringly.

"You don't understand, I was flattered at first, and welcomed it. Whatever it was, it got me writing, got me thinking and remembering, all these interesting ideas swirling in my head. I thought it was great, like I was special. Chosen. Then one night I was trying to sleep, but before I did, I woke up with more messages, more ideas. I pulled out my book to write them down, and all of a sudden I had this moment, like, wait a minute, who are you and why are you interrupting my sleep? What gives you the right to pop into my mind anytime you want and give me instructions? I feel like I've been manipulated. Finally I told it, 'I'm not your monkey, I'm not here to dance for you.' Well, it hasn't stopped, but at least I haven't been woken up again."

Esther and a few members talked through Maeve's experience. Esther asked what her intuition was telling her, and asked if she could separate herself from the information she was receiving.

"Just because you receive the information, even put it out there in the world, that doesn't mean you have to believe it yourself," said Esther. "And for the record, I thought you were special before you were chosen by this consciousness."

Before long, Dick Harris was speaking again, and brought the discussion back to UFOs.

"I'd like to share something if I could," said Dick, pulling a folded yellow lined piece of paper from the breast pocket of his brown sport jacket. Esther thought him to be in his early forties, but he had a round, boyish face that gave him a younger appearance, and eyes that seemed to always be wet, giving off a little reflection as he spoke. "As I've shared before, I have some sources on the inside, I mean deep inside, and sometimes I get some information. Well, a friend shared this with me, and I'm probably not supposed to, but I'm going to share it with you."

He looked around the circle raising and lowering his eyebrows to show that what he had to share was privileged knowledge.

"How would you like to know what God is according to the 'Greys'. You know, the grey aliens," Dick said, gently waving the yellow paper.

"How…how would you or someone else know that? Where did that come from?" asked Neander skeptically.

Dick responded excitedly. "UFO crashes. We've recovered discs, and in those discs, bodies. Some of them were alive and were taken in to study. And this is what they learned." Dick put on a pair of reading glasses and unfolded the paper.

"Okay, what is God according to Grey ET culture? First," said Dick, reading from handwritten notes, "time, space, everything in the universe, is the behaviour of a single universal consciousness."

"Well, that's something many of us have described experiencing," said Esther, trying not to show her skepticism of what Dick shares here.

"Many of you know my love of Merton," said Cormac, of the priest and monk Thomas Merton. "I may not get this exactly right, but he said: 'Compassion is based on a keen awareness of the interdependence of all living things, which are all part of, all involved in one another.'"

"Perhaps Merton had been talking to the Greys," said Dick with a smile before turning back to his notes. "Second, this consciousness behaves spontaneously, without forethought. Third, the minds of living things are part of this consciousness. This consciousness has looped in on itself, creating separation and individuality."

"I have certainly felt that in some of my experiences," said Esther, noticing the man with the thick round glasses giving the smallest nod.

"Next, through evolution humanity has developed higher cognitive complexity. As life continues to complexify, it will influence the single unitary consciousness that is the universe. Lastly, as life proliferates and complexifies, it leads the unitary consciousness to higher cognitive functions, and eventually, self-awareness. So…what do you think?" asked Dick, refolding the paper and looking around at the group.

The group had a discussion about how some of these points intersected with their own beliefs and experiences, with some disagreeing.

As the discussion progressed, Esther asked Dick again, "Can you tell us again what your source is for this? And why did you want to share it?"

Dick unfolded his paper again, looked at it, and smiled at Esther. "Source: A visiting superintelligence," he said. "And I just thought it would start a discussion. Which it did. Job done."

As the group finished for another week, Esther headed towards the door to try to catch the newcomer before he left. It turned out she didn't have to, as this time he lingered while the other group members left. He was standing across the room, looking at the god and goddess statue that had been in this church from the beginning, tipping his head up to look in detail through his glasses. Esther approached him.

"The Triple Goddess and the Horned God," she said, joining him in admiring the statues. The man turned and looked at Esther, not speaking. Esther felt something between them, as though there were some message, some information that was hanging in the air, waiting to be plucked. Esther closed her eyes and paused for a moment, before a word appeared in her mind.

"Noosphere," she said, a look of confusion on her face, wondering where this word had come from.

The man with the thick glasses smiled. "I'm Ray," he said. "For the past few weeks, I've been sitting here repeating that word in my head, wondering what might happen. And well, you certainly passed the test."

"What test?" asked Esther, feeling confused by, but also drawn to this man. To a kindness, a familiarity he shared. "And what does noosphere mean?"

Ray smiled. "Would you have time to get a coffee? Or even better, a martini?"

"So what is the noosphere," Esther started as the server placed two martinis on the table, "and why on Earth were you repeating it in your head?"

Ray smiled, seeming a lot looser and more personable compared to his stoic demeanour at the Experiencer Group.

"Hah, I suppose that was an odd introduction. Basically, I had heard about you, about what you do in the community, and that perhaps you have some, well, psychic abilities."

"Who did you hear this from?" asked Esther.

"Oh, let's just say it's the word on the street," Ray said coyly.

"And noosphere?" asked Esther.

"Well, I just picked a word to repeat to see if you would pick it up. The Noosphere is a concept worked on by a few people, including the Jesuit priest Pierre Teilhard de Chardin. Think of the Earth as having three spheres. The geosphere, all the rocks and water, the inanimate matter. Then the biosphere, all the living stuff. And humans as part of the biosphere have manipulated the geosphere. Well, the noosphere is the third, the emerging one, where consciousness, human cognition lives. And as human cognition progresses, it will affect the biosphere in the same way we've affected the geosphere. Anyways, I had been reading about it before my first visit, and thought it was appropriate," Ray said, finally pausing to sip his martini. "Now, can I ask, why do you do this work? Why do you host this Experiencer Group week after week?"

Esther looked at Ray for a moment, feeling very comfortable and open around him, despite knowing nothing about him.

"Well, it kind of happened by accident, but I found that I just love to work with experiencers. I've found there's one commonality among experiencers: they're generally kind and gentle. They are usually very sensitive people. They are so beautiful, and often because of their experiences, so broken," Esther said.

"Even Dick Harris?" asked Ray with a grin, indicating to Esther that Ray had his reservations about him as well.

Esther found herself inclined to be completely honest with Ray. "Dick is a spook. He's a disinformation agent, from what I've heard and what I've gleaned from him."

Ray nodded and sipped his drink, as though he was pleased to hear Esther was able to see through him. "Why do you let him stay in the group?"

"Hmm," said Esther, "I don't like to police the group, who is a real experiencer and who isn't. And I think some of what he says is true. I think he shares both truth and lies, and I guess I like trying to figure out which parts are which."

Ray smiled as though Esther gave the right answer. "That's what they do, disinformation agents. They give you a bit of truth along with the lies, so that when people repeat them, the truth is polluted by the lies. And then truth becomes fairytales and folklore."

While Esther was enjoying her meeting with Ray, she was getting impatient for clarity.

"So, Ray, what is it that brought you to my group, to find me and repeat a word in your mind just to see if I'd hear it?" asked Esther.

Ray smiled and sipped his martini, looking as though he was ready to finally disclose his motivations. "Esther, do you believe that your consciousness is non-local? What I mean is, well, what if I told you your consciousness could travel, that you could get information about far off places. Even far off times?"

Esther looked around the bar, the space bright, but sparsely attended on a weeknight.

"I think I might believe you. I've…never been able to control it. But there have been times, in dreams, in meditation, even daydreaming, that felt like more than imagination. More than dreaming. Mr. Ray, are you here to tell me that I've not been dreaming?"

"I could tell you that, but how about instead I show you? Are you busy tomorrow?"

With traffic it took Esther an hour to drive to Menlo Park, crossing the Dumbarton Bridge and getting a spectacular view of the whole Bay area. She pulled into the parking lot beside the sprawling brick research building, walked under the treed walkways to the entrance, and asked for Ray Jarmark.

Ray smiled through his thick glasses when he came out to greet her.

"Esther, welcome to the Stanford Research Institute, SRI for short. I'm glad you're here. I wasn't sure if you were actually going to come," he said, adding with a laugh, "I guess that's why I don't do the psychic stuff around here."

"Well, I suppose you have me intrigued," Esther said skeptically, looking around the professional office space. "This is not really what I expected for a psychic research facility."

"Let me guess," Ray said, extending his arm to lead Esther down the main hall towards the SRI offices, "you expected more tie-dyed? Of course, what we have here is by design. We are scientists doing scientific work. You'll see that our interview rooms where we do our experiments are not much more than four white walls and some recording equipment. Basically, if we want to publish and have the scientific community take us seriously, our research doesn't have to be solid, it needs to be bulletproof. And even then, many won't take it seriously. But here I am getting ahead of myself. We actually have some paperwork to do before I can really tell you more about our work."

They entered the SRI offices, and Ray brought Esther to the office of one of his colleagues, who had her fill out a personal information form, and ran through a strict non-disclosure agreement.

Esther read through it, hesitated with the pen, then signed with a sigh. "I'm too curious to put up a fuss," she said.

Ray led her into an interview room which was indeed four white walls, a couch and two chairs, a small desk, and a cart with recording equipment.

"I'm just going to give you a high-level overview," he said. Esther took a seat on the couch and Ray sat in the chair across from her. "And if you decide you want to work with us, of course then we can get into detail."

Esther's eyes widened and her voice sounded surprised. "Work with you? I don't remember a job offer."

"Oh, yes, I thought you understood that," Ray said. "The question is whether you feel this is the place for you. Let me explain. We do a variety of research studies on psychic phenomena here, but most of our work is contracted by various intelligence agencies, and the military. For these agencies we do what's called 'remote viewing'. Technically, remote viewing is the ability to acquire information about spatially – and temporally – remote geographical targets. Or put simply, Esther, it's psychic spying. I mention this because not everyone is comfortable doing work for the military or the government. But I assure you, our work doesn't get anyone hurt. Instead, it's usually trying to get information about what our adversaries are developing, even helping in search and rescue, that sort of thing."

"I see," Esther said slowly, trying to digest this information.

She had always thought of herself as a pacifist, and struggled with the idea of working for the military in any way. At the same time, she wondered what she might learn and experience here.

"How does it work, Ray? The remote viewing. How do you do it?"

"Quite simply, really. There are protocols we would go through, but imagine getting very relaxed, like in a meditation, setting your intention to a certain place and time, and waiting for impressions to come to you. It requires a lot of patience, and ability to discern information from noise. But you see, Esther," Ray said, his voice getting excited, "it works. It really works! We can get a set of coordinates given to us, and more often than not, we can gain information, useful information, about that place. Now, the more work we do, the more we can prove it scientifically. Do you know what it means if can prove that it works, prove that humans innately possess psychic ability?"

Esther nodded in understanding. "It means everything we know about how things work is wrong."

Ray smiled and pushed his glasses back up on his nose. "Exactly. Does our consciousness travel? Is there some invisible information field we have access to? We have to rethink the whole way we look at the universe. Here, let me show you something."

Ray led her from the interview room into a small observation room. On the long wall was a large two-way window, looking in on an active interview room. Ray closed the door behind them and flipped a switch, turning on the audio from the interview room. Through the window Esther saw a man sitting on a couch, looking as though he were having a nap after a big meal. The man had short dark hair with a short beard and a wide face. Esther looked at his face closely and saw that he wasn't sleeping. He was actually talking. It was the voice she heard through the speaker.

"He looks so familiar," Esther said. Ray smiled and nodded. "What is he saying?"

"He's in a remote viewing session, and he's simply describing what he sees, what impressions he's getting, shapes, colours, noises, smells."

"Smells?" Esther asked, surprised.

Ray nodded. "Emotions. Words. Messages. Sometimes these can get downright spooky. That's what the martinis are for."

Esther leaned her ear towards the speaker, trying to pick up his words as he spoke groggily.

"…yes, it's in this locked room, under a desk. It's a square box, it's a…a safe. Like a little vault. With a dial to enter the code."

"And can you pierce the safe? Can you see what is inside?" said the voice of another man, only the back of his head visible to them.

"It's…it's a picture," the remote viewer continued after a stretch of silence. "Not a photograph, a piece of paper. It's the only thing in here."

"Do you have any impressions of what's on the paper?" asked the faceless moderator.

The remote viewer seemed to take a couple of long, slow breaths, then blurted out, "Bird. Yes, a small bird, I see it from the side. It's perched on something, a branch I think. A cardinal maybe? I'm getting the impression of the colour red."

Ray let out a deep, audible breath, and flipped the switch to turn off the audio. He reached into the inside breast pocket of his brown jacket, pulled out a folded paper, unfolded it, and held it out for Esther to see. It was a glossy page that looked like it had been ripped out of a magazine, with a closeup picture of a cardinal perched beside a nest.

"A photocopy of this is locked in a reinforced steel safe in a locked office in the basement, two floors below us. I locked it in there this morning, two hours before he arrived," Ray said, still incredulous in this work despite years of research and witnessing unexplainable experiences.

Esther mouthed *wow* and shook her head.

"But here's the thing," Ray continued, "the Xerox machine I used only produces black and white copies. He said it was a 'red' bird, which you can see, it is. But the photocopy in that safe isn't a red bird. It's a black and white copy of a red bird!"

Esther laughed, feeling the goosebumps all over her body start to settle. "Okay, are you having me on here? What is this?"

Ray shook his head. "No, Esther, this is the kind of thing I want you to be part of. This particular remote viewer, he was once asked to remote view Jupiter. He was reluctant, because he only wanted to do experiments that were verifiable, so that we could confirm if he was accurate, and at the time we didn't yet have closeup pictures of Jupiter. Anyways, he was finally convinced to do it, and he described a lot of interesting things, but most notable was that he described rings around the planet. And everyone thought oh, it didn't work, or maybe he was looking at Saturn for some reason, because everyone knew that Jupiter doesn't have rings. So, the experiment was a bust. But…a few months later, the Pioneer 10 flew by Jupiter and snapped pictures, sending us the most detailed images of the gassy giant we had seen. And guess what?"

"Jupiter has rings," said Esther, still shaking her head at all she was hearing.

"Exactly. They confirmed what this one man already knew," Ray said, pausing for a moment. "Except he didn't need to physically travel there to find out."

"It's…incredible," said Esther, overwhelmed by this place, the research, and the possibilities it pointed to.

"So Esther, let's talk about you working here. He uncovered Jupiter's rings," Ray said, pointing through the glass at the remote viewer. "What mysteries will you uncover?"

Chapter 11

"The present issues from the past, and the future from the present. Everything is made one by this continuity. Time is like a circle, where all the points are so linked that one cannot say where it begins or ends, for all points precede and follow one another for ever."

Hermes Trismegistus

Ib was startled awake. He looked around, and realized that he had drifted off and woke himself with his own snoring.

He looked at the passenger seated beside him, smiled, and held up the book he had been reading. "Don't blame the author for my snoring. It really is interesting."

His seatmate, a woman looking to be in her late thirties, her long hair organized in two braids, smiled and waved his apology away. "I've never been able to sleep on flights," she said, "so believe me, I was jealous of your snoring."

Ib smiled, and looked at the cover of the magazine she was reading, an issue of *The Economist*. The headline in big, bold letters read, *THE GREAT UNREST*, with a cover picture of a crowd of young men clashing with police in riot gear.

"Can I ask, what is that about?" Ib asked, pointing to the cover. The woman flipped to look at the cover, and looked back at Ib with subtle confusion.

"This article you mean?" she asked.

"Yes," Ib said. "The Great Unrest. What is that?"

"You…haven't heard the term?"

Ib realized he had asked about something he should have known, had he been living in the world with everyone else the past two years, rather than on some cosmic, time-bending adventure.

"Let's pretend I've been living under a rock," he said and smiled.

"Well, it's…it's about all of the unrest. The protests and the riots. The media started calling it 'The Great Unrest' because the first couple months of the year it seemed like there was a coup or an attempt almost every week, somewhere in the world. It seems like it's calmed down, but for a while the protests seemed to keep spreading, rich countries, poor countries, it didn't matter," the woman said, a pang of sadness in her voice. "Including in my home country."

"Oh, I'm so sorry," said Ib. "From your accent, you are South African?"

"Zimbabwean," the woman said. "I'm Edith, by the way."

"Ib," he said with a nod, "Ib Johanson. What will it be like when you arrive? Is it safe?"

"I think so," she said, "I just need to go and check in on my parents and make sure they are doing okay. They live rurally and so far it seems pretty safe where they are."

"Well I certainly hope that they are," said Ib. "You live in the States?"

"I do," she said. "I'm a psychologist, but not practicing, I'm a researcher."

"I'm a researcher too," said Ib. "What do you study?"

"I research neurodivergences in kids. ASD, ADHD, for example," Edith said. "I'm neurodivergent myself, so it's personal."

"Interesting. And how does that affect you, or maybe put better, how does that inform who you are?"

Edith looked up, considering her response. "You know, it's just a little extra hard. Like I don't quite fit in. I guess I wonder why life, this world, is easy for most people and so hard for others. Emotionally hard. It seems like the people I meet in my research are all a little extra sensitive. Like most kids, most people sort of cruise through the world with ease, while some of us are feeling the suffering of people half a world away."

Ib nodded and smiled. "I think I understand. I think I have some friends that that would resonate with. Well good for you for doing that work. It sounds important."

Edith smiled, and went back to her magazine, and Ib opened his book. After a few minutes of silence, Edith spoke again.

"I um…wasn't sure if I was going to say anything, but I know that book. I'm actually in that book," she said, pointing at the book in Ib's hands.

Ib looked at her, looked at the book, and started to flip the pages.

With a small laugh, Edith said, "I don't think you've made it that far yet. There's a chapter in there about the Ariel School landing."

At that moment, the fasten seatbelts sign came on, and the captain's voice came over the PA letting them know that they were approaching Frankfurt and would begin their descent. Ib put the book in his lap and buckled his seatbelt.

He looked at Edith, his eyes wide with curiosity. "Let's say again that I've been living under a rock. What is the Ariel School landing?"

"Well, it was back in 1994, when I was just a kid, and I was a student at the Ariel school, a rural school in Zimbabwe. One day we were out playing in the field, when a silver craft flew over us and landed in the next field over. Some of us kids ran to the field hoping to get a look, including me. When we got there, the craft had landed, and two little men, two beings came out. They had big eyes and wore black clothes. And they talked to us, talked to me, but not with their mouths. It was telepathic," Edith said.

Ib had a look of wonderment on his face.

"I know, most people don't believe me, that's why I don't usually talk about it. But I'm quoted in that book, from back when I was a child."

Ib stammered, trying to form the right question. "What did the beings say to you? Oh, and I believe you, by the way, I really do."

Edith smiled kindly at Ib's reassurance. "Well it wasn't exactly words. It was a message, but more like a feeling. I said at the time, and it's in the book, that they were warning us about technology, and about protecting our environment. But that wasn't quite it, I just didn't have the right words for it when I was a child."

"What is it really, then?" asked Ib.

"I think they were really saying that our technology doesn't matter. That it's kind of a distraction for us. That everything we need is on the inside, our souls. And that the Earth's environment is far more important than technology."

Ib nodded reflectively. "I think I understand that. Look at this airplane. I mean we are flying high in the atmosphere, it's incredible. But how impressive is it when you realize your soul, your consciousness, can fly, travel to anywhere?"

Edith nodded, a look of gentle appreciation on her face at having someone really understand her. "A fellow traveller?" she said.

Ib smiled. "Well, here I am sitting next to an experiencer who is in the very book I'm reading. Now how's that for a coincidence?"

"You know," Edith said, "it's funny you say that. From that day on I stopped believing in coincidences."

Ib nodded in agreement, and they quietly looked out the window as the plane came in for a landing. Ib exited the plane and scanned for directional signage. When he figured out the direction towards his gate, he turned to find that Edith was already on her way, pulling a rolling luggage bag behind her, headed in the opposite direction. Ib walked briskly towards his gate and his flight to Copenhagen, wondering, if it were not a coincidence, what was the meaning of that meeting?

Ib pushed the back of his head into the headrest of the blue fabric seats, wishing his chair could tilt back just a little. He then rested his head against the wall of the train, the vibration lulling him to sleep until his head slipped onto the cold train window, startling him awake. Out of the window he saw the dual spires of the Roskilde Cathedral rising high above the passing city.

The eight-hundred-year-old red bricked cathedral had long been the burial site of Danish monarchs. He remembered touring the cathedral on a school trip – *at least forty years ago*, Ib thought with a sigh – and learning this fact, imagining skeletons and decaying bodies under the floor of the church. He imagined the inside of the cathedral wouldn't have changed much, even if he and the world around it had.

As the church spires disappeared from the window, Ib pulled his phone from his pocket and opened his email app again, looking for a response to the simple message he sent before boarding the train: *I will be there at 1 p.m. today.*

The app opened and he saw a new message: *I look forward to seeing you then, Ib.*

He scrolled down to read the original email, the one that had arrived just as Ib and Barry had emerged from their lengthy disappearance. The email that made Ib hop on an airplane and fly across an ocean, less for the content of the message and more for the mystery, the intrigue. How had she known Ib had resurfaced, and what did she know about the mysteries surrounding him? He read the email dated June 21st, 2026:

Dearest Ib,

It's time we talked, don't you think? Please meet me at Fanefjord Church at your earliest convenience. I will be in the area until Wednesday. Let me know when I can expect your arrival.

Yours,

Jette Kirkegaard

Although she had been the chair of the board of directors of PSI, the Perceptual Studies Institute, for Ib's whole tenure, he had only met her in person once, the board meetings taking place typically by conference call. Despite hearing her voice on all of those calls, Ib knew very little about her, other than that she was American with Danish ancestry.

He thought back to that night at Rory's Tavern when they celebrated Tomi's first eight-martini remote viewing session. Tomi had asked Ib how he had come to work at PSI. Ib had asked her if she had read Philip K. Dick. She had not.

'Well, Philip K. Dick once gave this incredible speech,' Ib had told Tomi, 'where he declared that we live in a computer simulation, and that other worlds exist right beside ours. That his stories are actually from these other worlds. In that speech he said that it's a common theme in his stories that a dark-haired woman would show up at the protagonist's door and tell him his world is delusional. Anyways, I loved that line, and sort of wished that would happen to me.'

'Do you know what happened, Tomi?' he had asked her. 'One day a dark-haired woman showed up at my door and told me my world was delusional,' he had said.

He could almost taste the martini, so vivid was his memory.

'I had a visit from the Board Chair of the Perceptual Studies Institute. She told me that our material world, time, our accepted reality, none of it was real, and she wanted me to prove it,' Ib had told her.

The next thing he knew he was living in Durham, running PSI, and trying to prove just that. *And what did I prove? Actually accomplish?* wondered Ib. His journey with Tomi showed him that Jette had been right, that the material world, our accepted reality, was indeed an illusion. But even if he knew it, the rest of the world ticked on none the wiser, continuing down a dangerous path.

He rested his head on the wall of the train and drifted off again, the slow rocking of the train making sleep inevitable.

After dozing for what felt like a few minutes, the ticket collector tapped Ib on the shoulder. Ib looked at him, jetlagged and momentarily confused about where he was.

"Vordingborg," the man said flatly, and pointed out the window at the train platform. Ib looked out the window, his mind waking up and reminding him where he was heading.

"Oh, tak for det," Ib said, thanking the ticket checker, grabbing his rolling luggage and stepping off the train just a few seconds before the automatic doors closed and the train proceeded down the line.

He rolled his luggage down the platform, to the front of the train station, and got in the first taxi in the lineup along the street.

"Jeg skal til Fanefjord Kirke," Ib said to the driver, setting his destination. The driver pulled away, and within a couple of minutes they passed through the small town of Vordingborg. The route took them through more small towns and sleepy villages, and across a few bridges as they hopped islands. Ib mostly stared silently at the farmer's fields, feeling a sleepy calmness looking at the landscape of his youth, peaceful and pastoral.

"The fields," Ib said to the driver in Danish, breaking the pleasant silence, "they don't look right for the summer. What's going on?"

"The cold," the driver replied with a deep, raspy voice, "it just hasn't been warm enough for anything to grow much. Pig farmers will be fine, but any farmer growing crops isn't expecting much of a harvest. There's already talk about a farmer bailout."

Ib nodded and felt a chill, hoping this cold snap was temporary. *You can bail out the first year, but what about the second, or the third if this continues?* Ib wondered, as he saw a road sign pointing towards Fanefjord Church. At that moment, he noticed a woman standing in a farm field beside a small hill, a short jaunt down a small gravel road. It was Jette, the dark-haired woman who had once shown up at his door and told him his world was delusional.

"Stop here!" Ib declared to the driver. The driver pulled the car over, and explained that the church was a little up the road. Ib said that was okay, paid the driver, and got out at the side of this rural road with his rolling suitcase. Jette, just out of shouting distance, waved Ib towards her.

His luggage bounced along the thin gravel road – really two tire tracks of gravel with a patch of grass in the middle – towards Jette. As he approached, he saw that the hill she stood beside wasn't an ordinary hill. Covered in grass, it was almost rectangular, with huge stones placed around the edge of the hill on all sides. He got closer and saw that at the centre of the top of the hill was placed a huge, wedge-shaped stone, like a slice of cake on its side.

Ib finally caught up to Jette, a tall black-haired woman in her forties. Jette continued looking at the hill as Ib approached, the red roof and white walls of Fanefjord Church just off in the distance.

"Grønjægers Høj. This is how we used to bury our royals," Jette said without looking at Ib. "It's said a king, Grøn Jæger, is buried here, along with his wife Fane – hence Fanefjord."

Out of breath from dragging his luggage behind him, Ib looked at the hill, then to the church in the distance, then back to Jette, and thought he might explode. Had he really taken three flights, a train, and a taxi, then dragged his luggage down a rough gravel road, sweating in a cold breeze, just to get a history lesson? He bit his tongue. *She summoned me here, let her tell me why*, he thought to himself.

"So here we have this sacred megalithic site, and right by it an eight-hundred year old church. All around the world it's the same. A holy site for the ancients becomes a holy site for the next people to come. Ever wonder why the ancients picked these sites, and why subsequent people found them holy, too?" she asked, finally turning to look at Ib.

He shrugged and let out a big sigh as he wiped sweat from his brow with his sleeve.

"What I wonder is," she continued, ignoring his agitated demeanor, "was it these megalithic builders who decided this place was holy? Or were there people before them who turned this into hallowed ground, and they just inherited it, like we did. And were there others before them?

"And who," she continued, her deep green eyes beginning to droop, her face subtly sad, "who will come next, Ib? Who will replace us and make this place their own holy ground?"

Ib shook his head slightly without changing his tense facial expression.

"Of course, by then I bet the church over there will have long collapsed and crumbled. But this mound, these stones, they will still be here," she said, pointing back at the mound. "You know what's strange? At megalithic sites around the world, it is often the base of the structure that is most impressive, has the most advanced stonework. The parts that were added after, well, it's like the people forgot. We lost the expertise, the knowledge. Maybe one day in the future when they find this place they will compare them, the ruins of that church, and the intact monolith here, and conclude that ours was a civilization in decline. I mean Ib, name one thing we've built in the last century that will still be standing five thousand years from now."

"Costco," Ib said flatly.

Jette laughed, and smiled at him. "I don't know where you've been Ib," Jette said, as though Ib's joke interrupted her monologue and reminded her why she had summoned him here. "I don't know what happened. I'm in the dark. But I do know some of the people you're in trouble with. And I'm worried about you."

Ib remained silent, ruminating on if she brought him all the way here to tell him she was worried. She had emailed the same day he returned. He didn't believe she was really in the dark. He cleared his throat and looked at the mound.

"I am here for you, Ib, to help you find your way home," she continued. "I feel responsible. I recruited you and put you into this role, and it's got you mixed up in something dangerous. I feel responsible. So, was able to get you a pass. A get out of jail free card."

"A pass," Ib said flatly. "What do you mean you got me a pass?"

"Think witness protection program. A new life you can step right into. Ib Johanson, you have a job, a cushy job as a professor with lots of time for research. And you have a beautiful home right in the centre of Aarhus. It's all set up and waiting there for you," she said, her gentle face smiling as she gave Ib this gift.

Ib shook his head. "No. Thank you, but no."

"Ib, you can't say no," Jette said sternly. "You don't know how hard it was to arrange this. This is your only choice. You will get to live a quiet, affluent, peaceful life. Otherwise, I…I know these people, Ib. They won't think twice about disappearing an eccentric old professor. The kind of person who can disappear for as long as you have, and nobody notices."

Ib stared back flatly, his head still shaking slightly.

"Ib, how many emails did you have waiting for you? I bet only mine. Well, I remembered you. I got you this deal, and it's a damned good one. You know that things are unwinding, Ib. You know something is coming," she said, turning and waving her hand towards their surroundings. "I mean look at this place. Peaceful, sparsely populated, wealthy, a country full of farms. You can live out a good life in peace here, Ib, sheltered from the chaos that's coming."

Jette reached into the pocket of her jacket and pulled out an envelope, handing it to Ib. "In here you'll find instructions for getting to your house in Aarhus. And a key. You will find that everything you need is there. Also in the envelope you'll find a card for your contact at the university. Just let them know when you're ready to start. It's all been negotiated. You'll be taken care of."

Ib held the envelope, feeling the weight of the key slide around inside. He opened his mouth to speak but nothing came out.

"You're going to love your home. You may also like to know that your ex-wife Dagmar lives close by." She reached out and squeezed his hand. "It's not too late for a good life, Ib."

Ib nodded his head just a little. "Why are you here in Denmark? You have a Danish name, but when we met I understood you to be American."

She nodded. "That's right. My grandmother's farm is just down this road. So, this place is going to be my ark. Nobody's talking about it Ib, but everyone with the means to do so have been preparing for it. They are buying up land and building homes – compounds, really. New Zealand is the most popular with the billionaires. But this here feels like the right place for me. It's time to go home, Ib. That's what we do when we need to feel safe. We go home."

"Because something is coming," he said sadly.

Jette nodded.

"Do you know what it is?"

"No. But you can feel it, can't you? Come on," she said, pointing towards the tall white church a field behind them, "I have a car parked over there. There's a train leaving shortly to Aarhus. Come on, I'll take you to the station."

Ib nodded but didn't move, looking back at the massive stones lining the hill. "Do you remember when we met, you told me that our accepted reality, all this, it wasn't real. And that you wanted me to prove it."

"I remember. And I'm sorry for that. I got you caught up in a dangerous game. You're not some protagonist, some hero in a mystery novel. You're just a good, kind man Ib. And whether this material reality is real or an illusion, either way, I'd still rather not experience violence. Or hunger. Or death. And these things are coming. So let's go," she said, grabbing his hand and heading towards the church, "let's get you on that train home."

Ib sat at a café table along the Aarhus River, watching the city go by. Groups of young, stylish people went shop to shop, while a couple shared a beer perched on the concrete ledge beside the water, and two women strolled slowly by pushing prams. The city was so vibrant and peaceful, Ib had trouble imagining something awful could ever find its way here. Something that could disrupt this peaceful way of life.

He paid for his americano, then strolled aimlessly down the pedestrian streets in the centre of the ancient Viking city. Eventually he came to a major street and, finding a taxi stand, hopped into a car and asked to go to the university.

Ib was dropped off among neat yellow brick buildings with ivy growing up the sides, set around a sprawling green campus of grass and trees. He walked alongside a pond, the waters calm and flat with families of ducks floating idly. Students walked busily around campus despite it being summer, with others on bicycles hurrying by. Despite the cool weather there were people gathered in the grass socializing and studying, dressed as though it was early spring.

Eventually Ib came to Nobel Park, a newer part of the campus named for the university's Nobel laureates. Here, the university buildings switched from older yellow to newer red brick. He admired the architecturally pleasing set of buildings, connected by a bridge of staircases encased in glass. He imagined himself climbing those stairs on his way to class, followed a group of students dishing about their research.

He stopped and sat on a bench, his North American lifestyle not preparing him for the pedestrian lifestyle in Aarhus. He reached his hand in his pocket and felt the key that Jette had given him.

He hadn't gone to his home right away, instead choosing to acclimate himself to the city before taking that next step. In truth, he had been avoiding it, afraid he may feel too comfortable there, afraid that a feeling of home, of safety, may tempt him to do what Jette advised: stay. Live. Bow out of this crazy mission. Keep his head down, as John had suggested.

Ib pulled out his phone and found the address on the map. His legs aching, he decided to call for a taxi. The taxi dropped him off a short walk from his address, the tiny street not wide enough for, and closed off to cars. Ib smiled when he saw it – Møllestien – as he had long regarded it as the prettiest street in Aarhus. Perhaps all of Denmark.

Ib walked down the narrow street, cobblestones laid long before the combustion engine and rubber tires. The small houses along each side of the street – mostly one story but a few with a second floor – were built side by side, each one unique and brightly painted. The houses, built hundreds of years before, looked almost miniature, more fit for elves than the tall, well-nourished Danes of the twenty-first century.

The cobblestones went right up to the houses, but each had little pocket gardens, and some had under-window planter boxes, resulting in a street lined with flowers. *It's perfect*, thought Ib, *simply perfect.*

Ib spotted his address, a tiny one story home painted maroon, with a bright white door and white gabled windows. He stood in front of it, feeling almost guilty, as though entering it made him disloyal to Tomi. Still, his body ached and he was exhausted. And curious.

He stepped towards the house – *two arm widths across*, Ib thought, *maybe three* – and reached into his pocket for his key. He noticed a small heritage plaque affixed to the wall beside the front door: *In 1688 two women living here were sentenced for witchcraft*, the plaque read. Ib sighed, both horrified to think of the terrors they must have gone through, but also enchanted by the novelty. It seemed that Jette knew how to play him like a fiddle.

The home was small inside, but more spacious than you would suspect from its elven exterior. It had been recently and elegantly renovated, with a beautiful modern kitchen and a small loft bedroom in the attic. It had modern fixtures but kept some exposed brick and wooden beams.

As Ib looked around, he realized that many of the contents of the home were his. The furniture was all new, but somebody had collected his clothes, books, and other important possessions, and integrated them into the house. In the small living room area, beside the hearth, which had been converted to a modern electric fireplace, was a built-in wooden bookshelf. He ran his hand along the spines of a row of books, as he liked to do, as though reaching out and touching old friends.

He pulled out a Philip K. Dick book and flipped it open, confirming it was indeed his copy that he had left in his home in Durham some eighteen months ago. He flipped to a page he had dogeared, and smiled as he read a sentence he had underlined with pencil: *'My schedule for today lists a six-hour self-accusatory depression,'* *Iran said.*

He put the book back and flopped on the couch, finding it firm but comfortable. On the side table was a remote for the fireplace. He clicked it on, and an imitation fire immediately appeared. He gave his head a small shake, imagining the witchcraft they would have accused of him in 1688, creating fire on demand.

Ib drifted off into a deep sleep, at some point pulling a blanket off the top of the couch and stretching out. He woke up in the morning with a beam of sunshine on his face, remembering only a dark, dreamless sleep.

A French press and a hand-crank coffee grinder had been set on the counter in his kitchen, just waiting for him. He put on the kettle, made himself coffee, and sat on a chair placed beside his front window. Every so often he would hear people talking and laughing, their shoes clicking along the cobblestone outside.

When he finished his coffee, he placed the mug on the windowsill beside him, pulled out his phone, and opening the Signal app, pressed to make a secure call to Barry.

"Ahem…Ib?" Barry said groggily when he answered the call.

"Oh woops, I must have woken you," said Ib, "I'm sorry, I hadn't thought about the time difference."

"Yeah that's no problem, what happened with the board chair? What did she say to you?" asked Barry, becoming more alert as he spoke.

"She um…it was nothing really. Don't worry about it," Ib said, with a pause. "I'm ready. To meet you in the UK. I'm ready to go find Arthur Minear."

Chapter 12

"Are these 'somethings' aspects of a greater existence, distorted perhaps by the subject's perceptual filters? Are they first glimpses of a 'larger Earth'? To a frog with its simple eye, the world is a dim array of grays and blacks. Are we like frogs in our limited sensorium, apprehending just part of the universe we inhabit? Are we as a species now awakening to the reality of multidimensional worlds in which matter undergoes subtle reorganizations in some sort of hyperspace? Is visionary experience analogous to the first breathings of early amphibians? Are we ourselves coming ashore to a 'larger Earth'?"

Michael Murphy

It felt like she was walking in a dream. A dream where your surroundings are unknowable, shrouded in fog. As they strolled through this dreamy, cloudlike place, Esther shared her story about the experiencer group, about meeting Ray, and about visiting SRI for the first time. Tomi walked beside her grandmother, absorbing the story, seeing it in her mind as her grandmother spoke. She found herself so focused on experiencing the story that she wasn't thinking about what to say when the story was done, as she would have in the Material Place, the name she had given for her old reality. Instead, she was at peace, sucking in her grandmother's words as it played visually and vividly in her mind's eye.

As they walked, Tomi noticed that the ground below them would vary, as sometimes they walked on stone, other times dirt, and even on pavement. *The Earth is here below our feet and all around us,* Tomi thought, *and yet it's still like a different world. A new Earth.*

She looked down at her bare feet, seemingly stepping on the ground, but not feeling the dirt or hard surfaces. Instead, she felt her feet glide over the ground, like a flat stone skipping across water.

From time-to-time Tomi would perceive something out the corner of her eye: a movement, or a figure. Perhaps another human. If she turned to look, the figure was gone.

Tomi remembered back to the time Kirsten had told her about her abduction experiences, and how it had made her struggle with, even question reality. 'I just always felt like there was something else, just off to the side, like just past your peripheral vision,' Kirsten had said. 'Just…something there that shouldn't be, some other reality. But if you didn't look at it, just ignored it, it wasn't there.'

Maybe Kirsten was right, Tomi thought. *Maybe she was seeing this reality in her peripheral just as I'm now seeing hers.*

Tomi smiled and felt warm thinking about her. She wondered where she was walking now, and where Kirsten might be, wishing she could get a glimpse of her, even just from the corner of her eye.

Suddenly, Tomi stopped walking, stopped hearing her grandmother's voice. She stopped seeing the world around her and felt herself pulled into a vision, feeling a sudden and deep connection. A force was pulling at her, drawing her in like a magnet. As though her perception were put into a maze, she felt it twisting and turning, travelling to bring her consciousness to Kirsten. *Don't freak out and ruin it this time,* Tomi reminded herself. *Just let the vision unfold.*

She felt her consciousness take a turn, switch directions, and suddenly she was pulling away from Kirsten, drawn towards a stronger magnet. As though someone flipped a film projector on, a vision lit up Tomi's mind. It was again as though she were floating within a glass sphere, but instead of Kirsten's bedroom, she was in a small office meeting room, the walls bare white. In the centre of the room was a meeting table, where she saw a figure seated, hunched over on the table. *Where am I?* Tomi wondered.

As the vision got clearer and more detailed, Tomi could see that the man was wearing a blue Air Force uniform. He had his face in his hands, looking like he was crying. She saw the man then rub his eyes, as though he were waking, raise up his head, and sit up straight.

It's John, Tomi thought. She felt an initial pang of alarm but tried to quiet it. She remembered her grandmother saying that these visions, seeing into the Material Place, could be hard to navigate. While she wanted to retreat immediately, find that pull towards Kirsten, she assumed she was seeing this for a reason, and felt a wave of calm wash over her. *I can't be hurt here*, she thought to herself. *I'm safe.*

John looked slowly around the room. She could see that he was young, very young, looking as he had when they had first met. His eyes travelled to where Tomi was viewing from and stopped there. He was staring right at her. Again she tried to suppress the feeling of alarm, but he continued to stare.

Suddenly there was movement and he looked away. Another man entered the room, closed the door behind him, and sat down. It all happened so quickly that Tomi wasn't able to make out the man's face, seeing only the back of his head and shoulders as he sat down across from John. The man was also wearing Air Force blues.

"*Your date was three days ago, John,*" the man said without a greeting. "*I'd like to think that your silence means your mission is going very well, and not that you're having second thoughts.*"

John's face was stoic but slightly pained. "*It's…going very well. Honestly, she's amazing. Our date turned into the whole weekend. She even told me about her grandmother, though she didn't really know much about her remote viewing work. Her mother had told her that it was top secret, so she was worried after she told me, and had me promise I wouldn't tell anyone.*"

"*Well, John,*" said the man, seeming to tell a joke though his tone still serious, "*it's a good thing I'm not anyone. It sounds like you're doing good work here. Just tell me you're being careful.*"

"*Like…with protection?*" asked John awkwardly.

"*Jesus John,*" said the man, his voice littered with impatience, "*with your feelings. You won't forget your mission? Where your loyalties lie?*"

John looked down and shook his head. "*No, I know what my mission is. I know what I'm signing up for.*"

"*Good, and if you get along well in that way, all the better. But John, this is a big opportunity for you. You stick with this, stick with me, stick with that woman, and you'll go far,*" said the man, leaning back in his chair, lighting a cigarette.

"*I guess what I don't understand is, why this way? Why not just hire her and train her in remote viewing?*" asked John.

"*Here's the thing about these top remote viewers, the people best at this stuff: short life expectancy. They disappear. They die. They end up in*" *poor health or end up with psychiatric problems,"* the man said as he exhaled smoke and, the room without an ashtray, tapped ashes onto the floor. *"We've got enemies, John, and if our psychic spies are good, they might end up kidnapped, murdered, compromised. And surely you don' want that for her, do you? So instead, John, what if we had a psychic spy that didn't even know she was a psychic spy? Maybe then she won't end up like her grandmother."*

John nodded his stoic face. *"What did happen to her? Esther?"*

The man shook his head. *"A story for another day. You know I saw her, Esther, in action before. If she's anything like her grandmother, Thomasina will be a great asset to us. So keep it up. Charm her, make her fall in love with you. In a few weeks, we'll bring her in. But we'll block those memories from her. John, she can't know, or we will lose her."*

John nodded and feigned a smile. *"Operation love and marriage, I've got it."*

Tomi heard the man speak, his voice growing more distant as the vision began breaking up and pulling away. *"As the man said John, 'may you live in interesting times.'"*

The vision went to black before reforming to her current reality, her body flopped on the ground, surrounded again in fog, feeling her grandmother's arms around her, feeling her grandmother's higher vibration flow into her as she worked to process what she had just experienced.

"You had a vision you hadn't expected, didn't you?" said Esther, embracing Tomi.

"It…it was John. From the past, back when we first met. He was using me for his career. I just feel so stupid," Tomi said, her body feeling heavy against the ground for the first time in this reality.

"Oh baby girl, I'm so sorry you are feeling that," said Esther, "but I am glad you experienced it. If there's a place where you can process these things and get perspective, it's here."

"You know, in Kirsten's near-death experience, my spirit came to her and asked her to protect me. It said that I'm trusting and can be taken advantage of," said Tomi. "Seeing that vision makes me wonder about everyone. Who can I trust? How do I know Ete isn't using me also. Maybe she's tricking me, too. How do I know any of it was real?"

"You think the best of people and that makes you beautiful," said Esther. "As for Ete, does it matter if what Ete says is true or not after all you've experienced? After what you're experiencing now? I mean, look where we are! You have gnosis Tomi, knowledge, direct experience of the divine universe. Try to put your trust in that."

Tomi sat quietly, being held by her grandmother, feeling a transfer of higher energy from Esther, like a battery being recharged. After some time, Tomi felt more balanced and deeply calm, which seemed to be her natural state in the Other Place. The vision, this new knowledge, quickly felt more and more remote, something that happened in that other world, some other place and time that was so removed from this new reality.

"Okay, I think I'm ready to keep going," Tomi said eventually, her light body easily standing up in the fog.

"Good, I think we're almost there," said Esther.

"How do you know?" asked Tomi. Surrounded by fog, she had no idea where they could be, no idea how anyone would navigate in this place.

"I can feel it," said Esther, turning slowly before proceeding, as though she were listening for which direction called to her.

They walked in silence for some time, their movements slow and graceful, until the fog became lighter and lighter and the view in front of them opened wide.

"You asked where the other humans are," said Esther. "Here are some of them."

The fog cleared in front of them, and Tomi found herself standing on a hill, overlooking an expansive city made of stone. The city was a wide circle, the circumference made of a seamless stone wall that hugged the outside of the city. It was big but not massive, grand but not grandiose. All of the buildings inside looked to be made of stone; not megaliths eroded by time, but stones cut with precise straight lines, the stone pieces cut to interlock perfectly. All of the buildings were short, one storey, except for one. In the centre of the town was a circular island, enclosed on all sides by a circular waterway, forming a ring around the centre island, where a large, impressive structure rose above the city.

"That's the temple, in the middle there," said Esther, pointing to the structure, a four-sided pyramid. Instead of enclosed walls, the pyramid was open, exposing the stone base of the structure. Four pillars of stone emerged from each corner, slanted and meeting in the centre, with a capstone on top.

Tomi gazed down at the settlement, feeling her emotions, her vibration rising from seeing something so grand, so masterfully constructed.

"How did they do this? Create this?" asked Tomi, her voice full of wonder.

"They've been here a long time," said Esther. "A long time."

"Who are they?" asked Tomi.

"Ancestors," said Esther, "the ones left from before the last cataclysm. The civilization that came before."

Tomi looked at Esther. "Atlanteans?" she asked.

Esther looked back, her face glowing with wonder. "Atlanteans."

As Tomi and Esther stood gazing at the small city, they sensed a movement behind them, a sudden change in energy. Tomi turned around to find Ete stepping through the fog, her Other Place body roughly the same shape as her Material Place body, tall and lanky, but like Tomi and Esther, she was also naked, the contents of her body seemingly a container for a liquid energy – *plasma bodies,* Esther had called them.

"Ete, you are here!" exclaimed Tomi, feeling the energy, the vibration of her body ramping up with her excitement.

As in the material place, Ete spoke into Tomi's mind telepathically. Tomi realized she and Esther had been speaking telepathically here, too.

"Tomi, do you remember," Ete said, "in one of our first meetings I showed you a vision, a cataclysm, the destruction of a great city?"

"I do," said Tomi, "it was so horrible. I remember calling out, asking for you to do something, to save them."

"And what did I say to that?" asked Ete.

"You said: 'We did,'" said Tomi, feeling as though her whole body was smiling, making the connection between that event and this smaller Other Place replica of the city.

"Of course, it wasn't just a city that was destroyed, Tomi," said Ete, her long legs moving her slowly and gracefully towards the two women, standing on the hill. "It was a civilization. A global civilization."

"So everyone died, except the ones you saved?" asked Tomi.

"No, not everyone," said Ete, standing beside Tomi and looking out at the circular stone city. "There were pockets that survived. The people who knew the land survived, the ones who could adapt. Not every human in the world was part of their civilization, just as not every human in your time is part of your civilization. Your civilization calls them 'uncontacted tribes,' communities of people who live in communion with the Earth. There were many like that during the time of the cataclysm too, who survived and continued on. You see, humanity can survive cataclysm. Your civilization will not."

Tomi thought about an article she had read about the Sentinelese, who inhabit an island in the Indian Ocean, and have been hostile to contact, throwing spears and shooting arrows at anyone who dares to try. She had shared it with John and remembered him being bothered that they lived in isolation, him saying, 'It's not right. Hell, they don't even know we put a man on the moon. It's crazy someone could live in this world and not know that.' They'd had an argument about it, him thinking it wasn't fair that we don't make contact. 'Think about all the medicines, all the good things we could share with them, all the technology. They should at least get to know what we have out here, give them the option.'

Tomi had asked him when contact had ever been good for the people being contacted, when it had ever not been followed with disease and violence and death. *Of course, our technology obsessed culture thinks billionaires flying us to Mars will save humanity*, Tomi thought, *when really it's people like the Sentinelese. The people who live in communion with the Earth, as Ete put it.*

"So you saved them and brought them here?" asked Tomi.

"No," said Ete, "just like with you, our role is not to be your saviours. But we did help to teach them to ascend, as we did with you two. Some of them were doing it already. They were advanced in their spirituality the way your civilization is advanced in your technology."

Tomi looked at Esther and noticed her nodding as Ete spoke. She realized Ete had probably told her this before, since Esther had known to bring her here. "So they ascended and just stayed here? They don't go back?"

"They have to go back," said Esther, "just like us. This isn't a permanent place for humans."

"So…where? How would we not notice Atlanteans?" asked Tomi. While this conversation should have been overwhelming, mind-blowing even, Tomi instead took this information in with a sense of wonder and patience. Being in tune with the information field, as Esther had called it, much of this information felt easy to grasp, even familiar.

"You didn't notice us, did you?" asked Ete with amused energy, a feeling Ete would share in place of an audible laugh. "Or notice any of the others living on or around the Earth. Or the beings who live here, in this place, who might cross over."

"The universe is abounding with life," said Esther with a tone of excitement.

"I've heard that," Tomi said to Esther, remembering the vision Ete had once shared with her, a glimpse into the overwhelming diversity and preponderance of life in this universe. "I don't understand though. They are human, just like us. Why would they hide from us?"

"That was part of the agreement. You see, the Earth is special, and special to many species, many civilizations, not just humans. And because of that, we must cooperate to preserve it."

As Ete spoke, Tomi felt herself pulled into a vision, as though Ete's eyes were a film projector and Tomi's mind was the screen.

The Earth was in front of her, glorious and bright, swimming in immense darkness. As though viewing the Earth in fast forward, she saw the Earth changing, getting colder and frozen over until the ice eventually melted and the green took over. She saw glimpses of life booming then receding, adapting and changing, destroyed and flourishing again. She was overwhelmed with feelings of love for this chaotic and nourishing planet and a deep feeling that it was rare and truly special.

She began to see faces, some of them human, or almost human, while others were very not human. Faces like Ete's, with her oversized cat eyes, and the Greys, with their teardrop-shaped heads and large eyes, much like the tattoo on Sixto's hand. There were faces that looked like reptiles, but the eyes were extremely intelligent, almost human. And another like an insect, similar to a praying mantis, but again, intelligent, advanced. The faces intrigued her but also gave her pangs of fear and anxiety. They weren't all from Earth, or from this Other Place, but they all had an interest, an agenda, with the Earth. And they had an agreement. A federation. An understanding: *leave the Earth alone.*

She also understood that this rule applied to Ete's people. Ete had just said that they were teachers, but that they could not be humanity's saviours. For the first time Tomi understood that it wasn't that Ete's people couldn't save us; they wouldn't because they had agreed not to. *Humanity is surrounded by life,* thought Tomi, *but we're all alone.*

Then she saw the people, the Atlanteans, some ascending before the great cataclysm. But they were not only Atlanteans; people from other civilizations, other empires, ascended as one people, and when they did, they joined in the agreement. Their time had come and gone; they had moved on from a purely materialist life. They, too, would leave alone the ones who came after.

The vision faded to black, and Tomi's consciousness returned and she found herself sitting with Esther and Ete on that hill, looking out at the city. "I…I see," said Tomi, finding herself surprisingly not overwhelmed receiving this information, her Other Place state instead feeling calmed by these insights. In her material body, these experiences would leave her exhausted and overwhelmed; here, new information, a new understanding seemed to energize her even more.

Tomi was looking at Ete while she talked, but in her periphery she saw a movement that drew her attention. They watched as a ship, a long cylindrical craft, shiny and metallic, rose from the stone city, slowly at first, then disappeared, winking out of existence. Tomi was unsure if it disappeared or shot off at an impossible speed.

"You gave them the craft," said Tomi. "You taught them."

"Yes," said Ete simply.

"And you will give them to us," she said.

"Yes," said Ete. "When you are ready."

Tomi didn't ask Ete to explain. She already knew. That we weren't ready to have this kind of power, that we possessed the intelligence, the ingenuity to use it, but lacked the spiritual awareness needed to not exploit it and turn it to destruction. She looked at the stone city, the people who had ascended, and understood that this could be her path, our path. To survival. To ascendence.

"Leave the Earth alone," said Tomi. "That's the understanding, the agreement. But you've been in contact with me, with us. What about abductions, all the sightings?"

"We are not to reveal ourselves, not directly interfere, but that doesn't mean there is no contact," said Ete. "Remember when I told you each species has its own agenda with the Earth? Agreements come with compromise. Leave the Earth, leave humanity alone, doesn't mean no contact."

"Right," said Tomi. She looked down towards the stone city again. "I have many more questions, but right now I'd like to go see this city. Meet these people."

Esther laughed. "Oh, I remember saying the same thing when Ete showed this to me."

Tomi looked to Ete. "I'm sorry Tomi, until the right time, it's just not permitted."

"But, I mean, it's right there," Tomi said. "We've already ascended, we're here in the Other Place, this place. And they're human, just like us. Surely they would like to meet us?"

"Surely they would," said Ete. "When they came here, when it was understood that there could be no contact, they protested. They had come so far, learned so much, and with human civilization destroyed, they wanted to share. It was agreed that they could give some gifts, some knowledge, but only the seeds of civilization. So they returned, they shared their knowledge of agriculture, writing, of spiritual understanding, but only bits, only the seeds, and the rest would be up to you. That was and still is the agreement. Until then, this city is off limits."

Tomi thought about her conversation with Arthur Minear, how he talked about a cataclysm wiping civilization off the Earth, like erasing chalk from a blackboard. He believed human civilization was cyclical, rising and falling, and that civilization today isn't actually our first try at it. We are just the latest rise. And the next to fall.

"Were they the first then?" asked Tomi. "The first human civilization to take this step, to ascend?"

Ete didn't answer in words. Instead Tomi could see – *feel?* – from looking in Ete's eyes that the answer was no.

"Let's sit here and meditate for a while," said Ete. "I've said as much as I can right now. But perhaps, Tomi, the universe has more to share with you."

Tomi looked at the circular stone city and wondered how they did it, how they created such a seamless structure with heavy stone, and thought about them sharing this gift, this talent and technology with the ancients and seeing them become master stone builders themselves. Even on this cyclical Earth there was continuity, across cataclysms a sharing of knowledge.

She closed her eyes and felt herself instantly fall into a deep state of inner peace. She held onto the darkness and enjoyed the sensation of her body's vibration, leaving her both at peace and energized. Tomi felt herself tuning in, connecting to the vibrations around her, and felt herself aided by her friends, and by her surroundings. She expressed an openness to receive, to see what she needed to see.

An image started to form in her mind, coming together slowly. She saw the colour green, and as though someone were drawing lines, the green started to break up into individual trees, then individual leaves, moving and swaying slowly. In the centre of this forest a figure emerged. At first Tomi was confused by the shape she was seeing, initially thinking it was a butterfly until the details became finer. It was a person, and she was looking down on them from above. They were seated cross-legged, and their shoulders and bent legs had at first looked like the wings of a butterfly.

Though she had been expecting a vision that would teach her more about the ancestors, she found the setting, the trees familiar. Tomi noticed the long blond hair on the person, and knew immediately who she was looking down upon: *Kirsten*. She paused to regulate her excitement, not wanting to lose the vision like before. She needed to be an impartial observer.

Unlike the other visions, she was far from Kirsten, looking down on her from a height. Again it was as though she were seeing this through a transparent sphere, but she was more distant than in the other visions, hanging above the treetops. She wanted to get closer but found that she wasn't moving, as though she couldn't delve below the treetops. Tomi tried not to get frustrated so as not to disrupt the vision.

She tried calling out, *"Kirsten! Up here!"*

Kirsten did not look up, staying still in her seated position.

Tomi told herself to be patient – an impartial observer – and focused on the trees, watching the leaves sway gently in the breeze. She imagined being back home, back at the cabin, sitting with Kirsten, sharing that breeze. Tomi felt a pang of homesickness for her life in the Material Place, but before she could dwell on it, something in the vision changed. It was small, a slight change, but something was moving. It was Kirsten. She got closer, just a little closer to Tomi, yet her posture hadn't changed, as she was still seated cross-legged among the trees. *How is she closer?* wondered Tomi.

"*Kirsten!*" she shouted again.

Tomi thought Kirsten moved closer still. She imagined herself reaching out, as though her arm could stretch and her hand could almost touch Kirsten. *She's floating*, thought Tomi. *Levitating.* She imagined herself reaching out even closer to Kirsten, but before she could touch her, Tomi felt her pull away, as though she had fallen back to the Earth, to the ground, away from Tomi.

The vision went to black, but it didn't feel like it was over. Tomi found her consciousness travelling again, surfing an ocean of information, looking for one specific drop. She started to see a colour palette forming again, as a new vision came together in her mind. Again, it started with green. As the picture became defined, she found that she was sitting in a hilly green field with craggy rocks embedded into the ground, bounded by tall wild grass. The field was bordered by fog, making Tomi think that she was seeing something in the Other Place.

To her left she saw a large rough stone, looking like it was dropped onto the side of the hill years ago, the bottom of the stone now part of the hill. From behind this stone Tomi saw movement. She looked directly at it and saw nothing for a few moments, before a face emerged again from behind the stone.

The head and face were humanlike but small, the size of a toddler's. The features were sharp, the nose, ears and jaw seeming to end in abrupt angles, and there were grey streaks of hair on each side of the head, looking almost like horns above the ears. The being's eyes were dark and intense, and it stared directly at her, its mouth stretching into a chilling smile above its long, pointy chin. When she first came to the Other Place, she couldn't imagine finding danger here, but now she felt scared and threatened. Instead of the chills and goosebumps she would have felt with her material body, here she felt slower, less energized, less clear in her thought.

The being crawled out from behind the stone, its smile widening even more. Tomi saw that it was indeed small, like an old person in the body of a toddler. It crawled on all fours for a few steps, holding eye contact and smiling, then stood up and moved quickly towards her. It was so close Tomi could see its yellowed teeth, seeing what looked like two rows of teeth when it opened its mouth wide.

Tomi broke eye contact and looked at the being's small hand, reaching towards her. She suddenly heard her grandmother's voice, something Esther had told her, a memory from childhood she had long forgotten: 'Count the fingers, count the knuckles, count the teeth,' her grandmother had said, a moment long forgotten but remembered at just the right time. 'If they don't have the right number, you might just be dealing with the fae, the fairy folk,' her grandmother had said.

Tomi looked at the small hand and counted seven digits: six fingers and a thumb. Just as the bony fingers were about to touch her body the vision faded to black. She felt immediately safe, as though the memory of her grandmother's lesson had protected her. She sat in the peaceful darkness for some time, focusing on her emotions and vibration, resetting herself before her consciousness was sent in yet another direction.

And in another direction it went, as a new vision swept into her mind. Tomi again found herself in the sphere, floating and watching a scene. She saw brown, and as the picture came together, she saw that the brown was wood: wooden floors, a wooden desk and bookcase. She was floating within this room, as though she were a fly high in the top corner of the room. There was a wall with pictures and certificates hung symmetrically. It was familiar. The door opened and a person walked in. It was John. She was watching him in his home office.

Tomi felt a moment of panic, thinking she would be spotted, then remembered she was just a fly on the wall. John wasn't young this time, instead looking to be roughly the age he was the last time she saw him. Another man entered the room behind him, wearing a black golf shirt tucked into beige dress pants. At first she didn't recognize him without his uniform. But she quickly knew. It was the General.

As he spoke, his voice connected several memories in Tomi. It had been him in that white room, talking to a younger John about her, about his mission. And she knew it was a voice she had heard many times before. She remembered the vision of her grandmother remote viewing the moon. The man, the moderator whose face she hadn't seen. It was him then, too.

"*I know you're not going to like it, and I know you are protective of her, I respect that,*" said the General, walking behind the desk and settling into John's leather chair. John took a seat on the leather couch facing the desk. "*You care about her, John. I need you to understand that I care about her too. She's important to us. But she hasn't given us what we need.*"

"*So what do you have in mind?*" John said cautiously.

"*You're going to bring her into the Perceptual Studies Institute. PSI. It's here in Durham. We've already been contracting with them, so the relationship is already there, but they can't know about Tomi. I want you to bring her in through your consultancy, as a ruse. You're testing their work, so to speak, by bringing people in just for the experience, to learn about remote viewing. And you know, John,*" said the General, "*what she can do. She will be a standout. Then I will contract with them and have them bring her in. Simple.*"

John listened without interrupting, the General being his superior, but Tomi knew John, knew his faces and body language, and could see he was uncomfortable.

"*Why?*" John asked. "*What will be different than bringing her in the way you have been?*"

"*We're under pressure to get results, John,*" said the General. "*We've kept the work secret even from her, so that she's not conscious of the work she's doing. We've had advice that perhaps she can't reach her full potential this way. That her abilities may be enhanced if she puts her full self into it. If she knows what she can do and has confidence in her abilities. If she's passionate and wants to do it. In doing it this way we can wind her up, let her go, and see what she can do for us."*

John stood up from his chair, looking at the pictures on the wall. *"So, you want me to support her to become a remote viewer, a psychic, in the open."*

"I didn't say I wanted you to support her," said the General, standing up and stepping towards John. *"Do you know how to lead a pig into a butcher shop, John? You see, pigs are stubborn. If you try to push it into the door, it'll push you right back. But if you turn the pig around and push, it'll push back. It'll push you back all the way into the butcher shop."*

"Right to its death," said John, looking like he wanted to say more but respecting rank.

"We're under pressure John. We're getting closer to a point where we don't control the narrative. We need to make progress before the big secret is out and all hell breaks loose. We need results. We need her to close her eyes and read their user manual for these craft. Without it, John, I'm not sure what happens to this country," said the General.

John remained quiet, facing his wall of pictures, avoiding looking directly at the General.

"We good, John?" asked the General.

John looked down for a moment before turning to face him with a stoic face, giving one solid nod. The General nodded, stood up, and started towards the door, whistling while he walked.

Tomi was still watching from within her orb, hovering just above the door. As the General walked towards the door, Tomi thought she saw him give a quick glance up towards her before exiting the room, like he knew she was there.

She looked at John, falling back into his chair and rubbing his face with his hands. The vision went to black, and Tomi felt her meditation ending, awakening to find herself seated on the hill overlooking the stone city, Esther and Ete both facing her.

"Tomi, how do you feel?" asked Esther. "Are you okay? We could sense, could feel that you were experiencing something difficult."

Tomi felt positively energized from her surroundings, and from Esther and Ete being here watching over her. Despite all that she had just experienced, she found that she rebounded quickly, feeling safe and secure despite these painful and terrifying visions.

"I…I saw a lot. I'm not sure I'm ready to talk about it all, but being here now with you both, I feel okay," said Tomi. "Nana, when you did your remote viewing of the moon, do you remember the man who was the moderator of that session? His name?"

"No," said Esther. "I'm not sure I ever knew it. But I can meditate on it. Why?"

"I believe that man was the General. The one that was hunting me. Had John working me, manipulating me. I believe that was the same man, and that he was working you, too. What do you remember about him?" asked Tomi.

"Tomi, that might be a breakthrough. I told you some of these visions might not be pleasant, but we seem to find the ones we need. You are seeing these things for a reason. But as for that man, I don't remember much about him. I remember he was well spoken, a bit intense but always professional. He was an outsider, not someone who worked at SRI, but came in for certain missions. Oh, but there was that one day," said Esther, trailing off as she retrieved a memory.

"One day, what?" asked Tomi.

"Well, there was one day, we had just finished the session and he was about to leave the room, when he turned and said something to me that made me think he knew something about me, more than just that I was a remote viewer at SRI. He turned and he said, 'That was certainly an interesting session. It almost sounds like the kind of thing Dick Harris would come up with.' And before I could say anything, he walked out the door."

If Tomi had the physiology to do so in the Other Place, she would have felt chills. "And Dick Harris was the one from your experiencer group. The one you thought was a disinformation agent."

"That's right," said Esther. "And I believe that was the day we did the remote viewing of the back side of the moon. Because I don't think I ever saw him again. That was one of my last remote viewing sessions before I met Ete. And left with Ete and came to this Other Place."

Tomi sat with this new information, adding so many new details to this mystery, but prompting so many more questions. She looked around, feeling herself energized by her surroundings. She looked at Esther and Ete and felt safe, reassured.

"Will you tell me how you first met Ete?"

Chapter 13

"In Egypt was located the Great Lodge of Lodges of the Mystics. At the doors of her Temples entered the Neophytes who afterward, as Hierophants, Adepts, and Masters, traveled to the four corners of the earth, carrying with them the precious knowledge which they were ready, anxious, and willing to pass on to those who were ready to receive the same. All students of the Occult recognize the debt that they owe to these venerable Masters of that ancient land."

Three Initiates

Kirsten turned onto a gravel road, the roadway getting narrower, wide enough for only one vehicle, as the forest closed in on both sides of the road. She pressed the seek button on the radio, as the radio station she was listening to was getting more and more staticky the more remote she drove. The radio scanned through the bands, picking up nothing until it finally caught a talk radio broadcast.

She slowed down as the road forked and poked her head towards the windshield, trying to stretch her memory back to the last time she made this trip. Of course, that time she had written directions provided by Ib; this time she was trying to find a remote cabin in West Virginia by memory.

She sighed and looked at the time, worried she would end up in a maze of mountain roads in the dark. She wished Tomi were riding shotgun with her. *She wouldn't need a map*, Kirsten thought, *she could just do some psychic shit and we'd be on our way.*

Kirsten turned down the radio and closed her eyes. "Help me here, Tomi," she said quietly to herself. She waited, hoping some message would pop into her head. Instead she felt a sensation in her abdomen, a sudden pop of energy, and she opened her eyes. *To the right, climb in elevation, to the left, the colour blue*, Kirsten thought. She turned up the radio, pressed the gas, and after slipping on the gravel, the car pulled off to the right.

"Today the *Bulletin of the Atomic Scientists* made an announcement about the Doomsday Clock, a measure of the likelihood of human-caused global catastrophe. In an unprecedented move, the clock has been changed for the second time in a calendar year and now sits at sixty seconds. One minute to midnight," the voice on the radio said.

Kirsten turned the volume up. She felt as though she had woken from a coma into a world that was familiar but not quite right.

"In January the clock had been moved to seventy-five seconds, that's one and a quarter minutes, which was the closest to midnight it had ever been set. In an action the *Bulletin* has never taken, they have made a mid-year change, and set the Doomsday Clock to a new time just months after the last change."

Kirsten felt her skin break out into goosebumps as she steered left onto the narrow road she had anticipated.

"The *Bulletin of Atomic Scientists* cite the reports of nuclear warheads going missing during recent coups in central Asia, accelerating weather events due to climate change, and the rapid decline in global trust in institutions. What do you think? Are we headed for catastrophe, or is this just a lot of hot air? We're going to open the phone lines now–"

Kirsten pressed the power button on the stereo and the voice was immediately silenced. She slowed the vehicle to a crawl, feeling like she was getting close.

The car inched along the rough road, with overgrown trees brushing the side of the vehicle every so often, producing scraping metal sounds. She was about to hit the gas, thinking she had been mistaken, when she saw it: an almost hidden driveway to the left, marked with a blue triangle atop a white circle painted on the trunk of a tree.

She pulled onto the overgrown drive, the car now being brushed by pine branches, before the car emerged in a clearing with a small cabin at the centre. Beside it was parked an old blue Ford pickup.

The same one, Kirsten thought, *he had said he would take to pick us up at the other side of the mountain*. Of course, they had never made it, and none in the group had seen him again.

Kirsten opened the car door and stepped out, pausing for a moment to stretch after hours of driving. Suddenly she heard a voice from behind her.

"I feel like I've seen a ghost."

Kirsten turned and found a man with chin-length sandy hair and an ungroomed beard, dressed as he always did, as though he were about to start a hike in the woods.

Kirsten gave an apologetic smile. "Hello, Sixto."

Sixto helped carry Kirsten's bags from her car inside his cabin. Kirsten looked around and found that not much had changed, besides his already full bookshelves looking more like an overstuffed cornucopia. His record player, an old wooden unit beside his bookcases, was spinning, the needle catching the edge of the record and making a scuffling sound.

Sixto set the needle back in place, then moved to the kitchen while Rodriguez began to sing through the stereo. "'Cause I lost my job two weeks before Christmas; And I talked to Jesus at the sewer; And the Pope said it was none of his god-damned business…'"

"Have you ever tried makgeolli?" Sixto asked as he picked up two small clay bowls and a clear bottle with a milky liquid inside. "It's Korean rice wine, I have a friend who brings it when he visits." Sixto joined Kirsten on the couch, and poured the white liquid into each of their bowls. "Cheers," he said.

Kirsten took a sip and frowned, slightly repulsed yet wanting more.

"It's an acquired taste," said Sixto, lifting the bowl with both hands and taking a sip. "Now, down to business. I know the four of you got out somehow. I have some friends on the inside, and I got that much out of them. But then nothing, I heard nothing for what, a year? Two years?"

Kirsten nodded apologetically. "I'm sorry we weren't in touch with you and left you wondering. Let me try to explain."

As Sixto refilled his bowl with makgeolli, Kirsten explained their encounter with the General, John, and the soldiers, how she had been shot just before they were all saved by Ete. She told him about being picked up by Ete's craft and travelling to the Hilly Island, their trip through space, about Ete's underground home, Ib and Barry's departure, and finally, Tomi's mission. Her ascension. Sixto listened patiently, a few times almost interjecting to add other similar experiences he had heard about, but he held back and let Kirsten finish her wild story.

"And now she's gone. She's gone to what we call The Other Place. It's like a different, or higher dimension, or something. There we were in Ete's meditation room, under a mountain. One minute Tomi was meditating, and the next minute, she was gone. Just, poof," Kirsten said, making fireworks with her fingers and trying to hold in tears.

"Poof! That's…wow, that is far out! What a story!" said Sixto excitedly. "And then what? Will she come back?"

"I…I think so. But I'm not waiting around. I know that she needs me. She told me so. Well, her soul told me so," said Kirsten, struggling to not doubt herself as she presented this unbelievable story. "So, that's my goal. My mission. Tomi and Esther and Ib and Barry have their missions. Mine is to follow Tomi, find her, and protect her. I've come to believe that she can't do this without me."

"So, you want to go interdimensional too," said Sixto, expressing no doubt or disbelief in Kirsten's story, as though the Other Place was just some other state or country.

"Yes, well, yeah, that's my hope. The other day I had a meditation that felt promising, but when I woke myself up from it, I just knew that I needed to come here. That this was the place for me to go to move forward. So…any ideas?"

"Well, going interdimensional, that's not something I have experience with," said Sixto, "but it's something I've heard about. And suspected. Hey, actually I do have an idea!"

"You do?" said Kirsten, encouraged. "That's great. I can't seem to get deep enough in my meditations."

"I think you should talk to our forest friends," said Sixto simply.

"Our…forest friends?"

"Yeah, sasquatch," said Sixto, as though the answer were obvious. "Bigfoot. They're interdimensional, too."

Although Sixto had told them about his sasquatch gifting experience, and though the apple that had been sitting on the Gifting Stump had disappeared with Tomi and Kirsten sitting just beside it, and although Kirsten's experiences told her that many things were possible, she still struggled to take sasquatch seriously. Sixto had believed her story without reservations, so she tried to hide her own.

"Sasquatch is interdimensional?"

"I think so," said Sixto. "And it explains so much. Why a body hasn't been found, why they can be sighted one second and gone the next. Get this, one night I was in the forest, and I heard something up the mountain a ways, so I pulled out these thermal binoculars I have. Now, if you see a human using these, you'll see their body, their form, but usually the head shows up red-hot while the body is colder. Can you guess why?"

Kirsten shook her head. "Clothes?"

"Yes, clothes!" agreed Sixto. "So on this night, I saw a human form. But it seemed way big in comparison to the trees. And the whole body was red hot, not just the head. So I figure it was either a Bigfoot, or the world's tallest man taking a naked midnight hike on the mountain. Now, which scenario seems more likely? Anyways, I was watching it through my binoculars, when I slipped on the rock under my foot. The rock rolled down the hill and made just the slightest sound. I could see the figure turn towards me, then," Sixto snapped his fingers, "just like that the figure was gone. Disappeared, the heat signature was just gone, like it was never there. Isn't that wild?"

Kirsten nodded her head slowly. "It sounds a bit like Tomi. Here one minute, gone the next. But it took Tomi a long time, a lot of practice, before this happened. Could it really just disappear, or ascend, or change dimensions, with the snap of a finger?"

Sixto didn't skip a beat, excited to share his experience and theory with a willing listener. "Evolution! There's actually a word for it: crypsis. It's the ability of a species to go undetected. What if that's how they evolved? Or maybe they originate in the Other Place, as you call it, and just come here to visit. Maybe they are just built for interdimensional travel in a way that humans aren't?"

"Maybe," said Kirsten, unconvinced. "But I don't think Bigfoot is going to sit down and give me instructions."

"Probably not," said Sixto, "I've been trying to introduce myself for years. Tomorrow you could bring an apple up the mountain, put it on the Gifting Stump, and meditate there. Maybe something will come to you, or a little of their magic will rub off."

"Maybe," said Kirsten slowly. Even if she didn't really believe in sasquatch, the idea of them gave her chills. "Okay, I'll try that tomorrow."

"And here's another thing. Most pictures of them are blurry. Maybe that's because they are interdimensional, sort of both here and not here," said Sixto. He then smiled and let out a big laugh. "Do you know the great Mitch Hedberg? He was such a great comedian. One of his jokes was," Sixto said, clearing his throat and trying his best Hedberg impression, "'I think Bigfoot is just blurry, it's not the photographer's fault, and that's extra scary, there's a large, out-of-focus monster roaming the countryside. Run, he's fuzzy, get out of here!'"

Kirsten trudged through the forest, rising in elevation, scanning for something to help move her in the right direction.

"You'll find a small clearing with an upside-down tree. Then you'll be close, just another minute or two of climbing and the land levels off, and that's where you'll find the stump," Sixto had told her.

She scanned the trees, looking for one that was upside-down, unsure what it would even look like without having a frame of reference.

"What do you mean upside down? Like it's fallen and landed upright somehow?" Kirsten had asked.

"Oh no," said Sixto. "This is intentional. Imagine something walking through the forest, something big and really strong, that pulls a tree out by its roots, then impales the top of the tree into the ground, so that it stands tall with the roots on top instead of branches and leaves," he had explained.

Kirsten dropped her head again to watch her steps as she hiked higher up the mountain. As she passed a dense patch of brush, she felt a twinge in her stomach telling her to look to her right. She continued for a few steps as she watched, seeing only ordinary trees in a forest, straightened her gaze, then looked to the right again.

"Holy fuck. How did I miss that?" Kirsten muttered to herself, her body suddenly frozen, goosebumps forming all over her body as she gazed at this ordinary object – a tree – almost unrecognizable to her brain by simply being flipped upside down.

Sixto's description was simple – a tree sticking upside-down from the ground, roots on top – and yet it took her two glances and a few moments before she recognized it right in front of her. She remembered once reading a myth about the Indigenous people in Australia not seeing Captain Cook's ships approaching, as they were so outside of their context, it was like they didn't see them until they were right in front of them. It was just an upside-down tree, and yet it was like her brain struggled to make sense of it.

She approached it to get a closer look. Just as he had promised, the tree was driven straight into the ground, the massive root structure joining the forest canopy.

What could have done this? Kirsten asked herself, rubbing the goosebumps on her forearms.

Feeling an urge to move away from the upside-down tree, she continued the climb until she arrived in the small clearing she had stumbled upon once before with Tomi. Kirsten thought back to that day and remembered telling Tomi about the mycelium network, the secret underground fungal communication network that links the forest together, just under our feet and out of sight. She remembered it was then they had found the gifting stump with the red apple placed atop it.

Kirsten scanned her surroundings, seeing only more forest. She felt a tension, like an early summer day where the weather looks clear and beautiful but the air is heavy and electrically charged. She approached the stump, pulled a green and red apple from her cargo pant pocket, and placed it on the stump.

"I…I come in peace," she said timidly, feeling embarrassed to be making peace treaties with the forest and its exotic creatures. Then she thought of Tomi, and her voice gained a tone of confidence. She closed her eyes. "I just want to find my friend. And I need your help."

Kirsten paused and listened, hoping the breeze would be carrying some instruction, some interdimensional password. She listened, but heard nothing. The forest had gone quiet. No birds sang, no critters moved through the brush.

Kirsten opened her eyes, blinked them into focus, and found herself gazing at a large old oak tree at the edge of the clearing. Though it had obviously been there on her last visit, she hadn't particularly noticed it, but now found herself energetically drawn to it. As she lifted her foot to step towards it, the birds resumed their songs, and the breeze whistled through the leaves again, as though someone turned up the volume knob for the forest.

She put her hand on the craggy bark of the old tree, and rubbed her fingers along it as she circled it. Kirsten couldn't believe what she found on the other side. There was a huge cavity at the base of the tree, as though something had somehow hollowed out the trunk, creating a cavern inside just big enough for a human to crawl into. She looked up and found that the branches of the tree were extensive, all covered in healthy foliage. *How is this possible?* Kirsten wondered. *How can this tree still alive?*

She touched her hand to the trunk of the tree, and knew what to do. She bent down, crawled inside the tree cavity, and found there was just enough room for her to sit cross-legged. She touched her hands to the inside of the tree, as though they were shaking hands in greeting. She closed her eyes, and began to meditate.

Kirsten focused on her breathing, and visualized her chakras lighting up with energy, eventually seeing her seven coloured chakras pulsating not just in her body, but within the body of the tree, as though they had merged into one. She continued breathing gently to this visualization until it began to fade and a new image started to form.

As the image came together, she felt as though her consciousness was on the move, flowing down the roots of this hollow tree, through the network of life underground, and into the roots of the gifting stump. Only it wasn't a stump she saw. As though she had travelled back in time, the stump was but a young sapling growing in the forest. Kirsten was the sapling, the young gifting stump, looking out on its surroundings.

At first she thought she was receiving this vision from this tree, but being this tree felt so familiar, so personal, she wondered if this wasn't a vision she was receiving, but instead a memory, a past life she had lived before. In this moment of meditation, she was this tree.

The world felt so different as a tree. Without two eyes pointing forward, she could see and sense the forest surrounding her in a circle. Kirsten felt time slow right down – *tree time,* she thought. It felt like an instant and yet she saw all of it, every slow, boring second as she grew tall with the forest around her.

The seasons passed, each feeling like an eternity and the snap of her fingers simultaneously. The winters were slow but peaceful, and as spring came she could feel her body, the body of the tree, wake up from its winter slumber. Like pins and needles in her limbs after being seated for a long time, she felt her circulation return as the weather warmed. In the summer she could feel her girth growing all around, the season feeling like a big inhale without an exhale to follow. In the fall she felt her body slow down again, as though she were tired after a long and productive day. But most of what she felt in the fall was gratitude.

The life was long, the forest her world since she couldn't move. But it wasn't boring, and it wasn't lonely. Her life as a tree was slow and peaceful, and filled with deep and meaningful connection. Unlike in her human life where each individual has its own inner world, the trees were networked, connected to each other, with no sense of competition, only comradery and love. Together they were the forest, each individual integral to the whole.

Then it was the day the loggers came. The peace of the forest was disrupted, taken over by the smoke and squealing of the chainsaw. Though it was done quickly, her death was not fast. It was slow, painful, and heartbreaking. She was decapitated from her base, and unlike a human death, she continued to feel every cut of every limbs. The forest wept for her.

She felt so sad and so scared, she pushed this vision out of her mind, and it faded to black. She eased out of her meditation, and found her face wet, her eyes shedding tears. She sat in the cavity of the tree for some time as the deep emotions she had just experienced slowly faded away. When she was ready, she touched the inside of the tree again, giving it thanks from one conscious being to another.

Kirsten crawled out of the tree, and walked back towards the stump, stretching out her legs as she moved. The apple remained on the stump where she had left it. She thought to move towards the stump, but the experience had been so overwhelming, she instead headed down the mountain, back towards Sixto's cabin, feeling deflated.

Sixto was excited for Kirsten's return, and asked about her experience.

"It was, uh, well let's say I had a very deep meditation," said Kirsten, "very deep, and also difficult."

"Well that sounds great!" said Sixto enthusiastically. "That's what you want, right, to go deeper until you do the interdimensional thing?"

"Yes, well I don't know," said Kirsten. "I got deep, but then I had this vision, and it was painful and kind of scary. I'm just not Tomi. I can't make it to where she can. When I try I end up scared or confused and snap myself out of it. I realized today I'm never going to be able to do it. To get to her."

Sixto frowned at hearing this, then straightened his face as a thought came to him. He quickly went to his bedroom and came back with a small book.

"You're not going to get there unless you believe," said Sixto, flipping the book open. "Not just believe. Know you can. You can do it if you believe you can do it. Here, I was reading this and underlined it while you were off on your meditation. What are the chances I read this just now? This is from the Hermetica: 'But if you shut up your soul in your body, and abase yourself, and say, *I know nothing, I can do nothing; I am afraid of earth and sea, I cannot mount to Haven; I know not what I was, nor what I shall be*, then what have you to do with God?'"

Night had fallen as Kirsten and Sixto finished their fire-cooked dinner in silence, the fire, the moon, and the light from his cabin fighting off the growing darkness.

"More wine?" Sixto asked holding up the bottle while Kirsten poked at the fire with a stick.

"Why not," Kirsten said, picking up and holding out the metal camping mug that passed as stemware to Sixto. "You know, I was thinking about this fire on my drive up here. I was thinking about the night we sat out here with Tomi and talked about Plato's Allegory of the Cave. About how it applied to experiencers. I was thinking about how it made sense to me at the time, but now, after what I've been through, well I was thinking it feels like more than an allegory. And I wondered why the hell I ever got up and left the cave in the first place," she said with a sarcastic laugh.

"Right, I remember," said Sixto, placing the bottle on the ground beside him and sipping from his mug. "But you didn't get up and leave, did you?"

"I…what do you mean?" asked Kirsten.

"The prisoner in the cave. They didn't just get up and wander out of the cave. Someone dragged them out," said Sixto. "They didn't see the sun by choice. They were dragged out against their will. Just like you."

"Right," Kirsten said, drawing out the word as she remembered this detail. "But was I dragged? I mean I went with Tomi willingly. I chose that."

"Sure, but you were an experiencer before you ever met Tomi, right? Did you have those experiences by choice?"

"My god," Kirsten said, having a moment of realization that often takes time for victims to reconcile. "I was dragged out of my bed. By beings. I was dragged out of the cave."

"And even Tomi," Sixto said, his voice growing quieter and more serious, "who introduced you to her? Who pulled her into these experiences? I've never met an experiencer who was an experiencer by choice."

"Something is dragging us out of the cave," Kirsten said.

"Something or someone, or some*ones*, or some force is dragging us from the cave," said Sixto. "All over the world people have experiences, whether with non-human intelligences or near-death experiences or with cryptids or travels to mystical realms. Something is definitely dragging us out, deciding it's time for us to see the sun."

"So, I was right then," said Kirsten. "Maybe it's not an allegory at all."

"Maybe it's not an allegory at all," agreed Sixto.

They sat in silence for some time, staring into the fire, until Kirsten said, "I need a distraction from today's meditation. Tell me, what whacky ideas are you exploring these days?"

"Oh!" said Sixto excitedly, drinking back the last of his mug and lifting the bottle for a refill. "I've been diving into quantum mechanics! Or at least I've been trying to. I'm not sure I understand it at all, but it doesn't seem like anyone else really does either, so maybe I do understand it?"

"Interesting, tell me more," said Kirsten, welcoming the distraction.

"Okay, dig this. So scientists had a debate about light, whether it behaved like a particle or like a wave. They did this experiment called the double slit experiment, where they shot light through two slits against a wall to see how the light behaved. When they did it, they found an interference pattern, which indicated it was a wave. Think about dropping a few stones in still water, the way the waves will hit each other, that's the interference pattern."

"So light moves like a wave then?" said Kirsten.

"Right! But then the experiment was done again. This time they fired individual packets of light called quanta, and instead of interference, the light made individual dots on the screen, which seems more like a particle. But when they shot more of these quanta through, they ended up making the same interference pattern. So basically, the quanta were interfering with themselves, meaning that they went through both slits at the same time!"

"What? I don't think I understand this," said Kirsten.

"Me either!" said Sixto enthusiastically. "And that's not the crazy part yet. So they added a detector that would be able to see this while it's happening. But guess what? That's not what it saw. It saw the quanta going through one slit or another with no interference pattern!"

"So…particle then?" said Kirsten.

"Well, they remove the detector, and guess what?"

"Wave," said Kirsten, starting to follow where this was going.

"It was a wave," said Sixto, shaking his head in disbelief. "So when we're not watching, it's a wave, but when we are watching, it's a particle. Apparently, the very act of observing actually changes the way light behaves. And not just light, all matter does this. I mean doesn't that just make your head explode? It's like the universe is designed to act one way when we're not looking, and another way when we are. I mean, *pwah*," Sixto said, using his fingers to animate his head exploding.

"That's…wow, that is so confusing," said Kirsten, "I'm not sure how to feel about that. So, what does that actually mean?"

Sixto thought for a moment and leaned forward, the light of the fire casting shadows, deepening his serious expression. "Honestly, fuck if I know," he said, tipping his head back and howling a laugh.

Kirsten burst out laughing, appreciating Sixto's wise humour on a difficult day.

After a few moments of laughing, Sixto calmed down and continued. "But really, I don't know. I don't understand this stuff enough to draw any conclusions. But I just love this experiment and how confusing and counterintuitive the results are. It almost feels like some cosmic middle finger reminding us that every time we think we know something, it turns out we actually don't. For example, how old is the universe?"

"Oh, isn't it like thirteen billion years?" said Kirsten, the number feeling familiar.

"Right!" said Sixto like an encouraging teacher, his academic past always apparent in these conversations. "At least it was. While you were away – you know, under a mountain somewhere – they added another ten billion years. We have a new telescope that can see farther back and whoops, turns out the universe is ten 'billion'-with-a-b years older. And to me, that's fine, as we get new data we have to go back and revise. That's a good thing, that's what we should do. But it's also what made me so frustrated as an academic because for the most part, whatever the current understanding is must be and can only ever be the truth. And to me that attitude takes away our wonder, curiosity, a humbleness in our knowledge."

"Agreed," said Kirsten.

"And I suppose that's what I get from the double slit experiment," said Sixto, "a reminder to be intellectually curious and be open to new ideas. Hey, maybe that's the attitude you need in your meditation. Find a way to be curious instead of scared. I don't know."

"Yeah," said Kirsten, "you're right. I need to just keep pushing."

They sat in silence, the forest around them quiet, the hissing and crackling of the dying fire filling the air around them.

"So, something is coming," said Sixto, his usually excited voice taking on a sombre tone. "That's what Ete told you?"

Kirsten nodded, realizing she slipped that tidbit in when she caught Sixto up on their adventures, not considering how jarring and destabilizing that message could be.

Sixto nodded back in confirmation. "It's starting to fall apart. All of it. The systems. Relationships. The climate, the wars. It's all starting to break down. You see it in the news every day. But more than that, I can feel it. In my bones. And not just me. A few of us in my experiencer group have been having the same dream. Just destruction, cataclysm. And then light. Looking up at a light in the sky like it's the first time seeing the sun. And the words 'something is coming.'"

Kirsten wiped a tear from her eye, thinking about the vision Ete had shared. Thinking now about Sixto, about her parents, about everyone she'd ever met or would hope to meet all hurtling through space, completely exposed and fragile.

"It's okay," said Sixto, "I'm a hermit in the woods, remember? The apocalypse is kind of our thing," he said with a laugh, then settled and spoke softly. "Did Ete say when? Do you have a date?"

Kirsten leaned forward. "If I did, would you want to know it?"

"Good question," Sixto said with a smile, putting his fingers to his chin in thought, the teacher becoming the student. "You know what? Don't tell me." He tilted his head back and yelled to the sky. "Surprise me, God!"

Kirsten laughed and then smiled, always enjoying conversations that can swing emotions so comfortably. "That's good because I don't know. I'm not sure Ete knows. But they seem to think it's soon."

Sixto nodded. "Well then, we have no time to waste. I've been thinking, I know someone who I think might be able to help you. And I know you're here on the lam, but I trust him. He worked on the inside on all kinds of super top secret programs. I mean remote viewing, UFOs, all kinds of out there stuff. But he's retired now. I'm just thinking about the remote viewing connection. I know he knows a lot more than he's told me. I just figure that if Tomi and her grandmother have figured it out, it's likely he knows something about it. What do you think?"

Kirsten closed her eyes in thought. She didn't really see the connection and felt nervous about the exposure, but trusted Sixto's intuition. Why else would she have come here? "Okay," she said, opening her eyes and nodding. "I'll put my trust in you."

Chapter 14

"These creatures show a very disturbing interest in the human soul."

Dr. Karla Turner

Esther was chilled. Not only had she just encountered a being while remote viewing the far side of the moon, this man, the client, had just referenced Dick Harris from her experiencer group. She had already suspected that Harris was a disinformation agent. Did the man bringing it up know about Harris' disinformation work from the inside? Or had he been spying on her, doing some kind of background check? What else did he know about her?

"Hey Patrick, who was that guy?" Esther asked, coming out of the interview room and around the corner into the observation room.

"Which guy?" Patrick asked, distracted by labelling the audio tapes of the remote viewing session. Patrick was part of the SRI team and in charge of data collection.

"The guy," said Esther, "the client. He just left."

Patrick's head remained down, focused on labelling the tapes, but his eyes shot up to Esther over his glasses. He spoke in a whisper. "I don't know, but he gives me the creeps."

"You must have a name, position? Military? Intelligence?"

Patrick lifted his head to look directly at Esther. He no longer whispered, but kept his voice low. "Honestly, I don't know. I'm not sure who knows. We get some like that where it's so highly classified we don't get any background at our level. But, I've heard that he might head up some secret, inside remote viewing program. Perhaps with the CIA, but that's just hearsay."

"If he headed a remote viewing program, why would he need to come here and contract with us?" asked Esther.

Patrick shrugged while he put the tapes into their cases. "Your guess is as good as mine. My assumption with him is that it's better for me not to know anything. Why do you ask about him?"

"Oh, just, something he said before he left, just…" Esther trailed off as she thought about Dick Harris and the experiencer group, where she had met Ray. "Hey, do you know if Ray is in today?"

Patrick shook his head as he stood up and started to collect his things. "No, Ray's away. For a couple of weeks I think."

Patrick was about to leave the room before he stopped and picked up two envelopes, waving them as he spoke. "Oh, this reminds me, could you come in for an RV session on Friday? The client left a couple more targets they wanted to take a look at. They wanted *you* to look at, actually. They wanted a consistent viewer for each target. I guess that makes you the chosen one," he said with an awkward grin, oblivious to Esther's chilled insides.

Inside the sealed envelope was a card with only a location and a date written on it:

February 20, 1954.

Location: Edwards Air Force Base, California

Esther laid on the couch of the interview room, working through breathing techniques and clearing her mind for the remote viewing session.

She had wobbled on coming in for it at all. The way that man had brought up Dick Harris, then just left, she knew it was designed to mess with her, to leave her wondering if she was being monitored. He was showing her that he knew more than she did. Was more powerful than she was.

Like Patrick, the man gave Esther the creeps, but not in a sexual or violent way that some men emanate. That wasn't the energy he gave off. This felt coldly patriarchal, about power and control. Esther, someone deeply attuned in reading people, didn't feel a good energy or bad energy or evil energy from him. There was no moral attached to it. Just power and control.

But in the end, she was too intrigued, too curious. That last session, while it ended uncomfortably, had been such an incredible experience for Esther. Her vision had been so clear she almost felt like she had in fact travelled to the moon. Then seeing the being, feeling a sense of communication, a sense of communion with it. *Fuck him,* she finally thought to herself, *I have to see where this goes.*

"Okay," Esther said quietly, in a deep state of relaxation and clarity, "I'm ready to begin."

Patrick read into the record: "Remote viewing session two. Session begins at 10:47 a.m., October 21, 1989. Subject has spent twenty-three minutes to get into a meditative state. Okay Esther, are you ready to receive your target?"

Esther breathed in gently, cleared her throat, and quietly said, "Yes."

"On the table beside you," Patrick said, sliding the sealed envelope towards her, "is a sealed envelope. Focus on the instructions in the envelope. They will guide you to the target."

Esther focused on her third eye, putting her energy into receiving a vision, trying to be patient. After a few minutes of little flashes or movements, lines started to appear, eventually joining together to create shapes.

"I see a sort of rectangle. And there are lines going in different directions. Not lines, roads I think. They are all completely straight, except for one that is curved and kind of wraps around it all," said Esther. "It's a building. The rectangle is a big building. Wait…"

After a few moments of silence, Patrick nudged her. "The raw data is good, you don't need to interpret."

"I can see it more clearly now," Esther said quietly, her voice relaxed, distant. "It is a building. An airplane hangar. The roads are runways for planes. I'm kind of seeing it from above."

"What else do you notice?" asked Patrick.

"I'm kind of zooming in, and I can see some of the airplanes. They are military I think. Yes, this must be a base. But the airplanes don't look like they do today. They seem new, but older. Like I'm seeing in the past…" Esther said, trailing off.

"No need to interpret where you are or when you are, just describe what you see," Patrick said, reminding Esther to focus just on her impressions.

"There is something drawing me to the building," Esther said.

"Good, follow that."

Esther took a few minutes to move her focus and let a new image emerge.

"There are people outside the building," said Esther. "In lines, like they are standing in order. Military formation. The front of the building is open, there's a huge door for the airplanes to get in and out."

"Do you have a sense of why they are gathered there?" asked Patrick.

"There's someone here. There's an airplane and some people are coming off," Esther said. "It's more of a passenger airplane."

"Can you get any detail about the people coming off the plane?" asked Patrick.

"Important. That's my feeling. It seems like all these people are waiting for them," said Esther, pausing for some time to gather more detail. "He's older, a man, in I think a grey suit. Kind of bald, I almost…I am picturing Eisenhower. President Eisenhower."

"That may be overlay, again, don't worry about interpreting," said Patrick.

"The other man is dressed in all red. A bright red. A little red cap on his head. A religious figure I think."

"Do you have a sense of why they are there?" asked Patrick.

"No, I…" started Esther, before pausing, finding information appearing for her, not as a visual, but as a knowing. "Something just happened. Someone gave an order to shut off the equipment. Like the radar, the tracking equipment. They turned it all off."

"Did you see them turning it off?" asked Patrick.

"No, I just sort of know. And now they are waiting."

"What are they waiting for?"

"A visitor," said Esther, her speech becoming less clear as she got deeper into the viewing. "Wow, I'm seeing this so clearly, detailed. There are lights in the sky. I see red lights. Five of them, in a V formation. They are approaching quickly. It feels tense, like none of the people are talking or moving. Everyone is looking up at the lights in anticipation. The lights are craft, I can see as they approach, silver craft. They land right there in front of the building. Five of them landing, landing in a V formation."

"Can you describe the craft?" asked Patrick.

"They are all circular, saucers but kind of fat, tall," said Esther groggily. "Four are smaller, and the one at the front, the centre of the V, is bigger, maybe twice as large. They all have legs that come out the bottom for landing. I don't see any windows, or…"

Patrick waited a few moments for Esther to continue, then prompted her. "You don't see any windows or, what?"

"The large craft opened, a ramp opened at the bottom," Esther said. "Three people stepped off. Three beings? I don't know."

"What do these beings look like?" asked Patrick matter-of-factly, not the first time he'd heard someone describe 'beings' while remote viewing.

"Human," Esther said, inflecting at the end of the word as though it were a question. "They are tall. Two have long hair, more white than blonde. Their lips, I don't know, they are different, they have no colour. They have on a sort of white robe kind of outfit. But the third has the white cloth wrapped around like a skirt. The chest is bare and they are wearing a huge headdress, like a bird. They have jewelry and head decorations. They look magnificent. Almost an Ancient Egyptian feeling. Like hieroglyphs."

"You see hieroglyphs?" asked Patrick.

"No. Like these people walked off of hieroglyphs."

"What happens after they come off the craft?"

"Movement, people are moving. There's a greeting of some sort, and the people from the craft, they divide up. The two in the robes seem to be showing the military people their crafts. The one with the bird headdress went back into the craft, and the man from the plane followed him on. To talk I think."

"Do you think you could enter the craft and find out?"

Esther drew in a deep breath, letting it out slowly. When she moved it wasn't like travelling from point A to point B, but rather the vision in her mind faded, then re-emerged as a new scene.

"They are sitting in the craft, it's like a large room, all metal. I don't see windows or controls or anything. Just two seats, like stools, and they are sitting on them facing each other."

"Can you hear what they are saying?" asked Patrick.

"Yes…" Esther said, trailing off as she processed the information. "Not hear. Think. They are not talking with their mouths, they are thinking the words."

"Telepathic?"

"Yes, that's the word," said Esther, her speech slow and groggy. "They are speaking telepathically. I can sort of get what they are saying. Almost like I can read it, the information is coming in so different."

"What are they discussing?" asked Patrick.

"A deal," said Esther. "The man with the bird headdress is offering a deal with the other man. The one that looks like Eisenhower."

"What is the deal? What are they offering?" asked Patrick.

"No…deal is the wrong word. Covenant. That's the word. They're offering technology. Their technology. The crafts. Energy. But more. Wisdom. Spiritual wisdom. But Eisenhower says no."

"Why did this man say no to this, this covenant?" asked Patrick, accepting Esther using the name Eisenhower for ease of communication, but unsure if she was simply having overlay. *She would have been a kid when he was the President. How many times would she have seen Eisenhower's face in her life? Her brain could easily connect the face to a similar looking man.*

"It would be for everyone," Esther said. "All people, their technology. And wisdom. And they want our nukes. All the nuclear weapons, we would have to destroy them all. But the man, Eisenhower, says no."

"Why do they want us to destroy our nuclear weapons?" asked Patrick. "To protect us from ourselves?"

"Yes…" Esther started, then paused. "No. It's more than that. They do something, the nuclear weapons. Time and space or something. Like we hurt more than just ourselves."

"How does the being, the one with the headdress, respond?"

"There's more he is offering. Asking. I have the sense that he, the being, is representing more than his people, his kind. There are others, and he is representing all of them. A federation, some sort of alliance or agreement.

"What is this federation offering?"

"A mission. An exchange. They will bring some people and we can send some people and learn about each other."

"Did the man in the suit agree to this?" asked Patrick.

"Yes," said Esther. "And more. They want to take people. Not like with the exchange. Secretly, they want to take people. For research."

"Did he agree to this?"

"Yes," said Esther, her groggy voice sounding confused. "The man, Eisenhower, wants names. The beings can do this but they have to share the names of people they take."

"What else is discussed?" asked Patrick.

"That's it," said Esther. "They will meet again. They walk down the ramp and exit the craft."

"Can you follow them out?"

"There's a handshake. Between the being and the man, Eisenhower. Then the beings are getting back on their craft…" Esther said before trailing off. "I'm just…they are about to leave, and I'm just drawn to one of the crafts. The one at the left point of the V."

"Can you follow that? Enter the craft?" asked Patrick.

Esther breathed quietly for a few moments before letting out a simple "Oh."

"What do you see?" asked Patrick.

"It…there's a being inside, but it's not like the one from the last craft. This one knows I'm here. I feel like it knows I'm here, but it's not surprised."

"Does it look like the other beings?"

"Oh no," said Esther. "This is something very different. It's taller, so tall, very thin and lanky. It's skin is green, I guess. Or brownish. It's hard to see, it has a kind of shine. A shimmer. Tight clothes on its thin body. Its head is big and its eyes, they are like the eyes of a cat. But so big. And such depth."

"How do you know it's aware of you?" asked Patrick.

"It's talking to me. Telepathically again. I just can't quite understand it. It's…like a warning. I…oh my. I just saw something. It shared something visual with me. Some kind of accident. On a bridge. Or bridges. It's like a warning about bridges, I think. I'm not completely sure."

"What else is it communicating with you?"

"That's it. It's gone. The craft are gone. The airplane, the passenger one, is gone. It's over," said Esther.

Esther finished the viewing and worked herself back to full consciousness.

"Another eight martini session?" said Patrick, returning to the room after gathering his recordings.

"Oh, not for me," said Esther. "That was intense. I need some rest."

Esther headed to her car, feeling sleepy, not looking forward to the long drive home. The image of the bridge, the destruction, came into her mind again. She thought about her drive across the bay, and decided to check in at a nearby motel and not risk the drive.

It was several days before Esther was called back in to SRI for another remote viewing. After the earthquake – a big one that flattened a portion of the Bay Bridge – the building needed to be inspected for structural safety before the SRI staff could return to work.

This time she didn't waffle about returning to SRI. She was still very put off by her interaction with the client, but these sessions, first viewing the moon, then viewing this meeting with technologically advanced beings had her too curious about this remaining target to pass it up. Plus that being she met at the end of the viewing, what that being had shown her. She hoped she could meet it again. She wanted to say thank you.

While Esther relaxed and focused herself, preparing for the viewing, Patrick placed an envelope on the table. The card inside read:

The planet Mars.

Time of interest approximately 1 million years B.C.

"This sealed envelope contains instructions about the target. When you are ready, access the target and report back the raw data you receive," said Patrick.

Esther's moderator Patrick had several coordinates he asked Esther to access. Esther saw a hostile landscape. She saw the remnants of an ancient civilization – roads, an obelisk, settlements dug deep in Martian rock, and of course, pyramids.

She saw shadows of people, an ancient civilization, and sensed the trauma their environment was facing. Esther entered a megalithic structure and found these beings meditating, waiting for a signal from their advance team telling them that a new home, on a new planet, has been found.

"I see the beings more clearly now," Esther reported back. "Three of them, but one closer to me. They seem to be meditating. Oh wow…I just get the sense that they are very spiritually advanced."

"What are you seeing?" asked Patrick. "What do the beings look like?"

"Tall, very tall and thin. I think…I think it might be the same kind of being I saw in my last viewing. The one at the end. Wait…" Esther trailed off as she watched the being turn its head towards her and open its large, catlike eyes. "Yes. It's the same kind of being."

"*We meet again,*" the being said. As in the last viewing, the communication was telepathic, the being not opening its mouth or making sound, the words simply appearing in Esther's mind.

"Are you able to communicate with it?" asked Patrick.

"Let me try," said Esther.

"*Is it you? The same being I met last time? You saved me,*" Esther thought, hoping her thoughts were shared telepathically. "*You showed me the bridge. The earthquake made part of it collapse. You were warning me. I hoped to see you again to say thank you.*"

"*That was me you met,*" said the being, "*but in the future, in a different body, but the same soul. We met in a different life.*"

"*I…I don't know what to say,*" Esther thought to the being. "*Do you mean you reincarnate?*"

"*We all reincarnate, Esther,*" the being said. "*Life, real life, cannot be destroyed. A soul cannot be destroyed. It would be like destroying the universe itself.*"

Just as with the destruction of the bridge, a new scene swept into Esther's mind, a vision shared by the being. She saw a sphere, bright in light and transparent, with swirls of colour moving and mixing inside, the outside of the sphere gently bulging then retreating, like a gelatinous glob settling after being flicked. Esther peered deep into the sphere, deeper and deeper until she saw swirling galaxies, then the sun, then the Earth, then zooming even faster towards her body, laying there on the couch at SRI.

It's the universe, thought Esther. *It's everything. It's all one. It's the most incredible thing.*

Esther zoomed back out and watched as the inside of the sphere – the universe, the one – began to pull apart into smaller pieces, then broke again into ever smaller pieces, each piece pulling away from each other but still held tight, together, within the sphere. These pieces, small bits of the universe, shimmered and glowed in all colours of the spectrum. Esther understood what she was seeing. These tiny pieces were souls, glowing and impossible in number, looking like all of the stars in the universe.

They are so beautiful, Esther thought as the meaning became clear in her mind. *They are souls, all kinds of souls having all kinds of lives.*

Again her vision zoomed in and Esther found herself viewing from inside the sphere, floating and surrounded by these bits of the universe, these star-like souls, each shimmering and shining beautifully, swirling with different coloured light energy, each unique and magnificent. She looked closer into one of the souls and found contained within it was a tiny universe, a miniature mirror reflection of the bigger universe, inside and outside, the part holding the whole.

Esther thought she might be crying, it was so overwhelmingly beautiful. She looked closer at one of the souls, this swirling glob of the universe, and noticed thin, almost invisible tendrils connecting the soul to other souls. She looked around and realized they were all connected by these tendrils, these strings tying each soul together into a matrix of life.

They are all still one, thought Esther. *They look disconnected but they aren't.*

"Esther," said Patrick, pulling Esther's focus away from the vision, "what are you experiencing? Were you able to communicate?"

"Just…just a minute," said Esther, her words slurred as though she were talking in her sleep.

"*So you see*," said the being, pulling Esther out of the vision and back inside the megalith, looking at the seated being with the catlike eyes. "*Death is not possible in this universe.*"

"*What…why divide up into all these souls?*" thought Esther. "*What's the purpose?*"

"*I wonder*," said the being, "*what an infinite number of souls with an infinite number of lives, could experience. Could learn.*"

"Esther," prompted Patrick.

Esther felt annoyed having him interrupt this experience. She knew she needed to report back, but paused, questioning whether she wanted to share any of this with that man, the client. This experience felt like it was just for her.

"Sorry," Esther said, "I thought I might be able to communicate but I wasn't able to."

"That's okay," said Patrick, "what are you seeing now?"

"*What is the point of it all?*" thought Esther to the being. "*With all of those experiences, what is it all for?*"

"*That may not be something we get to know,*" said the being. The being blinked its catlike eyes, then closed them, and turned its head back to where it was when Esther first viewed it.

"*Please,*" thought Esther, "*please tell me more. Show me more.*"

"*There is so much more I will share with you,*" said the being. "*At another time. May I contact you again?*"

"Esther, what are you experiencing?" asked Patrick, getting frustrated with Esther's lack of reporting.

"Sorry, it's just…" Esther said, trailing off.

"*Yes,*" thought Esther. "*How will you contact me? And what is your name?*"

As soon as she thought the word 'yes,' her vision quickly chipped apart, replaced by darkness.

"*Call me Ete,*" the being said through the darkness.

"Esther?" prompted Patrick.

"I…I lost the vision. Lost the target," said Esther. "I think I'm done for today."

"No problem," said Patrick, "take your time resurfacing."

Esther lay on the couch for some time with her eyes closed, reviewing what she saw, what she heard, not wanting to forget a moment of it. Eventually she got herself up, went to the washroom, and instead of stopping to debrief, headed right out to the parking lot and to her car, and drove home. Exhausted, she flopped into bed and fell immediately asleep.

When she woke the next morning she remembered no dreams, only a deep, dark sleep. But she awoke with a knowing that she would be travelling today. She got up and opened the top door of her dresser and pulled out and unfolded a map of California. She didn't need to look at the legend. Her eyes darted to the right location on the map. She found the words that were on her lips the moment she awoke: Mount Shasta.

Esther stepped out from the mountain path into a clearing with a small stone hut placed in the middle. She read the trail sign: *Welcome to the Horse Camp*. Her shoulders went limp to let her backpack fall from her body. She raised her arms to stretch her back, lengthening her body and gazing at the snowy peak stretching up to the darkening sky.

She flopped down onto the grass, exhausted, wondering what she was doing at the base of this old volcano.

Forty-eight hours prior, Mount Shasta had no relevance to her life, a place she had heard of before, but not one she had ever visited, or ever thought to. Then she woke up yesterday morning and Mount

Shasta was all she could think about, was calling to her, telling her that she needed to be there.

Esther had done some camping and hiking in the past, so she went down to her basement, pulled out a sleeping bag, tarp, raincoat, knife, and a few other essentials, and put them in her old hiking backpack, one she hadn't used since she was a much younger woman. But today, she would use it again.

She got herself dressed, put on some comfortable socks, pulled on a pair of old boots, and walked out the door. She stepped towards her car, then stopped in her tracks. *No*, she thought to herself. *I will go by bus.*

Esther walked to the bus station wearing her backpack, knowing nothing about her destination or what she even hoped to find there. She bought a ticket for Mount Shasta, found her way to the bus labelled Seattle, and sat in silence with strangers, all heading north towards the Cascades.

After a long and gruelling bus ride, Esther started seeing signs for the village of Mount Shasta. She saw advertisements for motels, lodges, and bed and breakfasts, and felt reassured that she would be able to find a warm bed tonight before hiking to the mountain the next day.

Esther stepped off the bus and turned to walk back towards a roadside motel she had spotted from the bus window, an older, rundown motel that belonged to another era. When she had passed it, it reminded Esther of the motels she had stayed in with Joanna when they had crossed the country on motorcycle, the nostalgia drawing her in.

After checking into her room, she opened the windows to clear out the musty air. She stepped outside under the overhanging roof and breathed deeply, watching the gentle rain fall and taking in the peaks of Mount Shasta in the distance.

"A lot of mysteries up on that mountain," said a voice coming from her right. She turned and found a man seated on a folding deck chair, enjoying a cigarette outside his room. Esther hadn't noticed him when she had come out. He was older, perhaps her age, or slightly younger, but with a wrinkled face that comes with a difficult life. Esther hadn't planned on talking with anyone, as this obsession with Mount Shasta felt like a solo journey, a secret quest. But Esther wasn't one to be rude.

"Oh?" she replied. "What kind of mysteries?"

"UFOs. A lot of UFOs have been spotted up there," said the man, pausing to take a drag. "Shadow creatures. There's even a story of a city hidden under the mountain, with an advanced civilization living there. From Lemuria. Ever heard of it?"

Esther nodded, familiar with the story of Lemuria, the legendary Atlantis of the Pacific. "I've heard of it. Do you believe and of that?"

"I'd like to believe a lot of stuff," the man said with a laugh that turned into a cough. "But I'm from Missouri."

Esther smiled, and the man leaned back in his chair. Esther was about to turn back towards her room when he spoke again.

"And it's holy, you know. The first people here said their creator spirit lived there, that he descended onto the mountain and defeated the spirit of the underworld by throwing hot rocks and lava."

"Interesting," Esther said, "I guess the lava would make sense with it being a volcano."

The man nodded. "An active one, too. That volcano is overdue for a major eruption. Could happen any time."

"You sure do know a lot about this mountain," Esther said. "Are you a guide or something?"

The man laughed, interrupted by another cough. "Hah, do you see me making the trek up there? No, not in this life." His facial expression grew sad as he dropped his cigarette into a beer can and leaned forward in his chair, towards the mountain. "Strangest thing. I've read all kinds of paranormal or alien stories, some that have involved that mountain. So I've always been interested in it. But a couple days ago I just had this sudden urge to get in the car and see this mountain. Like something is going to happen here, something incredible is coming. And well, I'm not a hiker, so I've just been waiting here and watching."

Esther felt the universal urge to spill her story, find comfort in another having a similar experience. To explain that she too had a sudden obsession with this mountain. But she bit her lip, feeling again that this journey was hers to have alone.

Instead, she smiled kindly. "And have you seen anything incredible?"

He looked at her and gave a quick, almost embarrassed smile. "Not yet," he said, his boyish smile fading as he looked back at the mountain. "Sounds crazy, I know. It just feels like something's coming. Here. And if I am crazy, well at least it's a great view."

"It sure is," Esther said, looking back at the mountain once more before turning towards her motel door. "Well, goodnight. I hope something incredible happens for you."

The next day she stepped out of her room and saw that the man had gone inside for a rest. Esther wondered what was drawing him – drawing them – there.

She caught a ride with a couple of hikers at the motel to the Bunny Flat, bought a park ticket, and started her hike. It was slow going for Esther, her hiking days long behind her. She took frequent breaks, and said hello to hikers heading both up and down the mountain. During the day the trail was busy enough, but somehow when she arrived at the Horse Camp, she found herself alone.

After a short rest in the grass, she willed herself up, hoisted her backpack onto her body, and headed for the lonely stone cabin at the centre of the Horse Camp clearing. The inside was sparse, with a few wooden tables and a fireplace at one end. While the heat of the fire would have been a welcome comfort, she was too exhausted to put in the effort. Instead, she pulled her sleeping mat and sleeping bag from her backpack, got her bed laid out, and sat on it cross-legged, eating some bread, cheese, and nuts she had hastily bought from a convenience store before heading to the mountain.

Once she was fed and watered, she climbed into the sleeping bag, the hard floor exacerbating her sore back. Nevertheless, she fell asleep almost instantly, and snored through the darkness, until she awoke in the night, startled from a dream. She sat up and looked around for a moment, remembering where she was, before recalling her dream. There was a hand that was reaching out to her. It was a big and thin hand, and though she couldn't count the digits in her dream, she knew they weren't right. It certainly wasn't human.

She lay herself back down and gave a little laugh. "Just laying here alone on a volcano having nightmares about alien hands," she said to herself. "Nothing strange here."

Esther closed her eyes for just a moment before sensing a flash of light. She sat up immediately and looked around, wondering if someone was arriving and had shone a flashlight in the window. She froze. Then she saw it again. It had come through a window, brighter and coming from a larger source than a flashlight. The light was now consistent.

Esther slipped on her boots, grabbed her flashlight, and slowly opened the door, peering around. With the light of the moon, she could make out the shape of the mountain. Then she saw the source of the light. There it was, a red, crimson red light coming from just behind the peak of the mountain. For just a moment her stomach twisted, thinking that the volcano chose this night to finally erupt after an eight-hundred-year hiatus. But it wasn't lava and it wasn't the volcano. Something else was coming.

She turned her flashlight off and crouched down to watch, the initial fear just washing away, replaced by awe. The light grew larger, a circular orb eclipsed by the mountain peak. It grew brighter, until it finally rose up and travelled over the peak, this glowing red orb.

As it grew, Esther realized it was descending in her direction, towards the Horse Camp. As it approached, she could see that the red light seemed to be a bubble, like an orb, with a triangular metallic craft protected inside.

The object got closer and the red light, the bubble around the craft, faded away, while the craft seemed to silently hang in place in the sky over the Horse Camp. Esther drew in a deep breath, stood up, and stepped further into the clearing, surprised by her lack of fear. She knew in that moment that this was why she was to come to Mount Shasta.

"Something is certainly coming," Esther said to herself, thinking of the man back at the motel. She held up her flashlight and flicked it on and off three times. As soon as she did this, the craft descended, this time not resting on legs, instead hovering silently just above the ground.

A door on the bottom of the craft slid open, and a ramp descended onto the grassy ground. Esther froze. She saw a being stepping slowly down the ramp, a being almost as tall as two humans, its body and limbs so thin and lanky. Then Esther saw the eyes, the catlike eyes she had seen before. It was the same being from her remote viewing of Mars. Ete. Here in real life.

Ete got to the bottom of the ramp and reached out her hand, just like in Esther's dream, and Esther knew that Ete reached out in welcome. She stepped forward, reached out her hand, and touched Ete's long, bony fingers. When they touched, she felt something, a flash of memories, a feeling of nostalgia.

"*Please come*," Ete said to Esther telepathically. "*There is much work to do.*" Ete turned, and they walked side by side up the ramp and into the craft.

Back at the roadside motel, a man dropped his cigarette, stood up from his folding chair, and leaned against a pillar for balance as he watched a light, beautiful and bright like fire, zoom around the mountain then descend into the trees below.

"Something came," he said to himself. He didn't think to pull out his camera, and as soon as the object descended out of view, he went back in his room and fell immediately asleep.

Chapter 15

"Thus the path of evolution for all living things is to raise this fire, whose descent made their manifestation in these lower worlds possible and whose raising brings them into harmony once more with the superior worlds. This myth of the life force that came down and took upon itself worlds is found among all the civilized nations of the Earth."

Manly P. Hall

Ib ran his fingers along the smooth wood on the dashboard, clenching for a moment when he looked up and saw Barry turning onto the left side of the road. *England*, Ib thought to himself, amazed at how bizarre it felt to sit as a passenger on the opposite side of the car.

"I don't understand, this doesn't seem like a typical rental car. What is this?" asked Ib. When Barry had picked him up at Heathrow, Ib was so focused on catching up with his friend, he forgot to ask about the unexpected vehicle.

"It's a seventy-three Jaguar," Barry said with a faint smile. "Classic British engineering. You should feel this engine when you really step on the gas."

"It's beautiful, but I don't recall ever hiring a car at the airport and getting something like this," said Ib.

"You don't. But if you arrive in London before your friend and you have the time, you just might be able to rent one online," Barry said. "Think of it like Airbnb for classic cars."

"Well let's hope this Arthur Minear is a car guy," said Ib, "and it distracts him from the surprise of the two of us showing up unexpectedly at his door."

Barry gave a laugh. "I know, the car is silly. And indulgent. And terrible for the environment driving this thing around, I'm sure. Sometimes it's hard to teach an old dog new tricks, even if you are the old dog."

Barry hit the gas to pass a slower vehicle and continued. "You know what's amazing, my nieces and nephews, you try to talk about cars with them and they couldn't care less. I mean our generation, we loved them. The engineering, the horsepower, faster, more comfortable, more gadgets. What would they come up with next year? We just took it for granted that cars were good."

Ib nodded. "We have taken a lot for granted. You and I have lived in the most opulent and indulgent generation in human history. And most of us don't think about it. Or realize it."

"Ain't that the truth. We assume that every year there will be more than the last. We just think this is the way it should be," said Barry.

"And always will be," agreed Ib. "And as a generation, I'm not sure we feel guilty enough for what this wealth has cost us. Has cost the kids."

"If we feel any guilt at all, we aren't showing it. God, we've been so fucking selfish, haven't we? I mean look what we've done. Here we are driving through southern England in July and it's what, forty-eight, fifty? In American degrees, of course," said Barry with a laugh, knowing Ib's feelings about American exceptionalism when it comes to weights and measures.

"Don't you get me started on your Freedom degrees," said Ib with a smile, always ready with a rant about the benefits of the metric system. "In Denmark the farmers were very worried about this weather. This sudden shift in the ocean currents. They were staging truck and tractor protests around the country demanding a bailout. But what if it's not just a blip? What if it doesn't change back to normal?"

"Have you been reading up on this Great Unrest?" Barry asked.

Ib nodded solemnly. "It feels like everything is spinning out of control."

"The centre cannot hold," said Barry, quoting Yeats. "It feels bigger. I think it's more than unrest. What if it's actually the start of a Great Unravelling?"

"Unravelling?"

"Collapse. You know how I feel about this," said Barry, shooting Ib a sombre look before returning his eyes to the road. More than once over martinis they had discussed civilizational collapse, Barry believing we were close, and Ib mostly not wanting to think about it, arguing human ingenuity would prevail.

"Ten billion people mostly reliant on stable weather, global shipping, and electricity. Do you know how fast things can unravel? I mean, imagine if the electricity gets turned off. Or someone explodes a nuclear weapon in the atmosphere and creates an EMP, knocking out all the electrical infrastructure."

"What then?" Ib asked, again running his finger along the wood grain of the dashboard.

"In America? We would have anarchy within a week," Barry said, shaking his head at the outcome. "Think about how many of us rely on refrigeration. For both food and medicine. No electricity, and the supply chain breaks down. Then it's a question of who gets the food that's left. Who gets the medicine that keeps them alive. Think about how many people rely on insulin to stay alive. And what parent of a diabetic child wouldn't take up arms to make sure their child got every drop of it they could. Multiply that by hundreds of resources, and you've got anarchy in no time. And what if no one was coming to the rescue? I'm telling you, civilization is a veneer on wood. It's that thin."

They sat in silence, feeling the variations and bumps in the road as the rubber tires sped over them, sending the vibration up the axle, through the body of the car, and into the bodies of the passengers.

"Of course, we both saw what Ete showed us," said Barry, "the cataclysms. You ever hear that saying that the Inuit have fifty words for snow? Feels like we have fifty ways to watch it all collapse."

"Fifty ways to leave your lover," said Ib with a smile. "In this case I guess our lover is Earth."

Barry smiled, appreciating gallows humour. He pointed ahead, drawing Ib's attention to a fast approaching sign that read: *Welcome to Cornwall – Kernow A'gas Dynergh.*

"You know, you said earlier that this is the most opulent generation in human history. I wonder if Arthur Minear will agree with you, what with his theories on lost civilizations. Human history is a long time, after all."

"I'm happy to revise my statement if it means he will help us," said Ib.

Barry nodded. "I just hope he agrees to talk to us. He's known to be very private. It wasn't easy locating him."

"How did you manage that, by the way?" asked Ib.

Barry smiled. "Let's just say someone in the Intelligence Community overestimated their chances at beating me in a game of pool."

"Barry Class, part time spy and part time billiards shark," joked Ib. When he noticed Barry pulling the car off the motorway, he asked, "Where are we going? Do we need gasoline?"

"Just a quick stop," said Barry, glancing at the directions on his phone. "There's a megalithic site I've always wanted to see. It's on the way to Minear, I promise."

"Stonehenge?" asked Ib.

"Ib, Stonehenge is for the tourists," Barry laughed. "I joke of course, Stonehenge is incredible. But no, the Hurlers are actually *three* stone circles. Wait 'til you see it."

"It is a pretty car, Barry," said Ib, admiring the four round headlights, steel grill, and metal jaguar statue leaping from the hood.

"Come, they're this way," Barry said, pointing towards the trail leading from the small gravel parking lot, about half full with a few other visitors already parked.

"Welcome to the Hurlers," Ib said, reading from the sign near the trail. "So this is an ancient stone circle?"

"Late neolithic," said Barry, matching Ib's slower pace. "And it's three stone circles. Three circles all lined up in one direction."

"Does the name have some meaning?" asked Ib, interested in these ancient sites but nowhere near as versed in them as Barry was.

Barry smiled. "The legend around here was that some giants were playing a sport called hurling on the Sabbath, and got turned into stone. Thus, the Hurlers. Close by there are two larger standing stones called the Pipers, because they -"

"Were piping on a Sunday?" Ib guessed.

"Exactly. Here they are," Barry said, pointing to the scene in front of them. Ib stopped to look, zipping his coat to protect himself from the cool breeze. The wind blew over the rough grassy landscape, the vegetation more brown than green in many spots. Small hills rolled outside of the stone fields, and several horned black and white cows were grazing beside the stones.

"Granite, from around here," said Barry, as they approached the first stone, reaching his hand out to touch it. "Not like Stonehenge where they dragged some of them all the way from Wales. And only about half the stones are still here. They did excavations to figure out where all the stones were originally. And they are of course weathered now, but they had been hammered smooth."

Ib approached a larger stone, the tallest coming up to his chest. "So three circles, all in a line. What was the purpose?"

"The theory is that it was for ceremony, for funerals. But it has some celestial alignments, so perhaps they used that to hold them on certain dates, like the solstice," said Barry. "And it's not just the Hurlers and the Pipers, there are sites all over here. The Hurlers point towards burial sites, also built with massive stones."

"What I don't understand about these megalithic sites," said Ib, strolling around the inside of the circle, "is why here? I mean okay, the stone was nearby, but why this specific spot? What's so special about here?"

"And in the cases where the stone isn't nearby, like Stonehenge, or Giza, it just shows how important a specific location was to them," said Barry. "Or Pumapunku! The stones had to go up a mountain. The site had to have been pretty damned significant to put that much effort into moving huge stones there. And then there's the stone. What was so special about the stone in Wales that they would quarry it and drag it all the way to Salisbury? Surely they could have found a closer source of stone. So what made that stone so special?"

"Hmm," responded Ib. "Isn't it funny that for thousands of years, around the world, all sorts of cultures, every continent, we made these. All around the world, humans thought doing this, creating places like this, was important. We marked the sky on the ground in giant stones. And then one day we stopped thinking they were important. Stopped making them. Stopped even knowing how."

"Or even knowing why," agreed Barry. "God, I just love the mystery of it."

"Oh look, those must be the Piper stones," said Ib, pointing towards two larger stones in the distance. As Ib spoke, Barry turned his head in the opposite direction, seeing a flash of darkness. A dark figure seemed to vanish, or move behind a stone, off in his periphery. When he turned to look, he saw no figure, nothing out of the ordinary. He breathed in and tried to will his goosebumps away.

"Are you okay?" asked Ib, seeing the surprised look on Barry's face.

"Yeah, it's nothing. We should probably get back on the road, we still have a ways to go."

They walked back to the car in silence, and Barry steered the car back towards the motorway.

"Can I ask you," said Barry, looking straight ahead at the road, "were you worried getting on the plane to come here?"

Ib sniffed in a breath, thought, and nodded. "You mean was I afraid my flight would have a malfunction and plunge into the frigid North Sea? The thought may have crossed my mind."

"You know, with what you were told in Denmark, and John approaching you at the airport," said Barry, "and knowing what I know about the IC, well, part of me thought it might happen. Even would happen. And you know, I thought I saw John in the airport on my way here. He didn't approach me, and it was just for a second. Of course I might just be being paranoid. I feel paranoid."

"Well," said Ib, "maybe paranoia is what we need right now. Is healthy, even."

They drove on in silence, crossing the Cornish countryside, until Barry pointed to a small roadside sign.

"Mousehole," said Barry, "we're here. This is where Arthur lives."

Barry steered the Jaguar down increasingly narrow streets as they entered town, the car looking down on the idyllic, almost Mediterranean-looking Cornish town. The narrow streets were crowded with grey stone homes, the town built to hug the harbour and the Atlantic Ocean. Barry followed the map on his phone and parked his car around the corner so that they could walk the narrow laneway to Arthur's house.

They approached the nondescript grey stone home, looked at each other, then Ib gave three knocks on the door.

A small, older man with thin grey hair and a gently wrinkled face swung open the door, and began to say, "You're early," before stopping, surprised to find two strange men at his doorstep.

"Mr. Minear," Ib said, "we apologize for bothering you at home, but we–"

"No, no thanks," Arthur said firmly, beginning to close his door.

"Please, my friend and I have travelled a long way to speak to you," Ib said, putting out his hand to prevent Arthur from closing the door.

"I don't care if you hate my work or love my work, I don't take visitors, it's just not safe," said Arthur, pushing the door closed. Just before he could, Barry stepped his foot out to block the door.

"Mr. Minear, I think you would be interested in this," Barry said, holding out the etched green stone he had been carrying since Ib entrusted him with it back at the airport in Charlotte.

"Where did you…" Arthur started before trailing off, his face softening as he gazed at the small stone held out before him on this stranger's palm.

"Tomi told us to show this to you," Barry said.

Arthur drew in a deep breath, looking first to Barry, then to Ib, then back to the stone.

"Well, I suppose I should put the kettle on."

Chapter 16

"There are countless sightings of objects that changed size and shape in front of the viewers or split into several smaller objects, each going off in a different direction. In some cases, this process was reversed, with several small lights converging together to form a single large one, which then went dashing off. Over and over again, witnesses have told me in hushed tones, "You know, I don't think that thing I saw was mechanical at all. I got the distinct impression that it was alive."

John A. Keel

Vibrations spread like waves throughout her body, the buzzing of a billion tiny particles giving Kirsten the impression that she had separated from her rocky perch, from the very Earth that cradled her.

In her mind's eye she imagined the world around her, the trees, the forest, Sixto's cabin just down the hill. Like a royal perched on an elevated throne, Kirsten sat atop a massive stone jutting out from the soil, looking down upon the forested mountain sloping below. She imagined moving her hand from her folded legs, and touching her fingers to the hard granite under her body. Her body continued to buzz, the feeling of vibration lulling her into a deeper meditation, as strings of morning sunlight made their way through the gaps in the mesh of leaves and branches of the tree cover above her, warming her skin.

Today was the day that Sixto's friend would arrive with, Kirsten hoped, some guidance or advice to help her move further in her meditation, far enough that she could reach Tomi in the Other Place. She had continued her meditation practice twice daily while staying with Sixto in his cabin, waiting for this mysterious guest to come. She had reached some deep states in her practice – *heightened states,* Kirsten thought – where the vibration had taken over, making her feel as though her body was becoming lighter, higher, ready to float away. Each time Kirsten put up resistance, and the feeling broke. *Am I too scared? Fighting it? Or am I blocked somehow?* Kirsten asked herself.

On this morning, after announcing her meditation time to Sixto – 'I'm going to try again,' she had said, as she did each time she meditated – she had stepped outside and was hit with a memory of the time she had been here with Tomi. She remembered them rushing out of the forest trail and into the clearing around the cabin, Tomi urgently wanting to use Sixto's computer to contact Arthur Minear. She remembered that Sixto had been perched in meditation on this granite stone, overlooking the cabin.

On this morning it was Kirsten using this stone as her meditation perch. Kirsten used a few trees to help pull herself up the hill and onto the stone slab. She had sat down on the stone in full lotus position, closed her eyes, and began her meditation.

Now here she was again, in a heightened meditation, feeling her body vibrating, feeling light as a feather, as though she could float on a breeze right off of the stone. In her mind's eye, she saw her fingers breaking contact with the stone – the Earth – below her. Her legs were crossed, with her left hand resting palm-up to the sky. Her body remained seated and still, while the world around her seemed to drift, as though her body remained in place while the mountain, the Earth itself, floated away from her.

She saw the leaves and branches approach, then drift away below her as she rose above the treetops. Below her she could see the individual trees weave themselves into a unified forest. She floated faster, as the very mountain below pulled away, and she entered a huge cumulous cloud, her surroundings seeming to be replaced with a thick, foggy shroud.

Kirsten wondered if this was it, if she was finally breaking through to the Other Place. She let the thought pass by, not giving in to indulging excitement, and continued breathing. Soon, the cloud surrounding her drifted away, as though blown by a gentle breeze. When the fog lifted, it revealed a lush garden. In her mind's eye, patches of green turned into individual stems and leaves, the vision gaining clarity slowly like a Polaroid photograph taking form.

When the vision became clear and detailed, and the garden presented itself, Kirsten gasped, though she was unsure if it happened in her mind, or if her meditative body actually huffed out a sound. The garden was a large circle, with a continuous stone walkway that formed and encircled a labyrinth, with Kirsten at the centre of it, standing under a round pavilion. The lush plants grew up between the walkway, forming living walls that defined the maze. All kinds of flowers bloomed, some small and bountiful, others large and prominent, the petals seeming to have a slight luminosity to them. Kirsten saw her hand reach out and cup a large flower, examining the lightly glowing petals. She looked around the circle at the magical glowing blooms, noticing that every flower in the garden shared the same deep shade of indigo, the colour jumping off the petals, set atop the lush green plants that held them up to the sky.

Kirsten looked beyond the labyrinth and saw that this big round garden was perched atop a plateau, partway up a huge hill. Below the plateau she saw a meadow rolling gently down the hill towards the ocean below.

It's the Hilly Island, Kirsten thought, *from my dreams. From our adventure with Ete. Tomi's Hilly Island.* Kirsten experienced a warm breeze spiralling around her, as though the Island was wrapping her in a hug. She felt a deep sense of peace, and a feeling that she was cherished.

Then she saw a figure, a human-shaped figure moving up the hill, following the thin, rocky path leading into the circular garden. She watched the figure enter and traverse the labyrinth, zig-zagging through the garden, surrounded by glowing indigo flowers. It seemed to take a remarkably long time, and no time at all.

The figure was wrapped in a hooded robe, covering all but the face. Under the hood, the face was glowing brightly, so brightly it was impossible for Kirsten to make out any details. As the figure made their final turn in the labyrinth and approached Kirsten, she felt a deep sense of calm. When the hooded figure stepped into the pavilion, they gently pulled the hood of the robe from their head, allowing the glow from their skin to disperse, revealing the face of Kirsten's high school art teacher. Ms. Bacon's thick grey and white hair was pulled back into a braid, her large, blue-framed glasses resting on the end of her bulbous nose, her mouth forming the resting smile that had always made Kirsten feel safe to be herself with her teacher.

"*Ms. Bacon, you came to see me,*" she heard herself say. Kirsten felt waves of emotions, and she tried to let them flow through and not distract her, centring herself in this vision. She felt so happy to see Ms. Bacon's face, the woman who had given her confidence in her art and told her it was special, the woman who had pulled out old art books and spent lunch hours sharing beautiful works with her, inspiring her love of art and design. She had been a retreat, a source of safety through some difficult teenage years.

"*Well, well, if it isn't my favourite student,*" Ms. Bacon said, reaching her hand up to Kirsten's cheek.

"*You're not really Ms. Bacon, are you?*" Kirsten said, an energetic knowing telling her this was an avatar, a costume. Still, she was enjoying this moment with her old mentor. She looked into Ms. Bacon's eyes but saw only warm white light.

"*That's right,*" Ms. Bacon said, gently pulling her hand away, maintaining her smile.

"*You're a guide,*" Kirsten said, the sense of knowing seeming to arrive as she spoke. "*You're my guide. You helped guide me into this life.*"

"*That's right Kirsten,*" Ms. Bacon said. "*You remember.*"

"*No,*" Kirsten said, trying to pull up the memory, wanting to go back to that place, the place we go between lives, to remember being guided here. But the memory didn't come. *"I don't remember. I just know."*

Ms. Bacon smiled wider, the way she did when Kirsten gave the right answer in class, or when she shared a poignant insight into a painting. *"And you know that I am taking a form that is comfortable to you. I could also be powerful."*

Kirsten's vision suddenly whirred and swirled. Ms. Bacon disappeared while a commotion filled the air, and a huge shadow darkened the garden. Kirsten stepped to the edge of the pavilion to look up in the sky. She saw two huge red wings flapping, pushing the air down and causing the garden flowers to swing and sway in the swirling wind. Above her a massive dragon beat its red, leatherlike wings, breathing puffs of fire from its nostrils as it swirled smoothly through the sky.

"Or weak," Kirsten heard Ms. Bacon say, the garden suddenly at peace, the sky now clear and still, the dragon gone. Kirsten noticed a bird's nest, like a small woven bowl, resting on the railing of the pavilion. She stepped towards it to look inside. She saw the remnants of a shell, but no bird. Then she saw a slight movement below. In the dirt, below the railing, was a baby bird writhing and stretching, trying desperately to get its body to work, to get itself back to its nest before a predator came by, or before it baked in the warm sun.

Kirsten started to reach down towards the bird, to help it, when it disappeared. Her guide took on the form of Ms. Bacon again, standing beside her, smiling kindly, pointing to show that the bird and the nest were gone.

"It's okay," she said, *"I can take any form you like because I am not physical."*

"You aren't physical," said Kirsten, *"but you are visual. You need a form for me to see you."*

"As a human, can anything really exist for you if you can't see it?" Ms. Bacon asked. *"Come. I want to show you something. We need to go down. Deep down."*

Ms. Bacon turned to stand beside Kirsten, putting one arm around her shoulders, and raising the other up, pulling up slowly as though she was pulling on a heavy lever. The ground, the Hilly Island, cracked open, like a giant sinkhole, exposing a magnificent, sprawling castle, an ancient structure surrounded by lush green fields. Another world, another layer of reality, had been just under their feet.

Kirsten's vision dissolved, then reformed, placing her and Ms. Bacon at the entrance to the ancient castle, the huge wooden doors propped open for their arrival. Inside the gate she saw people going about their lives, selling wares, pushing wooden carts over the stone ground.

"It's a whole Kingdom!" Kirsten said, feeling like she had been suddenly immersed in the Middle Ages.

"Queendom," Ms. Bacon said, correcting her. *"Take a look at them."*

As though her eyes had zoom lenses, Kirsten focused in on the people inside the walls of the castle. They were women, all of them. They were working together, one helping the next, as they went about their efforts.

"*They are my ancestors,*" Kirsten said with a sense of knowing and appreciation.

"*You need to know how deep this goes, Kirsten,*" said Ms. Bacon. "*In your human life you have lineage, you have generations of ancestors to pull on. The wisdom of your mothers and grandmothers. Remember it. They are always here for you.*"

Kirsten's vision reframed again, and she found herself back under the pavilion in the circle labyrinth garden standing beside Ms. Bacon, the hilly meadow island back in one piece.

"*You have the divine in you, Kirsten. You are made in the image.*"

"*Made in the image sounds more like a look-a-like,*" Kirsten said. Despite years of therapy, struggling to ever feel she was good enough, she still found it difficult to accept this concept.

"*No Kirsten, the divine is you, just as you are the divine,*" Ms. Bacon said, taking Kirsten's hand and placing it between hers.

Kirsten nodded, knowing that accepting this would be necessary to ascending, to reaching Tomi. "As above, so below."

"*One consciousness having infinite individual experiences. All one. You know this,*" Ms. Bacon said. In a flash, Ms. Bacon had the hood of her robe back on, and was walking the labyrinth path, unwinding her arrival, until she exited down the stone path, back down the hill, disappearing.

As soon as she departed, the indigo garden and the Hilly Island too disappeared, and Kirsten found herself again immersed in the haze of the cloud, again sitting in full lotus position, floating above the forest. Once again she noticed the vibrations spreading around her body. She felt her body buzzing, rumbling deep, as though she were being shaken by a powerful speaker. This is it, Kirsten thought, trying not to suppress her fears, but let them flow into and out of her consciousness, allowing the vibration to grow.

Amid this moment of peace, a pang of worry hit her. She heard nothing, but felt like someone had called her name, someone in distress. Through the fog she saw a movement, a swirl, then suddenly, there she was, emerging from the shroud of fog from above, travelling downwards: Tomi. Kirsten tried to yell, to scream, but no sound emerged. For just a moment, she saw Tomi's face clearly, saw her mouth open as though she were talking – *or screaming* – though Kirsten heard no sound. She tried to reach out, to grab Tomi's hand, to connect with her, stop her movement, wrap herself around her and not let her go, but Tomi zipped past her in a flash, gone before Kirsten could touch her.

Bang. Sudden pain. Kirsten opened her eyes and reached down to grab her knee, which had somehow smacked against the flat stone perch she was sitting on. She started to cry, rubbing her knee but not crying in physical pain. She had been so close, she had felt it, only to have her soulmate flash by her, lost in some cosmic soup.

Kirsten rubbed her eyes, sniffed, and started to stretch, preparing to stand up with her sore knee. She looked out in front of her and saw Sixto standing down by the cabin, looking up at her and not breaking his stare, despite a car pulling into his driveway and parking just a few feet behind him. Kirsten saw a man get out of the car, say something to Sixto, and watched Sixto finally turn around to greet his guest.

Sixto stepped out of his cabin and into the sunlight, linked his fingers, and pushed his palms up to the sky, stretching out his body after being seated cross-legged for the past ninety minutes.

While he had tried to keep a regular meditation practice for many years, he was inconsistent, with laziness or hyperfocus on another project eventually taking his attention. Since Kirsten had arrived, however, he had been inspired to make meditation a focus, but he kept it to himself, a little shy about sharing this. Each time Kirsten would announce that she was going to meditate, he would wish her well, then find his own secluded spot, trying to match her meditation efforts each day. At this point, having done this for several weeks, he felt even more shy about sharing this, feeling silly that he kept it a secret to begin with.

At first he wasn't sure why he felt shy about it, but in today's meditation he had had an insight, coming to an understanding about why he kept it to himself. There were two reasons. First, despite years of meditation, years of studying the paranormal, the occult, human consciousness, despite his beliefs, he didn't believe enough in himself. He could believe that Tomi and Kirsten could reach some other dimension – it wasn't for lack of imagination or belief in the mystical – he just didn't believe that *he* could.

The second reason was that it rocked his beliefs. He had such an openness to alternative beliefs, a certainty that our accepted reality is a myth and that something far more complex was going on behind the scenes. But belief was easy. The idea that he could close his eyes and achieve ascension, that he, Sixto, could just meditate and transcend material reality, made our accepted, mainstream beliefs suddenly seem a lot more likely.

But he wanted it, wanted so much to stretch his consciousness beyond this cabin, beyond this physical reality, reach a new level of understanding mystics had been hinting at for millennia. He secretly, guiltily hoped that Alexander's visit would provide a spark, something that would get not only Kirsten to this Other Place, but would take him as well. This reclusive hermit suddenly didn't want to be left behind.

Finishing his stretches, he meandered around the outside of the cabin towards the gravel driveway, scanning the forest that rose up behind the cabin. That's when he saw it. A flash, a movement, something that pulled his attention.

Sixto held his hand over his eyes like a visor, focusing in on the treetops to his left. Squinting, he saw it again. It was a light, an orb, a glowing circle in the sky. But it wasn't a satellite, not a plane high in the sky reflecting sunlight. This seemed close. A small ball of light hovered over the treetops.

The light, the orange-hued orb, hovered in place.

"Hello," Sixto whispered, feeling as though the orb was looking back at him.

That's when it winked. The light wiped away, then wiped back into existence, hovering in place for a moment before moving quickly, zig-zagging a few times, then disappearing again.

Sixto waited for it to reappear, blinked deeply, and scanned the treetops, but the light did not return.

"Come back," Sixto whispered, still shielding his eyes from the sun, now scanning lower in the forest. He stopped scanning and forgot about the orb the moment he saw her.

Kirsten was meditating on his rock platform. At first Sixto was impressed that she was still meditating, knowing how uncomfortable that hard stone could be after a while. Then he leaned his face forward. Something was off. It was as though Kirsten was blurry, like he couldn't see the level of detail he should at this distance. He rubbed his eyes and looked again.

"What the–" he muttered to himself. His vision was still blurry, but it looked as though Kirsten wasn't sitting on the rock at all, but was instead floating just a few inches above it. Her body seated, legs crossed, levitating above the rock.

"Sixto! Sixto my man," came a voice from behind.

Sixto had been so transfixed, so immersed in this experience, he hadn't noticed the car pulling down the gravel drive and parking just behind him, hadn't noticed the engine shutting off and the car door opening and closing as his guest arrived.

"Sixto? What are you looking at?" came the voice again.

Sixto blinked deeply again, opened his eyes, and found that he could see Kirsten fine. She wasn't levitating. She was sitting on the big flat rock looking back at him, stretching and rubbing her leg.

A long-lapsed Catholic, Sixto made the sign of the cross, cleared his throat, and turned around with a smile.

"Alexander," he said, his voice a little uneven as he pushed down the rush of emotions he had just experienced. "Sorry about that, I was sort of just having a moment there. You ever wonder if you can trust your lying eyes?"

"That's easy. You can't," said the man flatly but with a smile, stepping forward to shake Sixto's hand, leading to a one-armed hug.

"Of course," said Sixto, starting to feel lighter. "It's great to have you here, Alexander."

"It's great to finally be here," said Alexander, breaking away from the hug and looking just beyond Sixto, "and it's great to finally meet you."

Sixto turned to find Kirsten approaching, looking groggy after her long meditation, and walking with a little shuffle.

"Ah yes, I am so excited to introduce you two," Sixto said, "I just love introducing good people! Kirsten, this is my friend Alexander."

Kirsten stepped forward and reached out her hand to the man. He looked like a retiree, a man in his early seventies, dressed finely with blue pants and a brown sport jacket. Though older, he had a full head of white hair, and boyish features that made him seem more youthful. Kirsten felt he had friendly eyes that made her immediately more at ease.

"It's a pleasure to meet you," said Kirsten.

"Oh, I assure you, the pleasure is mine," he said, holding eye contact with Kirsten, his eyes twinkling a reflection of the bright sun.

Alexander crouched down to blow on the bottom of the fire, getting the dried leaves and bark burning. He watched closely as the flames caught onto the kindling and started to spread. He watched it burn for a few minutes, then placed two quartered logs gently on top, propping them against each other. An older man, he groaned as he worked to get up from the ground, and gave Kirsten a smile.

"I tell you, if I had to choose between a campfire and all of today's technology, I choose campfire every time," Alexander said as he settled back into his chair. "It's my favourite smell in the world."

Kirsten nodded politely and looked towards the cabin, wondering when Sixto would be out with dinner. Alexander seemed kind enough, but Kirsten was struggling to engage after the otherworldly meditation she had this morning. Not only had she felt like she was on the cusp of breaking through and missed it again, she had that awful vision of Tomi zipping past her, just out of reach. She wondered what it meant, and found it left her feeling farther from Tomi than ever.

"Sixto tells me that you have quite a story to share, that you are looking for help. Some advice," Alexander said, his voice quieter, more personal than when he was waxing about fire.

Kirsten nodded, then looked back towards the cabin, seeing Sixto's form moving around the kitchen through the screen door. She did want Alexander's help, it was true, though she would have taken anyone's help if it pointed her towards Tomi. At the same time, she was uncertain what or how much to share. She trusted Sixto, at least enough to come to his cabin when she needed help. But she knew whatever they were all wrapped up in was big, big enough to be able to fake a world tour on her social media. Big enough to have gotten her shot. Mostly, she just didn't want to say anything that could put Tomi at risk.

"To be honest, Alexander, I'm…well it's hard to know what I should say and what I shouldn't," said Kirsten kindly. "It's not that I don't trust you, I–"

"That's okay, you shouldn't trust me. You shouldn't trust anyone," he said, pointing at his abdomen, in the area of the body that Kirsten had been shot, "especially with what you've been through."

"You– "

"Yes, I know," he said, settling back in his chair and emitting a laugh. "I'm old, in case you haven't noticed. So I'm retired. But I still do some work as a contractor. Thirty years on the inside, it's nice to finally get paid well. Anyways, I know about this, about Tomi, about what you're all wrapped up in. Well, I don't know it all I'm sure, but I know a few things. So how about we make a deal. You don't have to tell me anything that you don't want to, because I'm certainly not going to tell you everything I know. And I'm sorry about that, but I just can't, it's not worth the risk. But that doesn't mean I can't talk to you about things, well, more generally. It doesn't mean I can't help you. What do you say?"

He extended his hand. Kirsten looked at his kind face, the growing darkness hiding his wrinkles, highlighting his boyish facial features. Kirsten shook his hand as Sixto exited the cabin carrying a pot in his hands.

"Veg chili," he said, nudging a grill over the fire pit with his foot and placing the pot over the fire. "I've had it on the stove all day, but we'll let the fire finish it off."

"Thank you, Sixto," said Kirsten, so appreciative of how he had taken care of her this past while. She then turned to Alexander. "So, where do we begin?"

"Well, like I said, you don't have to tell me anything you don't want to," Alexander said, "but maybe you can set some context for me."

"Well," started Kirsten, wondering where she should start. It seemed he knew about Tomi and about the confrontation with John, the General, and the soldiers. She decided to start with what they learned from Ete. "Something is coming. Something bad. Destructive."

Alexander held eye contact with Kirsten for a long moment before nodding gently and saying sombrely, "Yes, I know."

"You know?" said Kirsten with surprise.

"Cataclysm. We know."

"How…how do you know?" asked Kirsten, wondering how far this man's knowledge went.

"Now that, I can't say," said Alexander, "sources and methods. But we know something's coming. A cataclysm so big it could erase our civilization from the face of the Earth. And, we also know it won't be the first time we've gone through this. Humanity, I mean."

"There are cycles," said Kirsten, glancing over to Sixto stirring his chili, eyes wide as he listened to this conversation, "that reset civilization. And the next one is coming. That's what we learned."

Alexander nodded as though he was confirming old news. "Like I said, we know. Of course, we weren't the first to know, if you think of the Mayans or the Hindu yugas. The cycles, the ages. I mean, the American government didn't need to invade Babylon to find this out, though of course we still did. I mean, there's enough evidence to fill the Grand Canyon that confirms that this, our high global civilization, isn't the first go-around for humans."

Kirsten was stunned. "I don't understand. This is known, but is kept a secret? Why?"

Alexander leaned back in his chair and smiled as though Kirsten had asked a childish, naïve question. "You probably think UFOs are the big secret. That the government knows there's a non-human intelligence present on this planet, and is keeping it hidden from the public. No, that would be quaint. I'm afraid the big secret is so much bigger than that."

"And this is part of the big secret," Kirsten said, suppressing the pangs of rage she felt at being kept in the dark. "Why would cataclysm be kept a secret?"

"Well, the idea of cataclysm isn't, of course. I mean we all know what happened to the dinosaurs sixty-five million years ago. Less well known is what happened to humans twelve thousand years ago. It's cyclical cataclysm that we don't want to talk about. It's a dangerous idea."

"Dangerous?" asked both Kirsten and Sixto in unison, smiling at each other after.

"It's dangerous, yeah. Here's an example, something you don't know, or know as a fact, that is part of this big secret. There's a ninth planet."

"Pluto," said Kirsten. "At least it was the ninth planet until they demoted it. Still not over it."

"Well, I have to admit I agreed with Pluto's demotion, but no, that's not what I'm talking about," said Alexander with a smile before turning more serious again. "Imagine Pluto was a big planet. Really big, like Neptune. And imagine instead of a circle, this planet has a long elliptical orbit, meaning it swings way out beyond the solar system, but when it swings back it swoops in much closer to the Sun. And the Earth. Think about what our little moon's gravity does to the Earth. It creates the tides, gently pulling and releasing the oceans. Now imagine what the gravitational pull of a planet the size of Neptune would do to the oceans when it swings through the neighbourhood. And that's just one possibility for a cataclysm. So yeah, we know about it alright."

"Yes, I've heard about this," said Sixto with a tinge of excitement, his love of big ideas trumping existential dread. "Planet Nine, Planet X. Nibiru. I've heard a lot about this."

"Right, you've heard about it, probably in some internet conspiracy forum," said Alexander, "and maybe some of what you've heard is even true. But officially it's junk, right? Pseudoscience. Part of our job is to keep it that way."

"But why?" started Kirsten, her voice emitting both anger and impatience. "Why is this a secret? What's the danger in being honest? Maybe we could prepare if we knew."

"Let me ask you, do you use toilet paper?"

"Uh, yeah…" replied Kirsten, thrown off by this turn of the conversation. "I mean to be honest I prefer a bidet, but sure, yes I do."

"Remember back when the pandemic first hit and we were going into that first lockdown, and there was so much uncertainty about how long it would last? Do you remember the one item that people immediately went out and bought up, hoarded for themselves? Toilet paper. Take away the two-ply, and people will riot.

"Now, let's say one day you find out that no matter what you do, you're going to face absolute horror and destruction in the near future. You and everyone you care about will die in a horrible way. Burned to death, drown. Maybe you hang on long enough to die from starvation in some nuclear winter. Tell me, if your full-time job was to make toilet paper, and making toilet paper took up five days a week of what precious time you have left, are you going to show up for your shift at the mill the next day? Hmm?" Alexander asked.

Kirsten shook her head.

"Me either. But here's the thing: I like toilet paper. And cars and electricity and running water and air conditioning and property rights and a functioning civil society. And so do the people keeping this secret. We only have those things, this society we have, if everyone shows up for work on Monday. Everyone plays their part."

"Capitalism is a hell of a drug," Sixto said, ladling chili into bowls and handing them out over the fire.

"And in the case of Planet Nine," said Alexander, pausing to blow on his dinner, steaming in the cool evening air, "there's nothing we can do. This isn't an asteroid hurtling towards us that maybe we can intercept it with nukes. How would you intercept something the size of Neptune? You don't. Besides, if it isn't Planet Nine, it's something else. I mean look at what's going on, the upheaval in the world. Did you hear that last week the Thwaites Ice Shelf in Antarctica collapsed? They call it the 'Doomsday Glacier' because once it goes, a whole lot more will follow. Barely made a blip in the news. And it looks like the cold snap in Europe is here to stay."

"And the trees," added Sixto. "There's some new tree virus ripping through boreal forests. I read about it this morning."

Alexander nodded. "Yeah. Something is coming alright."

They sat in silence for a moment, Kirsten stirring her chili around without an appetite. This conversation just made her want to reach Tomi even more. *If a cataclysm is coming, I want to go through it together*, she thought to herself before breaking the silence.

"What does this have to do with Tomi?" asked Kirsten, her voice on edge with frustration. "The big secret, the remote viewing, them using her and monitoring her. What does any of this have to do with Tomi?"

"Right. Well let's say a flood is coming, and you have a lifeboat, but nobody knows how to inflate it, how to make it float. Nobody, except maybe Tomi."

"What's another word for lifeboat?" asked Sixto with a slight grin. Kirsten shook her head. "An ark, of course."

Kirsten rolled her eyes. She usually ate up Sixto's offbeat humour, but tonight she was impatient to get some useful information from Alexander. "Okay, so what is this lifeboat? This ark?"

"Well, flying saucers of course," said Alexander, as though it were a given. "Though most of them don't actually look like saucers. Some are triangles, some are cubes, rods, acorn, bell shaped, you name it."

"How many do they have?" asked Sixto? "We have, I guess."

"Enough," said Alexander. "Enough that we should have been able to reverse engineer them by now, understand how they work, at least be able to fly them. But we can't. I mean, I'm talking about nine decades we've had them, nine long decades we've been trying to crack the code. And the clock is ticking."

"So they need to figure out how to fly them," said Kirsten, "because they know about a coming cataclysm, and these craft could take us to safety."

Alexander leaned his head back and smiled. "You'd think that, wouldn't you? That we would be figuring them out so save as many people as we could. No, no, no. They want a weapon. Sure, saving humanity from destruction is nice, but these are military guys, remember. All they're thinking about is winning the next war. They are the hammer, and the world is a nail."

"Same as it ever was," said Sixto.

Kirsten noticed a certain sadness in his voice whenever he talked about war, about violence. She nodded to him, wondering how she could bottle that attitude and share it with everyone.

"Why can't they use them?" Kirsten asked. "Why haven't they figured it out?"

"Well, because the crafts are bullshit," Alexander said, pausing while helping himself to more chili, letting them sit with that statement for a moment.

"Bullshit?" Sixto finally asked.

"Bullshit. They're nonsense. Okay, imagine you want to know how a car works. So you pop the hood, right? But inside you don't find an engine and power steering and electrical system. Instead, there are maybe a few play cables, hoses that connect to nothing. Some wires that don't seem to have any purpose. Like it's just for display, a plaything."

"So they're what, they're not real? Hoaxes?" asked Sixto, his eyes wide and curious.

"No, they are the real deal. Thing is, we think of them as technological. Nuts and bolts. And they are, in that they are real physical things you can touch, but…okay, here's one theory I will share. Let's say they don't come from some far off galaxy, but maybe come from a different reality. Another dimension, say, where the technology makes sense. And when they manifest here, in our reality, they look technological, they look physical. But it's like they are projected into our reality in this nonsense way. I don't know. If anyone really understands it, they never told me."

"But…" Kirsten started, having a hard time understanding this when she had had first-hand experience on Ete's craft, had watched both Tomi and Ete control the ship. "I mean, but they do work. They aren't nonsense, they really fly, I mean…believe me, they do."

"Oh they do, they definitely do operate in our reality. They work. They fly. We just don't really know how, and the nuts and bolts don't make sense. That's why some of us believe they aren't operated physically. That it's consciousness, somehow. Some kind of consciousness machine."

"Far out," said Sixto nodding, his eyes still wide.

"So here we are, nine decades later and we still haven't figured them out. And the secret is slipping out into the public a little bit more each day, so on the inside, there are some very impatient people. They want a breakthrough. The thing is, they've been putting engineers on it, and guess what, engineers can't work out how to back-engineer a spirit machine. But convincing these people to look at it as a consciousness problem, rather than a mechanical one, has taken a very long time. And so, I guess you could say that Tomi is part of the even-more-secret back-engineering program, even if she didn't know it. Basically, they hope that Tomi can make the crafts work."

I know Tomi can make them work, thought Kirsten, remembering Tomi putting on the helmet and using her consciousness to guide the craft.

"Where are all these craft? Area 51?" asked Sixto, his tone a mix of facetiousness and excitement. While Sixto had been friends with him for some time, Alexander had not been as open with him as he was being today.

"Oh, probably at points of time," said Alexander, his tone serious and sombre. "What's sick is that they are mostly not in government hands anymore. They're in the hands of private aerospace. Military contractors. People ask how could the government hide these things? Well, they don't. They buried them within the private sector to hide them from any oversight. We have the most incredible, magical objects, these incredible spirit machines just locked away for private military research. We put the Holy Grail in the lobby of a casino."

"Moneychangers in the temple," said Sixto.

"So these crafts, cataclysm, this is the core of the big secret?" asked Kirsten.

"Oh, my dear," Alexander said with an exaggerated laugh, "believe me, it goes a lot deeper than that."

"How deep? Next you're going to tell us the JFK assassination is part of it," said Sixto, only partly joking.

"Maybe if you add MLK and RFK and Malcolm X and DJT and a whole lot more people you have and have never heard of," said Alexander, again speaking with seriousness and gravity. "People always say about these things, 'How could a secret that big possibly be kept by so many people?' Well it's pretty simple. Dead men don't spill beans. Period."

"So people have been, what, *disappeared* to keep these secrets?" asked Kirsten, knowing the answer but asking anyways, wishing a government by and for the people couldn't really go that far.

"How else could you maintain it?" replied Alexander flatly. After a pause, he looked at Kirsten and continued. "Look, I've told you a lot more than I ever should have. But I'm telling you these things because you are in danger. Your friend is in danger. You're both alive today because you are both still useful. They hope to get something from you, that you will lead them to answers. But there may come a time when you stop being useful and instead become a problem. A liability."

"And then they will kill me. Us," said Kirsten coolly, but with a layer of fear in her voice.

"Like I said, a lot of people have died to keep this secret. Believe me, I know too well," said Alexander, mumbling the last part as though he were talking to himself. "I think that's all I will say on that topic. Do you have anything else you need to ask me?"

"Well…how do I ask this?" started Kirsten. She hadn't told Alexander where Tomi was, what her mission was, having a feeling that she should hold back. But without context, she wasn't sure how to ask with any precision. "Sixto thought that you would know a lot about meditation, about consciousness. I'm wondering, how does one…raise their consciousness, I guess I'm asking. How do I raise my vibration?"

"Hmm…well, do you exercise frequently? Keep a strict routine of physical challenge?"

"I mean…yeah, I try," said Kirsten, surprised by Alexander's questions.

"Do you meditate daily, striving to refine your practice?"

"Multiple times a day," said Kirsten, then adding "well, lately I have been."

"Do you avoid coffee, alcohol, and drugs? Do you eat a strict vegetarian diet, making sure you walk softly on this Earth?"

"I…yikes, maybe not the first three. But I have been vegetarian since I was a teenager."

"Well, some people say that these practices are really important. Now, I've met some truly spiritually connected people, people who have used their consciousness in truly magical ways. Some of them were overweight, never exercised, and were pretty dedicated carnivores. Sometimes it's that as well. We don't really know."

"You see," started Sixto, as Kirsten gave him a glance to remind him not to say too much, "Kirsten is trying to use meditation to raise her vibration. To connect with Tomi."

"I see," said Alexander, "well, I'm not really sure I can help with that."

Sixto's face looked immediately drained, disappointed by Alexander's response. He then turned to Kirsten, wearing a face of reassurance. "I believe you are going to find her. I think you are close. Remember that you and Tomi are made of the same stuff. One and the same."

Kirsten looked down and scuffed her boot along the dirt, feeling frustrated. She remembered the night under the stars when she had told Tomi that we are made of start stuff. 'I want to be made of star stuff!' Tomi had replied. 'You are,' Kirsten had told her. Now she didn't feel any of that magic.

"Yeah, I…I feel like I don't know how that works."

"Like sparks from one flame," Sixto started, his tone shifting to one of wonder. "From drug trips to abductions, mediums to prophets, near-death experiences and meditation, we're always told the same thing: we are one. Not just humans. The Universe. Consciousness. God. I mean how many different ways can the universe tell us this simple fact? And that's why I believe you can find Tomi. Because hey, you are God or the Universe or whatever you want to call it, right?"

Kirsten gave Sixto a forced smile, appreciating what he was trying to do. "Thanks. I get that, and I've felt it. I just don't understand how it works. I mean, I get it as a spiritual concept, but here I am, Kirsten, here in this body. I don't just close my eyes and bingo, there's Tomi, easy peasy, because the universe is one. I get the oneness, I just don't know how to be that oneness instead of being Kirsten."

Sixto nodded reassuringly. "I think the goal is to become both of those things. Kirsten and the universe at the same time." Sixto paused for a moment, looking off into the distance as he retrieved a memory. "Hey, I remember learning about this concept in Hinduism called Achintya-Bheda-Abheda. It means 'inconceivable oneness and difference,' which, first, what a great phrase! Yes, it's a oneness with God, and yes, our current experience is different from that oneness, and yet there's no contradiction in this. Struggling to grasp it? Hey, it's inconceivable to us, anyways."

"I like it. I'll meditate on it. Thanks Sixto," said Kirsten, patting him on the knee.

"I think you are in good hands with your friend here," Alexander said to Kirsten. "But now that I think about it, I actually do have one suggestion for you."

Kirsten leaned forward.

"Perhaps you should travel to a window place."

"What…I'll go anywhere I need to go. But what is that?"

"A window place is a place where the veil is thin, basically where there is a window to another place. Another dimension. The veil between realities is thinner there, and so it may be easier to cross over."

"Yes," said Sixto, with excitement. "That makes so much sense."

"This is a real thing?" asked Kirsten. "Where?"

"Oh yeah," replied Sixto. "The ancients knew this and treated them as holy places. Planetary grids, ley lines, dragon lines. We wonder today why temples and monoliths are built where they are, well this is why."

"I'll write down a few ideas for you," said Alexander, turning his body to face Kirsten directly. "I think that about concludes my usefulness, so with that, I am off to bed. Kirsten, I wish you the best of luck. I really do."

"Thank you," she said with a smile. "Can I ask you one more thing? Why travel all the way here to talk to me? Why risk it?"

"Sixto promised dinner over a fire with a beautiful woman," Alexander said with a laugh, then turned serious. "I'm an old man, and I'm tired of the secrecy. Not only is it just wrong, it's not in our nation's best interests. And I just hate what this big secret has done to people. People like you and Tomi."

"Well, I think it's brave," said Kirsten.

"No, it's not. I'm only saying these things because we're in the middle of the woods and I know how paranoid Sixto is about privacy. Would I say these things to you out in the world? No. Out in the world I don't know you, have never talked to you, and any stories you tell are just the ramblings of a delusional person. That's how I protect myself."

"I understand," said Kirsten, chilled with a feeling of isolation.

"That doesn't mean I'm not rooting for you. They will try to stop you eventually. You might not even learn who 'they' are. They might not even know why they're trying to stop you. But remember, you have people on the inside who are rooting for you. Never underestimate the power of people actively believing."

Chapter 17

"Yes, in modern times."

Robert Oppenheimer, when asked if Trinity was the first detonation of a nuclear weapon

"Peggy, this is…actually I don't think I asked your names," Arthur said, waving for them to take a seat at his kitchen table.

"Ib Johanson, Dr. Ib Johanson, and this is my friend Barry Class. It's very nice to meet you," Ib said, smiling at Arthur's wife, Peggy, an older woman with a truly kind and welcoming smile, who was already filling up an old cast iron kettle and putting it on the gas flame.

"Ib Johanson, Dr. Ib Johanson, and this is my friend Barry Class. It's very nice to meet you," Ib said, smiling at Arthur's wife, Peggy, who was already filling up a kettle, an old cast iron pot, and putting it on the gas flame.

"Ma'am," said Barry, nodding to Peggy and looking around the cozy house, full of antiques and unique treasures, the walls bearing many framed maps and photographs of ancient buildings and dig sites.

"So we'll be four for tea then?" said Peggy kindly.

"That would be nice, thank you," said Barry, not realizing that by agreeing to tea he wasn't just getting a hot drink, but a meal as well.

"So," said Arthur, done with pleasantries, "may I examine the stone?"

Barry started to reach into his pocket and paused looking to Peggy, wondering for a moment if this conversation should be confidential.

"Oh, don't worry about that," said Arthur, recognizing Barry's body language. "There are no secrets between Peggy and I, even with my work."

"He needs me around to tell him when he's being daft," said Peggy, smiling at her guests while preparing food.

Barry smiled back, muttered, "of course, sorry," and placed the stone on the table in front of Arthur.

Arthur moved his glasses down his nose and gazed upon it, his mouth slightly agape. He rustled in his pockets, pulled out a jeweler's loop, and examined the finely etched characters. Ib and Barry sat quietly and watched as Minear carefully examined the stone. Eventually he put the stone and the jeweler's loop on the table, lifted his glasses to rest on his forehead, and examined Ib and Barry.

"I remember speaking with Tomi," Arthur said finally. "I remember talking to her on the computer. And I remember the story she told me. Completely outrageous, I thought she was a total nut. And yet I was challenged to believe her, because she knew something that was impossible for her to know. That I told her in a dream."

"Atlah-Toa," said Ib. "An early name for Atlantis."

Arthur nodded seriously. "That was some time ago that I spoke to Tomi and heard her story. What, almost two years ago? And here you two show up at my home, the location of which is meant to be private, with this stone," Arthur said, holding it up again, the chipped piece of the Emerald Tablet that Tomi had sent Ib and Barry off with. "I just don't know what to make of this. Can you explain how you came into possession of this? Assuming it's the real deal, and of course that requires study, this would be an almost miraculous find."

"Well, umm, where to begin…" Ib started, looking to Barry.

"Do you remember Tomi talking about Ete? The…alien, I guess you might say," said Barry, making eye contact with Peggy as she looked over at him while preparing sandwiches. "I know, it sounds ridiculous."

"I remember," said Arthur, his face expressing only seriousness, determination for the truth. "Tomi was trying to connect with this Ete, psychically, as I recall."

"And do you remember the advice you gave her?"

Arthur thought for a moment, before his serious face finally broke and he surprised himself with a hearty laugh. "It's possible I may have suggested she try a psychedelic."

"That does sound like you, love," said Peggy, with an adoring laugh and a pat on his shoulder.

Barry smile. "Well, she did, and it worked."

"She connected with this Ete?" asked Arthur.

"She did. And in that experience, Ete handed this to her," said Barry, pointing at the piece of stone, one edge rough, having once belonged to a larger whole. "And when she woke up from her experience, well, it was in the palm of her hand."

Arthur stared at Barry as though he were waiting for more information, then looked to Ib, scanning them both for believability. "Well, I said before that this would be an almost miraculous find. It sounds like the 'almost' was unnecessary. What happened then? Where is Tomi now?"

Barry and Ib took turns explaining their near-capture and extraordinary rescue, their journey on Ete's craft, their time under the mountain, Tomi's current mission, and their current quest. As they spoke, Peggy began setting plates of food on the table along with four cups and saucers, pouring from the teapot into each. Peggy listened with interest and interjected with a few "wows" and "ohs", while Arthur listened stoically, his face serious and unchanging.

"So as far as we know," said Ib, scooping a spoonful of sugar into his tea and stirring gently, "Tomi is still with Ete under the mountain. Or perhaps she has made her way to this Other Place, whatever that might be."

Arthur reached out to take a few sandwich quarters, then forked a pickle onto his plate. "When I spoke with Tomi I told her I wasn't a UFO guy. I'm not an Ancient Aliens guy. So this story sounds outrageous to me."

"Yes, I realize it sounds–" started Ib before being interrupted by Arthur.

"But then there's this," said Arthur, rubbing his finger on the etched characters of the green stone. "How long were you underground?"

Barry looked to Ib and they both smiled. "Depends," said Barry. "A few weeks. Or so we thought. When we returned to the surface, to civilization, more than two years had passed."

"Hmm," sounded Arthur, his face still serious. "About eight hundred years ago, here on this island, some villagers found two lost children, brother and sister. But these were not normal children. Their skin was green, they spoke an unknown language, and would only eat raw beans. The boy grew sick and died, but the girl eventually learned to eat different foods, her skin lost its green colouring, and she learned the local language. When she did, she explained that they had come from an underground land, Saint Martin's Land, a place where the sun didn't shine, but there was always light. They had been exploring, got lost, and found a passage to the surface."

"Wow. This is historic, documented?" asked Ib, flashing a smile to Peggy as he helped himself to another scone.

"Documented folklore, you might say," said Arthur. "Like I said, I'm not an alien believer, or a believer in the paranormal, perhaps just because it's not been of interest to me. What does interest me are the mysteries of our human past, and I'm one who puts a lot of stock in our ancestors, what ancient people actually said and believed. I often talk about the great flood, and how this flood, this ending and restarting of civilization, is talked about by people all over the world. Well likewise, all around the world our ancestors spoke of people, or beings, who lived underground. Sometimes human, sometimes not, sometimes friendly, sometimes not. Usually a more advanced people, sometimes inhabiting the most remarkable underground cities."

"Shambhala," said Peggy, "Agartha. The Nagas in India, Xibalba in Peru. And here of course, with the fae."

"Precisely," said Arthur, smiling and placing his hand on Peggy's.

Ib smiled watching them, the special beauty of old people in love. "For me, when one culture has a belief or myth, it's interesting. When every culture has a variation of the same myth, to me it starts to feel more like evidence. And why do people, cultures hand down these stories from generation to generation?"

"Because they're important," said Barry.

Arthur nodded, his serious face slowly morphing into one of excited engagement. "They wanted us to know these things, to help us. Protect us. Like Pillar Forty-Three at Gobekli Tepe, which I believe contains a warning for us about a coming cataclysm."

"Hmm," nodded Ib, enjoying Arthur's passion for the subject but wondering how to get him focused on solving their own mystery.

"And that's not to mention the human cultures who have lived underground," continued Arthur. "I believe that around the end of the Younger Dryas, a time of extreme cataclysm, that many humans went to live underground. Derinkuyu, for example, in Turkey, is an underground cave city that could have housed twenty thousand people, their animals, industry. And it's just one of many underground cities in the area. Now, archeologists have dated it much later, because of inscriptions and items that have been found. But for me these only tell us when a people lived there, not when it was built, since we can't date the stone."

"That's fascinating," said Ib. "I wonder if you have any thoughts on the mission Barry and I have been assigned?"

"Right, your mission," said Arthur, leaning into his chair and tilting his head back in thought. "You didn't just come here to listen to an old man ramble. Please, remind me of why you came here?"

"Well," said Barry, "we told you about this pyramid. This dark underground pyramid."

"Something I sure would like to get a look at, if such a thing exists," said Arthur.

"Right, of course you would," said Barry, "except Tomi's mission is to destroy it. To do that, she needs some kind of weapon that me and Ib have been tasked with finding. Ete said it is something that is both ancient and highly destructive. Tomi sent us here hoping you would have some advice for us."

Arthur sat quietly in thought, fiddling with the green stone on the table in front of him. "Would you give me just a moment?"

Ib and Barry both nodded and watched Arthur stand up and turn around the corner into another room. They smiled at Peggy.

"I know this all must seem crazy," said Ib, "us showing up at your door with a story like ours."

"Nonsense, this is a house where crazy stories find refuge," Peggy said, smiling in a way that put them at ease.

"Well, let's see if it's a match," said Arthur, returning to the room and to his seat. In his hand he held a piece of green stone that looked much like the one they had brought here. Arthur held a piece in each hand and examined the edges. He pressed it together in one configuration, then another, examining the chiselled characters. He eventually turned one piece over, and pressed the edges together.

"It's a match," said Arthur, quietly at first, then with a laugh. "It's a match! This truly is the most remarkable thing."

He sat quietly for a few moments, examining the reconnected stone. The piece that Tomi manifested filled in the bottom section, while Arthur's piece fit onto it to form the upper-left portion. It appeared that a third portion, of a similar size, would complete the stone. The tablet. Eventually he put both pieces back on the table and looked at his guests.

"I don't know," he said. "Something ancient and highly destructive. I just don't know. But with some thought perhaps it will come to me. I propose that you both stay here tonight, unless you have other arrangements. And we regroup tomorrow."

"We don't have other arrangements," said Ib, "and would be so grateful for your hospitality."

"It's nothing fancy," said Peggy, "but I can get some sheets on the pullout. And we will keep you well fed, of course."

"It sounds perfect," said Ib.

"Now," said Arthur, "I wonder if you would indulge me, I am dying to spend some time analyzing this stone."

"This is what I wanted to show you," said Arthur, pointing at an inscribed stone obelisk protruding from a stone wall, the wall itself enclosing an old stone church. "This here, this is the resting place of Dorothy Pentreath. She was born the daughter of a fisherman in Mousehole, and died here in seventeen-seventy-seven. She was said to be the last native speaker of Cornish."

"Wow," said Barry from the passenger seat. It turned out that Arthur was in fact impressed with the Jaguar, and had suggested an outing, a stroll in a place he liked to go to think. On their way Arthur had pulled the car over to point out the memorial.

"That's very sad but also amazing to have that recorded, known who the last one was."

"Of course it's not true," said Arthur. "Or probably not true, there are stories of other speakers. But she was known far and wide in her old age as the last native speaker. She claimed to have not learned English until she was an adult. It was also said that if you crossed her, you were in for a long torrent of curses in Cornish. She died at over a hundred, and with that, Cornish itself."

"It's nice that they have this memorial, that people honour her," said Ib from the back seat.

"You know, this stone was put up about a hundred years later by one of Napoleon's nephews," said Arthur with a small laugh as he pulled the vehicle back onto the road and drove off. "What a strange world it is sometimes."

"You know, my home country is not very big geographically," said Ib, leaning his head between the two front seats to be heard over the rumble of the engine, "but it isn't that long ago that people in one region would sound completely different from another region. I remember visiting my father's mother, my grandmother, and she lived in another part of the country, and she still spoke with that region's dialect. It sounded so different to me, it was like something from a different time. Today there are accents, sure, but basically everyone sounds just about the same. In just a few generations."

"Such a sad loss," said Arthur while making a turn, "the loss of language. There is so much culture wrapped up in language. But then sometimes I wonder: how many languages have there been? In all of human history, how many distinct languages have we created, have we seen die, replaced by something else, or evolving into something new. I mean hundreds of thousands of years, perhaps longer, how many words for 'bird' have there been?"

"And how many more will there be?" said Barry with a note of sadness, thinking about the cataclysmic visions Ete had shared with them.

They drove on for a time down rural roads, the landscape of farms and rough rolling hills pulling by.

Arthur eventually made a turn and parked the car in a small gravel parking lot. "As I said, this is a place I come to walk and think," he said, stepping out of the car. Arthur led them towards a few stone stairs, with a stone marker beside it reading *Mên-an-Tol*.

The trio hiked up the stairs and set out through the rough field, largely void of trees but full of wild vegetation, until they spotted the ancient granite standing stones.

"One-zero-one," said Ib, noticing the middle stone to be a large flat circle with a hole bored out of the centre, bookended by stone pillars on either side, looking like the numbers 1-0-1 from the right angle.

"Isn't it amazing," said Arthur, approaching them and laying his hand on the round stone, standing just shorter than him. "Though this isn't how the ancients knew it, created it. It was once part of a larger stone circle, but this is all that's left."

Ib ran his hand along the rough inner edge of the holed-out stone. "How did they do this?" he asked.

Arthur just shook his head, his eyes focused on the stone in front of him, but his voice sounding as though he were far away in thought. "Did the ancients create anything that didn't leave us in wonder? I once had a young man come up to me after a lecture I gave, and asked me, if the ancients were so advanced, as I believed, why did they build using stones and not with concrete, steel, or plastic?"

Arthur's face was still serious, but he let out a loud laugh. "I told him they showed they were advanced *because* they built out of stone. They didn't build disposable, they built to last. Not for a hundred years, but for thousands and thousands of years. And the things they were able to create are still beyond our comprehension today. They seemed to have advanced knowledge of quarrying, cutting, and moving stones. And maybe some knowledge about the power of these stones. You know, the legend here is that if a woman passes through this round stone backwards seven times on a full moon night, she will get pregnant. A superstition, surely, but these sites are so often associated with health and healing and fertility.

"And of course it's not just here, they did it in Europe, the Americas, Africa, Asia. We're just on the cusp of discovering more amazing sites in Oceania. It appears there's a massive, buried pyramid in Indonesia that looks to be nearly thirty thousand years old."

"Thirty thousand?" questioned Barry. "That's…well that's well beyond when humans were able to build. Had a society that could build something like that."

"Is it?" replied Arthur. "Sure, that's what we're taught. And that old Minear is grasping at straws again, because civilization only started six thousand years ago with the Sumerians, right? But then we found Gobekli Tepe, and that six thousand years started to look older. We have geologists looking at the weathering of the Great Sphinx and concluding that it is actually much, much older.

"You know," Arthur said, stepping away from the stones and starting to stroll through the field, his hands resting behind his back.

Ib and Barry followed like dutiful students.

"People don't realize how quickly the Earth erases evidence. Rising and lowering sea levels, centuries of deposition burying the evidence. In Zambia, archeologists recently found the oldest known human made structure. The wood that was used was uniquely preserved, and they dated it to over four hundred thousand years. Everything keeps getting older. And how many more have we not found? What else have humans accomplished in our distant past that has been erased by a world in a state of constant change?" Arthur started to curve his direction, walking back towards the car.

"How old do you think it goes?" asked Ib, trailing a few steps behind Arthur.

"I don't know. And it shouldn't be considered 'dangerous' to say that we don't know. You see unless you have the hard evidence, academia will just say that you're making up stories. But if we look at the breadth of evidence, it's pointing us backwards. Then there are the Kings Lists. So many ancient cultures have documented lists of rulers that would take their civilizations back much further than we believe possible. So, we say that these kings were just mythical. It just doesn't make sense to me why we only came up with civilization six thousand years ago, when modern human brains have been tromping around the world for hundreds of thousands."

As they completed their loop, they stopped again to look at the three standing stones.

"I wonder," said Ib, fascinated by Arthur, but struggling to see how any of this helped them on their mission. Helped them to help Tomi. "Has this walk helped you in your thinking? About our mystery."

Arthur stood looking at one of the pillar stones, his hand gently resting on it, his facial expression unaffected by Ib's question.

Eventually he pulled his hand away and spoke. "Yes," he said, "it has helped, but I'm still thinking. I'm not ready to share yet. Come, let's head back home. I'm dying to spend more time with your stone."

"I also wonder," said Ib, following behind Arthur as he set off towards the parked Jaguar, "why the Emerald Tablet? How does it fit in with Tomi's…mystery, I guess I'll call it."

Arthur slowed his pace slightly while he formulated an answer. "It points us towards something. Ancient knowledge. Suppressed, hidden ancient knowledge. And power. These Hermetic texts have the power to crack open an ancient religion, a philosophy, that may have been more in tune with our spiritual reality. An understanding of the immaterial nature of the universe. I mean Hermetics is core to the occult and alchemy with it, saved just below the surface, knowledge passed generation by generation, and built upon, stretching back to Ancient Egypt, and perhaps much farther back, perhaps even to Atlah-Toa."

Arthur's stride came to a stop, and he turned to face Ib and Barry to conclude his lecture.

"We are talking about knowledge that has been suppressed over time, ideas that have been considered dangerous, yet passed down over generations, often in secret and with great personal danger, especially for women. And what do we see today? Many of these ideas, it turns out, are borne out by scientific discovery."

Finishing his sentence, he pivoted, and started again towards the car.

"That's my hypothesis, at least. Perhaps there is something chiselled in those pieces of stone that we've yet to discover. Come, we will discuss more at home."

When they returned, Arthur retreated to his study, wanting to spend more time with Tomi's stone, her piece of the Emerald Tablet that fit so perfectly together with his own. Barry and Ib spent some time examining the museum that was Arthur and Peggy's home, with souvenirs and trinkets and art from around the world, each piece painting another brushstroke of their life story.

Later, when Peggy returned, they joined her in her garden to harvest some vegetables for dinner, Peggy remarking more than once that the weather had turned her garden barren, and that they needed to come see it in a normal year. The trio worked together to make dinner, enjoying Peggy's casual hospitality and stories about the couple's expeditions and book tours.

"But nothing, no place we've visited has drawn us away from our home," she said, setting places at the table as Arthur entered the room with a classroom-sized globe in one hand and several books resting on the palm of his other hand. He sat down, pushing the plate and flatware to the side to make room for his collection.

Peggy smiled as he did this, finding his hyperfocus endearing, knowing that he probably didn't even notice that dinner was about to be served.

"I knew that a walk around Mên-an-Tol would get me thinking. I have some ideas for your mission. Sit," Arthur said, gesturing towards the chairs around the table.

While Ib and Barry took their seats, Peggy circled the table, plating the food. She stopped to leave a loving kiss on Arthur's head, then pointed to the food and reminded him to eat, before seating herself.

"Something ancient and highly destructive. There is no shortage of weapons used and described in histories, religious texts, legends. At first, I thought about the powerful way that Ezekiel was taken to Heaven. And I thought about the Vimāna in Hindu and Jain texts, these powerful flying chariots the gods would fly around in."

Ib and Barry nodded, Barry eating while Ib had pulled out a little notebook and scribbled ideas down. Peggy gave Arthur a motion to pick up his fork. He complied, took one bite, then continued.

"And that certainly isn't the only interesting, powerful thing described in Hindu texts. Listen to this from the Mahabharata. It's describing an unknown weapon."

Arthur picked up one of the books he had brought to the table, flipped to a bookmarked page, and read: "The hostile warriors fell down like trees burnt down by a raging fire. Huge elephants, burnt by that weapon, fell down on the earth all around, uttering fierce cries loud as the rumblings of the clouds. Other huge elephants, scorched by that fire, ran hither and thither, and roared aloud in fear, as if in the midst of a forest conflagration."

"That, well that certainly sounds highly destructive," said Barry.

"Maybe that will lead you somewhere on your search," said Arthur. "I also thought about the Great Pyramids, supposedly tombs for kings, yet no graves have been found. There is some conjecture that these could actually be machines, massive power plants. And there are rumours of great underground caverns, particularly under the Sphinx, which are said to be kept hidden."

"That…well that sounds more like a task for Indiana Jones than for Ib Johanson," said Ib.

"I would pay to see you dressed like him, hat and whip and everything," laughed Barry.

"You may not be that far off. I thought about it and realized that if I were starting on your mission, there's one thing that would be at the top of my list, both ancient and highly destructive," Arthur said, pulling the globe in front of him, giving it a half spin, and placing his finger on it. "And this is the first place I would go to find it."

Chapter 18

"This critique also misreads the Copernican revolution. Yes, our perceptions misled us about our place in the universe. But its deeper message is this: our perceptions can mislead us about the very nature of the universe itself. We are prone to falsely believe that certain limitations and idiosyncrasies of our perceptions are genuine insights into objective reality."

Donald D. Hoffman

"What a story!" said Tomi, grateful to have finally heard the story of her grandmother's meeting with Ete. "Picked up on a craft on a mountain like that, it sounds like it could be a movie."

"Of course, I'm not the only one that was picked up in a craft on a mountain," Esther said, referencing Tomi's rescue from John and the General.

"Right, of course," said Tomi. "Maybe that will be for the sequel."

Beyond just hearing the story, Tomi was privy to visuals, as though she were able to slip into her grandmother's eyes and relive it from her perspective. Tomi felt so fortunate to be in this Other Place, to have these kinds of insights and experiences.

Tomi looked out upon the circular stone city in the valley below them. She looked over and saw Ete seated in meditation again, her tall, lanky energy body seeming to glow, charged by the clarity and connection to information the Other Place affords. Tomi wondered what Ete was seeing, experiencing. What she was watching.

Tomi felt her own energy shift into receiving mode, as she felt another vision coming on. She looked to her grandmother, and saw that Esther was also entering a meditation.

Tomi closed her eyes – *if I really have eyes here*, she thought, still unsure of her physiology.

Almost immediately Tomi was tuned into her vibration, felt the energetic vibrations around her meld with her body, entering and flowing through her like blood through an artery. It seemed the more time she spent in this Other Place, the faster and deeper she could access information, these downloads, these visions. She was feeling more confident in her ability to predict and control these experiences.

As though many colours of paint were dumped on a canvas and swirled around, she saw colours mixing as they created an image. It was a silhouette, a figure, shaded so that she couldn't make out details of the being. Golden light backlit and defined the figure, the light surrounding it, like the piercingly beautiful light of the chromosphere peeking out from behind the moon during a solar eclipse.

The figure seemed large and powerful, humanlike in form but with bulges coming off the shoulders, as though wings.

An angel, thought Tomi.

Details of the figure slowly emerged, and she saw that the figure wore a dark robe. What she thought were wings on the shoulder was simply the shape of the being's body. The face never became distinguishable, instead only emitting a beautiful, golden light energy. Tomi felt good, strong and energized in the being's presence.

"Before you return, you must know how important the human soul is," the being said – or rather shared – telepathically. Instead of audible words, each word carried a feeling, a meaning that provided for deeper understanding. The vision shifted, and Tomi saw the Earth, and like the vision Ete had shared with her, she saw all kinds of beings, some from Earth, some visiting, others from the Other Place or still other places. *The covenant*, Tomi thought, thinking of the agreement these beings had made: *leave the Earth alone. Leave humanity alone.* For the first time, she realized this agreement, this covenant, was to protect the human soul.

Tomi saw an oasis in a desert, animals crossing great distances to find this rare wellspring of life amidst the barren surroundings. *Earth is the oasis*, she thought, remembering how beautiful and fragile the planet looked floating in the darkness of space. She then found herself surrounded by water, watching as a huge blue whale surfaced, clearing its blow holes and breathing in the air. Her vision zoomed, and Tomi was looking at a single, tiny cell, an essential but almost insignificant part of the whole of the giant whale. *The cell is the human soul*, she thought. Separate but indistinguishable from the whole.

Her vision zoomed out again, presenting an overview of the ocean below, and she watched as the waves moved, intersected, mixed, and rolled on. *Each wave is a soul, distinct and separate, but always part of the ocean whole*, Tomi thought.

The images subsided, and Tomi was again looking at the being's silhouette. Although the being was set in darkness, she felt deep, positive energy flowing to her.

"You are a being of good and light," Tomi said telepathically.

"Of course I am," the being replied. "A being of good and light, of sadness and darkness. Just like every being in the cosmos."

"Are you real?" Tomi asked, wondering where this information, this visitor had come from.

"As real as anything in this universe," the being replied. "Remember this Tomi, remember what I have showed you. Remember the work you need to do."

As the being finished this message, the vision was wiped to darkness, and Tomi felt her consciousness on the move again, seeking out the next vision, the next piece of information flowing through the ether and into her mind.

The darkness was gone, and Tomi's inner vision was again flooded with colours. It was Earth, the Material Place. From above, she looked out over a big green field surrounded by forests. She zoomed in closer, and saw many people in this field, in the forests, camping in tents or campers, sleeping in vehicles.

Tomi could feel their energy, their emotions, as though their vibration melded with hers. They were afraid, these people, frightened by the future, lost in the present. She got closer and saw people in all kinds of clothing, some in colourful tie-dyed, others in sarongs and wraps, some in t-shirts and jeans, still others nude, their skin exposed to the bright sun.

Tomi knew they had come here seeking guidance, solace in rituals and community. They came here desperate for guidance in a rapidly unbalanced world. The people were gathered in the field, all looking towards the west. Tomi followed their eyes and saw herself, Tomi, standing in the field, in her human, Earthly body, her skin luminescent, nude in the bright sun. Her view zoomed in closer, and she could see every supposed flaw in her body, every wrinkle and scar and roll that she had stared at for hours in mirrors throughout her life. She expected to feel shame, but instead felt overwhelming unity, unity between her human body and all the bodies around her, all different, all the same. *We are not just a human body*, she thought. *We are humanity.*

In her vision, she saw herself facing the group of people, who all looked to her, Future Tomi, standing completely still with her eyes closed. *This is the future,* she thought to herself. *The last vision was a visitor, a lesson. This vision is the future. My future.*

Future Tomi opened her eyes and slowly formed a smile, looking around lovingly at the faces in front of her. She heard the beat of a drum, and watched as the vibration, the resonance of the sound seemed to pull all the people closer, towards Tomi.

As though she had stood up quickly and found her legs asleep, Future Tomi's knees buckled, and she collapsed to the ground, still smiling, then laughing, running her hands through the grass as though she were hugging, loving the ground.

She then turned her head and looked up to the southern sky. The crowd of people followed her gaze towards the sun, which grew rapidly larger, as though it jumped towards the Earth, zigged and zagged, then moved back into position, casting multicolour rays of light through the sky. The crowd was frozen, staring at the sky in silence, before a child started cheering and clapping. Then the adults joined in, cheering at the sky, as the crowd moved closer to Tomi and helped her back to her feet.

The vision faded to black. Tomi felt her consciousness return, as she again became aware of her body, seated on the hill. She looked out again at the circular stone city below, then to Ete and her grandmother. Ete was no longer meditating, and Tomi felt that they had been waiting for her to emerge from her own meditation.

"Tomi," Esther said gently, placing her arm around Tomi, Tomi feeling her heightened vibration interacting with her own body. "Ete had a vision and has received a message. It's time for us to leave the Other Place, to descend. It's time for us to go home."

"No," said Tomi, feeling her energy drop, "it can't be time to go back already. We just got here! There must be so much more to see."

"Tomi," said Ete, "I think you will be surprised how long you have been away."

"You remember how long I was away?" asked Esther. "Here in the Other Place, it felt like a flash."

Tomi looked around, wondering what was just beyond the fog, what more she could see and experience. She looked back towards the city, and found that the fog was setting in, making it harder and harder to see.

Tomi focused on her grandmother's arm, the energy her grandmother was sharing with her. She was devastated. She didn't want to leave. Here in the Other Place, she felt so assured, energized, so deeply connected, knowledge and experiences surrounding her in the ether. She had lived most of her life desperate for a purpose, for a direction. Every moment here felt deeply purposeful and delightfully without direction.

But she had seen the vision, saw her future self – back in the Material Place. She had seen a woman with a purpose. As disappointed as she was, she had also felt it in that vision. It was time.

"Okay," Tomi eventually said, "I understand. So, what's next? How do we do it?"

The three sat together as three points of a triangle, their bodies touching. Tomi closed her eyes and felt herself tune in to the vibration, the resonance of her surroundings.

"Much like you did when you ascended, you will reach a deep, interconnected state," Ete had told her. "You will focus, tune in to your body, matter and energy always in motion. As you lower your vibration, a path will open up. Follow it, let the path guide you. We will see you on the other side. In the Material Place."

Tomi was immediately reassured as she felt herself in motion, felt her body connect, synch with the vibration around her. As though she were turning a dial down, she felt her vibrations slow as she moved out of synch with her surroundings.

In her mind's eye she saw an opening, as though a doorway opened and created a path.

"Let the path guide you," she heard Ete say again.

The path was not in front of her, but was off to her side. 'Off to the side,' Ete had called the Other Place the first time she had talked about it.

Tomi let herself relax and surrender to the pull, to the pathway drawing her in, and felt herself move over to the side, clicking into a different speed of vibration, like gearing down on a bicycle.

Then, there was a sudden pull. It felt like something rose up, grabbed hold of her, and pulled her down, down another pathway. She was surrounded by darkness, feeling like the was floating in space, hurtling in one direction with nothing to anchor herself to.

Flying through the void she saw glimpses, mini-visions, like images on a television screen, flying out of her view as fast as it had arrived. They were memories, moments of her life, moments from other lives, other places and times. She saw Ete's people, a long time ago on a lush Mars, constructing their pyramids. She saw groups of them carrying massive stone blocks without strain, as though the block were made of nothing heavier than Styrofoam. She saw others, tall and lanky, just like Ete, using instruments, metal spirals they would ding with sticks, filling the air with sound. It seemed as though the soundwaves pushed the stone blocks up into levitation, and those carrying them just needed to guide them into place. She looked down and saw that she had been playing one of the instruments.

In another vision she saw Kirsten seated in meditation, surrounded by trees. She wanted to reach out to her, pull herself through this in-between and back into a reality she shared with Kirsten. She felt herself trying desperately to reach for her, but in an instant the vision was gone.

Then in a forest clearing, standing by a pot over a fire, with primitive wooden buildings surrounding her. A child ran by laughing, followed by several more, chasing the first. A group of people emerged from the forest carrying something. *Food*, Tomi thought. *For all of us.*

A feeling of connection, of community filled Tomi, energizing her, but again, it felt like she was grabbed and pulled down again, no longer floating in some in-between, but landing painfully on a floor.

Everything felt heavy, and the sense that she had a physical body quickly returned. Then more pain, a burning feeling, as though a friction burn. She felt herself open her eyes. Everything was blurry. She was groggy and disoriented. She saw carpet, and realized that was where the friction burn was coming from. She was being dragged across the floor.

Again darkness, then again another room, then darkness. Time passed. She didn't know how long, but her sense of passing time had returned. She was not in the Other Place anymore.

Again, she opened her eyes. The peaceful, connected feeling of the Other Place was gone. Instead, Tomi felt nothing but terror as she gazed upon the face in front of her.

"Welcome back, Thomasina," said the General.

Chapter 19

"1) The truth, certainty, truest, without untruth.

2) What is above is like what is below. What is below is like what is above. The miracle of unity is to be attained.

3) Everything is formed from the contemplation of unity, and all things come about from unity, by means of adaptation.

4) Its parents are the Sun and Moon.

5) It was borne by the wind and nurtured by the Earth…"

Arthur Minear tilted his lamp head slightly, rubbed his eyes, and looked through his lens, magnifying the tiny inscriptions on the green stone. While he had enjoyed meeting Barry and Ib, enjoyed the excitement and intrigue of their visit, Arthur had been aching for some time alone to examine this stone – this second fragment of the Emerald Tablet stone he had found in Turkey, the one that on the reverse side of the stone seemed to tell the story of Atlantis – or Atlah-Toa, as it was called on the stone.

After waving Barry and Ib off as they headed to the airport, off for their great mission, Arthur hurried inside, made himself a cup of tea, and got right to work examining the stone. He had been so happy that his new friends entrusted him with their stone, with the hopes that his examination may lead to useful answers.

Arthur was so hyper-focused he hadn't noticed Peggy coming into his office, leading him to jump as she put her hands on his shoulders.

"Ooh, you need to take breaks you know," Peggy said as Arthur placed his hand over hers. "Let me guess, you are starting with the Atlantis side."

Arthur smiled and nodded. She knew him so well. "Anything interesting?" she asked.

"Oh, it's so early," he said lightly. Then his voice had a tone of boyish wonder. "But this one, right here, I think this might be the end. I think it's talking about a location, perhaps where to find them. And this character, well I think it says to find them in the side. Or to the side. Of course, I may be wrong. Nor do I know what that would even mean."

"Well," Peggy said, squeezing his shoulders and planting a kiss on his thin grey-haired head. "If anyone's going to find them, my money's on you, Arthur."

"Have you ever been?" Ib asked Barry as they shuffled into their seats, Barry beside the window and Ib in the aisle seat.

"Here?" Barry asked, holding up his boarding pass. "No. I've never even been on the continent. You?"

Ib shook his head. "Same. Always dreamed of it. Although I perhaps imagined visiting as more of a tourist. I mean, I appreciate the direction we got from Minear, and the faith Ete showed in us, but I wonder what Ib Johansen and Barry Class bring to crack this case that Arthur or the Templars or the Nazis didn't?"

Barry laughed. "Don't forget Indiana Jones."

The airplane lurched as it began to taxi away from the gate. As it reversed, Barry looked out the window towards the terminal, seeing people sitting and waiting, others walking in all directions. He saw a man standing in front of the window, watching their airplane. *John*, Barry thought, but the plane pulled out of view before he could ask Ib to take a look.

Clunk. The plane grunted and lurched again as it switched into forward gear, heading towards the runway. Barry closed his eyes and took a deep breath, his anxiety around flying only heightened by the warnings they had received.

"Have you read about these billionaire bunkers?" Ib asked, pulling a magazine away from his face and showing Barry the article. "Basically, everyone with means has been buying up land and building massive doomsday bunkers. In New Zealand especially."

"What a surprise," Barry said sarcastically, "the rich are looking out for themselves. I guess with all of the climate stuff, and the Great Unrest, as they call it, I'm sure a lot of people are pretty spooked."

"Yes, but it says here that this trend started in 2010. It's like someone tipped them off and they all started preparing."

"I wonder what they know that we don't," said Barry.

"Or if they know what we know," said Ib.

The airplane was stopped at the beginning of the runway. Barry pressed his head back against his seat as the jet engines revved up, and the airplane moved forward, slowly at first, then shooting off the runway and into the sky. Barry's stomach was in knots.

"Something ancient and highly destructive," Barry said.

"That's our job," Ib said. "For Tomi."

"6) Every wonder is from it

and its power is complete.

7) Throw it upon earth,

and earth will separate from fire. The impalpable separated from the palpable.

8) Through wisdom it rises slowly from the world to heaven. Then it descends to the world combining the power of the upper and the lower.

9) Thus you will have the illumination of all the world, and darkness will disappear…"

"I see that he wrote down a few," said Sixto, looking at the note that Alexander had left for Kirsten. "Window places, I mean. Do you know where you will go?"

Kirsten was combing her long hair, having just taken a shower. "Well, I figure I'll start with the closest one and work my way out. Until one of them gets me to Tomi."

"That's a smart plan. I made you some lunch for the road," Sixto said, holding up a paper bag full of drinks and sandwiches.

"Thank you. I mean for everything, Sixto. You've really been there for me. For Tomi, too," she said, giving her friend a hug. "Now…I don't see my bags."

"While you were in the shower I loaded up your car," he said. "I thought it would be helpful."

"It is," Kirsten said, smiling gratefully to Sixto, who she could see was sad she was leaving. *Perhaps his hermit life is a little lonely*, she thought.

They exited the cabin, and Kirsten saw her bags loaded into the back seat. It had seemed like excessive luggage when she had first headed here. Now, with no return home in sight, she was glad she had overpacked.

"Oh, this isn't mine," Kirsten said, pointing to an old red backpack, the kind hikers use for multi-day treks.

"Yes, well that's um, that's mine," said Sixto sheepishly. "Feel free to say no. But I wonder if you might need some company. Someone who can watch out for you. Maybe someone who could help you."

Kirsten felt herself tear up. "You want to come with me, Sixto?"

"If you think it would be helpful," he said. "Helpful for Tomi."

Kirsten acted like she was unsure, humming and hawing, before laughing and telling him to hop in. Sixto jogged back to the cabin, grabbed the packed lunch, locked the door, and jogged back to the car, getting into the passenger seat.

"Don't worry," Sixto said, placing the bag of food on the floor beside his feet. "I packed lunch for two."

Kirsten smiled. "I'm glad you're coming. Well, off we go," Kirsten said, while reversing the car and turning away from the cabin, wondering what all might happen between now and bringing Sixto back to his home.

Esther opened her eyes and immediately cringed, reminded at how unpleasant returning from the Other Place could be, like a hangover, extreme jet lag, and a panic attack rolled into one.

The light was dark and heavy, a deep inky indigo. Esther knew immediately she was back in Ete's underground home, in the indigo meditation room.

"Where…" she started, then stopped, disoriented and scanning the room. "Tomi, where's Tomi?" Her eyes were adjusting to the light, and she looked around the room and saw Ete seated on a floating meditation stool, with two more of her kind standing nearby. Esther could see that they were communicating with each other telepathically, but not so that she could hear.

"Ete, where is Tomi?" she asked again. Ete raised her hand to the other two beings, indicating that she needed a pause.

"*Tomi is not here*," Ete said to Esther telepathically.

"Not here?? Well, where is she?"

"*We don't yet know*," Ete said.

"Don't know? I don't understand. Did she manifest somewhere else?"

"*It doesn't appear she has manifested in this reality*," said Ete.

"So what, she's back in the Other Place?" Esther asked. "Let's go get her!"

"*It doesn't appear that she is in the Other Place*," either, said Ete. "*Tomi seems to be somewhere else entirely. We don't yet know where.*"

"Somewhere else?" said Esther, her voice becoming more and more panicked. "Where else could she be?"

"*We do not know*," Ete said, projecting calm telepathically. "*This was not supposed to happen.*"

"I…I don't understand," said Esther. "Aren't you the watchers? You didn't see this? Can't you meditate and see where she is?"

"*We did not see this, nor have we been able to see her*," said Ete. "*We are the watchers, but we only see what is shown to us.*"

"So what now?" asked Esther, her voice desperate for an answer.

"*Now we wait. And watch. And hope they will show us Tomi*," said Ete.

"10) This is the power of all strength – it overcomes that which is delicate and penetrates through solids.

11) This was the means of the creation of the world.

12) And in the future wonderful developments will be made, and this is the way.

13) I am Hermes the Threefold Sage, so named because I hold the three elements of all wisdom.

14) And thus ends the revelation of the work of the Sun."

The Emerald Tablet by Hermes Trismegistus,

translated by Idries Shah

Before she could open her eyes, she could feel the sore on her bum, thighs, and lower back, the raw feeling of a friction burn.

I was dragged. Dragged across the carpet, Tomi thought, so confused by where she was and what had happened, she was reminding herself of her most recent memories.

She opened her eyes and saw pale blue flooring, that flat, tight carpet used in offices. She saw what looked like an old coffee stain, and areas where the carpet was worn. She looked around and found herself in a large empty room with pale yellow walls. She remembered being dragged through other rooms with other colours; light blue, beige, off-white. On one wall to the left of her was a door.

Tomi remembered this place, remembered when she had been blocked in her remote viewing, always finding herself stuck in these old and musky empty offices, one door leading to another and to another, but never leading anywhere. These backrooms.

She tried to move her arms but they didn't budge. She looked down and saw that she was seated in an office chair, her arms and legs duct-taped to the arms and legs of the chair. She tried to scream but her mouth wouldn't open. She realized her mouth was duct-taped, also.

Then she heard the door open and close, and in he walked, wearing his Air Force blues, his chest covered with medals and commendations. *The General.*

He walked over to Tomi and crouched down in front of her.

"Welcome back, Thomasina," said the General. His stern, wrinkled face stretched into a smile. "I'm so glad you're here. We have a lot of work to do."

She tried to wrestle her arms out and kick her legs, but she was stuck. She tried to scream, but was silenced by the duct tape. Tomi closed her eyes and started breathing deeply, trying to stave off the panic that was overwhelming her body.

She focused hard to picture Kirsten, tried to feel the love she had for her, pictured Ib and Barry and Ete, and of course Esther, her grandmother, hoping their faces could bring her some calm.

Tomi thought back to being on Ete's craft with her friends, looking over the Earth, a fragile blue oasis passing through the cold and dark of space. All of them were on this planet, everyone she'd ever loved in this life, coasting along with eight billion others, all immersed in their daily lives, mostly unaware and unaccepting of the magical universe around them, forgetting that they are actually cosmic travellers hurtling through the universe, completely vulnerable to asteroids and comets and gravitational anomalies, solar flares and pole shifts, climate change and nuclear war.

All these people living their lives, unaware that all the while, something is coming.

About the Author

CJ Dearlove is a writer, artist, and community builder from Cambridge, Ontario, Canada.